"A WITTY, SAVVY, URBANE ROMP OF A BOOK."
—*Detroit News/Free Press*

"MURDERING MR. MONTI introduces a different Viorst, but you won't have any trouble recognizing her unique, self-effacing wit.... Brenda is a perfectly groomed vigilante. If she doesn't make you laugh out loud, she'd advise you to loosen up."
—*Chicago Tribune*

"Funny ... Wacky ... Viorst infuses her premiere adult novel with the quicksilver pace, naughty optimism, and heartwarming humor of her bestselling nonfiction."
—*Kirkus Reviews*

"Barbing her trademark insight with humor, the multitalented Viorst hits another bull's-eye with this mystery.... Readers, laughing their way to the last page, will be glad to have made this Mom's acquaintance."
—*Publishers Weekly*

"This novel is a delightful read, doused with Viorst's usual humor and insight into the human psyche.... Wildly funny."
—*The Phoenix Gazette*

Books by Judith Viorst:

Poems
THE VILLAGE SQUARE
IT'S HARD TO BE HIP OVER THIRTY AND OTHER
    TRAGEDIES OF MARRIED LIFE
PEOPLE AND OTHER AGGRAVATIONS
HOW DID I GET TO BE FORTY AND OTHER
    ATROCITIES
IF I WERE IN CHARGE OF THE WORLD AND
    OTHER WORRIES
WHEN DID I STOP BEING TWENTY AND OTHER
    INJUSTICES
FOREVER FIFTY AND OTHER NEGOTIATIONS

Children's books
SUNDAY MORNING
I'LL FIX ANTHONY
TRY IT AGAIN, SAM
THE TENTH GOOD THING ABOUT BARNEY
ALEXANDER AND THE TERRIBLE, HORRIBLE, NO
    GOOD, VERY BAD DAY
MY MAMA SAYS THERE AREN'T ANY ZOMBIES,
    GHOSTS, VAMPIRES, CREATURES, DEMONS,
    MONSTERS, FIENDS, GOBLINS, OR THINGS
ROSIE AND MICHAEL
ALEXANDER, WHO USED TO BE RICH LAST
    SUNDAY
THE GOOD-BYE BOOK
EARRINGS

Other
YES, MARRIED
A VISIT FROM ST. NICHOLAS (TO A LIBERATED
    HOUSEHOLD)
LOVE AND GUILT AND THE MEANING OF LIFE,
    ETC.
NECESSARY LOSSES*

Published by Fawcett Books

MURDERING MR. MONTI:

A Merry Little Tale of Sex and Violence

Judith Viorst

FAWCETT CREST • NEW YORK

A Fawcett Crest Book
Published by Ballantine Books
Copyright © 1994 by Judith Viorst

Library of Congress Catalog Card Number: 93-37919

ISBN 0-449-22355-8

This edition published by arrangement with Simon & Schuster Inc.

Grateful acknowledgment is made herewith for permission to print the following lyrics:

"Unforgettable." Words and music by Irving Gordon. © Copyright 1951 (renewed) by Bourne Co. Used by permission of Bourne Co. All rights reserved. International copyright secured.

"These Foolish Things." Words by Holt Marvell, music by Jack Strachey and Harry Link. © Copyright 1936 (renewed) by Bourne Co. Used by permission of Bourne Co. All rights reserved. International copyright secured.

Manufactured in the United States of America

First Ballantine Books Edition: January 1995

10 9 8 7 6 5 4

for my two beautiful and beloved daughters-in-law
Jane Hamill Viorst and Hyla Stacey Viorst

CONTENTS

Deciding to Do It

- *September 21*

1

•

THE MURDERING KIND

I am not the murdering kind, but I am planning to kill Mr. Monti because he is doing harm to my family. I don't look like the murdering kind, being a short, blond, rounded, very married lady, with bifocals and a softness under the chin. On the other hand, I don't look like the kind who, just a few weeks before her forty-sixth birthday, slept with three different men within twenty-four hours. And since I indeed did do that, I might indeed be able to murder Mr. Monti.

Nine months ago Mr. Monti's daughter Josephine told him that she was engaged to marry my Wally. Five weeks ago poor Josephine was having a nervous breakdown and Wally was being accused of stealing a large sum of money from Mr. Monti's safe.

"I know you didn't do it," I said to Wally in my most reassuring maternal-supportive voice. "But could you just explain how a hundred and fifty thousand dollars happened to be in the trunk of your Chevrolet?"

"It's a really long story, Mom," he said, so we sat in the living room and he told me the story. And then he kissed me goodbye and disappeared.

I have complete confidence in Wally. Jeff, my other son, the older one, is a whole different matter. I mean, who could have complete confidence in a real estate developer? But Wally, who is going for his Master's in Social Work at Catholic University, is a good boy, a truly lovely person. And it doesn't hurt a bit that in the right light, with his perfect profile and roguish blue eyes, he is definitely a Mel Gibson look-alike. In fact, if someone told Mel Gibson that he looked like Wally Kovner, Mel could take it as a major compliment.

Though I ought to have known better, I tried, on the second day of Wally's disappearance, to talk over possible plans of action with my husband, Jake. Not the murder part, which I hadn't come to yet, but several other thoughts I had on the subject. Jake did not wish to hear about them.

"We've got a lawyer handling this now, Brenda. So I'm going to ask you, nicely and politely and with a great deal of respect for your autonomy, to back off." He took a big sip of coffee and resumed reading *The Washington Post*.

We've been married forever, but I continue to be fascinated by the way Jake can push a button in his brain and switch off the outside world as if it's a TV program he no longer wishes to watch. Lately, however, I have noticed that I am the TV program that Jake keeps switching off. Who could resist a line like "I've got something desperately important to discuss with you"? Who could ignore a statement like "What I have to say could totally alter our lives, the lives of our children, and perhaps the lives of our future grandchildren as well"? Jake could, can, does, and—that second day after Wally's disappearance—did.

I tried again. "I know you're feeling annoyed with me," I told him, trying to sound hurt but not reproachful. He swigged down the rest of his coffee, got up, gave me an insincere pat on the behind, and was out the door and into the car before I could finish the rest of my sentence. I was going to say ". . . and I can even understand why you might feel that way," which would have added just the right tone of empathy *and* humility. I often tell my readers that if you put yourself in the other person's shoes and display a little good-natured self-effacement, you will greatly enhance your communication skills.

It's a shame that my column (which appears in 372 newspapers around the country) doesn't run in *The Washington Post*, where Jake might stumble upon it from time to time. I believe he is confusing the name of my column—"IN CONTROL OF OUR LIVES"—with my character, which he seems to view as far more controlling than I am emotionally or philosophically capable of being. Indeed, I often make the point, in the 750 words allotted to me three times a week, that (as Spinoza or somebody very much like him once said) "Freedom is the recognition of necessity." Which means that, when confronted with a stone wall that is blocking your path, you need to recognize its stone-walledness and not go banging your head against it. But which also means that you could dig a tunnel under it, walk around it, climb over it, dismantle it, or find another road to where you want to go.

This is an attitude that has equipped me to help hundreds of thousands of readers (and two dozen or so of my closest friends) with troubled marriages, difficult children, midlife crises, aging parents, and blasted dreams. This is an attitude that has also equipped me to provide them with a wide array of useful household hints (including foolproof gourmet recipes), the names and phone numbers of first-class psychotherapists, thoughtfully annotated book and film recommendations, and (though there is not a lot of call for this) the lyrics to vast numbers of popular songs from the nineteen twenties, thirties, forties, and fifties.

In other words, what we've got here is a "can-do" attitude, which is something quite quite different from "controlling." So I don't intend to sit around and wait for a lawyer (who may be more into necessity than freedom) to protect my family from harm when there is, in fact, something I can do. Like murder Mr. Monti.

You must understand that never once, in my column, have I recommended murder. I am, however, in favor of capital punishment. My problem here is that I have recently lost some of my once starry-eyed confidence in judges and the jury system, and therefore would want to be the one who personally decided which criminals merited the death penalty. I acknowledge that this philosopher-king approach (derived from Plato's *Republic*, a surprisingly good read) is at odds with my basic liberal-humanistic-ACLU bent, but—as I often tell my readers—the capacity to live with ambivalence is a necessary (though not sufficient) condition of healthy adulthood.

Jake doesn't think that I live with ambivalence. He thinks that I am absolutely positive about absolutely everything. He has always thought this about me, but when, at age eighteen, I was absolutely positive that he was the man with whom I wished to lose my virginity, he thought I was adorable. And when, at age twenty, I was absolutely positive that he was the man with whom I wished to spend the rest of my life, he thought I was irresistible. Over the years, however, his enthusiasm for my certainties has waned, and he now insists on seeing me as a black/white, day/night, wrong/right, unnuanced kind of person. I could resent his failure to appreciate my subtleties, but instead I accept responsibility for his misperception and intend to keep working (marriage, I tell my readers, is a full-time occupation) at correcting it.

Actually, if you want to see a truly unambivalent, unsubtle, absolutist controller, take a look at Mr. Monti. A nonnegotiable Roman Catholic, he has bullied his wife into pious submission and made sure that his two older daughters married in the faith. When Josephine began dating Wally, a distinctly Jewish person, last autumn, Mr. Monti brought out priests, nuns, and other big guns, but failed to prevent Josephine from continuing to see Wally and very quickly falling in love with him. When, during the Christmas-Chanukah season, Josephine agreed to marry Wally, Mr. Monti, moving to his next line of defense, launched into a passionate pitch for conversion. He told Wally and Josephine that this was the kind of accommodation—okay, call it sacrifice, even—that people in love were more than willing to make. Such sacrifices, he said, were good not merely for the marriage but for the soul. Wally completely agreed with him and went on to praise his sensitivity to the needs and obligations inherent in all committed human relations. (Wally has learned a lot from me over the years.) He also said he was certain that Mr. Monti would understand if his soul took a while to get used to the whole idea. Accustomed to having his way, Mr.

Monti confidently waited through the first three months of the new year. So in April, when he was informed that Wally wouldn't be converting, he felt not only defied and disdained but personally and publicly humiliated.

Mr. Monti has no sense of humor and no sense of proportion, both of which are also necessary (though not sufficient) conditions of healthy adulthood. He is a large, vain man who, though vision-impaired without his tinted glasses, instantly whips them off when there's an attractive woman around, the better to dazzle her with his expressive eyes. He also seems quite enamored of his overly styled black hair, through which he fondly runs his fingers while bragging about his vast wealth, extraordinary business acumen, and the fact that he has never ever ever lost a fight. It's true that his suits fit him to perfection, but he wears a bit too much gold to make a favorable impression on us less affluent but more tasteful types. (I confess to being hostile to gold chains worn by men of a certain age. Make that any age.) As for his pinky ring . . . Well, suffice it to say that Mr. Monti—with his bullying and boastful ways, his manicured nails, his custom-made shirts with the monogram on the left cuff, and all that gold—would not be my first choice for one of my future grandchild's four grandparents. But if that's what he was going to be, I have to say I was pleased that this hypothetical grandchild was going to be raised by a Jewish father. Pleased not only because I wished to perpetuate our heritage (which I did), but also because (and I grant that this is a deeply unattractive part of my character) it gave me a lot of pleasure to screw Mr. Monti.

Which, to get back to an earlier point, I had already done.

What I mean is that, while I wouldn't ever choose a person like Joseph Augustus Monti to be one of my future grandchild's four grandparents, I had in fact chosen him to be one of the three men I went to bed with just a few weeks before my forty-sixth birthday.

I could plead insanity, but I won't. As I often tell my readers, all of us—if we wish to call ourselves adults—must take responsibility for our actions. Despite unhappy childhoods. Despite social and economic inequities. Despite life's cruel, random blows. We are responsible and, within the limits imposed by necessity, we are in control. No one is forcing us to have sexual congress with burly, bullying Italians who wear gold chains and pinky rings (though he did, in response to a moan not entirely of pain, have the courtesy to remove the ring). We make—I made—that choice.

I had taken the coming of age forty-six very hard. This may well surprise my readers, to whom I have confided that, despite an innate optimism (which has carried me through many a dark moment), I have long possessed a tragic sense of life and been well aware that someday I too would grow old and die. I had presented myself, and had thought of myself, as someone who had come to terms with mortality.

Several months before my birthday, however, I became increasingly obsessed with a grim statistic: My grandmother had died at sixty-nine. My mother had died at sixty-nine. And so had her only sister. As a rational person committed to staring unflinchingly at the truth, I had to conclude that, given this relentless family history, officially my life was about to be two-thirds over.

As a rational person I then had to ask myself, Why am I taking this so hard? First of all, I still had twenty-three years left. Second of all, I had already enjoyed a richly fulfilling life: Love and work. Marriage and the family. Personal satisfaction and public recognition. Good friends and good health. Indeed, I had often proclaimed that, were I on a plane that was going down in flames, I could not complain that I was being significantly cheated of life's delights. Except . . . Except . . . Except for one thing. Sex.

I am embarrassed to say this, but as one who has lived by the guiding principle Know Thyself, I could not let shame, guilt, or anxiety deflect me from facing facts. And the fact was that I felt sexually deprived. Let me hasten to add that I did not feel deprived of sexual *pleasure*. I have always had plenty of that, thanks to a certain natural talent on Jake's part and to my willingness to accept (as I urge my readers to accept) full responsibility for my own orgasms. No, I felt deprived not of sexual pleasure but of sexual *variety*. I had married young and committed myself to marital fidelity and now I was going to go to my grave having had carnal knowledge of just one man—my husband.

At first this realization struck me as unutterably sad. But after many sleepless nights and much self-analysis, it began to strike me as intolerable. I asked myself, as I often do in such situations, What would you tell your readers? My answer was that I'd tell my readers a lie. I'd say that instead of finding sexual variety by going to bed with many different men, they could find it by going to many different beds with the same man. I've actually written several columns advocating this viewpoint, waxing quite eloquent about the thrill of taking a long lunch hour at an in-town motel with your husband, about the thrill of spending a Saturday night in a Jacuzzi (and don't forget the wine and candles!) with your husband, about the thrill of slipping off with him to a deserted corner of the beach on a sultry summer evening and . . . These are not bad ideas, but they do not answer a couple of urgent questions: What would it be like with another man? And, perhaps more important, what would *I* be like with another man?

As all my readers know, I am philosophically opposed to adultery. It involves lying, sneaking, and cheating. If you are an essentially decent person, you will not adjust well to lying, sneaking, and cheating. Therefore you will either confess, unconsciously arrange to get caught, feel morally rotten, or provoke your mate so that he or she will wind up behaving badly enough to justify your being morally rotten. All of the above (and I haven't even mentioned sexually transmitted diseases) are serious threats to personal happiness and matrimonial stability. So even though I'm well aware that my same-man-in-different-beds prescription leaves an enormous amount to be desired, I still believe I'm correct in telling my readers that they must say no to adultery.

I myself decided to say a mature, responsible, rational, can-do yes.

Three days after Wally took off, he telephoned me from Rehoboth, Delaware, where a friend had lent him a house right on the beach. I was in the kitchen, washing and drying lettuce leaves, which I then stored in plastic Baggies and refrigerated until ready to use (I have found this the ideal way to prevent soggy salads), when the phone rang.

"Mom, I've been worried that you're upset and I don't want you to be," he said, which is the kind of thing that makes me so crazy about him. "I'm safe, I'm fine, and I know exactly what I have to do."

"And what is that, Wally?" I asked, bagging the last of the romaine as I moved freely around my kitchen thanks to the modern marvel of the portable phone.

"I have to get Josephine away from her father and that phony psychiatrist he's hired to work her over," Wally said.

"She's in bad shape," I reminded him, taking out the chicken breasts and starting to marinate them. "I don't think she can manage without some sort of therapeutic help."

"But the right sort, Mom. Not that Dr. Phony. So I'm just going to slip quietly into town and rescue her."

"Is that what she wants?" I asked.

"Not at the moment, I guess. But when she comes to her senses, she will."

"Except at the moment," I pointed out, "what you're planning to do might come under the heading of kidnapping. May I make a few alternative suggestions?"

"You did that the other night, Mom. I rejected them. So . . . are you going to help me with this, or what?"

I thought about Jake and sighed. "Your father would—"

"He would if he knew." Wally's voice turned soft and cajoling. "Why does he have to know?"

It is my observation that there are mother's sons and father's sons. Wally has always been a mother's son. He

clearly thinks that I married a man who is too insensitive to fully appreciate me, and that I deserve someone
better, perhaps someone more like himself. But beyond
the usual Oedipal business, Wally enjoys my company,
trusts my judgment, and confides in me. Over the years
we have kept many small, but potentially irritating,
items of information from his father. Now that we were
moving into big-time secrets, however, I was feeling
rather uneasy.

"What do you want me to do?" I asked him as I set
the table for dinner. (I tell my readers that it's quite all
right to eat dinner in the kitchen, as long as they use
cloth napkins and never serve directly from the pots to
the plates.) By the end of our conversation, after sup-
plying a few creative modifications, I had agreed to par-
ticipate in Wally's rescue (or kidnapping) of Josephine.

I provided an edited version of my conversation with
Wally when Jake came home exhausted from Children's
Hospital. It was better that way.

Jake is a pediatric surgeon rather than a general surgeon because he deeply believes in specialization. I do
not. It is Jake's view that pediatric surgeons operate on
children, psychiatrists practice psychiatry, architects design houses, and lawyers handle legal matters. It is my
view that we should develop informed opinions on a
wide range of subjects and not mindlessly defer to the
so-called experts. Now I wouldn't, of course, attempt to
do a kidney transplant on a two-year-old (unless it had
to be done immediately and there was no one else
around), but I have never hesitated to contribute my
psychological insights, my architectural esthetics, or my
legal opinions. Or my extralegal opinions, for that matter. I am basically committed to law and order, but

when my child's life is being endangered by a pinky-ringed Italian psychopath in a $1,200 suit, it is my opinion that we ought to bend a few laws.

Mr. Monti was wearing one of those fancy suits five weeks ago, on Tuesday, August 18, when he came driving up to our house at about ninety miles an hour in his red Porsche with JAM (for Joseph Augustus Monti) on his vanity plates. The three of us—Jake and Wally and I—were just finishing our main course (sautéed shrimp with pesto sauce, served on orzo), taking full advantage of the unmuggy air, a very rare treat in August, by having dinner out on the front porch.

There are lots of front porches in Cleveland Park, our gracious but somehow unpretentious neighborhood, where big old Victorian houses like ours compensate for bad pipes and inadequate wiring by virtue of lofty ceilings and multiple fireplaces. With raccoons in our yard and squirrels in our attic and boisterous bird song at dawn in our skyscraping trees, I can feel as if I'm far from the madding crowd. But the White House—we've not been invited as yet—is just a brief car ride away. And right down our steep Newark Street hill, a five-minute walk from where we live, is everything a civilized person needs: A branch of our public library. A bookstore. A video store. A movie theater. Markets, carry-outs, restaurants galore. And the Metro, our still-spiffy subway system, which even the richest folks in Cleveland Park ride.

In other words, I've got supplies an easy stroll from home and sweet serenity outside my door, a sweet serenity about to be blasted by Joseph Monti in full attack mode.

"I knew he was a bum, but I didn't know the bum was also a crook," he bellowed, storming up onto our porch and dragging a tearful, reluctant Josephine behind him.

Wally got up and reached for Jo but Mr. Monti, planting a hand on his chest, shoved him back into his wrought-iron seat, knocking over the saltshaker in the process. Mr. Monti stared for a moment at the salt he had spilled, then scooped it up with his fingertips and tossed it over his left, and then his right, shoulder. "I can never remember which shoulder," he said, in a normal tone of voice, "but why risk bad luck—what's so hard to do both?" He turned back to Wally. "Bum!" he snarled. "Bum! Crook!"

Jake stood up and said, in his best surgical-strike voice, "I don't know what your problem is, Mr. Monti, but I suggest that you get off this porch immediately or I will have to call the police."

"Feel free," said Mr. Monti. "But when they arrest your son, just remember who invited them to this party."

Josephine was sobbing hysterically. Her father pointed to our beautiful antique white wicker rocking chair (it's amazing what a can of spray paint and a new fabric on the pillows can do). "Sit. Blow your nose. Wipe your eyes. And listen. Maybe you'll finally learn something."

As Josephine headed for the rocking chair, Wally yelled, "Jo, honey!" and got up again. Again Mr. Monti shoved him back in his seat, this time with such force that on the way down Wally's head hit one of our hanging geranium plants and set it swinging wildly.

Jake reached for our portable phone, punched 911,

and awaited a human response, which you shouldn't hold your breath for. "Excuse me," said Mr. Monti, his face instructing me in the definitive meaning of the word "sneer." "Do you want to report to the police that your son has just stolen a hundred and fifty thousand dollars from my bedroom safe?"

"No way!" yelled Wally. Josephine sobbed louder. I decided it was time for a constructive intervention.

Fortunately, I was looking real good and, as I often remind my readers, shallow though it may seem, let's not underestimate the confidence we gain from feeling pleased with our physical appearance. I had the best tan you can acquire with Presun Number 29 sun screen, the pale streaks in my cropped curly hair could almost have been natural, and the eye lift had done wonders for my upper-eyelid droop. While no one would ever confuse me with Goldie Hawn, I will in all modesty note that we might very well be mistaken for first cousins.

Anyway, I asked Jake to please get off the phone for a few minutes while we tried to work this out like civilized human beings. I asked Wally to please stay in his chair for a few minutes while we tried to work this out like civilized human beings. I gave Josephine a soothing pat and a few paper napkins (no, I'm not being inconsistent; I believe paper is permitted at dinner when dining outdoors) to mop up her tear-stained face. Then I told Mr. Monti to stop being disrespectful to my husband, to keep his fucking hands off my son, and to please elaborate upon his grotesque accusations.

Mr. Monti pulled a chair up to our wrought-iron table and shook his head. "Some nice family you've got here. The doctor has two malpractice suits hanging over him and his hospital—"

"Both of which are entirely without merit and will be resolved in our favor," said Jake in his best surgical-icicle voice.

"And the lady of the house has—"

"Has what, Mr. Monti?" I asked him, knowing full well that he was never going to spill the beans about our . . . brief encounter.

"Has some filthy mouth on her. What did you call my hands? You called my hands *what*? That's how you talk in front of a girl who had never missed a mass until she met your son, a girl who had never been touched any place personal until she met your son, a girl who . . ." As Mr. Monti's rage mounted, his fingers—seeming to possess a life of their own—reached into the orzo and pulled out a pesto-drenched shrimp. He popped it into his mouth, nodded appreciatively, and then helped himself to another. The shrimps seemed to exert a calming influence.

"And congratulations on your sons," he said, his voice returning to conversational level. "Both bums. Your real estate genius, I'm taking bets, before the end of the year will be begging on street corners. And your master of social work—this bum right here—stole first my daughter's virtue, and now my money."

There was a yowl of protest from Josephine, and Wally started getting up from his chair yet again. I shook my head warningly and he subsided. "Mr. Monti," I said, "let's put the subject of Josephine's virtue to one side for now and concentrate on the money. What are you trying to say?"

"Not trying. Saying. This afternoon your son entered my bedroom and removed all the cash from my safe."

"You saw him do this?" I asked.

"The money was there this morning. Josephine was there all day. She will confirm that the only three people who were in the house today were me, her, and—" pointing a fat thumb in the direction of Wally—"him."

"Mr. Monti," Wally said, trying to emulate my calm, reasoned approach, "I did not take your money. I do not have your money. I drove directly from your house to my house. Search me. Search this house. Search the car."

"What did you do—figure it would be days, weeks, before I checked my safe again? Bad figuring, bum." He put out his hand. "Car keys."

I found it hard to believe that Mr. Monti was actually going to search Wally's car. We all did. Jake said, "This is ridiculous. What are we having for dessert?" I was telling him that dessert was a lemon sorbet topped with strawberries soaked in crème de cassis, when there was a roar of triumph over by the Chevrolet.

"I want everyone to see this," said Mr. Monti. "I want everyone to see with their own eyes."

We all rushed to the curb and peered into the trunk of Wally's Chevy. A lot of money was stacked up in rubber-banded piles. Wally said, "What's going on here?" Jake said, "I'm calling our lawyer." Josephine fell into her father's arms, back to heavy-duty sobbing. I returned to the porch, cleared the plates from the table, and served the dessert. I even had enough class to bring out desserts for Josephine and Mr. Monti.

Fortunately our lawyer, Marvin Kipper, also lives in Cleveland Park, just a few blocks away. In response to Jake's call, he said he was going out for his evening run and would run over to our house. He was there within four minutes, sweaty and panting but ready for action.

Wally swore he never took the money. Josephine, completely undone, said she didn't know whether he did or not. Jake asked how Wally could possibly open the safe. Mr. Monti turned to the kids and asked them to tell the assembled throng why Wally knew the combination to the safe. Without waiting for their answer, he reminded them with a big gotcha grin that Wally, while still persona semi-grata, had attended a Monti family dinner at which Mr. Monti let slip that the combination of his safe was the same as Josephine's birth date. Wally confirmed this with a "right," Josephine with a grim nod of her head.

In his faded red shorts, tattered T-shirt, and bargain running shoes, Marvin was no match for the sartorially splendid Mr. Monti. In a film of his life, Marv's lovable shlumpiness could best be captured by Woody Allen in his pre-Ingmar Bergman phase. But Marvin is one of those low-key, high-fee attorneys who inspire confidence, and his thin reedy voice carried authority when he told Mr. Monti that if he wanted to go to the police with his accusations, go right ahead. All of us stared at Mr. Monti, who pushed aside the strawberries and vigorously attacked the sorbet, noting between spoonfuls that in fact he preferred not to go to the police. He said he just wanted his money back, his daughter back, and Wally permanently out of their life.

Josephine had stopped sobbing and was looking practically catatonic. Her eyes were blank, her face was dead-white, and she was twisting and turning a long strand of dark-red hair around her finger.

"Say something, Jo," Wally begged her. "Say you believe in me."

Josephine didn't answer.

"Tell him he's a bum and you never want to see him again," Mr. Monti instructed her.

Josephine didn't answer.

"It's going to be okay," I said to Josephine.

She shook her head from side to side in a violent, silent no, no, no. Then she left the porch and got into the front seat of her father's car.

A moment later Mr. Monti, having polished off his dessert, and his daughter's too, made his departure. "Talk to your client," he told Marvin, "and I'll talk to you around noon tomorrow." As he opened the door to his Porsche he tossed off one last instruction: "Take good care of the money, folks. I'll be counting every bill when it's returned to me."

"That son of a bitch. That son of a bitch," Wally muttered as the Porsche took off.

"You didn't do it, right, kid?" asked Marvin.

"Didn't do it," said Wally.

"So who did?"

"There's only one person could have done it, but—" Wally rubbed the back of his head where it had crashed into the geranium plant. "Hey, I've got a really rotten headache right now. Could we wait and discuss this tomorrow, at your office?"

"Absolutely," said Marv. "And think about the offer Monti made you. Innocent or not, maybe you don't want to get mixed up with a cuckoo family like that."

Wally launched into a "Josephine is the woman I intend to marry" speech, but I tactfully cut him short and sent him to bed, recommending for his aching head two pillows, two Bufferin, and an ice bag wrapped in a towel. Jake pointed out that we couldn't leave a hundred and fifty thou in the trunk of a car, even on a quiet street like ours, so I brought out a giant green garbage bag and the three of us hastily stuffed the money into it. "I'll pick it up tomorrow on my way down to work," Marvin offered, after Jake had dragged the bag inside. "Now how about—" he hitched up his drooping running shorts "—a cup of your coffee."

The three of us sat in silence for a while, listening to the crickets' raspy chorus. A light breeze stirred our bright-blossomed crape myrtle and a couple of squirrels played last-game-of-tag-before-bedtime in one of our pines. The scene was serene, but I was certainly not. Sitting here at home on our leafy street on our wraparound porch, I had been feeling so sheltered and so safe. But Mr. Monti had clomped up the steps, disturbing the peace and reminding me what a mean and menacing place the world could be.

I explained to Marvin how deeply distraught (make that crazed) Mr. Monti had been about the conversion decision. I explained how I had tried on several occasions, unsuccessfully, to charm and argue and beg and press Mr. Monti into letting these sweet kids alone. I added that I thought that Mr. Monti would do anything—even something as wildly extreme as taking cash from his safe and putting it in the trunk of Wally's car—if this would discredit him in Josephine's eyes.

"He would do such a thing just because of this disagreement about converting?" Marvin asked me.

"No," I answered. "He would do it to win. This is a man who always has to win."

* * *

Jake never suffers from insomnia, and that night was no exception. He said he was sure that after Marvin and Wally met, Marvin would have some expensive and useful recommendations. I told him I thought we were dealing with psychological, not legal, issues here. He said we should first see what Marvin had to say and that I should try to get a good night's sleep. I said that I assumed that he and I would be going to Marvin's office with Wally. He didn't answer because he was fast asleep.

Around 1 A.M. I went down to the kitchen and began eating my way through a large bag of Hershey's Kisses. A few minutes later I heard Wally's feet on the stairs. We took the bag into the living room and when we reached the end of our conversation, the only kiss that was left was the one he gave to me before he disappeared.

I waited until six before I awakened Jake with the news that our son had taken off. Sparing him the details, I simply told him that Wally was feeling upset and needed some time by himself to think things through.

"Great," Jake said. "Now he's a fugitive from justice."

"No, he's not," I explained. "He hasn't been charged with a crime. He is perfectly within his constitutional rights if he wants to go away for a few days to clear his head."

"Is that what you told him, Brenda?"

"More or less. But only after he asked."

When Jake gets angry his voice becomes softer, not louder. By the time he was finished with what he had to say, he was almost whispering. Then he called Marvin, who said that he had a couple of legal tactics that would put Mr. Monti on hold for a few days. He added that although he wished that Wally had talked with him first, he hadn't been charged with a crime and was therefore perfectly within his constitutional rights if he wanted to . . .

I was listening in on the extension, but when the conversation was over I didn't gloat. Instead, with tears in my eyes I told Jake that the tone he had taken with me displayed an absence of love and affection, not to mention considerable disrespect for my autonomy. (I strongly urge my readers, in marital disputes, to use the more-in-sorrow-than-in-anger approach if they're looking for an apology from their husbands.) Jake apologized.

Have I mentioned that Jake has a slim, muscular body and that from the neck down he looks almost as youthful as the twenty-nine-year-old who was another of the three men I went to bed with in those twenty-four hours shortly before my last birthday? Sometimes when I'm feeling unappreciated by Jake, I forget to acknowledge how attractive he is. And he is, even from the neck up, where his fifty years have pouched his eyes and stolen most of his hair, but have left him with the somewhat battered appeal of a—well, try to imagine a Jewish Sean Connery.

Furthermore, Jake has never been one of those surgeons who confuse themselves with God. He is reasonably modest, a very hard worker, a devoted father, and, until recently, a tolerant husband who had been perfectly happy to allow me to be in charge of human relationships and culture. But now, in indirect and not so indirect ways, he seems to be suggesting that my column is bringing out the worst in me. I wonder if he's jealous. I wonder if he thinks I'm confusing myself with God.

Actually, neither Jake nor I could possibly be God. The title has been claimed by Philip, an internationally known television personality whose name would be instantly recognizable to you if I weren't calling him Philip, which I am doing because he's the third of the men I went to bed with in those twenty-four hours before my forty-sixth birthday.

It has been quite a year. My birthday took place five months ago. Wally took off five weeks ago. And yesterday I decided to kill Mr. Monti.

2

•

YES TO ADULTERY

Once I had chosen to say yes to adultery, I was faced with some tricky questions: (a) How could I be an adulteress (or are we saying adulterer these days?) and still feel like a basically good human being? (b) Was there a way to minimize the lying and sneaking and cheating while also making certain I didn't get caught? (c) How many different men would it take to meet my need for sexual variety? And (d) What could I do to avoid the quite unwanted complication of falling in love with any or all of these men?

Now there are people all around us who maintain their sense of goodness by denying the negative aspects of themselves, by indulging in the blind belief that they harbor no wicked thoughts or malevolent feelings. I am proud to say I am not one of those people. Instead, I am well aware that each of us, including myself, contains both lightness and darkness, both good and evil. And I therefore believe that a "good" person is not one whose heart is pure, but one who stares into, and continually wrestles with, her heart of darkness (a stirring phrase taken from the fine novel of the same name by

Joseph Conrad). Goodness, I tell my readers, is a struggle, not a settled state of grace. And even the best of us sometimes struggle and lose.

I suppose you could say I had lost the adultery struggle. On the extenuating other hand, however, I intended to commit adultery not in a spirit of self-indulgent lust but more in a spirit of intellectual inquiry. Indeed, it would not be farfetched to call it . . . research. If you add to this analysis the tit-for-tat factor (Jake had not been a man of total fidelity) and the helpful-to-my-readers factor (engaging in adultery would certainly broaden my range of expertise) and the preponderance-of-good-over-evil factor (in my wrestling matches with my heart of darkness I win about 92 percent—well, okay, 85 percent—of the time), my answer to question (a) is that I indeed could be an adulteress/adulterer and still feel like a basically good human being.

I also concluded that limiting my adulterous activities to a narrow—a very narrow—time frame would contribute both to my sense of goodness (I would not, after all, be making extracurricular sex a way of life) and to my ability to minimize the lying and sneaking and cheating (as well as the likelihood of getting caught). Furthermore, I decided that the best way to work adultery into my already tight and overprogrammed schedule was to get it over with as quickly as possible.

Frankly, I don't understand why adultery is as popular as it is, considering how time-consuming it is. I mean, it isn't just the time involved in actually having sexual relations. It's all the support systems, like locating matching bras and panties, plus panty hose without a run in the thigh. Like getting your hair done, a pedicure, a manicure. Like applying lotion not only to your hands but to your heels and elbows as well, which, of course, we should all be doing anyway—but do we? And then there's this constant searching for a working pay phone in order to call your lover without being overheard or (for the more paranoid) being tape-recorded by a less-than-trusting husband. There are so many time pressures on women today as they try to have it all (though, as I tell my readers, they *can* have it all but they can't have it all at once) that I am slowly coming to the conclusion that one of the best arguments for marital fidelity is the incredible convenience of it.

Anyway, to get back to question (b), I decided that setting aside no more than a week, say, for adultery (who dreamed I could do it in less than twenty-four hours?) was the best way to limit my lying, sneaking, etc.

As for question (c)—and as I also tell my readers—there is nothing like sitting down and making a list, either lettered or numbered, to give you a sense of clarity and control. I therefore sat down last November and listed the *types* of men I wanted to carnally know, focusing initially on the generic, not the specific, and choosing the types that I chose for assorted complicated reasons that only my former analyst need comprehend: (1) a younger man; (2) a married man; (3) a black man; (4) a political activist; (5) a genius; (6) a celebrity; (7) a man of a different religious persuasion; and (8), I blush to add, an identical twin. Actually, I thought it might be nice to carnally know both identical twins, simultaneously, but although, like Publius Terentius Afer, nothing human is alien to me, I immediately banished that thought as . . . overreaching. Besides, the number of men on my list, counting only one twin, struck me as a little bit excessive, and I decided I had to . . . not prune, really, but consolidate. Which eventually I was able to do, having established that I could satisfy eight different needs with only three different men, all of whom—it conveniently turned out—were already uncarnally known to me.

There was Louis, a dedicated black activist who, at age twenty-nine, also met the younger-man requirement.

There was Philip, the world-famous TV pundit who had been flirting with me for years at my friend Nora's New Year's Day parties and who, if you didn't listen too closely, could pass for a genius.

And there was Joseph Augustus Monti.

My concern about falling in love with the men with whom I committed adultery—question (d)—might strike you as rather outdated at a time in our social history when sex (despite its risks) has become regarded as a form of entertainment. Like bowling or bridge or going to the movies. Like ordering in a pizza with mushrooms and anchovies. No big deal. Nevertheless, I found it hard to imagine how people who take off their clothes and lie down together can "have sex" without "making love," without feeling a tenderness, a connectedness, an involvement with each other that could lead to major emotional complications. But as I contemplated the three men I had selected to become my short-term lovers, I realized that the danger of love was remote. Like Elvis Presley, whom in my youth I had passionately disapproved of and just as passionately lusted after, these men spoke to my loins, not to my soul. I could not fall in love with Louis. I could not fall in love with Philip. And I could certainly not fall in love with Mr. Monti.

Mr. Monti was not at all lovable when, the day after his appearance on our front porch, Marvin and I showed up at his office with the hundred and fifty thousand dollars and no Wally. "You wanted your money back and my client out of your life," said Marvin reasonably. "Your money is here. My client is gone. Your terms have been met."

Marvin stretched out his hands palms up, in a fair's fair gesture that complemented the sweet reasonableness of his voice. Behind his horn-rims, his eyes gazed steadily at Mr. Monti, his whole manner suggesting that while the practice of law might, for some folks, be viciously adversarial, men of good will could surely work things out. Knowing Marvin's reputation as one of the bigger barracudas in the Washington legal profession, I watched his genial performance with admiration. Only a slight tension in his tight runner's body execrably clad in a discount Syms suit hinted at his ability—should sweet reason fail to prevail—to viciously tear out his adversary's throat.

Most adversaries. Maybe not this one.

Mr. Monti leaned back in his desk chair and sighed. "You think so, huh?" he said softly. "You think that you can walk in here in those cheap hundred-and-forty-dollar shoes"—Marvin flushed with pleasure, having never spent more for shoes than $32.99 at Payless—"and sell me a bill of goods that my terms have been met?"

"That's my understanding of—"

"Well, understand this, Kipper. I don't just want your

client out of my life. I want your client out of my life *permanently*."

I decided that the moment called for a constructive intervention—something philosophical with a down-to-earth touch. I had on just the right outfit to strike that note—a black-and-white silk with a slit skirt to show off (let me not indulge in false modesty here) my fabulous legs. I was there without the approval, or even the knowledge, of my husband, and I can't say that Marvin Kipper was thrilled with my presence. But, as I pointed out to him while we were riding up in the elevator together, "Marvin you can never tell when my grasp of the human condition will come in handy."

I thought that time had come.

"Mr. Monti," I said, "what, after all, do we mean by permanent? Even our greatest symbols of permanence are subject to change. In time the Rockies may crumble, Gibraltar may tumble, and we all have to live with that reality. Even you, Mr. Monti."

"What's your point, Mrs. Kovner?"

"That Wally is gone. That as far as any of us, in any ultimate sense, knows, he is gone permanently. And that, until he stops being gone, your terms have—in fact—been met."

Mr. Monti rose from his chair, walked around his desk, and stood over me.

"I want it in writing," he said to me, bringing his face quite rudely close to mine. "No, I want it in blood." He smiled a dangerous smile and lowered his voice. "Symbolically speaking, of course."

Symbolically speaking is not, believe me, the kind of verbal expression that leaps to the lips of Joseph Augustus Monti. He learned it, I regret to admit, from me. He learned it one evening last January, in that delicate period after Wally and Josephine had announced their decision to marry but before they'd announced that Wally would not be converting. Mr. and Mrs. Monti had invited us four Kovners to dine with them, their three daughters, and two sons-in-law at their extensive and expensive spread in McLean, Virginia. Also in attendance were a professor from Georgetown University (I never quite caught his name but he bore an eerie resemblance to the somnambulist in *The Cabinet of Dr. Caligari*) and Father Pezzati, a cheerful, fat-cheeked, roly-poly priest. Wally had already met all the Montis, and all of us Kovners had already met Josephine, but this was the initial full-fledged family-to-family encounter, and I was eager for us to make a good first impression.

I was therefore relieved that Jeff, a tawny Michael Douglas type (What can I tell you? I've got two gorgeous sons), was looking untypically virtuous in pinstripes, having eschewed his signature chartreuse suspenders and diamond-stud earring for the occasion. We had picked him up at his Watergate apartment, and on the way out to McLean he had expressed his interest in "doing a deal" with the widely diversified Mr. Monti.

"The guy's made a bundle," Jeff informed us, "buying old rental properties real cheap, and then the neighborhood—whoosh—takes off, and he's selling these suckers for five, six times his investment." Jeff shook his head respectfully. "I don't know where he gets his crystal ball, but I'd sure like to take a look in it sometimes."

"Yes, but you won't get into all that tonight," I gently

asked and/or suggested, never quite sure where Jeff's hustling heart might lead him.

"Certainly not," Jeff answered in a huffy there-she-goes-underestimating-me-again tone of voice. "I just intend to lay a little groundwork."

Wally, looking divine in his gray tweed social-worker jacket and Mel's *Lethal Weapon* longish wavy hair, greeted everyone with hugs, kisses, and handshakes and his big, broad, utterly irresistible smile. Jeff laid some groundwork with his "honored to meet you, sir," greeting to Mr. Monti, accompanied by a smile which, though not as sincere as Wally's, can certainly warm up a room.

Although the boys inherited their great bodies and strong, even features from their father, they definitely got their knock-'em-dead smiles from me. It's not that Jake doesn't have a perfectly pleasant one; it's just that he often seems to be hoarding a portion of it for a more worthwhile occasion. Still, cautious smile, cautious blue suit, and all, he too, I thought, made a fine first impression. And, of course, I did my part as well, having enhanced my self-confidence with a trip to the hairdresser, where Lawrence of Elizabeth Arden clipped and colored my hair into a jaunty tangle of gold-streaked caramel curls.

In the interests of rapprochement, I had chosen to wear something with papal overtones—a bright-red dress with a high collar and long sleeves. It was by far the brightest item in the Montis' vast living room, which was decorated entirely in beige and white. Very traditional. Very tasteful. Very damask and velvet. Very beige and white.

As I often advise my readers, compliments should be

precise, never global. If possible, they should also be genuine. I found, as I looked around the room (so different from our own audaciously eclectic green, brown, gold, and rust interior), that I could sincerely praise the flower arrangements, which ranged from a single white rose set in an exquisite bud vase to masses of white tulips exuberantly bursting from a fat china tub. I also assumed, when I cooed to Mrs. Monti about the beauty of these flower arrangements, that I had embarked on a sweet and safe subject. I was wrong.

"Mommy is great with flowers," said Gloria, the oldest and most pregnant of the three Monti daughters. "But they're always white. Look, I'm not saying use every color of the rainbow, but why not *red* roses, why not *yellow* tulips? Branch out, live a little, I keep telling her."

"And I keep telling her," said Mrs. Monti, her voice trembling with emotion, "that she's got her own house to put red roses in. I don't want them in mine."

Annette, the middle and less pregnant of the daughters, shook her head with disgust. "But Mommy, you can't just keep doing the same white flowers year after year, decade after decade. You'll . . . you'll stagnate."

"Watch your mouth there, missy," warned Mr. Monti, as he poured wine into glasses set on an ornate silver tray. "I don't want to hear any 'stagnates' around here."

A silence descended upon the room. When Mr. Monti had finished filling the glasses, he walked around handing out the drinks. "I'm only serving wine," he said, "but you can have whiskey if you want."

There were no requests for whiskey.

Josephine, the youngest and (please, God) the only non-pregnant Monti daughter, roused herself from her customary reticence to make her contribution to the great flower debate. "If Mommy likes white, I support her right to white."

Father Pezzati who, as I eventually figured out, was not hard of hearing but merely inattentive, now eagerly joined the conversation. "Of course you do, my dear. Of course you do. I presume everyone in this room supports right to life."

Without missing a beat, the Monti contingent murmured their assent. Particularly enthusiastic were the sounds coming from the beige-on-beige striped damask couch, upon which languished—like three variations on the Madonna theme—Mrs. Monti and her two pregnant daughters, all built on a heroic scale, with thick black hair, flawless complexions, and magnificently reconstructed (it takes one to know one) noses. It was clear that their capacity for challenge and dissent had completely exhausted itself on the flower issue. They were now eager to return to the familial harmony which, as Wally had told me, was never breached (at least until he came into the picture) on anything more controversial than tulips and roses. Mr. Monti liked his women docile and devout. And while he was willing to tolerate a brief debate on the merits of right to white, right to life was a closed subject in the Monti household.

But not, needless to say, in the Kovner household. The question was whether integrity required us to state our positions or whether, in the interest of Wally and Josephine's future happiness, we should keep our mouths shut. Fortunately, the Georgetown professor leaped in with a lecture on when life begins. This, according to him, was not at conception but at the moment that you and your mate *decide* to conceive. Why this should be so was explained at great length, taking us through our drinks, the announcement that dinner was served, and the first course, a hearty cheese-encrusted onion soup. It was obvious, as we moved on to the beef Wellington and scalloped potatoes, that the Montis weren't into nouvelle cuisine.

"If life begins with the intention to conceive," said Jake, as he performed microsurgery on his beef, "I'd love to hear your definition of when life ends." He addressed his comment to the professor but Father Pezzati replied instead.

"In the deepest sense, my son, life never ends."

"Yeah," said Annette's husband, Victor, his sandy mustache quivering, his blue eyes alight with religious fervor, or maybe too much red wine. "That's what immortality is all about."

Gloria's husband, Albert, who, like Victor, was employed by his father-in-law, was eager to add his insights to the subject. "You ask a question like that," he reproached Jake, "and the next thing you know, you're turning off the respirators, you're taking out the food tubes, you're playing God."

"That's exactly right," said Mr. Monti.

Gloria patted Albert's hand and looked proud. Mrs. Monti purred, "Such a bright boy." Victor tilted his wineglass approvingly at Albert. Annette actually clapped.

There was a rustle from the far end of the table where Wally and Josephine, their dinners barely touched, their pinkies (his left, her right) tightly intertwined, had been sitting in a romantic stupor.

"Maybe God . . ." Josephine began, her huge eyes

wide with anxiety, her free hand rummaging through her long Botticelli curls. "Maybe God . . ."

Josephine was the only blue-eyed, red-haired Monti; the only small-boned, delicate Monti; and the only Monti female with a heart-shaped face, a Michelle Pfeiffer mouth, and her own (tiny and flawless) original nose. Furthermore, she was soon to become the only Monti woman to finish college, having already made it into her junior year at Catholic University. Unfortunately, she had also been the most intimidated of the Monti women—until she and Wally had met in the stacks of the library and he had started urging her to express herself.

"Maybe God," she began once again, "*wants* us to make these decisions. About the tubes. And the respirators. Maybe God wants us to take responsibility."

I smiled a private smile, recognizing that one of my favorite phrases—"taking responsibility"—had made the trip from me to Wally to Josephine. Now *that*, I told myself, is what immortality is all about.

"God does *not* want us turning off respirators," said Mr. Monti with the confidence of one who converses daily with the Lord.

"Render unto Caesar the things that are Caesar's," said Father Pezzati, "and unto God the things that are God's. Life and death belong to God."

"That is correct," said Mr. Monti.

"Then how come," asked Josephine, "with all those shoot-outs and murders and stuff, you're against gun control, Daddy?"

"Guns don't kill people; people kill people," said Mr. Monti. "Besides, the Bill of Rights guarantees the right of every citizen to bear arms."

Jake got into the act. "That's actually the gun lobby's distortion of what the Bill of Rights . . ."

I silenced him with a quick kick to the ankle, just hard enough to get his attention but not hard enough to cause him—as has happened in the past—to yell "Ouch! Shit! Cut it out, Brenda."

Josephine, terrified but persistent, was not yet finished. "And if death belongs to God, Daddy, how come you're in favor of war?"

"That's enough, Josephine," Mr. Monti replied.

"And how come—"

"I said, enough!" Mr. Monti thundered.

"—how come you believe in the death penalty, Daddy?"

"What a coincidence," I said, rushing in with one of my constructive interventions. "So do I. And speaking of penalties, what did you think of that foul they called against Georgetown last night in the last five seconds of the game? Was that highway robbery, or what?"

Sometimes I astonish myself. I mean, I never watch basketball but I can't always tune out Wally and Jake's morning-after rehash, which is how I learned about this injustice perpetrated against the Hoyas.

The conversation immediately lurched off in a new direction. The Hoyas, every man at the dinner table agreed, had been cheated out of their victory over Syracuse, and the outrage of it all took us through the salad and the home-baked apple pie à la mode. I didn't know that anyone in America ate like that anymore.

After dinner we returned to the living room, where we broke up into separate chatty groups. I found myself in a white velvet chair, alone with Mr. Monti, who removed his eyeglasses, cleared his throat, and said, "Let me ask you something."

"Go right ahead," I told him, hoping he'd ask me for a low-cholesterol diet, or what I thought about full-grown daughters who still call their parents Mommy and Daddy.

"You write a column. You give all kinds of advice. You're this big expert on people."

"Well, I don't claim to be a big expert. I just seem to have an empathic grasp of the . . ."

"Yeah, yeah. An empathic grasp. So just tell me this. Why, all of a sudden, after being a doll, an absolute doll, of a daughter, is Josephine questioning me, disagreeing with me, having all these—all these new opinions?"

"Perhaps she . . ."

"Is that what they teach you in college—disrespect?"

"Perhaps she . . ."

"Or could it be your boy? Could it be your boy turning my daughter against me?"

Ordinarily, anyone making nasty remarks about my children (well, let's be honest here—about Wally) would be the immediate recipient of the full, fierce force of my maternal fury. Instead, despite the fact that Mr. Monti was clearly a sexist and a tyrant, I found myself in touch with the loneliness, the pain, the feeling of abandonment, that quivered beneath his hostile inquiry. Furthermore, despite the fact that he was clearly a militarist, and maybe even a member of the NRA, I found myself in touch with the love he had for his wife and children and with his profound commitment to family life. I later realized that I felt in touch with these things not necessarily because they were there but because I was finding him extraordinarily attractive.

Recollecting my earlier description of Mr. Monti, I must concede that I've made him sound like a slightly sleazy Mafia cliché. It is true that this is how I see him now. But let me not deny that there was a time when his body seemed less burly, his hair less glossy, his jewelry less shiny, his soul less slimy, a time when I was tantalized by his full lower lip and those liquid bedroomy eyes, a time when his restless, eloquent hands seemed made for making a woman's body sing, not for fishing shrimps out of pesto sauce. Indeed, that night, the night of our first meeting, he was—to me—the spitting image of Joe Mantegna, not the violent Joe Mantegna of that third (and, in my view, quite disappointing) Godfather movie but the Joe Mantegna who, as the seductive con man in the fascinatingly enigmatic movie *House of Games,* asks Lindsay Crouse, "Do you want to make love with me?" And then tells her that what she craves is "somebody to come along. Somebody to possess you. To take you into a new thing." And then, knowing perfectly well what her answer is going to be, inquires, "Would you like that? Do you want that?" I drew my chair a bit closer to Mr. Monti's.

"Mr. Monti . . ." I said.

"Call me Joseph," he said.

"Joe—I mean, Joseph," I said, "I honestly think your daughter loves you a lot. But I also think she's trying to be a separate person, independent from you, and that's bound to create some temporary tension."

"Temporary tension? When she talks like that it's like she wants to kill me."

I gave him the full eye-contact treatment and said,

"Every child who breaks away must, in a sense, kill his parents." I then leaned forward, smiled my two-hundred-watt smile, and added softly, "Symbolically speaking, of course."

The evening ended with affectionate champagne toasts to the engaged couple, though there was a somewhat ominous note struck in Mr. Monti's "Good luck. Good love. Many children. And, keep the faith." With the meal I had packed away, I was grateful that my new winter coat still buttoned. Barely.

It had been snowing lightly on the way out to McLean, the flakes melting as they hit the ground, but by the time we said our goodbyes the temperature had dropped and the snow was falling hard. In the hopes of saving my hairdo, I pulled my handy fold-up umbrella out of my purse and was starting to open it up in the hall when Mr. Monti stopped me with a "No. You shouldn't do that. It's very bad luck to open umbrellas indoors."

I had been looking forward to a group analysis of the evening on the trip home, but with near-blizzard conditions assaulting Route 123, I had my hands full helping Jake drive. "Slower, please, darling," I suggested. And, "Why don't we just stay in the right-hand lane?" And, "Watch that guy in the Buick—he's driving as if he's drunk." And, a little testily, I admit, "Sweetheart, *must* you tailgate? In this weather? When it's so easy to skid? When just one little skid and next thing you know we'll wind up in one of those hideous twenty-car pile-ups?"

Despite the limitations placed on our conversation by my navigational duties—and by the car radio, which Jake plays at top volume whenever I start navi-

gating—we did have the chance to unanimously agree
that Mr. Monti was definitely no pussycat. It was then
that Wally presented me with a remarkable new item of
information. "And can you believe," he said, "that there
are *two* of them? He's got an identical twin who lives in
New York."

There was a picture of the identical twin—Vincent Theodore Monti—in Mr. Monti's office. He was indeed a
replica of Joseph Augustus Monti except, or perhaps I
imagined this, for the look of compassion in his eyes.
Joseph Augustus Monti was, I had by now decided,
compassionless. Nevertheless, Marvin Kipper—without
any further assistance from me—eventually succeeded
in striking a deal with him, agreeing that Mr. Monti
could take back his money and still retain his right to
accuse Wally of the theft, in return for which Mr. Monti
agreed not to go to the police with his accusations unless Wally reappeared in Josephine's life.

Marvin wasn't, he reassured me as we left Mr.
Monti's office, selling out Wally. He was simply, as
lawyers are wont to do, buying time.

"You know that Mr. Monti took the money himself,"
I (just for the record) reminded Marvin.

"I know that Wally told you that Mr. Monti took the
money," Marvin replied. "Now"—he pecked my
cheek—"I gotta run."

Mr. Monti's office is on K Street, within walking distance of my ophthalmologist, gynecologist, and periodontist, all of whom practice out of office buildings on
19th Street between K and L. (It's incredible how much
time you can save by selecting geographically compat-
ible doctors.) Miraculously (well, not so miraculously—

most of their patients were out of town on vacation) I
had been able to call first thing in the morning and line
up consecutive afternoon appointments, allowing half
an hour between each appointment for the usual
waiting-room time. (I can't tell you how much satisfaction I get from being able to schedule so efficiently!)
Anyway, I had brought along a novel (*The House of
Mirth*, by Edith Wharton—well worth a reread, and if
you've never read it before, a must) to keep me occupied when I wasn't checking out glaucoma, cervical
cancer, and gum surgery. But I couldn't concentrate on
Wharton. I knew that the truce with Mr. Monti was only
temporary. I also knew that Wally would not relinquish
Josephine. Furthermore, even if I could mobilize my
skills as a detective (I do have certain talents in that
area) and prove beyond a doubt that Mr. Monti and not
Wally had stolen the money, I feared that Mr. Monti
would keep pounding and pounding and pounding away
at my family.

If only, I thought (the first intimations of murder
piercing my consciousness), I could just snap my fingers and make him disappear.

When Jake and I had dinner that evening—cold
poached salmon with mustard-dill sauce, in our air-
conditioned kitchen; it was much too sultry to try to eat
on the porch—I let him tell me all about Marvin's
meeting with Mr. Monti. Marvin, who knows when to
keep his mouth shut, hadn't mentioned my presence at
that meeting, which greatly contributed to the serenity
and pleasure of our meal. When I (partially) described
what Wally had told me late last night, before he
departed—that it had to have been Mr. Monti who had

taken the money and placed it in his car—Jake was his usual irritatingly sanguine self. "It sounds as if Mr. Monti is having a temporary aberration," he said. "Watch—in a couple of days he'll calm down."

"This is not a calm man," I reminded him, sipping the soothing California Chardonnay.

"True," said Jake. "But I don't think he's a crazy man either."

"Or dangerous?" I asked slyly.

"Or dangerous." These last words, delivered in Jake's flat and-that's-that manner, tempted me to describe the rest of what Wally had told me during last night's conversation: That (though Wally wasn't quite sure how) Mr. Monti was involved with Jake's malpractice suits. And that (though I'd have to ask Jeff for the details—Wally did not want to tattle) Mr. Monti was doing Jeff in financially.

"That'll show you, you dumb insensitive bastard" was the mean-spirited subtext of my wish to tell Jake. But I controlled myself. I controlled myself because, first of all, I didn't want to pass on that information until I had thought about how it ought to be handled. And, second of all, I knew that whatever way I wanted to handle it, Jake would definitely disapprove. And, third of all, the kinder, gentler part of me didn't want to spoil Jake's mellow mood.

Jake had come home from Children's Hospital feeling really great, having reconstructed the severely damaged esophagus of a three-year-old girl named Lily Lopez, who was, he said, a honey and the sweetest little kid and doing just fine. He was high on fixing Lily and continued happily high on the Chardonnay, and he looked so yummy in his white shorts (he has even better legs than I do) and sleeveless shirt that I decided to try—by an act of sheer will—to put aside my anxieties and enjoy my husband.

"Enjoy your husband," usually followed by an exclamation point, is a bit of advice I frequently offer my readers. In the daily grind of marriage, I note, we tend to forget that—once upon a time—we had some excellent reasons for deciding to marry the man we are currently married to. Try to remember those reasons, I urge, and try to find in the person he is today some of those once beloved and admirable qualities. Mix with a video rental of *The Philadelphia Story*, add a pint of rum-raisin ice cream, and . . . enjoy.

Although I continue to believe that this is one of my better ideas, I've received some discouraging mail from a number of readers. The most memorable letter came from a "Grateful in Glendale," who wrote:

DEAR BRENDA:
When I tried to recall some of my husband's beloved and admirable qualities, I realized that he never had any and still doesn't. Who knows why anyone marries anyone? I did try watching *The Philadelphia Story* with him, but this only ruined the movie for me. On the other hand, I had never tasted rum-raisin ice cream before, and thanks to your tip I've discovered what a terrific taste sensation it is.

Jake and I skipped the rum-raisin and opened up another bottle of Chardonnay. "So what else was doing at Children's today?" I asked him.

With Jake this is always a good question. While normally not a talkative man, he becomes positively gabby about perforated intestines and intra-abdominal bleeding, about solid tumors and undescended testicles, about hernias and blockages and—his personal favorite— biliary atresia, which, he has taught me over the years, means very serious trouble with the bile ducts. In fact, as Jake was eager to report, his other operation that day was removing and replacing the shut-down ducts of a six-week-old baby boy. "Simeon Andrew Davenport-Kaminsky," he said, shaking his head in bemusement. "Why do they do that? His name weighs more than he does. Real cute baby, though. He's real, real cute."

I find it touching that supercritical Jake is so fond of all the children he operates on. Their parents are, of course, a whole other story. But from snarling, belligerent teenage punk to nonstop-screaming baby, he has never met a patient he didn't like. It is for them that Jake displays the full, unstinting voltage of his smile. It is for them that he exhibits a depth of patience and psychological sensitivity which, around our house, tends to range between slight and nonexistent. Back when I was a volunteer at Children's, I'd occasionally get to see Jake do his stuff, like the day he worked over a shivering six-year-old boy, a Bobby Something, who was scheduled for in-and-out hernia surgery.

When Bobby arrived that morning in the reception area, Jake was absorbed in tossing a softball around— up in the air, under his leg, behind his back, under his arm—so totally into his ball game (at least it seemed that way) that it took him a couple of moments to notice Bobby.

"You again? What are *you* doing here?"

"I'm having an operation."

"Oh, wow. Who's going to do it?"

"*You* are, Doctor Kovner."

"I am? You're sure? Who said so?"

Bobby began to giggle, feeling gratifyingly superior to this dumb doctor. "*You* said so!"

Jake reluctantly set down the ball. "Oh, yeah, I remember now. Well, I guess I better put on my baseball uniform."

"Your *baseball* uniform? You're going to wear a . . ."

Jake doesn't actually own a baseball uniform but he is in possession of a full gorilla suit, mask included, which he has on occasion donned for a needy patient. Contrary to rumor, however, he has never performed surgery in his gorilla suit. Yet. But there's no question that he is willing to make an absolute fool of himself if it helps a scared little kid feel a little less scared. When I think of Jake's beloved and admirable qualities, this is high on my list.

Along with kissing. Which, as we came to the end of our second bottle of Chardonnay (I swear they're making the bottles smaller these days), Jake enthusiastically embarked upon.

Jake is a world-class kisser. He likes doing it. He likes taking his time doing it. He never rushes ahead to the main event. He kissed me in the kitchen, and up the stairs, and into our bedroom with that same fine combination of intensity and tenderness that made me, when I was eighteen, so eager and so willing to take off my panties.

It still does.

I woke up the next morning stretching and purring like Scarlett O'Hara after her night of ecstasy with Rhett. I felt as if I'd been stripped and stained and polished, then slowly and thoroughly buffed to a golden glow. Despite or perhaps because of this, I also felt significantly guilty. I mean, what kind of woman—what kind of *Jewish* woman?—so totally abandons herself to the pleasures of the flesh that she actually forgets that her family is threatened?

At breakfast I tried, as you may recall, to talk to Jake in depth about Mr. Monti, hoping the past night's stripping and staining and polishing, etc., had co-opted him. No such luck. He was up. He was out. He didn't wish to discuss it. So I was left on my own to channel the full force of my intellect into strategies for defeating Mr. Monti. As I showered and dressed for the 98-degree weather, I daydreamed of how convenient it would be if Mr. Monti—his arteries choked with apple pie and pâté—should happen to drop dead of a coronary. Or if Mr. Monti—off on one of his trips in his corporate jet— should happen to slam into a fog-shrouded mountain. Or if Mr. Monti . . . Oh, well. Enjoyable though I found them, these fantasies were not resolving the problem. I slipped into my sandals and telephoned Jeff.

"How about lunch today?"

"What did I do wrong now?"

"That's between you and your conscience," I said briskly. "See you at the Four Seasons at twelve-thirty."

I arrived at 12:15 and settled into a private corner of the upstairs restaurant, which, with its plants and flowers and homey groupings of overstuffed couches and black wicker chairs, is my favorite place in Washington to have lunch. You can order a fresh fruit platter which almost always includes plump raspberries and blackberries, or an inventive warm salad of greens and pasta and seafood, and never gain an ounce unless you lose control and follow it up with their deeply, deeply evil flourless chocolate cake. Besides, there is valet parking, which is guaranteed to do wonders for my digestion.

I am always fifteen minutes early. Jeff is always fifteen minutes late. He headed for my corner with that slow and slouchy it-don't-worry-me walk, his jacket slung nonchalantly over one shoulder. He smelled delicious as he bent down to kiss me.

After the waitress had given Jeff his Campari and orange juice and me a frosty glass of spiced iced tea, I brought him up to date on Wally's current difficulties with Mr. Monti. I waited for him to confide in me, and when he didn't, I added, "Wally said Mr. Monti is also leaning on you."

Jeff put on his glasses and studied the menu for an inordinately long time.

"Do you want to say something?" I asked.

"The smoked salmon looks good."

"I mean about Mr. Monti."

"I know what you mean, Mom." Jeff had reverted to his old nervous habit of running the tip of his thumb up and down, up and down, up and down the cleft in his chin. I quietly reached over and pulled his hand away.

"I remember you talked a few times about wanting to maybe do a deal with Mr. Monti. Did you? Do it, I mean?"

"Yeah. I did. In fact, we went into a high-ticket project together."

"A high-ticket project?"

"*Very* high-ticket."

"You must be richer than I thought."

"Creative financing, Mom. There's a lot of creative financing in this business."

"Instead of money?"

"Yeah, well . . . Mr. Monti said we were almost relatives. He said relatives had to help each other. And trust each other."

"So he trusted you?"

Jeff got very busy trying to balance his knife on his spoon, and his fork on his knife. Then he said, "That isn't the problem, Mom. The problem is that *I* trusted *him*."

"Jeff," I told him, well aware that I shouldn't, but doing it anyway, "that was a big mistake. A big mistake."

Now of course he already knew this—better than I did—so why in God's name did I have to point it out? Don't belabor the obvious, I strongly believe and always urge upon my readers. But who among us, especially with our children, is able to exercise that kind of restraint?

I hoped that Jeff would somehow not notice my lapse.

He noticed.

"A big mistake, Mom? Why, thank you so much. What a helpful insight. Will there be others? I can hardly wait."

"Honey, I am really sorry I said that."

"You're always sorry. And you always say it."

"I'm slitting my wrists. I'm groveling. I'm begging on bended knee. Will you please please please please please accept my apology?"

I have to point out that apologizing is one of the things I do terrifically well. I mean, why not? As I often tell my readers, the capacity to fully and freely admit that you are wrong is a necessary (though not sufficient) condition of healthy adulthood. And if some folks do not feel they are receiving a full apology unless it comes with groveling, begging, etc., I say give it to them.

Somewhere in the midst of all this, the waitress—a shapely brunette with long legs and short hair—took our order, brought us our lunches, and replenished our drinks. "Is there anything else whatsoever you would like me to do for you?" she inquired huskily, directing her question to Jeff and hinting at sweets far far beyond the flourless chocolate cake.

"Not at the moment, thanks," Jeff answered, tossing her a conspiratorial smile. "But promise that you'll come back and ask me later."

Jeff is so good at this lady-killer stuff that he can do it in his sleep, which—as I examined him more closely—it was clear he could desperately use. I also noticed that underneath the tan, his feline face had a slightly greenish tinge. He started rubbing his cleft again. I took his hand from his chin and gave it a pat. "Just tell me this," I said to him. "On a scale from one to ten, exactly how much trouble are you in?"

"Eleven, Mom," he answered and then my cocky firstborn son began to cry.

The last time I saw Jeff cry was in seventh grade, when he was suspended from Georgetown Day School for cheating on a chemistry exam. He swore, and I believed him, that he had only sought outside help on one of the questions. He then defended himself by observing that since the chem exam had twenty questions his dishonesty quotient was merely 5 percent.

Jeff was not an easy child to raise. A moral corner-cutter with a fast mouth, he had many close encounters with the authorities. For all I know, he still does. He certainly still displays a devotion to hedonism that the rest of his hardworking family does not share—doing dubious deals, dancing and drinking half the night away, and wasting his substance upon glitzy, shallow women who could never be the mothers of my grandchildren. In addition (though I don't mean to sound petty) Jeff is never on time, he never phones when he says he is going to phone, and people tell me (I won't say who, but I've got my ways of knowing) that he almost never bothers to use his seat belt. I guess the good news about Jeff is that after a trip two years ago to the Sibley Emergency Room, he no longer snorts, smokes, or swallows controlled substances. That afternoon at the restaurant, he finally opened up and proceeded to inform me of the bad news.

Jeff told me that back in January, soon after the Monti-Kovner family dinner, he called Mr. Monti and said he would like some advice. Asking for advice, my shrewd but currently quite chastened son informed me, was the best way to ease into asking for bigger favors. Which he did.

"You've made some brilliant real estate moves," Jeff said to Mr. Monti when they met and had ordered their second round of drinks. "I'm into a little real estate myself."

"A profitable business," said Mr. Monti. "Even in these tough times. But if, and only if, you know how to figure it."

"That's just it," said Jeff. "With prices so low now, I'd like to buy some properties in the District, but the neighborhoods I'm looking at could go either way—up or down—and frankly, sir, I *don't* know how to figure it."

"Help me, O Real Estate Maven," was Jeff's unexpressed but unmistakable plea. Mr. Joseph Monti, for his own unsavory reasons (I'll get to them soon), chose to oblige.

"There's a very sweet deal coming up with a block of buildings in Anacostia," he told Jeff, who, as he listened to Mr. Monti describe it, almost fell off his bar stool with excitement.

According to Mr. Monti's source—a person he characterized as "my own Deep Throat"—an urban revitalization project was coming up in . . . he mentioned a section of Anacostia. "Some office buildings, a Cineplex, a mini shopping mall—the works. If you owned in this location you could sell and quadruple your money in just a few months."

"And who," Jeff asked him breathlessly, "gets to own?"

"Could be us, kid," Mr. Monti replied. "Sixteen buildings are up for sale, and I'll cut you in on eight—if you can find four hundred thou for the down payments."

Jeff gasped. "I don't have that kind of money," he said. "I was thinking of something smaller. A whole lot smaller."

"Never think small," Mr. Monti said. "Let's examine your resources—all of them."

At the end of the examination Mr. Monti offered to lend Jeff most of the money he needed for the down payments, with Jeff putting up as collateral the two houses he owned out in Rockville (bought, he explained to me, after a fabulous day at the races and on which, he explained to me, he still owed plenty), his Watergate condo (bought, he explained to me, in the wake of a brilliant stock-market killing and on which, he explained to me, he still owed plenty), his brand-new Jaguar (bought, he explained to me, with the winnings from a high-stakes poker game and on which, he explained to me, he still owed plenty), and the twenty-five thousand dollars that his grandfather had left to him (but which he would not come into until he was thirty).

In the contract Mr. Monti drew up, it said that his loan to Jeff was "payable in full upon demand." But, he assured Jeff, "that's just a formality, to keep my accountants happy. Listen, we're practically relatives— you shouldn't give the matter a second thought."

The buildings were purchased in March. They figured to sell them in early June when the project went public. That's also when Jeff intended to pay off the loan. But in May, Mr. Monti found out—though he neglected to notify Jeff—that the urban renewal project was dead in the water. Mr. Monti unloaded his buildings. Jeff did not.

"And then," Jeff said to me, "you know what he did? He called in my loan. He said he wanted payment in full, immediately."

What a surprise, I was tempted to say. I didn't. I bit my tongue and said, "What a shame!" instead.

I completely understood why Jeff had made this high-flying deal with Mr. Monti. My boy was greedy. I also had some thoughts about why Mr. Monti had chosen to do what he'd done to Jeff.

I think he had lent Jeff the money as a way of trying to get his hooks into Wally, who was far more independent than he liked the men in his daughters' lives to be. By helping Jeff make money, he would be saying to Wally, "Look what I've done for your brother. I'll do it for you—if you'll submit to me."

And when Wally didn't submit, when Wally appeared to mock and defy him on this stupendously super-charged issue of conversion, take-no-prisoners Joseph Monti took his revenge by striking out at Jeff.

Trying to look on the bright side, I said to Jeff, "You've still got the Anacostia buildings. Couldn't you fix them up—make something out of them?"

Jeff groaned. "I said I had trouble figuring out if a neighborhood's going up or going down. Well, I'm not having any trouble trying to figure *this* neighborhood out. It's going down. Fast."

He groaned again. "And Mom, so am I. So am I."

I once got a touching letter from an "Inadequate in Islip," who wrote:

DEAR BRENDA:
When it comes to the daily disasters of life I do great like you wouldn't believe. If my furnace conks out, if my tire goes flat, if my water pipes freeze and burst, I am cheerful and calm and on top of things because I always can say to myself, Could be worse. My problem is that when it *is* worse, when disaster really strikes, I fall apart at the seams and am incapable of rising to the occasion. I am not pleased, for instance, with the way I behaved when my husband embezzled this money from his company, and ran away with the bookkeeper on exactly the day I had surgery for my . . .

I won't go into the rest of the letter (which was quite poignant) or my reply (which was quite constructive). I simply want to say that although I, too, bring my can-do attitude to things like broken furnaces and flat tires, I find them harder to cope with than the big stuff. Indeed, unlike "Inadequate in Islip," I'm at my best when disaster really strikes.

Leaning over and giving Jeff a reassuring hug, I said in a voice of absolute conviction, "Don't worry, darling. Don't worry. I promise that we're going to straighten this out."

Now all I had to figure out was how.

3

•

OY, IS THAT A GENIUS!

A couple of years ago, at Nora's annual New Year's Day party, Philip Eastlake confided to me that he had been born an Epstein in Newark, New Jersey. He said he was telling me this because he sensed what he called a *"simpático* something" between us, a *simpático* something which, were we not married to two other people, would surely have burgeoned, he said, into something quite ... passionate. I think he fondled my earlobe as he confided this to me, but having consumed several cups of Nora's famous champagne punch, I was feeling far too fuzzy to be sure.

Last year Philip was at Nora's party with a Cher-like brunette approximately his daughter's age. Unhappily, he confided to me, his marriage of thirty-seven years was through. He added that although he was finding some temporary solace between the silken thighs of his well-toned companion, he remained convinced that the seasoned consolations of September were far, far richer than those of girlish May. He then plunged his eyeballs so deeply into mine that I felt that I had been ocularly raped.

Philip, who possesses the carved beauty of Gregory Peck in his middle years and whose silver hair is so magnificently coiffed that I have often been tempted to ask him the name of his stylist, flashed me his internationally famous TV smile. "If only . . . ," he began, but at that point girlish May beckoned to him across a crowded room. He sighed, pressed his cheek against mine, and departed, his padded shoulders drooping in an eloquent gesture of reluctant adieu.

This year, at the New Year's Day party, I was ready and waiting for Philip, for only a few days before I had begun to consolidate my final adultery list. Philip was the first (and thus far the only) name in my Definite Lovers column, and I wanted to convey that information. Indirectly. Adorably. Unmistakably.

Actually, Philip made it quite easy for me, having arrived at Nora's party both unmarried and alone, and more than willing to be led to the quiet of Nora's den for what I called (this is the indirect part) "our annual chat." I brought along a platter of Nora's miniature spinach crepes (elegant and attractive when served with a dollop of sour cream and red caviar), and soon Philip and I were playfully popping crepes (this is the adorable part) into each other's eagerly open mouth. When some of the sour cream dribbled onto Philip's finely sculpted lower lip, he reached for a napkin. I shook my head and gently pulled it away. "No, no," I said, "let me," and then I flicked out my tongue and (this is the unmistakable part) slowly and thoroughly licked his lower lip clean.

I figured that after about ten years of chaste New Year's Day flirting, my I'm-available message might take even faze-proof Philip by surprise. I decided to give him a little assistance in processing it.

"You're quite a remarkable fellow, Philip Eastlake," I said archly (though arch is not my strong suit), giving his lip a "there—you're all cleaned up" tap. "You know, I watched your program on the philosophy of Wittgenstein. And the one on Lebanon. And that program you did on Oriental art. And that program on the fantasy life of children. And—what can I say?—I'm absolutely staggered."

"I hope that means," Philip said archly (he's fabulous at arch), "that my humble efforts met with your approval."

"Yes, they did," I told him, lying only a little. "I was . . . well, I always knew you were brilliant, but—but the sensitivity, Philip. The originality. The . . . the wisdom."

What I was doing to Philip was, I'll readily admit, the verbal equivalent of licking his lower lip. Some might find it excessive. Philip did not. In fact, if I had to bet, I'd bet that my words were turning him on even more than my tongue had. The message in his eyes—those brooding, expressive, deep-set eyes—read, "Don't stop now."

I didn't. "And I was especially touched," I said, "by your insights into religion and the environment, when you said . . . Do you remember that part?"

Did he remember. Philip can quote himself extensively and accurately on any subject he has ever addressed in his twenty-three years as host of "Everything Under the Sun." He can also quote Gerard Manley Hopkins, W. B. Yeats, and Emily Dickinson—but not nearly as movingly.

"I said that there were many of us who, while having

no belief in a personal God, nonetheless believed in holiness." He smoothed the neck of his green velours shirt, just in case he was being televised, and kept rolling. "Believed in the holiness of our mountains and rivers and oceans, in the holiness of all creatures great and small, in the holiness of . . ."

I have often wondered where Philip, who is a graduate of Rutgers University in New Brunswick, New Jersey, acquired his classy accent, but there it is. William Buckley should only speak that well. Philip's voice is so modulated, so mellifluous, so mesmerizing, that even when he's full of shit he sounds profound. But, in fact, if we exclude how he talks when he's engaging in what he believes to be sexual banter, he really isn't full of shit that often. (*Time* or *Newsweek* once called his "lively and wide-ranging intellect one of our national treasures" and added, "Eat your heart out, Bill Moyers.") Well, I don't know about national treasure, but he sure is a whole lot sexier than Moyers, and he is—in a kind of fatiguing way—supersmart. Actually, I tend to think of him as the ultimate Bar Mitzvah boy, who first tasted glory at Temple Beth Shalom, and whose eagerness to learn and digest and explicate virtually everything under the sun derives from his wish to keep hearing the awestruck whispers that filled the temple when he was thirteen: "Oy, is that a genius or is that a genius!"

Philip had finished with the environment and was now regaling me with brilliant lines from his program on the fantasy life of children. While he spoke, I indulged in my own fantasy. Without going into details, I'll simply say that it involved the use of crepes, sour cream, and caviar in locations and combinations that hadn't been mentioned in the original recipe.

Just as my fantasy was becoming seriously weird, Jake stuck his head into the den doorway. "I'd like to get out of here in a couple of minutes, Bren. You want to start saying your goodbyes?"

It was time to reel in Philip. "I've really loved being with you," I told him, adding, with a little catch in my voice, "It's going to be a long time until next New Year's Day."

"Where is it written," asked Philip, who was gratifyingly eager to be reeled in, "that we have to wait until next New Year's Day? Can't we get together for lunch?"

"I'd love that," I answered, tossing him what I hoped was a sluttish smile.

And then I panicked.

I didn't want him thinking I was cheap. I didn't want him talking about me in bars. I wanted him to respect me the next morning. Everything my mother had ever said to me about sex in the days when she still believed she could keep me a virgin suddenly came surging into my consciousness.

"Listen, Philip," I told him, "I'm having lunch with you, I'm definitely having lunch with you. But you need to know that I usually don't—that it really isn't my habit to commit . . . lunch. In fact—and you can believe this or not, as you choose; I won't try to persuade you—I have never ever before committed lunch."

I could feel my face heating up (my God, was I blushing?) but I kept on talking, faster and faster and faster.

"Not that I'm trying to turn this into something sig-

nificant between us—certainly not. My eyes are wide
open. I'm seeing it for exactly what it is. I am, for heav-
en's sake, a consenting adult. But you need to know
that having lunch is a very very big step for me
and . . ."

Philip hadn't heard a word I said. He was too busy
flipping through the pages of his pocket calendar, looking for an opening in his schedule. "Hmmm," he said.
"Zurich next week, London the week after, Paris after
that, and then L.A. Looks like my next several shows
are on location. But wait. Wait just a minute. EX-
cellent. What about March eighteenth, twelve noon, the
Hay-Adams?"

Two months and seventeen days from now? I felt both
profoundly relieved (because I wouldn't have to *do it*
right away) and also profoundly offended (because he
didn't insist on *doing it* right away). My panic, however,
was definitely gone. I recalled the words of the great William Shakespeare, who once observed, "The readiness is
all." With plenty of time to get used to the thought of
adultery, I figured that, come March 18, I'd be ready.

I searched through my purse, tracked down my little
date book, and (in my first gesture of adulterous decep-
tion) entered my appointment with Philip in code:
P.E.H.A.B.C.

The P.E. was Philip Eastlake, formerly Epstein.

The H.A. was our meeting place, the Hay-Adams.

And because, as I tell my readers, the profoundly
passionate need not preclude the practical, the B.C. was
a reminder to Buy Condoms.

Months later, on a steamy August day, there I was at a
far-from-my-neighborhood drugstore, purchasing a pack

of condoms again. Except this time they were not for Philip and me, or for Mr. Monti and me, or for Louis and me. This time they were for Josephine and Wally.

One of these days I ought to do a column on purchasing condoms. I mean, there is so little guidance in this area. Do we want ribbed? Do we want lubricated? Do we want the old standbys—Ramses or Trojans—or is it better to opt for the newer brands? Do we want to flatter our partner by buying the extra-large or—if he's not extra-large—will the damn thing fall off? Even my best friend, Carolyn, who has had a quite remarkable number of lovers (considering that she has also been married four times), is not that informed about condoms, though she strongly recommends that you look the salesman straight in the eye when purchasing them.

Anyway, it had been six days since Wally had taken off for Rehoboth Beach, where he'd been holing up, planning and tanning. Today, however, was the big day he was coming back to the city. Today was the day he intended, with a little help from me, to rescue (or maybe kidnap) Josephine. He would then, having won her trust again, take her back to the soothing shores of Rehoboth, where he had already (what can I tell you? he's a *remarkable* young man) lined up a vacationing shrink to give the poor girl some decent psychotherapy.

Actually, Josephine had started seeing a therapist early in June. She should have started early in second grade, which was when, she once told me, she began to hyperventilate and sleepwalk and vomit every morning before school. But it seems that Mr. Monti treated any hint that his youngest child had emotional difficulties as a vicious personal attack on his fathering. "She's a growing girl," he'd say, whenever she started gasping for breath or throwing up. "She'll grow out of it."

And so she did, replacing her childhood symptoms with several inconvenient obsessive rituals and an awesome collection of allergies and phobias (including, along with the standard ones, a fear of contracting botulism from canned foods that had been improperly sealed). When Josephine's allergist strongly recommended psychotherapy, Mr. Monti found her another allergist. When Josephine's Aunt Minnie strongly recommended psychotherapy, Mr. Monti quit talking to Aunt Minnie. And when I, in a moment intimate enough to tempt me to try a constructive intervention, also recommended psychotherapy, Mr. Monti almost put on his trousers. "If my daughter's got problems," he finally said, in a very unloverly voice, "let her tell *me* about them. Why should I pay good money to some jerk who's going to teach her to hate her father?"

But then, in April and May, as the conflict between her father and Wally intensified, so did Josephine's rituals and rashes. In addition to which she lost—and she was a skinny girl to begin with—seventeen pounds. Just as the doctors were talking about putting Josephine in the hospital, Mr. Monti tuned in to a local talk show. And there was Dr. Phony (excuse me, Foley), a genuine certified psychotherapist, assailing the "disconnectedness of our perniciously individualistic society" and denouncing the current focus on independence and separation as "a psychoanalytic plot against family life." His message—that all neuroses stemmed from a failure to respect parental authority—spoke directly to Mr. Monti's condition. And when Mr. Monti learned that

Dr. Foley had a private practice in Washington, his joy was complete. Here, at last, was the therapist for Josephine. Here was the man who'd be able to restore his daughter's psychological health, while also restoring her to her father's arms.

Three days a week, from 2 P.M. until 2:50 P.M., Josephine had therapy with Dr. Foley, driven into the District and back by one of Mr. Monti's overpaid flunkies. The flunky would go for a snack at the diner on upper Connecticut Avenue, just a few blocks from where Josephine got shrunk, and my job—on that August day— was to intercept her before she started her session and somehow talk her into seeing Wally.

"Mrs. Kovner, hi, what are you doing here?" Josephine nervously asked me, as I came hurrying over to her in the lobby.

I had given my Josephine tactics a considerable amount of thought and had opted for the Grand Emotion approach. "Wally needs you," I said to her, gripping her thin arm. "Please—he's waiting around the corner. Please come with me."

Can I be frank with you? If I'd had my choice, I would not have been trying to coax Josephine into coming with me to see Wally. She was not the kind of girl I wanted for him. It's true that she was good. She was kind. She was loving. She was probably even intelligent. And she was—in her wispy, wraithlike way—quite beautiful. But when I thought of what I'd consider the ideal woman for Wally, I thought "feisty." I thought "zesty." I thought "competent" and "savvy." I thought "fun." I didn't think of someone who suffered from fear of botulism, had a tormented attachment to her father, and might, in my view (despite my deep commitment to growth and change), be a permanent basket case.

Don't imagine I didn't wonder why Wally had chosen to fall for a permanent basket case. Don't imagine I didn't have a few theories. But also don't imagine I would ever refuse, if Wally asked for my help, to help him to achieve his heart's desire, who was—at the moment—chewing on a cuticle and shaking her curly head in a slo-mo "no."

"I can't," she wailed. "I can't see Wally right now. Tell him I'm really sorry, but I can't."

The elevator arrived and Josephine, showing more backbone than I would have predicted, got in and pressed the button for the third floor. I was right behind her. I waited a moment and then I asked, as we rode up to Dr. Foley, "Maybe you at least could tell me why."

The door opened at 3 and an ancient woman hobbled on just as Josephine was about to answer. Josephine clamped her lips together and rode, without saying a word, back down to the lobby. The door opened, the woman left, the door closed, Josephine pushed the third-floor button and said, as we headed upward, "Because I promised my father and Dr. Foley."

"Promised them you wouldn't hear Wally's side of it?" I asked, as the elevator once again stopped at 3.

A man and a woman, quarreling in low hissing tones, entered and pushed the lobby button. The four of us, them still hissing, rode down together. When they were gone and the car was again ascending, Josephine sighed and looked at me with moist eyes. "Mrs. Kovner," she said imploringly, "I promised."

This time, when the elevator arrived at the third floor, Josephine was instantly out the door. "It's funny," I said to her T-shirted back, my finger pressed on Door Open, "but one of the things I never dreamed you were capable of doing was deliberately inflicting emotional pain."

Bingo! Josephine gasped, stood rigidly still, and then backed back into the elevator.

We rode down to the lobby together in silence. In silence we walked together around the block. And a moment later Wally was buckling Josephine into the front seat of his car, after which he gave me a kiss, said, "Thanks a million, Mom," and was heading his Chevy up Connecticut Avenue.

Just before my confrontation with Josephine, I had handed Wally a Care package consisting of my homemade curried squash and apple soup, my pasta primavera, a gorgeous olive bread from Marvelous Market, a bottle of Beaujolais Nouveau, and the box of condoms, "Just in case," I explained, as he set the carton of goodies in the trunk of his car, "you were too distracted to plan ahead." I had also made him swear that he wouldn't take Josephine to Rehoboth against her will. In turn I had promised that I'd be in charge of informing Mr. Monti that his daughter was—though I couldn't say where—in safe hands.

Remember the movie *Raging Bull*? It starred Robert De Niro, who gave a truly compelling performance as the brutish boxer Jake La Motta, a man whose violent . . . Well, you don't have to remember the movie—the title itself quite nicely describes how Mr. Monti took the news about Josephine. Which I bravely delivered in person, that day, at his office.

When Mr. Monti stopped raging, he smoothed back his hair from his forehead and said, "So now your son is kidnapping my daughter."

"She went with him of her own free will and volition."

"Never!"

"Yes she did."

"She went of her own volition with a person who stole money from her father?"

"You know that's not true about the money, Mr. Monti."

"You're calling me a liar? Don't you ever call me a liar. Don't you ever ever ever call me a liar."

Mr. Monti was moving back into his Raging Bull mode, but I refused to be intimidated. "I'm not calling you a liar," I told him. "I'm calling you a megalomaniacal sociopath with a severe narcissistic personality disorder and some heavy-duty unresolved Oedipal problems. You need help."

Mr. Monti flashed me a smile of the kind last seen on the nonhuman star of *Jaws*. "And I'm going to get some help," he said, as he reached for the telephone and dialed a number. He kept smiling his sharky smile as he waited impatiently until someone answered his call. "Hello," he said. "This is Joseph Augustus Monti—and I want to report a kidnapping and a theft."

Although my friend Carolyn's taste in sexual partners is awesomely catholic, she still couldn't understand why Joseph Monti had made my Definite Lovers list. Which, of course, he had done the moment I learned he was one of a pair of identical twins. Mr. Monti and I had seen each other a couple of times in the weeks shortly after our January dinner. Once, by accident, when we (with our spouses) ran into each other at the Kennedy Center. And again when Jake and I (at Wally's urging) invited the senior Montis to brunch at our house. Each time I saw him I mentally deplored his intellect and his ethical system, while also mentally tearing off his clothes. He was Catholic, married, and a twin, which covered three of the eight traits I sought in my liaisons, in addition to which he was someone to whom I kept on wanting to moan, "Oh, take me! Now!" So why, I asked Carolyn—shortly before Mr. Monti accepted my offer—shouldn't he be on my Definite Lovers list?

"It's just a gut feeling I have," she replied. "I think he's bad news."

"And since when has your gut feeling been reliable?" I asked her. "Cast your mind back to Gabriel, Kevin, Jimmy, Owen, George, that entire Argentinean string quartet . . ."

"No fair bringing up the string quartet," Carolyn grumbled, blowing strands of blond hair out of her eyes. "That was a scientific experiment. A sexual byway. A momentary lapse."

"And," I reminded her, "a big mistake."

Both of us were breathing hard as we spoke—not because of the sexual subject matter but because our discussion was taking place as we briskly pedaled away on Carolyn's side-by-side stationary bikes.

According to Carolyn, her relationships with men have been greatly improved since her purchase of that second bike. "It's a very bonding experience, pumping together for forty-five minutes," she told me. "In fact, I'd say there are many times when the pumping is much more bonding than the humping."

"And definitely better," I added, "for your calf muscles."

It was an unseasonably warm late February day, and

a mild breeze blew through the open bedroom window as we pedaled round and round. Carolyn's Cleveland Park house, just two blocks from mine, had been lavishly renovated, and her bedroom was three rooms combined into one vast suite with walk-in closets, a handsome tiled fireplace, and a bed that could hold all her past husbands at once. There was also plenty of space for the bikes, plus one of those giant-size television screens, plus a cabinet containing a fridge full of pricey champagne and boxes of Godiva chocolates. There was also Carolyn's favorite toy—her tape recorder—which she used to record all sorts of indiscretions. But she never turned it on when we got together twice a week to improve our bodies and relieve our souls.

"How much biking time left?" I panted.

Carolyn checked. "Seventeen more minutes. Then I've got to shower and get out of here. I'm having my legs waxed, my nails wrapped, and my hair done. Then I pick up my new Calvin Klein. And this is my afternoon to baby-sit Tiffany."

If you want to meet the living incarnation of the phrase "contradiction in terms," meet my friend Carolyn, who spends more on her body than anyone I know, who (thanks to an eight-figure trust fund) indulges her every materialistic whim, but who also engages in all kinds of gritty volunteer work—like baby-sitting Tiffany, a poor black two-and-a-half-year-old with AIDS, so her mom can get out three afternoons a week. Imagine a Big Is Beautiful (size 14–16) version of Grace Kelly and you'll have a pretty clear picture of Carolyn's gilded, polished, aristocratic good looks. But from what I've learned in our twenty-year exchanges of deep dark secrets, you'd need to be familiar with some

of the videos in the Adults Only section to get a sense
of Carolyn's sexual style.

I've been best friends with Carolyn since ten minutes
after we met, which happened soon after I moved to
Cleveland Park, when Jeff, beguiled by the host of
golden daffodils on her front lawn, addressed himself to
picking every last one of them. Carolyn had a warm
smile on her face when, hand in hand with Jeff, she
showed up at my house and told me the story. "You
have an *adorable* son," she said, "but he's got this thing
about daffodils. How can we stop him before he strikes
again?"

I loved her utter graciousness about the rape of her
lawn. She loved my ardent apology and the homemade
lemon pound cake I served with our tea. By the time
she left my kitchen we had begun a conversation which
we knew would never stop as long as we lived.

"So what makes you think Mr. Monti is seducible?"
Carolyn asked me, as she climbed off her bike at the
ding and removed her sweats. "For all you know he
takes that 'Thou shalt not covet thy neighbor's wife's
ass' commandment seriously."

I quit biking too, and followed Carolyn into the bathroom, sitting on top of the toilet seat so we could continue talking while she showered. "I don't think so," I
shouted over the din of her luxe eight-faucet stall
shower. "Remember when the Montis came for brunch?
Well, I had a few moments alone with him in the
kitchen—enough time to melt a little ice—and he gave
me this look and he said that people just don't understand that a woman's beauty is always found in her
eyes."

"Sounds innocent enough."

"Yeah. Right. Except he was patting my ass while he was saying it."

Carolyn came out of the shower and started toweling off briskly. "God, look at these breasts. Why do they keep staring down at the ground instead of gazing up at the heavens?"

"Only the left one is looking down. The right one is fine. Anyway," I continued, "when, instead of slapping his hand, I gave it a kind of reassuring squeeze, he suggested that we meet in his office soon—very soon—to discuss the Wally-Josephine situation."

"I still think he's bad news. Besides, don't you feel guilty—just a little guilty—about *her*? Mrs. Monti?"

"This from the woman who slept with her own sister's husband?"

Carolyn brushed some blusher across her alabaster skin and then went to work on her eyes with a blue-gray liner. "But I'm an Episcopalian. I can handle adultery."

"Well, so can I. And besides," I added, in my stuffiest voice, "one needn't conceptualize this as adultery."

Carolyn laughed. "Then how might one conceptualize it?"

"As a scientific experiment. As a sexual byway. As a momentary"—I sprayed myself with her million-dollar perfume—"as a very very momentary lapse."

Although I use a word processor when I write the final draft of my newspaper column, I always like starting out with a pencil and pad. I like to write by hand curled up in our big brown living-room chair, or sprawled on the flowered chaise upstairs in our bedroom, or settled on a bench in the Bishop's Garden of the National Cathedral.

The cathedral is right in our neighborhood, an easy stroll away, but Carolyn drove me there on the way to her waxing. I found my bench in the garden, which is sort of a Secret Garden—small, cozy, lovingly tended, hidden from sight—and checked out the greenings and bloomings that would shortly ignite into a spring spectacular. Spring is different for sixteen-year-olds than it is for forty-six-year-olds, I told myself. And what if you're seventy-six—what's it like then? On such idle musings, I've found, are some of my finest columns built. I fished out my pad and pencil and started writing.

What does the old lady think about in the springtime? What, in a time of rebirth and new beginnings, can possibly be her expectations, her dreams? In autumn's flaming finale, the old lady can find reflections of herself that speak to her glories as well as to her diminishments. But she will not find her reflection in the spring of fresh starts and everything-is-possible. So what exactly is springtime to the old lady? What does the old lady think about?

Every now and then I open one of my columns on this sort of poetic-melancholy note, but fear not—I instantly move on to affirmation. My column is, after all, intended to put people in control of their lives and to help them to develop a can-do attitude. Thus if spring means a new beginning, I go on to tell my readers, what all you old ladies in springtime must do is: Begin! Think about a new language you'd like to study, a new city you'd like to visit, a new book you'd like to read, a great new recipe you'd like to try. Is going back to school an impossible dream? No way. Alice Carney from Grand Rapids, Michigan, has done just that and she writes to me that she hopes to have her B.A. next year at the age of seventy-eight! Is learning to tap dance simply out of the question? Of course not! Marlene Walters writes to me from a nursing home in Tulsa that she can do a fan*tas*tic tap dance to "Puttin' On the Ritz"! And she does it sitting down!! In a wheelchair yet!!! (I try never to exceed three exclamation points.)

In this column I also said that the old lady could think, in spring, about the past, as long as she thought of the joys—not the regrets. And for my younger readers I urged that, before they become old ladies in the springtime, they should live a life that (without doing anything cruel, illegal, or too too irresponsible) "followed their bliss" and minimized their regrets.

I didn't really mean "follow their bliss" in the Joseph Campbellian sense, but it didn't seem terribly urgent to explain that. In its no-regrets message, I felt that the column spoke to every age and kind of bliss—though I don't agree with Carolyn, who insists that my much admired OLD LADIES IN SPRINGTIME was basically a sneaky, oblique, and deeply guilt-ridden effort to justify my own impending adulteries.

I have been writing my column three times a week for almost seven years and I'm proud to say that I've never yet missed a deadline, despite major family emergencies, heartaches of every kind, and some ongoing physical problems including—and here I'll quote my urologist—"the worst cystitis this office has ever seen."

I'm even prouder to say that I have managed to meet every deadline without shortchanging my family or my friends. And this is not, believe me, because I'm Superwoman. It's because I plan ahead and include a lot of room in my plans for the unexpected and never take on more than I can feasibly, realistically hope to accomplish.

However, when I came home from that confessional lunch with Jeff on August 20 and sat down at my Zenith to finish my column (my subject that day was LEARN WHILE YOU SLEEP), I was finding it somewhat difficult to concentrate. As I brooded about Jeff's impending financial disaster and my promise to him that I would straighten things out, I found myself briefly wondering whether I had taken on a bit more than I could accomplish.

But then I reminded myself of what La Rochefoucauld once said ("Few things are of themselves impossible") and what Carlyle once said ("The fearful Unbelief is unbelief in yourself") and what Publilius Syrus once said ("No one knows what he can do till he tries") and what The Little Engine That Could once said ("I think I can—I think I can—I think I can—I think I can"), and I put in a phone call to Louis, with whom (except for some moments of rapture back in March) I've enjoyed a warm but strictly platonic relationship.

Carolyn had met Louis three years ago when they worked together at a homeless shelter. She introduced us in the hope that I would be willing to write a column about Louis's concept of a national network of group homes for the homeless. Louis, a mere twenty-six at the time, was already so persuasive and so dedicated that I not only wrote the column (MAKING A HOME IN YOUR

HEART AND IN YOUR COMMUNITY) but also agreed to serve on the board of Harmony House, the group house he was setting up in the District. Louis was probably the most secure black man (or maybe man, period) I had ever encountered, the product of Washington's black upper-middle class, Yale University, and Harvard Business School. He wasn't especially handsome (unless you happen to think the Gregory Hines type is handsome) but whenever he entered a room there wasn't anybody else you wanted to look at. He had gone to business school sharing the basic make-it-big assumptions of his parents—that upon graduation he'd sign on with some major corporation and swiftly move onward and upward, straight to the top. But a funny thing happened to Louis in between the MBA and the CEO—he fell in love with Adrienne, and she radicalized him.

I met Adrienne once, shortly before she left Louis for a member of the Irish Republican Army, and found her awesomely intolerable. The trouble is that it's hard to tell you *why* I found her so awesomely intolerable without sounding (as she would immediately label me) racist, sexist, classist, gynophobic, and homophobic, plus phallo-, ethno-, Euro-, and logocentric. Adrienne was so politically correct that she once organized a feminist boycott of man-made fibers and demanded the firing of a professor who, she said, had displayed a demeaning attitude toward Asians by publicly using the phrase "a chink in his armor." Her definition of date rape included any consensual sexual act that ended without the woman's having an orgasm. And her response to a compliment (from me) on how wonderful she looked in her leather jump suit was a lecture on how the application of stereotyping standards of attractiveness invariably led to the un-PC sin of "lookism."

I learned long ago to stop asking why terrific people like Louis fall in love with major pains in the butt like Adrienne. I mean, maybe the only true answer is: "That old black magic has me in its spell." Or "Fools rush in where angels fear to tread." Or "Ah, sweet mystery of life." But maybe Louis loved Adrienne because, in her own profoundly obnoxious way, she forced him to question his habits of easy privilege, because—through the fog of her relentless rhetoric—he glimpsed some vision of nobility. (Or maybe the reason he loved her was because she did some amazing tricks in bed.) In any case, Louis loved Adrienne and that love completely transformed him politically, teaching him that his blackness counted more than his Yaleness or Harvardness, and eventually leading him out of the Fortune 500 and into the ghettos of Washington, D.C.

I was hoping that his insights into some of Washington's more beleaguered neighborhoods could throw some light on how I might help Jeff.

"What do you know," I asked Louis, "about this block in Anacostia?" I named the block.

"Stay away from it."

I nervously cleared my throat. "Well, um, my older son, Jeff, has recently purchased some properties there."

"Why would he do that?"

I explained about the urban revitalization project—about its glowing prospects and its collapse.

"Real tragic for the speculators," said Louis.

I decided to ignore that rather unsympathetic remark. "So how bad is the neighborhood?" I asked him.

"It used to be okay," he said, "and maybe it will be again. But right now it is strictly a shooting gallery."

"You mean shooting up drugs, or shooting one another?"

"I mean both," Louis said.

"I guess that's why all of Jeff's tenants are moving out."

"You got it, Brenda. And it's no place for that yuppie son of yours, no matter what kind of mogul he thinks he is."

"He doesn't exactly think he's a mogul these days. He thinks he's—may I quote the words of an eloquent former President?—in deep doo-doo."

I started out fairly calm but grew increasingly upset as I explained how Mr. Monti (with his trust-me sweet talk and his screw-you contract) was demanding full payment of money that Jeff didn't have. And explained how Jeff was about to lose his condo, his Rockville properties, his Jaguar, his inheritance, and his shirt. And explained how Jeff couldn't even pay the mortgages on his buildings in Anacostia, because if he didn't have tenants he didn't have rent, without which he didn't have the mortgage money. And explained how Jeff desperately desperately desperately needed to raise some money on those buildings. And explained . . .

"Whoa, wait a minute, Brenda," Louis interrupted me. "I just need a little clarification here. Like, is Jeff going to go to jail for this?"

"No. He's not going to *jail*. But he'll . . ."

"Anyone threatening to put a bullet in his back?"

"This isn't drugs. This is real estate."

"Are his wife and babies about to be deprived of food or shelter or medical necessities?"

"Cut it out, Louis. What are you saying? You know he doesn't have any wife or babies. But he's got a very big problem."

"And what's the worst thing that this very big problem could lead to?"

"He could lose everything he owns. Which admittedly is not starvation, or death or disease, or a prison term in Attica, or—I can't *believe* that you are acting so supercilious."

There was a long pause at the other end before Louis spoke again, this time in a much nicer tone of voice.

"I'm sorry, Brenda, I'm sorry. You're right. Hey, if I'm not careful I'll wind up sounding like Adrienne." He sighed. "I know that for Jeff this is big trouble. I guess I'm just trying to put it into perspective."

Don't think I'm opposed to putting things into perspective. Indeed, I have urged my readers in many a column to make an effort to take the larger view. And certainly I would never deny that if you compare Job on his ash heap, Jesus on his cross, Joan at the stake, and Jeffrey Joshua Kovner in bankruptcy court, Jeff is definitely the J with the least aggravation. Nevertheless, the fact remained that my son was in trouble and I intended to help him. So, as I said to Louis, "If you're able to help me help him, just *do* it."

Louis calmed me down, said he had some ideas, would make some phone calls, would get back to me. He apologized again for being supercilious and (I hope he was smiling) Afrocentric, and assured me that he was on the case.

Although Louis is only four years older than Jeff, he is much more mature. And although he is twenty-one years younger than Jake, he is much more street smart. In addition, Louis is much more direct and no-nonsense than either Philip or Mr. Monti, or for that matter any man I knew. Which was why I'd been able to say to him, after a meeting at Harmony House early in March, that I needed to go to bed—just one time—with a young black activist and hoped that he would be willing to accommodate.

Louis scratched his head as I spoke, then gave me a warm, slow grin. "I've got no problem with that," he replied. "Say when."

I recalled that Jake had mentioned that he had a conference in New York on the evening of the next Harmony House board meeting. Louis and I agreed to Do It then. It was only after we'd parted, and I had opened my little date book to enter the date, that I was reminded that I had already made some plans for earlier that day. There, on the March 18 page, was the information, neatly printed in capital letters: P.E.H.A.B.C.

4

•

THIGHS AND WHISPERS

*I*f anyone had asked me whether, and when, I planned to tell Jake that his older son was facing financial disaster, I would have replied that Jake already knew. (Wasn't he sitting right there on the porch the night Mr. Monti warned us that our "real estate genius" would soon be begging on street corners?) I would also have replied that in view of the fact that Jake had seen fit to ignore this warning, too bad for him. I would also have replied that nonetheless I intended to tell him about it . . . eventually.

The reason I wasn't in any hurry to talk to Jake about Jeff was that talking to Jake was difficult these days. He used to be a good friend of mine—CAN HUSBANDS AND WIVES BE BEST FRIENDS? was a column devoted to an affirmative answer—but in recent years our friendship has started to pale. And although I don't believe that the survival of our marriage is in question (as it was when Jake took up with Sunny Voight), it is suffering from something worse than the marital common cold. Like maybe the flu. Like maybe even pneumonia.

In any case I'm convinced that our rising tensions (I

think I'll ditch the illness imagery) are tied to the success of my newspaper column. Which has led, in the past few years, to lucrative speaking engagements, TV talk show appearances, and a certain (not unwelcome) amount of celebrity. But which also has led to the toppling of Jake from his long-entrenched position in the family as chief financial provider and leading authority. To call a spade a spade (which is not, despite what Adrienne says, a racist remark), I believe that Jake is resentful of my success. "No," he once said, his eyes frosting over, when I directly confronted him with this theory, "I only resent what success has done to your character."

I believe I've already mentioned that Jake regards me as controlling and simplistic. He also seems to think I think that I'm much smarter than he thinks I am. ("A little learning," he has taken to muttering ominously, "is a dangerous thing.") He also describes as "prurient" and "nosy" and "intrusive" my passionate interest in the human condition. And he has more than once accused me of using the power of my column "to recklessly mislead" my reading public.

That last accusation arises (you will not be surprised to learn) whenever I write columns on medical matters, which—since I don't have a Washington outlet—are probably being sent to him by some secret agent in the AMA. He absolutely hated STAND UP TO YOUR DOCTOR. He was enraged over NOBODY KNOWS YOUR BODY LIKE YOU. And last winter we fought an entire day about WHY ARE DOCTORS STILL SCARED OF ALTERNATIVE MEDICINE?

In my column I pointed to the closed-mindedness that afflicts too many members of the medical profession, making them ignorant of, and dismissive of, nontraditional forms of healing. While granting that the claims of holistic healers and other out-of-the-mainstream practitioners must be examined with a healthy skepticism, I offered some stirring vignettes of startling cures achieved by assorted unorthodox means. Many of my readers wrote to say that they'd found my column thoughtful and eloquent. Not Jake, however, who acted as if I had written a paean of praise to Joseph Mengele, the Nazi doctor.

"You're encouraging quackery," he snarled. "You're sending innocent, trusting people to charlatans."

"All I'm doing is asking them to consider a broader definition of health care. Which is something"—I smiled a mean smile—"you doctors seem temperamentally unable to do.'" (The "you doctors" was a mistake, but never mind.) "Furthermore," I continued . . .

I will spare you the rest of our argument, which began at the Phillips gallery, our number one favorite art museum in Washington, where we go from time to time to pay homage to the blissful Bonnards and Renoir's sensual *Luncheon of the Boating Party*. The Phillips, once a private home, is to grand museums like the Louvre what the Bishop's Garden is to the Tuileries gardens—not anywhere near as spectacular, but exquisite, human-dimensioned, user-friendly. Visiting the Phillips can sometimes be, for me, a spiritual experience, but not when I feel like bopping Jake with the *Boating Party*, whose fleshy, contented ladies and gents, lounging over lunch, stood in sharp contrast to us carping Kovners. Indeed, as I consider the deep dislike (okay, hate) we felt for each other that day, I believe it is all for the best that Jake does not get to see my newspaper column more regularly. He would not have appreciated, for instance, IT'S REALLY OKAY TO FAKE IT NOW AND THEN, which—though I continue to stand by every word I wrote—certainly provoked a lot of controversy.

Among the things I advocated faking now and then were geographical knowledge (nod thoughtfully and don't ask where Ouagadougou is), pesto sauce (Contadina puts out a pesto which, if you wanted to claim that you made it yourself, no one—and I mean no one—could tell that you hadn't), and orgasms (moan a few times and contract your vaginal muscles). I also relayed some crafty advice passed on to me years ago by an enterprising and quite large-bottomed lady who, whenever a lover was in residence, would strategically drape a couple of pairs of tiny bikini pants around her bedroom. She was absolutely convinced that these tiny bikini underpants—three sizes smaller than those she actually wore—would succeed in persuading her lovers, thanks to the power of suggestion, that her bottom was small enough to fit into those pants.

Now I happen to think that this is a funny story. Not massively hilarious, but cute. Yet although it drew a laugh from friends like Carolyn and from some of my readers (who wrote and told me so), there isn't a man among the four I went to bed with this year to whom I could tell it in hopes of sharing a giggle. At one time Jake might have laughed at this story, but now that he's into finding flaws in my character he would doubtless see this as proof of another flaw. Louis might *want* to laugh, but I suspect that Adrienne's spirit still whispers in his ear, "Beware of lookism." Philip wouldn't laugh, though he might murmur "Most amusing," and then he would turn it into a two-hour special, some meditation on women and beauty and the nature of truth called "Thighs and Whispers." As for Joseph Monti, I actually tried to tell him this story the day we set the date for our sex rendezvous. But although he was eagerly making plans to betray his wife and church, and caressing my left nipple while he was planning, he frowned at the mention of "underpants" and said that pretty women shouldn't soil their lips with smutty stories.

The planning meeting with Joseph Augustus Monti took place March 10, in the back of a white stretch limo that first drove me to National Airport, then him to McLean. I had offered—between my quarterly torture session with Sherman Schwartz, my periodontist, and the 5:30 plane I was catching to go to New York—to stop by his office to drop off what I hoped he might find a helpful column on children called LET THEM GO AND THEY'LL COME BACK AGAIN.

"You don't have to come to the office. Just call me up when you're done with your gums and I'll pick you up in the car," Mr. Monti countered. "We can talk about the children while I'm taking you to the airport on my way home." He assured me that the detour would be "no trouble, no trouble at all. In fact," he added caressingly, "a pleasure." I could tell right away that my unspoken goal—to set up an appointment to go to bed with him—was going to be achieved without much difficulty.

The chauffeur-driven limo, its smoked-glass partition providing privacy and its miniature bar providing a nice Burgundy, seemed made for an easy segue from "let's talk about Wally and Josephine," to a fraught-with-innuendo "let's talk about us." It didn't take long before

I was soulfully saying to Mr. Monti, "I married very young and I sometimes feel I missed out on . . . certain kinds of experience. On the other hand," I hastened to add, to let him know I wasn't unhappy, just horny, "I'm fortunate in having a wonderful marriage."

Mr. Monti confided that he too—"knock wood," which he knocked—was exceptionally fortunate in his marriage. "Three beautiful daughters. Two grandchildren on the way. A wonderful wife."

"She seems quite wonderful," I agreed, smiling and sipping my wine and sinking deeper into the plush upholstery.

"Quite wonderful is right," he said, as he poured more Burgundy. "A woman of great understanding. And acceptance."

I nodded solemnly, trying to look impressed. "Understanding and acceptance are wonderful qualities."

"Wonderful," he repeated, bringing our total number of "wonderfuls" up to six. "She understands my appetites. And she accepts . . . she accepts that I must . . ." He shrugged an excessive Italian shrug and tossed me an unconvincingly sheepish smile and reduced the space between us to practically nil. The limo was moving slowly through the afternoon rush-hour traffic, but Mr. Monti and I were starting to speed.

"Accepts that you must what?"

"Satisfy them."

"You *tell* her when you satisfy your appetites?"

"Sometime I tell her. Sometime she finds out."

"But when she doesn't find out, you always tell her?"

As the limo swung onto the Fourteenth Street Bridge, Mr. Monti finished his wine, then helped himself to mine, then got rid of the glasses, after which he swiveled toward me, one hand pressing my shoulder back into the seat, the other—palm flat—insistently rotating round and round and round against my shamelessly receptive left nipple.

"You mean," he said, "would I tell my wife about *us*?"

The hand that was pressing my shoulder had moved significantly southward and rapidly disappeared into the interior, setting certain sensitive sections to singing oh-my, oh-yes, oh-more, oh . . .

"Ouch!" My turned-to-mush body suddenly congealed. "Excuse me for saying this, Joseph, but I really don't think that's any place for a pinky ring."

Mr. Monti was deeply apologetic.

"Please forgive me, Brenda," he said, withdrawing his hand and removing the ring from his pinky. "The last thing I would want is to cause you pain." As he made his move to return to where he had been before being rudely interrupted, I pulled away and said, "Wrong time. Wrong place. But if, just for argument's sake, there should happen to be a right time and right place, I think you need to know that you would cause me *serious* pain if you told your wife about it."

"Just for argument's sake," said Mr. Monti, "what do you think would be the right time and right place?"

I knew half the answer immediately, though I certainly also knew that my response was more than a little bit kinky. Which didn't stop me from answering, "For argument's sake then, let's say March eighteenth. I've got some time available in the morning."

My trip to Manhattan included a sushi dinner with my older sister, Rosalie, and an early-morning taping of a cable television show on food guilt. The TV people had offered to put me up at the Berkshire Place, but with all I had to tell Rosalie I decided I'd spend the night on her living-room couch.

There are twelve years, ten months, and three weeks between the date of my sister Rosalie's birth and mine. For twelve years, ten months, and three weeks, as she is often wont to point out, she reveled in being our parents' only child. At the age of fifty-eight she has finally recovered from the shock of my arrival. But she still resents the fact that I am always going to be twelve years, ten months, and three weeks younger than she.

Tall and leggy and slender, with her jawline fairly intact, my sister looks good for her age the way Lauren Bacall does. Which doesn't quite do it for Rosalie, who would rather look good for Jodie Foster's age and who is heading toward sixty kicking and screaming, "Why me?" In her job as a conference coordinator, Rosalie shows the organizational skills that both of us inherited from our late mom, known in northern New Jersey as perhaps the finest president ever to preside over Fair Lawn Hadassah. In her chronic dissatisfaction, however, Rosalie seems to be taking after our dad, a life insurance salesman who believed that he sang better than Ezio Pinza and who felt that if he had only aimed for Broadway instead of Prudential, he would have been the man Mary Martin tried to wash out of her hair in *South Pacific*.

Our father, who died two years ago, sang decades of popular songs—from "Jeepers Creepers" to "Bésame Mucho," from "Goody Goody" to "White Cliffs of Dover," from "Some Enchanted Evening" to (keeping up with the times) "What I Did for Love." He sang at Bar

Mitzvahs and weddings and on trips down to the shore (during which Mom and Rose snoozed and I sang along), and although he was surely no Pinza he could put a lump in your throat with his "Once you have found her, never let her go."

Dad at least had a vision of what perfect happiness was: making beautiful music up on a stage. Rosalie, on the other hand, is forever revising her life and she still hasn't got a clue as to what she is going for. She has been an airline stewardess, sold real estate, run a gallery down in SoHo, worked as the pastry chef at La Folie. She has ranged, since her divorce, between defiantly single ("Who needs them?") and desperately single ("I'm nothing without a man"). Currently a blonde, she was briefly brunette with a stick-straight Lulu-in-Hollywood bob and has also tried her luck as a frizzy-haired redhead. She has also tried being a mother, which has worked out just fine with her dog, but not with her only human child, Miranda, an independent producer who is living out in Los Angeles and keeping in cautious touch with her mother by fax.

Remember that woman who dealt with bad times by saying "Could be worse"? Rosalie lives by the motto "Could be better." Which means that, wherever she is, it—by definition—is never the place where she wants to be. "How's the convention business?" I ask, and she gives me forty-five minutes on why she finds it deeply unfulfilling. "You know who's being fulfilled?" she asks me. "Landscape architects. I'm giving serious thought to a career change."

This career-change talk used to be the cue for *me* to do forty-five minutes on wasn't it time she resolved her identity crisis, and didn't she need to channel and focus her energies, and shouldn't she come to terms with her limitations, and why in God's name didn't she grow up already!

We irritated the hell out of each other.

I once confessed to Jake that I loved my sister but didn't like her. I believe Rose would have said the same about me. But when our father died and was laid to rest beside our mother in the Kedron section of the King Solomon Cemetery, we both resolved to make greater efforts at sisterhood.

I would make efforts to stop with the critiques.

And Rose—though she viewed whatever I did, including being born, as a critique—would make efforts to be less defensive and less touchy.

Which is why Rose tries not to tell me to shut the fuck up when I give her advice on how to live. Which is why—although my column advises everyone *else* how to live—I'm trying really hard to not advise *her*. Which is therefore why, instead of making my why-don't-you-grow-up-already speech, I said, as I finished the last piece of yellowtail at Hatsuhana, "Landscape architect—that's really interesting."

And then I told her some interesting stuff about me.

"I'm appalled," Rose said when I'd filled her in on my short-term adultery plans. "I'm fainting with shock and horror. Tell me more." We were at her apartment now (she has a nice place on East Seventy-fourth Street) and Hubert (Rose's Great Dane) was sprawled at our feet, the beauty of his countenance, his charm and wit and intellect and grace having already been commented on ad absolute nauseam by his doting mistress. Rose stared at me contemplatively as I brought her up to date with my back-of-the-limo encounter with Mr.

Monti, and then she said, "I disapprove. I really disapprove. God, this feels good. This feels great. I mean, this feels fabulous."

"What does?"

"Feeling morally superior to you."

"Well, okay, fair enough. You're entitled."

"And feeling more mature than you."

"Why do you say that?"

"Because what you're planning is very immature. You're not going to give me an argument on that, are you?"

I cleared my throat and fiddled with the zipper on my cozy flannel bathrobe. "Don't take this the wrong way, Rose, but if you were doing it, I'd think it was immature. My doing it is . . . is a, well, it's an exhaustively thought through, fully responsible choice. Not admirable. I'm not saying admirable. But when you look at the total picture—not immature."

You can tell how improved our relationship is by the fact that Rose just shook her head and laughed at me, after which she excused herself, hustled into the kitchen, and came right back with a bag of frozen Clark Bars. "Speaking of immature . . ." she said, and then the room fell silent, except for the snuffle of Hubert's stuffed nose and the sound of our busy teeth chomping through chocolate.

Rosalie yawned, "So tell me, on this TV show you're taping tomorrow morning—what are you going to say about food and guilt?"

I stood up and brushed the crumbs off my lips and licked the last of the chocolate off my fingers.

"I'm going to say that there's nothing that a woman

could do in bed that could possibly, in a million years, make her feel as guilty as eating four Clark Bars."

I'm getting concerned that I'm coming across as devil-may-care about guilt. Not true—I am a deeply guilty person. I'll go even further and say that I believe I am gifted in guilt the way some folks are gifted in athletics. A sense of guilt is a necessary (though not sufficient) condition of healthy adulthood. If I've said it once, I've said it a thousand times. But having asserted that principle, I must add that although guilt is good, we must not overdo it—a point I have underscored in several columns, like IT'S NOT YOUR FAULT THAT IT'S RAINING and FORGETTING HER BIRTHDAY DID NOT GIVE YOUR MOTHER A STROKE and (one of my profounder explorations of the subject) NOBODY'S GOD—MAYBE NOT EVEN GOD.

I believe I have learned to distinguish the things that I shouldn't feel guilty about from those things about which I most assuredly should. Like (despite what they taught me in parenting class) preferring Wally to Jake. Like (despite an excess seven pounds and a two-eight-five cholesterol) eating candy. Like (despite the fact that Mrs. Monti won't ever find out about it) sleeping with the husband of a wonderful wife and mother and future grandmother.

I knew at the time that Mrs. Monti would never find out about it because Mr. Monti had sworn a fearsome oath. I didn't know at the time that (even though our secret would go with us to the grave, and even though I posed no threat to their marriage, and even though I wasn't the first—or even the fifteenth—woman he had slept with) I would nonetheless feel I had injured Mrs.

Monti. I didn't know I would feel so small, so mean, so wrong, so unbelievably guilty.

I told you I'm good at guilt but, as I often explain to my readers, guilt must then be followed by forgiveness. We need to forgive other sinners—and ourselves. And so I'm in the process of forgiving myself for injuring Mrs. Monti, a process I am hoping to complete by the time I've managed to murder her husband.

It was while I stood in his office back on August 24, hearing him bellowing to the police that my younger son was a kidnapper and a thief, that I let myself think it: I want to kill Mr. Monti. Look what he's doing—destroying my Wally's life. But not so fast! It seems the police could not call Josephine "kidnapped" unless she was being held against her will. ("Find my child," Mr. Monti roared, "and when I'm finished talking to her, I guarantee she'll say it's against her will.") As for the theft of the money, "Yeah, okay, I got it back," he conceded grudgingly. "But that doesn't cancel out that I was robbed." He explained his deal with Marvin—"I retained the right to accuse this punk of the theft"—but that didn't seem to galvanize the officer, who clearly was not responding with a blazing-guns, call-out-the-SWAT-team sense of urgency to Mr. Monti's increasingly wild accusations. A few more rounds and Raging Bull was raging, "Family problems? I'm not talking family problems—I'm talking *crime*." And then he slammed down the phone with a red-faced, furious "Enough! I don't speak to sergeants. You've got my number—have the police chief call me."

He slumped back into his black leather chair, tap-tap-tapping the telephone with his pinky ring.

"I think I'll go now," I said with a smile as I took out my peach-glow blusher and brightened my cheeks. I looked fine. Mr. Monti was looking bruised. But not for long. "Don't think, Mrs. Kovner"—his venomous voice stopped me dead at the office door—"don't think that you are going to beat me out. If I don't get Wally on this, I'll get him on something, dealing drugs or even spying—I've got a couple of friends in the CIA." He laughed. "Yeah, I've got friends and they could fix him pretty good. Fix him for a while. Fix him forever."

I stared at him. He was trying to scare me, right?

"And it won't be, you know," he went on, "just little Wally who's going to get it. There's Jeff—you heard what's doing with him?" I nodded. "And then there's your husband. Your husband the fancy pediatric surgeon. Your husband and those two malpractice suits."

Mr. Monti was pushing hard, but I didn't intend to let him see I was shaken. "Those stupid lawsuits!" I snapped. "I can't *believe* those people are suing. They're being just incredibly ungrateful."

"Ungrateful?" said Mr. Monti. "These are heartsick, heartbroken people, their children's lives shattered by a surgeon's knife." He puffed out his cheeks and slowly blew the air from his pursed-up lips before he continued. "But lucky for them, a friend of mine—I've got my friends at the hospital—looked up their records and helped me track them down."

"Tracked them down to do what exactly?" I whispered, though I already knew the answer.

"To tell them it wasn't too late to sue the pediatric surgeon who messed up their children. And"—his (once so melting, now so menacing) big brown eyes locked onto mine—"to offer them my help with their legal expenses."

While I never refrain from criticizing the medical profession for being (this is a partial list) insensitive, greedy, arrogant, conservative, and patronizing to women, I also (where it's appropriate) am always willing to give the doctors their due. I have nothing but praise, for instance, for my artful cosmetic surgeon, who rescued me from upper-eyelid droop. I adore my nimble internist, who is the Jascha Heifetz of the sigmoidoscope. I am even willing to grant that the sadist who deep-cleans my gums four miserable times a year is, though made of stone, the finest periodontist in the Washington area. And I'm totally convinced that my husband, Jake, whatever his personal inadequacies, is a brilliant, gifted, dedicated surgeon. (You don't have to take my word for it; there are major—major!—hospitals in New York City, Boston, and Los Angeles where they're begging on bended knee for Jake to please be their chief of pediatric surgery.) So when, a few months back, I heard that the Tesslers and the Malones were suing Jake for malpractice in the treatment of Tara Tessler and Kenny Malone, I knew (and this was *before* I knew that Joseph Augustus Monti had put them up to it) that Jake was being persecuted unjustly.

At the time the suits were brought, it was almost impossible to get my husband to talk about them. He was evasive, dismissive, cryptic, and abrupt. He was also (although, of course, he would never admit this to me—but I knew) terribly hurt that the Tesslers and the Malones, whose daughter and son he had done so much for, would take him to court on such baseless and nasty charges.

I extracted the details one night in July when Jake had come home from Children's with a bad headache, and I offered to give him an almond cream massage. He flopped on his belly while I, on my knees, gently straddled his thighs, kneading his bunched-up muscles with the silky, slithery, almond-scented lotion.

"Ooooh, ahhh," he sighed. "I love that a lot."

"More?" I asked him.

"More."

"Happy to do it," I said. "But you've got to talk to me."

Which is how I finally got the straight scoop on the Case of the Shattered Spleen and the Case of Malrotation Volvulus.

Kenny Malone was the kid with the shattered spleen, which got badly smashed up (along with his leg) when he ran in front of a car at the age of six. Jake—in a race-against-the-clock emergency operation—saved Kenny's life by taking out his spleen. Jake also, in the post-op care, gave Kenny his all-out, you're-my-main-man attention, the kind he rarely gives unless you are scared and sick and under the age of eighteen. The Malones had sent Jake a lavish "Thanks, Doc, we'll never forget you" Christmas card every single year for the last five years. This summer—on the grounds that "due to the removal of his spleen Kenny Malone has suffered from, and will continue to suffer from, a life-long susceptibility to painful and potentially lethal infections"—the Malones filed a two-million-dollar suit against Jake.

The Tesslers' suit was for four and a half million dollars.

Another family that should have been singing Jake's praises instead of suing him, the Tesslers had brought Tara in with a twisted intestine, which, as I understand it, is the English translation of malrotation volvulus. As Jake explained it to me, when a person's intestine gets twisted, the twisting cuts off its blood supply, and without a supply of blood the intestine will die, and if a surgeon doesn't untwist the intestine and remove the part that is dead, pretty soon the person will be dead too. The reason Tara Tessler, now three, is just in the fifth percentile for height and weight and has chronic diarrhea and will spend her life on a highly restricted diet is that Jake took out part of her intestine. And the reason Tara Tessler did not die at five weeks old is that Jake took out part of her intestine.

Okay, so what we're dealing with here are very ungrateful parents, who got ungrateful after they met Mr. Monti. A man I thought, until yesterday, I'd know how to outmaneuver and control. A man I thought, until yesterday, was vengeful and mean but not *that* vengeful and mean. A man I thought I'd like to kill, which of course is totally different from *deciding* to kill, which— since yesterday afternoon, on Sunday, September 20, is what I decided to do to Mr. Monti.

As I often explain to my readers, our capacity to deny, repress, and split off isn't always, by any means, a bad thing. Indeed, it is this capacity that permits us to go about our daily lives while waiting to get the results of an MRI that will tell us whether we've got a brain tumor, while wondering whether our husband has decided he's going to leave us for Sunny Voight, or while worrying our hearts out over the safety and well-being of our nearest and dearest. Thus I was able—despite (on August 18) that unpleasant scene on our front porch, and despite (on August 20) Jeff's highly distressing real estate revelations, and even despite (on August 24) my ugly confrontation with Mr. Monti—to write my column, run my house, nurture my relationships, and (on August 27) serve my fabled red pepper soup, followed by veal tonnato and tabbouleh, followed by a simple lime sherbet with blueberries, to Marvin and Susan Kipper, Dave and Joan Goldenberg, and the McCloskeys, plus Carolyn and one of her former husbands.

The meal was a smash with my dinner guests, none of whom knew how much I had on my mind. For only that morning Louis had phoned to say he had come up with zip on Jeff's real estate problems.

"In case you hadn't noticed," he said, after he broke the news, "developers are going bust left and right. Please don't think I'm a wise-ass if I say to you that if your kid's wiped out, he's going to be in some very ritzy company."

What about that new group—that new Consortium of Black Business Folks—that Louis had established and was working with? Hadn't they been talking about some housing for the homeless in Anacostia?

Louis laughed. "Yeah, sure. I'll tell you what, get some fat cat philanthropist to buy up Jeff's houses and *give* them to CBBF. Then Jeff can pay off his debts, the fat cat can get a place in heaven—and a tax deduction—and CBBF will turn them into first-rate, well-run housing for the homeless. They'll even, I'll bet you, name it after the fat cat."

"This isn't," I told him, "a totally impossible idea. Semi-impossible, maybe. But not totally."

"And if that plan doesn't work, I think I could get you a couple of guys to torch the properties. Then Jeff could walk away with the insurance."

The little hairs on the back of my neck stood up. "You know arsonists? *Reliable* arsonists?"

"Yeah, I do, Brenda, but that was a joke, okay?" Laid-back Louis sounded a little ruffled. "I know all kinds of guys who do all kinds of crazy things, but I'm trying to *discourage* them from doing them."

"Of course you are," I said. "And I am with you a hundred percent. Anyway, I just might know a philanthropist who wants the family name on some homes for the homeless."

Actually, I'm acquainted with four seriously rich people, three of whom (the exception is Joseph Monti) would easily qualify as philanthropists. One is my friend Carolyn, whose vast sums of money, however, are tied up in what is called a spendthrift trust, watched over by bankers who get to say yea or nay (and mostly say nay) whenever she wants to spend money on save-the-world ventures. Another is Vivian Feuerbach, a magnificent eighty-two-year-old grande dame, the widow of a man who had been in oil when it was good to be in oil. She likes me a lot—the two of us always share season tickets to the Washington Opera—but Vivian only gives money to the arts, and most particularly to music. The other philanthropist in my life, or formerly in my life, was retired ambassador Edmund Standish Voight, whose grandchild had died of leukemia and whose central charity was children's diseases. Jake and I first met Edmund eight years ago at a black tie do at Children's Hospital, for which he had just grandly purchased a CAT scanner. He was there with his niece, the daughter of the youngest of his brothers, the blue-eyed, black-haired, beguiling Sunny Voight.

Sunny had just moved from Boston to take a job at the Smithsonian. Her Uncle Edmund was showing her around. And because we all took to each other, Sunny and Edmund and Jake and I found ourselves spending a lot of time together. And some of the time it was just Jake and me and Sunny. And some of the time (though nobody told me about it) it was just Jake and Sunny.

Do you remember Leslie Caron in *Gigi*? *Lili*? *An American in Paris*? Absolutely irresistible, right? Those expressive eyes! That graceful dancer's body! That accent! That style, so ingenue yet chic! Now combine her with the young Audrey Hepburn. Those expressive eyes! That graceful dancer's body! That accent! That style, so ingenue yet chic! And give her warmth and modesty, along with a Ph.D. in paleontology, plus a blind, irrational reverence for surgeons. Would you want a woman like this (who, incidentally, had Leslie's lush mouth and Audrey's fine cheekbones) anywhere near your beloved surgical husband, especially if his taste ran to the Leslie-Audrey type rather than to bosomy Playboy bunnies? Of course you wouldn't. No woman would. So why did I let her in? Was I that sure of Jake or of our marriage? I think that the answer is yes but I also think there's another answer: Although I couldn't compete with Sunny in body and eyes and accent and cheekbones and chic, I was light-years ahead of her in ingenue.

I'm embarrassed to admit that—even after the day I saw them together, leaving the Holiday Inn across from Saks—I couldn't believe I was seeing what I was seeing. I was willing for Jake to tell me that he had gone with Sunny to the Holiday Inn to help choose a room for Sunny's mother's next visit. I was willing to hear that they'd gone to Saks to secretly buy me a birthday present (my birthday was a mere ten months away) and Sunny had started to faint from the heat and Jake rushed her off to the Holiday Inn to lie down. I was willing to hear that there was this really spectacular view of upper Wisconsin Avenue which had to be seen from a room at the Holiday Inn. I was willing to hear almost anything except what I heard on that hot June day eight years ago, when Jake came home and I said to him, "Before we have our dinner, we need to take a walk in the Bishop's Garden."

"Taking a walk in the Bishop's Garden" was how Jake and I used to tell each other, in code, that we needed an urgent, private talk—immediately. We saved these walks for red alerts—like the time ten years ago when the doctor thought I had a brain tumor and I sat in the garden sobbing and clutching Jake's hand, and we wound up having a fight because he refused to swear that if I died of this tumor he'd marry my friend Marianne who, while admittedly not *that* sexy, would make a wonderful mother for our boys.

Words usually burst right out of me, but on this bad June evening all the words seemed pasted to my throat. We strolled through the Cleveland Park streets, past wide porches hung with trailing baskets of geraniums, and onto the grounds of our neighborhood cathedral, then took the stone steps that led by a trickling pool down to the heart of the Bishop's Garden, flamboyant this season with roses in red and yellow and pink and palest peach champagne.

"So," I asked, bending down to breathe the shy perfume of a newly opened rosebud, "are you and Sunny having an affair?"

Jake looked at me as if deciding whether he wanted to operate and if so where was the best place to plunge in the knife. "She didn't want it to happen," Jake told me. "And I didn't want it to happen."

I straightened up. "Then I guess it didn't happen."

"It happened," he said.

We sat—as far apart as we could—on a small wooden bench just beyond *The Prodigal Son*, stone figures draped in an all-is-forgiven embrace. I contemplated my wedding band. "Are you in love with Sunny?" I asked my husband. "And if you are, what are you going to do about it?"

"We love each other," Jake answered. "And—oh, Jesus, Bren, I'm sorry—but I swear I don't know *what* I'm going to do."

I had planned to maintain my composure while Jake explained that he wasn't in love, but merely infatuated, and hadn't the slightest intention (What was I thinking of? What was I, nuts?) of leaving me. But all of a sudden I'm hearing that our marriage could really be over, I'm seeing my life about to career off a cliff, and I started to sob even louder than I had on the day I'd sat sobbing about my brain tumor.

He pulled out a clean white handkerchief and handed it to me. I threw it back in his face and continued to cry.

"Look," he said, neatly folding the hankie and putting it back in his pocket, "I'll really understand if you want me out of the house while I'm thinking through—"

"You're leaving already?"

"That's not what I said."

"No discussion, no nothing? Eighteen years and it's over, just like that?" I wiped my wet eyes with the back of my hands and sniffed up the drip from my nose. "Tell Sunny Voight to go and get her own husband! Tell her to get the hell out of our lives!"

I then had to put up with Jake explaining that this was precisely what Sunny wanted to do. Because she was such a moral, compassionate person. Because she didn't see herself as a home-wrecker. Because . . . Well, despite the becauses, Jake had persuaded Sunny that she couldn't walk away until "we understood if what we had together was too big to walk away from." He actually seemed rather proud of this pretentious turn of phrase. I wanted to punch him right in his big fat mouth.

I suppose I should be grateful to Sunny Voight. I mean, until Jake met Sunny, I was basically a housewife who did volunteer work and tried to write on the side, occasionally selling an article to the *Washingtonian* or *The Washington Post*. After Jake met Sunny, and after Jake fell in love with Sunny, and after I realized I really might wind up divorced, and after I finally decided (though it was touch and go for a while) that I wouldn't make it easy for them by killing myself, and after three months of Jake and Sunny sorting everything out and deciding it wasn't too big to walk away from, and after my first full year of some heavy-duty one-box-of-Kleenex-per-session therapy, I decided I didn't want to be dependent, co-dependent, emotionally or financially dependent, or a woman who loved too much or herself too little or loved the wrong way, or . . . Anyway, what I mostly decided was that I was going to fix it so I'd never feel so frightened and helpless again.

By the time I had made this decision, Jake and Sunny were long done with their affair, and I was prepared to forgive—if not to forget. But I also was preparing—by writing several sample columns and getting them published in three small out-of-town papers, after which I wrote more sample columns and got them into seven larger papers, after which a syndicate started selling my columns to papers all over the country—I was preparing to be IN CONTROL OF MY LIFE.

Aha, you are doubtless exclaiming. So that explains it! That explains why Brenda (née Bromson) Kovner became the can-do woman she is today. Wrong. Wrong. Wrong. At least, partly wrong. Because, as Freud has taught us (though I can't, at the moment, put my hand on the reference) all of our acts are multiply determined.

Consider the fact, for instance, that my mother always possessed the—excuse me—iron balls of a Margaret Thatcher. Indeed, it was easy to picture, with just a few religious and geographical shifts, Maggie running Hadassah and Mom running England. I therefore submit that since I'd inherited my mother's potent organizational skills, my decision to be IN CONTROL OF MY LIFE was, at least in part, genetically programmed.

In addition to Sunny Voight—call her (a)—and my

mother's organizational genes—call them (b)—was
the looming empty nest syndrome—call it (c): the fact
that Wally and Jeff, then fifteen and seventeen years
old, were growing up and soon to be leaving home. So
I think it's fair to point out that this decision of mine
to be IN CONTROL OF MY LIFE also arose from develop-
mental needs—the need to stop defining myself as a
mother and a wife and to start to redefine myself as
a person.

And then there's—call him (d)—Dr. Milo Cunningham, my analyst, who helped me heal and redefine myself, who taught me that "admitting you're scared is not
the same as saying that you're helpless," and who
(though he has suggested that I took him a little too lit-
erally) encouraged me to be IN CONTROL OF MY LIFE.

In conclusion I'd like to remind you (as I often remind my readers) that the answer to most complex
questions isn't (a), (b), (c), or (d), but "all of the
above." On the other hand, when asked, as I am frequently asked these days, to whom I am indebted for in-
spiring me to BE IN CONTROL OF MY LIFE, I always
mention my mother and my "ever-supportive family"
and Dr. Cunningham. But the first name I always think
of is Sunny Voight.

Indeed, I was thinking of Sunny when I phoned Mr.
Monti on August 28 and, making no reference to the
unpleasantness of the twenty-fourth, asked if we could
have a little talk. (I was thinking, I managed with *her*;
I can manage with *him*.) Dressed in a pale-blue chemise
with a saucy flounce, and sporting a beige straw cloche
for the ladylike look, I arrived with a great big smile
and a well-prepared script which began, "I know we

can work this out. I know in your heart you're a caring and warm human being."

But Mr. Monti was hanging up the phone as I was ushered into his office, and the face I confronted was neither caring nor warm.

"My wife has moved in with Gloria. My wife has left me," he rasped. "And you know whose head this is on? It's on *your* head."

5

•

AND DO NOT FORGET THAT YOUR MOTHER, THOUGH DEAD, STILL LOVES YOU

/ suspect it says something bad about me that—although I have dined at her home, entertained her at mine, and slept with her husband—I haven't once mentioned Mrs. Monti's first name. But in my defense, let me note that this is a woman who, whenever she introduces herself, will say, "Hello, I'm Mrs. Joseph Monti." As I stood in her husband's office, however, recoiling from his curses-upon-you glare, it flashed in giant letters on my brain: Renata, shortened to "Ren," then homonymed into "Wren," then ornithologically generalized into "Birdie."

Who, from what I'd just heard, had flown the coop.

Mr. Monti's ashen face was precisely the shade of his gray Armani suit, and his suddenly deflated lips had turned the steely blue of his Hermès tie. Even in a state of shock, the man remained exquisitely color-coordinated. And unrelenting.

"Somehow—how, I don't know yet—this whole thing is on your head," he repeated menacingly. But

I had come to make peace and would not be provoked.

"Mr. Monti, Joseph," I said, taking him by the arm and thinking fast, "this is no time for blaming and reproaching. Come sit with me on the couch and tell me about it."

Sounding slightly dazed, Mr. Monti murmured, half to himself, "She calls me up and she says, 'I've put up with plenty over the years, but this time, Joseph, you have gone too far.' " He settled, with a heavy sigh, into the brown leather couch. I was right there beside him.

"Did she say what you had gone too far about?" I asked solicitously, removing my fetching cloche and fluffing my hair.

"Something to do with Josephine. Something—it didn't make sense to me—about Josephine. But then she started crying. And then she hung up."

Though I not only think of myself as, but am, a deeply compassionate person, I confess to faking compassion for Mr. Monti. For the truth is that Mrs. Monti's flight left me with only one (uncompassionate) question: Was this good news or was this bad news for the Kovners?

I was just about to explore this when there were cries of "Daddy! Daddy!" and Annette and Gloria burst into the office.

"I've never seen Mommy like this before," said Annette.

"She's up in my guest room," said Gloria, "sobbing her heart out."

"She says as of now," said Annette, "she's a single parent."

The Monti daughters, though no longer pregnant, still

looked larger than life, their Dolly Parton breasts and their showers and towers of raven curls occupying far more space than your average breasts and hairstyles tend to do. Standing tall in their strappy shoes, and encased in designer duds, Annette and Gloria would surely have seemed a dynamic duo anywhere but in the presence of their formidable father.

"Watch that tone of voice, missy," Mr. Monti snapped at Annette, the color flooding back into his face. "And Gloria, if you're walking around the city with skirts that short, I don't want to hear you've been raped. It will not be rape."

I silently waggled my fingers in a hello to Annette and Gloria, hoping I wouldn't be asked to leave what promised to be an informative family powwow. Lucky for me, the three throbbing Montis were far too overwrought to contemplate the propriety of my presence.

"You'd be on the rapist's side? Against your own daughter?" Gloria asked, uncharacteristically unsubdued. "Another good reason for Mommy to want an annulment."

"Annulment? What annulment?" roared Mr. Monti.

"And she's prepared to take it all the way to the Pope," Annette chimed in. "She says you've gone too far."

"I heard that already. And I say your mother's gone crazy. It must be—what's this new ailment all of the women are getting now?—that PMF."

"It's PMS, Daddy," said Gloria, "and it stands for—"

"In mixed company I don't want to hear what it stands for." With one reprimanding finger, Mr. Monti silenced his daughters and let the silence gather in the room. "And now," he said, "the two of you sit and tell me why your mother has left our home and is suddenly talking annulment."

Annette, alternating with Gloria, explained that their mother had packed a suitcase and left after Josephine telephoned her that morning.

"From where?" Mr. Monti interrupted.

"She isn't saying," Gloria said, trying to tug her skirt down over her kneecaps. "She told Mommy she's hiding out from you because—" She stopped abruptly and sank her top teeth into her lower lip.

"Because *what*?" Mr. Monti demanded.

"Annette will tell you."

"I'm not telling him. He'll kill me."

"What's this kill me? Have I ever even laid a hand on you?"

With that voice and that glare, I thought, who needs hands?

"I don't know," said Annette. "I mean, maybe I forgot."

"Repressed," corrected Gloria. "Josephine says that her doctor says that children tend to repress awful things like that."

"Things like what?" Mr. Monti rose from the couch and hovered over a now cowering Gloria. "What doctor?"

"Her new shrink." Gloria, feeling the heat, slipped out of her turquoise linen jacket and draped it over her rape-provoking knees. "Jo's already had four sessions with her—the last one just this morning, before she called Mommy."

Annette, the perspiration standing out on her creamy brow, decided to give her older sister some help. "Jo says Dr. X—she won't tell her name because she's worried you'll track her down—has already opened her eyes about her whole life."

"And when she opened Josephine's eyes," Mr. Monti asked, "what, I would like to know, did Josephine see?"

"That you didn't want her to go with Wally . . ." Gloria began.

"Or with any other man," Annette continued, "because—I cannot say this."

"Say it!" bellowed Mr. Monti.

"Because," Annette whispered, "you want her for herself."

"Sexually, that is," said Gloria, looking ready to faint. "Josephine told Mommy that the reason you're against Wally is because you secretly want to go to bed with her."

I have to confess that I was totally loving this Freudian seminar. Mr. Monti totally was not. Back in his Raging Bull mode, he swung out wildly and smashed a green-glass-globed lamp to the floor, then swung again and shattered a crystal ashtray. "I will not—" he reached out to swing once more, thought better of it, and jammed his hands into his pockets "—I will not have such filth spoken in my presence. Take your lies and get out of here, and you can tell your mother—" he took a deep breath "—you can tell your mother that if she can persuade the Pope to believe such filth, she can have her annulment."

In an instant, Annette and Gloria had vanished from the room, and I was alone with Mr. Monti's wrath. What, I asked myself, could I possibly say or possibly do to turn it away? It was clear to me that Dr. X had tried to help Josephine understand her father by pointing to the underlying unconscious (and, of course, uni-

versal) incestuous yearnings that fueled his fierce
refusal to let her go. (Give her a few more sessions and
Dr. X, I was virtually positive, would see Mr. Monti's
motives as not merely Oedipal, would see that his narcissistic need for control and domination was just as
profound an aspect of his pathology. Jake hates it when
I talk like this, but too bad.)

In any case, poor Josephine—who possessed, I'd already observed, a quite literal mind—had failed to
make the crucial distinction between unconscious
wishes and concrete actions. Misinterpreting Freud, she
had apparently decided that her dad was a clear and
present sexual menace. Furthermore, having decided
this, she was eager to share her new insights with her
mother. Who, from what I was learning today, appeared
to have an equally literal mind.

Let me say two things: I was more than willing to
think the worst of Mr. Monti. But I also was ready to
swear on my kids that, whatever else he might do, he
didn't do incest.

Perhaps I could earn his gratitude by essaying a constructive intervention.

"Listen to me, Mr. Monti," I began, in my gentlest,
most empathic voice, "your daughter Josephine is a bit
confused. I'd like to help straighten this out, if you'll
only—"

"Listen to *me*, Mrs. Kovner," said Mr. Monti in an
extremely ungentle voice, "and listen carefully. You
have torn my family apart. I promise you, I will do the
same to yours."

I had to admit to myself that Mr. Monti sounded
chillingly sincere.

"I hear what you're saying," I soothingly said,

though I truly loathe that phrase. "I hear that you are really, really upset."

"Upset?" said Mr. Monti, laughing unpleasantly. "You think I'm upset?" He raised his eyes to the ceiling, but I presume his destination was higher up. "May I never see my wife or my children or grandchildren again, may I end my days in poverty, may my—" here he faltered a moment "—my thing drop off, if I fail to exact full vengeance on your husband and your sons for what you have done to me."

He paused, turned his burning eyes on me, and intoned: "Vengeance on your husband, Jake. Vengeance on your son Jeff. And permanent—permanent—vengeance on your son Wally."

The temperature in the office suddenly fell about fifty degrees. A lump the size of a softball lodged in my throat. My body turned rigid. My stomach turned over. My thoughts turned to Victor Mature in *Kiss of Death*. This was the moment I recognized that Joseph Monti was basically unmanageable, that in spite of my profound grasp of the human condition I wouldn't be able to turn this man around. He had taken his vow—this corny, ridiculous, melodramatic vow—and I totally believed that he would keep it.

I believed him because he was seriously vindictive. Because he was mean. Because he needed to win. But mostly I believed him because he knocked wood, tossed salt over shoulders, never ever opened umbrellas indoors, refused to sing before breakfast (because, as he once explained, that meant he would cry before dinner), and would walk ten miles to avoid walking under a ladder.

The man was semi-psychotically superstitious. So I believed him.

I believed that *he* believed that he would lose his family and fortune and sexual organ unless he succeeded in tearing my family apart. They won't be safe till he's dead, I thought. I really want him dead, I thought. I really want to murder Mr. Monti.

In one of the many columns I have written on coping with stress, I strongly recommend the use of mind games, whose purpose, I tell my readers, is to give our tensions and torments a brief holiday by diverting us to trivial pursuits. Unlike board games, however, mind games require neither equipment nor a playmate. Mind games are played entirely inside the head. Which means, if we're having an MRI—where we lie in a narrow tunnel for forty-five minutes, feeling both claustrophobic and unshakably convinced that we have a brain tumor—we could, for instance, try to name seven songs which contain the name of a drink in their title. (Hint: "Kisses Sweeter Than Wine." They've Got an "Awful Lot of Coffee" in Brazil. "Tea for Two." Take it from there!) Or nine songs that bear the name of a fruit in their title. (Hint: "Tangerine." "Blueberry Hill." "Strawberry Fields Forever." And, counting for two, "Cherry Pink and Apple Blossom White.") Or, on a somewhat different theme, we might try to list all fifty states, alphabetically. (Hint: Eight of them begin with the letter *M*.)

The nice thing about these mind games is that they get you so obsessed that you simply cannot obsess about anything major. Which is why, when I left Mr. Monti and this voice inside my head started chanting murdermurdermurdermurdermurder, I drowned it out by trying to think of eleven movies starring Bette Davis. I had only thought of seven by the time the Metro had reached my Cleveland Park stop, adding *All This and Heaven Too* as I huffed up the Newark Street hill, and *The Letter* as I walked through my front door. I would have had my eleven, I'm sure, but the telephone was ringing. It was—I did not really need this—Philip Eastlake.

Philip had been pursuing me since our love in the afternoon back on March 18. He simply refused to believe that I would not be going to bed with him again. His surreptitious phone calls ("Are you alone?" "Is it safe to talk now?") assaulted my orderly short-term adultery plan, which involved, you may recall, a commitment to minimal sneaking around—and no second helpings. Louis, in contrast to Philip, had refrained from sexual overtures after our naughty night together (also, I blush to remind you, on March 18), having accepted my statement that I intended to limit our lust to a one-night stand as the prerogative of all free men *and* women (for which I must, reluctantly, credit Adrienne). I have to confess, however, that neither before nor after my afternoon with Philip did I ever mention the concept of one-night stand, concerned that he would find such limits insulting, and convinced that I could surely come up with another (more tactful) gambit to fend off future sexual complications. And so, when Philip throatily asked, as we lounged in the John Hay suite of the Hay-Adams, "How soon will we be able to meet again?" I offered him a rejection which I hoped he would interpret as First Prize.

"What happened between us this afternoon was the kind of thrillingly total soul/body experience that can—that often does—shatter a marriage. Which means, my dear"—could he hear that little tremor in my voice?—"that I do not dare make love with you again."

Is that a winner or what? The man is turned away with his ego not only intact but inflated ("thrillingly total soul/body experience"—wow!). And since I assumed that Philip had no wish to play Vronsky to my Anna Karenina, I had, with my "shatter a marriage," deftly warned him of the dangers of further pursuit.

Yes, thanks to my profound grasp of the human condition, I'd figured out exactly what to do. I had not yet figured out why it wasn't working.

Why did Philip keep calling me up? Why did he keep imploring me to come to the John Hay suite and take off my clothes? Why did he keep insisting, "Don't be afraid. You will always be safe with me, *querida*"? And, for that matter, why was a Jewish man with a William Buckley man-of-Yale accent using Spanish endearments like *querida*? (Perhaps it had something to do with that summer, many years ago, when he interviewed Ché and Fidel in a Cuban bordello. Or maybe he just thinks it's cute. Well, never mind.)

My point is that I was stuck with my thrillingly total soul/body story, and it wasn't making Philip leave me alone. Could it be that he was a selfish beast who would actually feel kind of flattered if, his name on my lips, I threw myself under a train? Could it be (this was Carolyn's view) that by letting him do the peculiar things that he wanted to do with me, I had turned him forever into my sexual slave? Or could it be (this was Rosalie's view) that Philip had seen through my story, and knew I had used-him and callously tossed him away, and wanted to prove that he couldn't be callously tossed?

In any case, what with Bette Davis movies on my mind, and murdermurder just beneath the movies, I didn't have the strength to fend off Philip when, that famous voice thick with emotion, he begged me to meet him immediately—or else he would come to my house and make a scene. I negotiated him down from the John Hay suite to the National Zoo, a manageable walking distance from home. Then, changing into my Reeboks, I trotted back down Newark Street to Connecticut Avenue, chanting my cheering mantra, "I can handle this."

I hadn't been to the zoo since Wally and Jeff were still young enough to be utterly awestruck at the sight of Ling-Ling and Hsing-Hsing, our prized giant pandas (one—sigh—now dead), whose inky eyelinered eyes and black-and-white stuffed-animal bodies looked like creations of Disney rather than nature. I had planned to return to the zoo, if my back and energy held out, after my sons had provided me with some grandchildren, to whom—as we toured the premises—I would offer my quasi-poetic zooey spiel on the poignance of pandas, the tension of tigers, the bluster of bears, the goofy grace of giraffes, and other alliterations that my kids had long ago quit putting up with.

But there I was in the smelly humidity of the elephant house, surrounded by the most massive of the mammals. Philip, an ad for GQ in his well-pressed white pants and striped cotton shirt of many colors, was contemplating a rhino who'd lost its horn. I came up behind him. "I'm here," I said, tapping him asexually on the shoulder. "But this is a terrible time for me. I've got a *lot* on my mind. And Philip, I need to say that I don't think it's right that you kind of blackmailed me into meeting you."

Philip's eyes, which usually glitter with the look of eagles, were glittering—to my amazement—with genuine tears. "Forgive the cliché," he said, "but all is fair in love and war. And Brenda, I believe that I am in love with you."

In spite of my profound grasp of the human condition, I have to admit I wasn't expecting this.

"Shh, please lower your voice," I urged, as a pair of tanned young mothers turned and looked with interest in our direction. Then, realizing that they had recognized Philip's unmistakable baritone, I tugged at his arm and whispered, "Let's get out of here."

The last of the summer tourists, sluggish and sticky under the hot late-afternoon sun, were dragging crabby children from ape to zebra, with time-outs to chase after vagrant balloons ("Did I *tell* you not to let go?") and to issue threats ("Whine once more and it's straight back to Tucson") and to urgently ask, "Quick! Where can we find the rest rooms?"

Walking briskly down the sloping path, we passed the bison and didn't stop until we reached the seals, where a woman read from a plaque to reassure an anxious boy that "If a gray seal is lying in the pool under the plastic pipe to your left, don't worry. It's asleep." Her penetrating voice sent us on to the bears, where Philip repeated his declaration, adding "and I believe you love me too. And I want you to know I'm prepared to accept—" he paused a pregnant pause "—the consequences of shattering your marriage."

And I want you to know that *I* was prepared to tell him, "Don't be ridiculous," but the proud and hopeful look on his face slowed me down. He reminded me of how Wally looked when, at the age of nine, he presented me with my Mother's Day gift—a hostess apron covered with pink-sequined poodles. Faced with that please-be-pleased face, I switched from dismissive to gently instructive, edging into rejection with "It's true we felt something quite special that day—"

"Not just quite special," said Philip. "Thrillingly total."

"—and it's tempting to see that experience as the basis for a continuing affair—"

"Not just an affair. I might want to marry you."

I almost choked on the "marry you," but pressed on.

"—but that wasn't really me you held in your arms that afternoon. It was an idealized, romanticized version of me."

A plump man in unduly short shorts and a pith helmet, herding a large batch of boys, crowded beside us to gape at the fearsome black bears.

"It wasn't an idealization," Philip protested, seizing my hand and steering me to the relative calm of a water-lilied pond and a rocky waterfall. "I tell you, I love you."

"Philip, trust me on this. The only reason you think you love me is that you saw me, that afternoon, through rose-colored glasses."

(What can I say? I happened to be undressed to kill that day in my sultry red silk panties and my matching peekaboo bra and, to complete the picture, a red lace garter belt.)

"Not at all," Philip protested. "I didn't see you

through rose-colored glasses at all. I saw where your bottom is starting to sag. I saw that fold of flesh above your waistline. I saw where the skin's getting loose on your upper arms. When the light hit your face a certain way, I could see those little laugh lines around your mouth. And I saw that without your makeup the shade of your skin changed from pinkish brown to a sort of beige-green."

A long, sustained screech from a ponytailed girl interrupted Philip, who seemed to be just warming up to this extensive documentation of his clear-sightedness. Before he could resume, I tersely said, "I do believe you've made your point."

"Is that Philip Eastlake?" An ample middle-aged woman, her T-shirt displaying the Stars and Stripes above the vainglorious message THESE COLORS DON'T RUN, rushed over to us, an autograph book in hand. "I never leave home without it," she said, her small black eyes aglow like two luminous jelly beans. "You just don't know—please sign here; I found you a space next to Jackie Mason—where you're going to bump into a celebrity."

While Philip turned on the charm (the noble head attentively cocked, the chiseled lips curved into a humane smile), I wandered ahead and promptly bumped into Leon Cooper and his daughter Daisy. Leon, like a couple of other ex-presidential aides of my acquaintance, had discovered the joys of fatherhood late in life, having maintained—in his journey to the best antechambers of the Oval Office—the most minimal relationship with his first family. Toward the end of the 1980s, when Leon was looking at fifty-five, he noticed that his last kid had left the house and that, as he put it to me at the

McCloskeys' annual Fourth of July pool-and-picnic party, "I'd missed it all—the entire parenthood thing." Which is why he divorced Bernice and married Brooke, who gave birth to Daisy and gave Leon his second chance at fatherhood.

In a column of mine called LIFE ISN'T FAIR—SO WHAT? I discussed the Leon Cooper phenomenon, concluding:

> Perhaps the reason that women tend to be more mature than men is that life offers women fewer second chances. If we don't get it right the first time, we must live with that failure and loss, work through that pain, use it to help us grow. When medical marvels succeed in giving the postmenopausal woman not only the complexion but the conception capabilities of a twenty-year-old, I wonder what the costs will be—for women, for men, and for the human race.

("I'll pay the costs! I'll pay the costs!" my sister Rosalie said after she had finished reading this column. "You want to be mature—with all the failures and losses and pain and the rest of that shit—go right ahead.")

Anyhow, there was Leon, a beaming, balding, slightly taller Danny DeVito, taking time off from his megamillion-dollar consulting firm to show his darling Daisy the *Panthera* tiger. "And I'm the one she cries for when she wakes up with a nightmare, and I'm the one who's there for her allergy shots, and . . ." On he went, as Philip, having escaped from his admirer, caught up with me and had the good sense to keep walking.

"What, by the way, are you doing here all by yourself?" Leon, as I'd expected, finally asked me.

"Research," I immediately replied, having had lots of time, while Leon was busy with his Doting Daddy routine, to concoct an alibi. "Research for a column on personal freedom I'm thinking of calling MUST WE—LIKE THE ANIMALS—LIVE IN CAGES?"

Which, I decided on the way home (Philip, to my relief, was nowhere in sight), was really not a bad idea for a column.

When I returned from the zoo I took a few deep, restorative breaths and decided to think about Philip Eastlake tomorrow. I also decided, however, that it was time to bring Jake and Marvin up to date on the Wally and Josephine situation. "You know, I have to bill you for this," said Marvin apologetically, when he rang our doorbell after his evening run. I handed him a cooling drink and said we'd be thrilled to be billed if he would use the money to buy some new running shorts. I then informed them that Josephine was down in Rehoboth with Wally, confessing my own involvement in her flight, and summarized—albeit with several significant omissions—my last two conversations with Mr. Monti.

(Among the omissions were Mr. Monti's instigation of Jake's malpractice suits, Mr. Monti's role in Jeff's real estate woes, Mr. Monti's malediction upon the Kovner family, and all of my innermost thoughts about first-degree murder. I had my reasons.)

When I'd finished my bowdlerized report, Marvin briskly summarized my summary: "Monti calls the cops on Wally for stealing his dough and his daughter and winds up with no daughter and no wife. Look, it wasn't the greatest idea for you to help Wally and Josephine run away together, but—"

Jake cut through Marvin's sentence with a series of slashing incisions. "Not the greatest idea? How about the most high-handed idea? The most arrogant idea? The most presumptuous, irresponsible—"

"—but," dear, unperturbable Marvin continued, "I think, at least for the moment, it turned out okay."

I modestly murmured that I agreed with Marvin.

"And how's Mr. Monti feeling about you breaking up his marriage?" asked Jake, most unfondly. "Is Mr. Monti saying, 'It turned out okay'?"

"Well, he didn't have much to say," I lied. "He just sort of mentioned his marriage problems in passing when I dropped by his office today to—"

"—meddle some more?"

"To reach out a friendly hand. To end the hostilities."

"Speaking of which," said Marvin, inching discreetly toward our front door, "I think I'll go now."

Jake was unrelenting. "So tell me, was your mission accomplished? Will there, thanks to you, be peace in our time? Or"—this wasn't my husband; this was the Grand Inquisitor speaking—"would you say the hostilities have been escalated?"

I think I could safely have said that the hostilities had definitely been escalated. I didn't feel like saying that to Jake.

Over the weekend I received one of those whispered phone calls from Philip. He woefully announced that duty had summoned him out of the city for a few weeks. I also spoke to Wally and Jo, with whom I tried—several times, and without success—to discuss the Oedipus complex, the Monti marital situation, and other matters. "We'll catch you later on all this stuff," Wally told me after my third or fourth call. "Can't do it now."

Jeff, looking even more drawn than he had looked at our lunch last week, had dropped by the house to have a quick cup of coffee and (the true point of his visit, as I learned when Jake left the room) to ask for a stave-off-Mr.-Monti loan. I wrote him a very large check from my personal, private, mine-to-do-as-I-please-with checking account. After he'd gone, I started my next column.

This column came straight from my soul, which had been burdened with recurring thoughts of murder, obsessive murderous wishes which, with every passing moment, my block-that-thought mind games were finding harder to block. How was I to deal with these insistent homicidal inclinations? My answer, which both relieved my soul and provided me with the subject for my next column, was to give up trying to fight them, indeed to thoroughly indulge them—via fantasy.

In FACING UP TO OUR FANTASIES I discussed the vital importance of fantasy life as a way to permit and contain unacceptable impulses. I took the view that all of us, deep down in our souls, harbor sexual wishes and violent urges that (for everybody's sake) shouldn't be acted upon out there in the world. But inside our heads, I maintained, we can find relief and even some psychic satisfaction by giving our wickedest, wildest desires free rein. So don't be afraid, I said to my readers, to use your fantasy life for the most unspeakable, most outrageous purposes. To make mad love to Paul Newman on the steps of the Lincoln Memorial, if you like. Or, if you like, to kill off all your enemies.

This column gave me permission to indulge myself fully and freely in fantasies of murdering Mr. Monti. I needed that permission. I planned to take it.

That Monday, when I awoke and started getting out of bed, the entire bedroom suddenly tilted sidewards. I closed my eyes. I took a deep breath. I opened my eyes again. The room still spun. I inched toward the bathroom holding on to the bedpost, my dresser, our chaise, but the walls refused to resume their upright position. Deciding to sit before I fell, I waited it out on the floor, my emotional state perplexed rather than panicked.

The good news was, I didn't have a brain tumor. The bed news was, my dizzy spells had returned.

My first encounter with dizzy spells was slightly more than ten years ago. One alarming day in late July. My mother and I had just returned from a transatlantic cruise—fifteen days on *The Empress of the Blue*. My mother had always wanted to travel by ship across the ocean, but my dad got intractably seasick even on ferries. So when the doctors announced that there was nothing more they could do about her liver cancer, I booked us a cabin, left Jake home with the boys, and off we went with our flashiest dresses (for Fully Formal Evenings), our checkered shirts and bandanas (for Country Western Night), and our purses stuffed with cash (for the blackjack tables).

Her energy far surpassing mine, my mother embraced every goody the ship had to offer, partaking (just before lunch!) of Low-Impact Aerobics, Ladies Shuffleboard, the Complimentary Dance Class with Chris and Christine, a tour of the ship's inner workings, a Better Your Bridge lesson, and a lecture on something like Secrets of the Deep.

"Come sit on the deck after lunch and we'll watch the ocean and read our books." My mother rejected my offer every day. She was making, in Cruise Crafts, an eyeglass case. She was playing a game of charades. She had to rehearse for the Passenger Talent Show. ("If only," she sighed, "I could sing a song like your father.") She spent half a day in our cabin preparing her costume for Masquerade Night, where, baring her midriff and wearing a whole lot of fruit, she won second prize for her chunky Carmen Miranda.

Every night, before and after the evening's Star-Studded Show, my mother, her golden curls bobbing and her baby-blue eyes aglow, shook her sequined tush in an unfettered cha-cha, having lured some willing (or maybe not-so-willing) widower onto the dance floor. And after the orchestra packed it in, we hit the gaming room, playing our slit-eyed, monosyllabic killer game of blackjack until we had exhausted our nightly gambling budget.

"How're you feeling, Mom?" I would casually ask as we strolled the windy deck after midnight. "I honestly never felt better," was her reply. Pointing up at the silvered sky, which was putting on its own star-studded performance, she said, "I haven't seen stars like this since they invented air pollution. Who wouldn't feel great with all this gorgeousness?"

She liked the ports we stopped at, and she liked my company—though she knew every person on board by the second day. But what she liked the best was the cruising itself—the movable feast of cruise activities.

"To be doing all of this," she said reverently, "while *at sea*," as if the waves themselves were transsubstantiating blackjack and bridge and the cha-cha into something miraculous.

I too began to believe that the waves were possessed of some mystical qualities, for my mother returned to New Jersey smiley and pink, eager to introduce my dad to the forty new best friends she had made on *The Empress* and looking, he said happily as he gave her a fond squeeze, "the picture of health." I had pretty much convinced myself that a transatlantic cruise was the cure for liver cancer when, six days after we docked, my mother was taken back to Beth Israel. Two weeks after that my mother was dead.

And two days after that I began getting dizzy spells.

So after my neurologist had done all those tests where you have to close your eyes and try to touch your nose with your index finger, he recommended an MRI "just to eliminate certain possibilities." I explained that I found it hard to understand technical terms like "certain possibilities." I told him, "I can handle the truth. Don't mince words." And after he had unmincingly told me that "certain possibilities" could mean a brain tumor, I passed out cold.

During the next eleven days, while I waited to take the test and get the results, Jake gave me the grown-up version of the treatment he usually saves for his six-year-old patients. Teasing me. Tickling me. Making me laugh. Bringing me dopey gifts. Holding me in his arms when I needed to cry. And one nutty night, having cut an incision in a strategic location, making mad love to me in his gorilla suit.

The next day I sewed up the slit in his suit and said,

"You've got to promise me that you'll never wear this with your second wife."

"Even if I agree to marry that pudgy cub scout leader you picked out for me?"

"Marianne Kimmel will not understand a gorilla suit," I said, flashing a spunky smile that quickly collapsed into a noisy boo-hoo-hoo.

Jake lifted my chin until I was looking straight into his eyes. "Brenda," he said solemnly, "who was the only one-armed baseball player in Major League history?"

"Why are you asking me this?" I snuffled. "You know I don't know."

"But *I* do. And I also know you're not dying of a brain tumor."

"Yeah," I said, "you're probably right," but what I said to myself was, If he tells me that he loves me—which he does about once every six or seven years—it means I'm done for.

He told me he loved me.

Threatened with death by the same disease that had knocked off Bette Davis in *Dark Victory*, I tried, like her, to be gallant and uncomplaining. I failed. I also tried to inspire myself by reciting those stirring lines, "Cowards die many times before their deaths. The valiant never taste of death but once." I wasn't inspired. Since I couldn't sleep through the night, I spent a number of pre-dawn hours down in the kitchen where, seated at the refectory table we'd picked up for a fortune in St. Michael's, I wrote my sons a series of letters sealed and marked "to be opened" on future birthdays well into the twenty-first century.

Full of warmth and wisdom, these letters provided

motherly guidance as my boys passed through their teens, twenties, thirties, and forties: Don't slouch. Don't mumble. Help the needy. To thine own self be true. Marry for character rather than for breasts. Never give up on poetry. Floss now or be sorry later. And do not forget that your mother, though dead, still loves you.

("This is the creepiest goddamn thing I ever heard of," said Carolyn when I placed my tear-stained missives in her safekeeping. "I'll tell you what's worse for kids than having a mother who dies young—it's having a dead mother who doesn't stay dead.")

I also, during those sleepless nights, reorganized and categorized all my recipes, less—I'll admit—for Wife Number Two than for my future daughters-in-law, whom I imagined sighing as they prepared my infallible brisket or oyster-and-artichoke soup, "What a remarkable woman she must have been!"

For those of you who would like to know the name of the Major League's only one-armed baseball player, the answer is Pete Gray, outfielder, St. Louis Browns. For those of you who would like to know the source of the "Cowards die many times . . ." quotation, the answer is William Shakespeare's *Julius Caesar.* For those of you who would like to know how to make my brisket and my oyster-and-artichoke soup, the answers appear in my recent collection of recipes and columns called *Brenda's Best.* And for those of you who would like to know the cause of my dizzy spells, since obviously I did not die of a brain tumor, the answer is that the doctors—that is, the neurologist-type doctors—had no answer.

Those dizzy spells lasted about a month and then they disappeared, returning two years later when Jake was deciding whether to leave me for Sunny Voight. This time, however, my dizziness was analyzed into submission by Dr. Cunningham, who also helped me recognize that my *first* set of dizzy spells had to do (you knew this already) with the death of my mother, and that they had served at least four different functions: (1) an identification with my mother—like her, I too would die; (2) a displacement of the mourning process—I couldn't weep for her because I was much too busy weeping for myself; (3) an expression of my dependency needs—I couldn't stand on my two feet without her; and (4) a punishment for failing to save her life.

When we spoke of my *next* set of dizzy spells—the Jake and Sunny dizzy spells, I called them—I put in a lot of couch time on point (3). The prospect of losing Jake was not only making me terribly sad, Dr. Cunningham told me; it was also scaring the living hell out of me. For as I imagined life without my mother—oops, excuse me, my *husband*—to lean on, I felt helpless, I felt powerless, I got weak in the knees, I got light in the head, I got . . . dizzy.

But all of that was years ago. I was now IN CONTROL OF MY LIFE. I wasn't supposed to get dizzy spells anymore. Which was why I was feeling perplexed as I quietly sat on my bedroom floor, waiting for the walls to stop their whirling.

Which, about ten minutes later, they finally did. After which, in order to reinforce my sense of control, I made myself a list entitled GOALS TO BE ACHIEVED BY THE END OF SEPTEMBER.

1. Find a philanthropist willing to help the homeless

(and bail out Jeff) by purchasing Jeff's buildings in Anacostia.

2. Talk to the Malones and the Tesslers about dropping their malpractice suits against Jake.

3. Put an end to Philip Eastlake's passion for me.

4. Help Wally and Jo with their short-range and long-range planning.

5. Locate a displaced homemakers support group in northern Virginia for Birdie Monti.

6. Try to figure out—on a strictly fantasy level, of course—how a person (I, for instance) could murder another person (Mr. Monti, for instance), and get away with it.

In addition to all the above, I had my newspaper columns to write, and I certainly planned to keep working on my marriage. (I've had the uneasy feeling that with every moment that passes, it's needing an increasing amount of work.) Looking over my GOALS, I had to admit that I was feeling a little pressed. But as I turned my calendar from August to September, I took a deep breath and told myself, I can handle this.

6

•

SHE MATES AND SHE KILLS

*I*f you think that it's easy for people like me to come up with a plan to kill somebody, all I can say to you is, "Think again." Indeed, having spent the first two weeks of September exploring the subject, I was full of admiration for your ordinary citizen who has managed to commit the perfect crime. Most of my research was done at home in front of the VCR, with rentals from Potomac Video. Watching and taking notes on films like *Black Widow*, *Double Indemnity*, *The Postman Always Rings Twice*, and *Body Heat*, I was sobered by the fact that only Kathleen Turner gets away with murder.

Perhaps Theresa Russell, the black widow of *Black Widow* ("she mates and she kills"), might have been just as successful as Kathleen if only she'd had the good sense to refrain from murder after husband number three. But smart as she was, she failed to grasp a fundamental concept—enough is enough—and Debra Winger nailed her in the end.

Yet in spite of Theresa's errors, I felt she had used the best technique—a poison injected by hypodermic needle into an unopened bottle of brandy. I also felt, considering the risks involved in having a partner in crime, that she'd used the best judgment by doing her dire deeds solo.

I mean, even devoted lovers like Lana Turner and John Garfield came close to betraying one another in *Postman*. And in *Body Heat*, Kathleen Turner—having conspired with William Hurt to kill her husband—set him up to take the rap alone. As for Barbara Stanwyck and Fred MacMurray, the death-dealing duo of *Double Indemnity*, they wound up treating each other quite abominably. The moral was clear: Either do it yourself, or else run the risk of exposing yourself to snitches, blackmailers, double-crossers, double agents, or unreliable bedmates.

(And you can't even count on your woman friends—see Demi Moore and Glenne Headly in *Mortal Thoughts*, where, sharing some ugly secrets about the untimely death of Bruce Willis, they give each other up to the police.)

"When two people are involved," Edward G. Robinson warned Fred MacMurray in *Double Indemnity*, "they're stuck with each other and they have to ride all the way to the end of the line." Unfortunately, the end of the line, said Edward, making Fred (and me) very nervous, may be the . . . cemetery.

Anyway, having given much time and attention to the matter, I wound up firmly rejecting the notion of letting others in on my murder plans. I also rejected guns and knives, explosives and ropes, and shovings off of cliffs—anything that involved hands-on violence or blood. My weapon of choice was the poison that Cary Grant was plotting to purchase in *Suspicion*, a poison not only untraceable and easily obtainable but also guaranteed to produce "a most pleasant death."

I waited, pencil eagerly poised, for Cary to let me know the name of the poison. He didn't.

Furthermore, in spite of several calls to the Poison Center, I could learn nothing about this promising potion. Indeed, as the days went on and my inquiries into the matter grew more insistent, and the people I spoke with began saying things like "Excuse me, what did you say your name was again?" I started to fear that I was about to become the star of a film called *Suspicion 2*. Putting my poison search on hold, I reviewed my movie notes and was struck by a line from *The Postman Always Rings Twice*, a line that referred to the fact that most serious accidents happen at home—in our own bathtubs.

At home. In our own bathtubs. In *his* bathtub. I sat quietly, staring into the middle distance. And all of a sudden, I knew what I could do.

What can I say? I was Bernard Castro inventing the Castro convertible, the Earl of Sandwich conceptualizing the sandwich, Jonas Salk discovering the polio vaccine, and whoever that genius was who thought up Velcro. I was peerless Cole Porter figuring out that "Fred Astaire" could rhyme with "Camembert," that "Inferno's Dante" could rhyme with "the Great Durante," and that (if you had the vision, the moral courage, the sheer audacity to *do it*) "the steppes of Russia" could rhyme with "a Roxy usher."

In other words, inspiration had struck, the creative juices were flowing, Newton's apple had bopped me on the head. In other words, having given free rein to my fantasies, I'd devised a way to commit the perfect crime.

During these same two weeks, I also talked with Tara Tessler's mother and father and, at a deeply disappointing breakfast at the McDonald's near her apartment, with Mrs. Malone. (Actually the breakfast itself wasn't bad. It was Mrs. Malone who was deeply disappointing.)

"I'm here because you said you thought we could settle this suit out of court," said Mrs. Malone, a homely-attractive Jamie Lee Curtis type with a mannish haircut, a fabulous body, and a wary expression in her pale-blue eyes.

"Woman to woman," I corrected her. "I said I thought we could settle this woman to woman."

"Whatever," said Mrs. Malone, as she methodically chewed her way through an Egg McMuffin. "So how much is the doctor willing to settle for?"

"I can see you must be wonderful at your work. So crisp and efficient. You work . . . where?"

"At the *Post*. In classified ads. Where we're used to very short messages. How about giving me yours, so I can get going."

I put down my cup of coffee and smiled warmly at her. "Won't you let me see a snapshot of Kenny?"

"Then you'll show me pictures of *your* kids, and then we'll ooh and we'll ahh? I don't have time for this. I'm walking to the office, and if I'm not out of here in two minutes, I'll be late."

I decided I'd better deliver my message fast. "I'm not a typical doctor's wife, Mrs. Malone. I don't think they're gods. I don't think they're infallible. Here, I

brought you some columns of mine"—I offered my
folder of clips, but she put up her hand in a way that
said hold it right there—"that will show you how
deeply I share your reservations about the medical profession." I set the rejected folder next to her plate.

"Good. That's very good," said Mrs. Malone, wiping
her mouth and applying fresh lipstick. "And when you
translate your reservations into dollars you get—what?"

"This isn't about money." I leaned forward and gazed
into her narrowed eyes. "I really don't think that money
should be an issue here."

Mrs. Malone stood up and slung her purse briskly
over her shoulder. "I was afraid of that. End of conversation, Mrs. Kovner."

Without another word Mrs. Malone was out the door.
I grabbed my purse and folder and hurried after her. She
was speed-walking down Seventeenth Street with her
arms pumping back and forth, her eyes straight ahead.

"I'll just walk with you a little way," I murmured,
trying to match my stride to hers.

"I don't own the sidewalk," she said, "but you're
wasting your breath." She speeded up. I speeded up.
She doubled her pace. I did too. But she wore serious
walking shoes and I wore my end-of-the-summer-sale
patent pumps. I knew, as she once more increased her
pace, that I wouldn't be keeping up with her much
longer.

"Could I just say a couple of things about humanity
and gratitude and justice?" When you're sweating and
gasping, it's difficult to sound eloquent, but I gave it my
absolute all.

Mrs. Malone stopped short. "We're pursuing this suit,
so I'll see you in court, assuming you plan to accom-

pany Dr. Kovner. But if I see you before that, I'll sign a complaint—against you *and* your husband—for harassment."

As she sped off, I leaned against a tree and did something irrational. I prayed. "Please, God," I prayed, despite the fact that I think of myself as a deeply committed atheist, "whatever you do, don't let Jake find out about this."

My encounter with the Tesslers, though far more cordial than breakfast-and-walking with Mrs. Malone, turned out to be every bit as unrewarding. I drove to their modest Silver Spring house early one evening, while Jake was out at a dinner meeting, and met what seemed to be a pair of twins. Both Mr. and Mrs. were freckled, snub-nosed, and sandy-haired. Both had a gap between their two front teeth. And both wore green cotton-knit pants and matching green-and-white-striped shirts on their interchangeably hipless, flat-bellied bodies. Tara, an adorable miniature clone of Ray and Felice, as they urged me to call them, played quietly with her dolls while the grownups conversed. What with the homey atmosphere and all of us on this friendly first-name basis, I felt sure I could dissuade them from their malpractice suit.

Unlike Mrs. Malone, they were quite impressed with my critical attitudes toward medicine, cheerfully assenting when I offered to read them passages from STAND UP TO YOUR DOCTOR and some of my other columns. "I think you'll see," I concluded, "that though I am married to a surgeon, I'm quite objective. I'm the kind of person who, if I believed he deserved to be sued, would tell you to go for it."

"And we appreciate that," said Ray.

"Really," said Felice.

"However," I said, and I launched into a brilliant discussion of malrotation volvulus, followed by a moving defense of Jake, without whom, I softly reminded them, "this beautiful child would not be alive today."

"You could be right," said Ray.

"Definitely," said Felice.

"You make some very good points," said Ray.

Felice supportively bobbed her head up and down.

"Maybe," said Ray, shrugging his shoulders and turning up his palms in a who-knows gesture, "the court will agree with you. So why don't we just let the court decide?" He poured me a glass of iced tea and added, with a gap-toothed smile, "Don't think we aren't grateful to your husband."

"Truly," said Felice.

I was starting to feel as if I was being pummeled by large, soft pillows. I shook my head clear and inquired, "Then why sue?"

"Because," Ray answered, "it's the American way."

"James Frommer of Hartford, Connecticut, tripped and broke his leg in a restaurant parking lot where he was trying to mug a departing customer. He is currently suing the restaurant for failing to keep the parking lot properly lit." One-word Felice was speaking, her hands clasped together, her eyes litigiously aglow.

"Viola Petrushansky, whose telepathic powers were so extensive that she could make long-distance phone calls without the phone, lost ninety percent of those powers after a double root canal in Bangor, Maine. Last year she brought suit against her endodontist."

I cleared my throat and tried to speak, but Felice had not yet completed her oral argument.

"Five women in Akron, Ohio, started a class-action suit against a local department store for causing traumatic stress by opening up their private sale to the general public and letting them get away with all the best markdowns. William Jones of New York, New York, whose plastic surgeon had promised him that he'd come out looking just like Sylvester Stallone, is suing his plastic surgeon because he came out looking more like Kevin Costner. The Wygands of Butte, Montana, whose five-year-old son started wetting his bed after he saw Bambi's mother get killed in *Bambi*, are suing . . ."

"Just one moment, please," I said, loudly enough to interrupt the flow. "Are you saying that these are meritorious suits?"

"It's not for us to say," Ray replied. "It's for the courts to say."

"Unquestionably," said Felice.

I moved into perilous waters. "But going to court is so expensive. If you've got a dubious lawsuit, does it make sense for people—for you—to be throwing all that money away on lawyers?" I waited to see if the Tesslers would mention the help that they were receiving from Mr. Monti.

Felice and Ray looked at each other, conferred without saying a word, and then turned to me.

"It's decent of you to worry about our legal expenses," said Ray.

Felice said, "Very."

"But people," said Ray, "have to do what they have to do."

He stood up. "It's time to put Tara to bed, so we'll

need to say good night. But be sure to give Dr. Jake our
best regards."

"Positively," Felice said.

Positively not, I said to myself.

I know there might be those who would see my Tessler-
Malone discussions as a defeat. But scorning such neg-
ativity, I preferred to call them a temporary setback.
Another temporary setback, I was forced to admit, were
my efforts to help Jo and Wally with their life plans. I
had many useful suggestions, for instance about when
they should get married (no earlier than next June, after
she was finished with college and he was finished with
graduate school and they both—God willing—were
gainfully employed) and who should marry them (Rabbi
Emmanuel Silverman, scholar and humanist) and what
major problems Josephine ought to be focusing on in
her therapy (just in case she'd forgotten one or two).

As I said, I had many suggestions, which I tried
very hard to offer to Wally and Josephine, who—mid-
afternoon on September 13—had finally returned from
Rehoboth Beach. It was time. With Wally no longer
afraid he'd be charged with theft, and with Jo—so it
seemed—no longer afraid of her father, they hadn't any
reason for continuing to hide out, particularly since their
classes at Catholic U had been in session since late August.

But hiding out was not the reason that Wally and Jo
had remained so long at the beach. They had stayed in
order for Josephine to continue her therapy sessions
with Dr. X, who had taken her into treatment and was
willing to see her regularly *even though she—Dr.
X—was on vacation!* And since Dr. X had decided to

stay at Rehoboth till the Sunday after Labor Day, so did Josephine. And so did Wally. Who was standing by his woman because, as I may have already mentioned, he happens to be a truly lovely person—caring, supportive, loyal, understanding, devoted, empathic, compassionate, etc. As I also may have mentioned, Jo wasn't exactly my first choice to be the object of all this wonderfulness, but I hoped that with Dr. X's help (supplemented by mine) she would shape up.

Unfortunately, I was having trouble supplementing. Both Wally (back living up on our third floor) and Jo (now living at Gloria's with her mother) were frantically playing catch-up with the readings and the classwork they had missed. In addition, Wally, whose graduate program included doing casework in his field, was always running out to see some schizoid Cheryl or manic-depressive Dwayne—clients with significant mental-health problems. As a result, whenever I tried to embark on a let's-discuss-your-future discussion, Wally and Jo insisted that they had too many obligations to take time to chat.

One afternoon, however, I came upon Josephine in my kitchen and seized the opportunity to speak to her privately. I started the conversation by saying, "It may not be appropriate, now that you're seeing a reputable psychiatrist, for me to involve myself with your private affairs . . ." and almost choked on my diet Sprite when Josephine replied, "You're right—it wouldn't be."

She gave me a chance to wipe spilled Sprite off my chin before she added, "I've got this really great positive transference going with Dr. X, and I wouldn't want to—you know—attenuate it."

Since when was Josephine using words like "attenuate"—not to mention "positive transference"? I was staggered. But, instantly regrouping, I said, "I wouldn't want to attenuate it either, Jo. So let me just ask you this—what are your thoughts about when you and Wally might wish to marry?"

"I'll be working that through with Dr. X," Josephine crisply replied, "and you'll be among the very first to know."

"And Wally?"

"Oh, I'll probably tell him even before I tell you."

"I mean, aren't you working your marriage plans through with Wally?"

"Not really, Mrs. Kovner. Right now my main relationship has to be with myself. Discovering my identity. Providing myself with my own self-validation. Learning to live with ambivalence. Stuff like that."

The Josephine I was listening to was not the quivering wreck who had crept into Wally's Chevy less than a month ago. I had to hand it to Dr. X—she worked fast. Still, remembering Jo's conviction that her father was about to pounce on her sexually, I wondered how her literal mind would process all of her new psychological know-how.

I also wondered why Wally hadn't stopped Josephine, down at the beach, from making the fatal phone call that had spurred her mother to walk out on her father. He had taken lots of psychology courses and surely he understood that Jo had confused the symbolic with the concrete.

"I tried to straighten her out—before the phone call and after the phone call," Wally told me, when I raised the question with him a couple of hours after my thwarted talk with Jo. "But she was too mad to listen then, and now I can't discuss it anymore. She has asked me—no, told me—to please stay out of her treatment. She doesn't want to attenuate the transference."

We were in Wally's room—an incredible mess, but, as I've repeatedly reminded myself, you cannot tell adult children who live at home to clean up their rooms (or to eat their vegetables, or to not drive the car when the streets are sheets of ice). Wally, eyeing his books, was making it clear that he wished our conversation to end.

"Can you and I make a date to talk about your future plans?" I asked, picking up a few stray socks and some underwear.

Wally looked uncomfortable. "Nothing personal, Mom, but I better not. Josephine feels our relationship is a bit too symbiotic. She says that it's hard for a man to fully commit to another woman when he hasn't separated from his mother."

I scooped up a soaking-wet towel that had fallen behind the radiator, then hung up a suit and a jacket that were crumpled at the foot of his double bed. "Maybe Jo should consider switching her major from English literature to psychology," I said, making heroic efforts not to sound snide. "She certainly seems to have taken to the subject."

Wally, who had noticed the snide despite my heroic efforts, said, "You shouldn't see this as an attack on you. It's just that Jo is killing her father—symbolically speaking, of course—and she's sensitive about controlling parents."

I guess I'd been feeling a bit more stressed out than I had actually recognized because I behaved in a quite untypical way. I was bending down to fish Wally's hightops and loafers and flipflops from underneath his desk, and instead of, as I'd intended, setting them neatly in a row on his closet floor, I stood up and threw them with all my might—one by one by one—against his wall.

"Why should I"—bam!—"feel attacked," I screamed, "merely because"—bam!—"I am being attacked? I'm a competent"—bam!—"can-do woman"—bam!—"and if people choose to mistake that"—bam!—"for controlling, well, boo"—bam!—"on them."

As Wally gaped with astonishment, I took a few deep breaths and returned to my more characteristic calm. "You've been happy to use my help in the past," I reminded my son with enormous dignity, "and whenever you wish to use it again, I'm available."

I gathered up an armful of sopping towels and dirty clothes and marched out the door. "If you don't think I'm being controlling," I told Wally as I departed, "I'll just go ahead and drop these into the hamper. And then I'll be writing my column. On INGRATITUDE."

On Sunday, September 20, I was sitting on my porch reading the *Post*. Jake had gone off to make hospital rounds. Wally, parked in front, was sweeping the rest of the beach sand out of his Chevy. He had just rolled up the windows and was hosing down the chassis when a plain black van came roaring up our street. Careening from side to side, with heavy-metal music blasting at top volume, the van abruptly took aim and bore down on Wally. I'm sure it would have smashed him if he hadn't dropped the hose and spread-eagled himself across the hood of his car.

"Hey, watch it, you asshole," Wally yelled, clambering down from the hood, as the van, its speed unchecked, went barreling past him. "What do you think you're—"

With a squeal of brakes and a grinding of gears, the black van slammed to a stop and went into reverse, aiming again for Wally, who stood in the middle of our street with an upraised fist. He ducked to his left; the van shot left. He ran to the right; the van was almost on him. And when he tore to the left again, diving over a hedge and landing facedown in the Dunlaps' pachysandra, the van spun around, crashed through the hedge, and moved relentlessly toward his helpless body.

Screaming, "My God, he's going to run over my baby boy," I raced off the porch and over to the Dunlaps'. But before I could get there, the driver braked, insolently gunned his engine three times, backed out over the hedge—and roared away.

"Say something, Wally. Speak. Let me know you're all right," I called to my son, my heart achieving heart-attack velocity. But he was already on his feet and brushing himself off when I and the Dunlaps, pulled from their house by the ruckus on their front lawn, got to him.

"I'm fine. I'm fine. No harm done," said Wally, plucking a couple of leaves out of his hair. "But that asshole!"

The Dunlaps, foreign-service types who had returned to Cleveland Park after several years with the embassy in Beirut, were smiling and shaking our hands with warm cordiality. A profile in *Washingtonian* magazine had recently characterized them as "unflappable and gracious through car bombs and coups." Clearly this vicious van attack—which had left me wondering whether to faint or throw up—was a piece of cake for the unflappable Dunlaps.

"Good morning, Brenda, Wally. It's a beautiful morning, isn't it?" said Mrs. Dunlap, as if she were at a State Department reception. And only after we had established beyond the slightest doubt that yes, it was indeed a beautiful morning, did Mr. Dunlap ask Wally, "Say, we hate to be nosy neighbors, but that person in the van—you've had a quarrel with him?"

Wally shook his head. "I don't know. I couldn't see who it was. Sorry about your front lawn, Mr., Mrs. Dunlap. But I kind of ran out of choices."

"Not to worry, Wally. Now, can we offer you both some coffee? Or would you prefer Perrier?" said Mrs. Dunlap, trying to sneak a glance at the condition of her hedge and pachysandra while maintaining her position as a credit to the Diplomatic Corps.

Maybe, I said to myself, she wouldn't be acting so composed if *her* son, not mine, had been inches away from death. On the other hand, I said to myself, as I heard her purr, "Bloody Mary? Herbal tea?" maybe she would.

We declined the drinks, and we and the Dunlaps finally returned to our respective houses, having agreed that the van attack was doubtless the work of some crack-addicted youth. Back on my porch, however, I said to Wally, as I sank, shaking, into my rocker, "That wasn't some crack-addicted youth. I'm positive he was sent by Mr. Monti."

"He's a pretty rough guy, but he wouldn't do anything physical," Wally said, in that subject-is-closed tone of voice he seems to have recently acquired from his father. "Anyway, whoever it was, he was just jerking my strings. He could have run me over when I was splat on the Dunlaps' lawn, but he backed away."

"Maybe we scared him off," I said, and then I added grimly, "this time."

Wally dismissed my concerns. "There's a lot of weirdos out there, believe me. This was just some weirdo getting his kicks. I doubt if he knew who I was. I really doubt this was anything personal. Unless . . ."

"Unless?"

"Well, my dean called me in the other day to blast me for starting school more than two weeks late. I tell you, this woman was majorly pissed at me. In fact, now that I think about it"—Wally gave me a big lighten-up-Mom smile—"I'll bet *she* was the person driving that van."

I held myself together until Wally went off to see Jo, and then I ran into the house and fell apart, shivering and sobbing as I let myself grasp the full horror of what had just happened.

That Mr. Monti had turned to physical violence.

That a new and brutal phase had now begun.

That he'd sent the van to show us his vile intentions.

That the vengeance, the permanent vengeance, he had vowed to wreak on Wally was death—the death of my precious, beloved son.

I saw that Wally didn't know, and needn't know, the danger he was in. He had, thank God, his mother to protect him.

The sounds coming out of my mouth no longer belonged to a human being. They were the sounds of a maddened mama bear. And suddenly I was screaming,

"I won't let him do this! I won't let him do this! I'll stop him! I'll kill him!"

And I suddenly understood that I really would—I really would—kill Mr. Monti.

In that column I wrote on the value of engaging in fantasies of sex and violence, I noted that if these fantasies became unduly obsessive and consuming, we might give some thought to getting outside help. But my column also suggested that we need not reject all our fantasies out of hand, that we need not always view them as unrealizable. Indeed, my column suggested that we might—with certain responsible modifications—dare to make some of these fantasies come true.

I underscored *modifications* and I carefully warned my readers that in trying to make their fantasies come true they must do so without breaking laws or causing harm to themselves or to others or blah blah blah.

But as I had lain in bed last night and contemplated my perfect murder plan, I knew I intended to disobey that warning.

This morning I purchased a Norse-blond wig styled in a tidy pageboy, a white nylon uniform with white stockings and shoes, supersized dark glasses, a sheet, a radio, a metal folding table, and those latex gloves that doctors and dentists wear. I also prepared a flyer that described certain interesting services available from a qualified professional. Obviously Mrs. Kovner would no longer be welcome in Mr. Monti's home. With a little luck, however, he would throw his doors wide open to Ingrid Swedenborg.

Daring to Do It

● *The Rest of September
and On into October 28*

7

•

HEAVY-DUTY RASKOLNIKOV-TYPE GUILT

Late Wednesday morning, three days after I'd made the decision to murder Mr. Monti, Rosalie flew to Washington to have a consultation with my friend Carolyn. I was not thrilled. Rosalie, now a landscape architect, had sent out a mailing to everyone she knew—and everyone *I* knew—announcing her availability as, and I cringingly quote, "a transformer of your exterior space into a true vision of loveliness." Carolyn, who had just decided to give her vast backyard a completely new look, expense no object, had invited Rose to make her a proposal. My concern was that Rose would talk herself into the job, get it halfway done, and then succumb to another career-change crisis, having reached the conclusion that her true calling in life was manager of a health spa or maybe an acoustical guitarist.

I yearned to tell Rosalie not to screw up but I managed to restrain myself as I drove her from the airport to Carolyn's house. In part I attribute my silence to my commitment to improving the sibling relationship. In part I attribute it to the fact that I had a lot of other things on my mind.

While Rosalie and Carolyn consulted about her yard, I went back home and started working the phones. I first called Birdie Monti, on whose behalf (unbeknownst to her) I had tracked down a displaced homemakers support group. Now was the moment to tactfully persuade her to check it out. I was even prepared to go with her the first time.

Once past the usual pleasantries about Wally and Jo and the grandchildren and the weather, I eased into "If you'll please excuse me for being a little personal, I just want to say that it must be hard, after all these years, to be a woman alone, without a husband."

"I'm getting by just fine," Birdie replied.

"But to find yourself stripped of your role, your self-definition, your raison d'être . . ."

"My what?"

"You know—the feeling that your life has some meaning, some purpose."

"Meaning? Purpose?" Birdie Monti sounded baffled. "With two new grandchildren, I have plenty of . . . raison d'être."

"I'm sure it feels that way," I hastened to say, validating (as one must) her experience. "But once again, as you did with your husband and children, you're living through others. You need to be tuning in to your own desires and needs, your undeveloped potential."

Mrs. Monti sighed. "That must be more of a Jewish kind of thing."

"Not at all," I assured her. "It's an everybody thing. This is the time to find out who you are. Not you, Mrs. Joseph Monti. Not you, mother and grandmother. You, Birdie. No! You, Renata. Who, after all, really *is* Renata?"

She said she wasn't rushing me but her granddaughter needed her diaper changed and was there something special that I had called about? I told her about the displaced homemakers support group that met once a week not too far from Gloria, and asked if she'd go with me to the next meeting.

Mrs. Monti was instantly solicitous. "Oh, my, I heard from Josephine that there were—well—some tensions around your house. But I didn't know you were having serious problems."

I explained, over the urgent screams of her grandchild, that the group was for her, not for me, and that she needed it a lot more than she realized, and that—before the depression and the anxiety set in—how about if I picked her up tomorrow night around a quarter to eight.

She sighed once more and said, less gratefully than I might have hoped, "All right. I'll go."

I next called Philip Eastlake, who had phoned me just before I left for the airport to let me know that he had returned to town, having completed his interviews for the first in his four-part television series entitled "Democracy in Disarray." Philip back in Washington. Rosalie coming to Washington. I suddenly had a fabulous idea.

"Join our family for dinner tonight," I urged him, an invitation he swiftly accepted.

After that, all I wanted to say was, "See you at seven-thirty." But Philip wouldn't release me quite that fast.

"I'll be counting the moments," he said to me, his magnificent voice aquiver with deep feeling. "It's been terrible having all those miles between us."

"Philip, please, don't start in," I said. "This is not an assignation. It's me and Jake and my sons and my very attractive unmarried sister. Attractive. Unmarried."

"I have no interest in your older sister."

"Older than me. Not older than you."

"Not interested. I'm coming tonight for only one reason, my darling."

"Believe me, Philip, you're going to like my sister. And I promise you'll go crazy for my brisket. It's guaranteed to put you in touch with your roots."

Fending off a couple of emotion-packed rejoinders, I got rid of Philip and telephoned Vivian Feuerbach, whose philanthropic concerns might be enlarged (with a little bit of assistance from me) to include some homes for the homeless in Anacostia. Vivian agreed to get together with me on Friday afternoon, though I was, I'll admit, somewhat vague about my intentions. And Louis (phone call four) agreed to help me make my homeless pitch to Vivian.

I was down in the kitchen working on my brisket when Rosalie, dancing with excitement, returned from Carolyn's house and twirled into the room. "She adores my ideas. The Japanese garden. The lily pond. The tree house for adults. She says I'm a true original. She wants me to get going right away."

Rosalie seized me in her arms and spun me around the floor, then stopped in her tracks, sobered up, and said, "Just one thing. Would it be a big imposition if, while I was getting going on this, Hubert and I moved in here for two or three weeks?"

I will spare you (as I spared Rosalie) my thoughts on the subject of having a dog as a house guest. I consoled myself with the fantasy that when Philip and Rosalie met tonight over brisket they'd fall in love immediately and profoundly. One happy result would be that I would put an end to Philip's passion for me. Another result could be that when Rose came to Washington to redesign Carolyn's yard, she and Hubert would go be *Philip's* house guests.

Rosalie had named Hubert after Senator, later Vice President, Hubert Humphrey, whom she adored. It turned out, however, well before we had finished our first course (a leek soufflé), that Philip had never forgiven Humphrey for failing to stand up to Johnson on the issue of the Vietnam War. It also turned out that bipolar Rose, who—only a few days ago—was moaning, "I can't live without a man," had swung to the opposite pole and was now in her "men—who needs them?" totally hostile mode. So instead of saying bewitchingly, as she knew how to do, "We'll have to agree to disagree about Humphrey," she unattractively sneered, "It's always the lesser men who crucify the great ones. On everything else but the war, his record's magnificent."

"There was no everything else," Philip answered haughtily. "The war was the central issue—it was the central moral issue of the sixties."

Rose spoke between clenched teeth. "Maybe your TV audience needs you gurus to explain to them what the central moral issues are. But surely all of us here can decide for ourselves."

This was as sweet as Rosalie got all evening.

I wanted a little help from the rest of the people at the table. It wasn't forthcoming. Jake was being deposed the next morning on the Tessler lawsuit. He was preoccupied. Wally had had a tiff (though he refused to say about what) with Josephine. He was also preoccupied. And Jeff, his skin drawn too tightly across his cheekbones, had whispered, just before we sat down, "My real estate lawyer has run out of moves. The vultures are closing in." He, too, was preoccupied.

"Hubert Humphrey aside," I said to Philip, heaping brisket onto his plate, "I suspect you and Rose are basically in agreement on a whole wide range of matters." I smiled at Philip and tossed Rose a shape-up look.

Rose spent the next two hours proving she wasn't in basic agreement with Philip on *anything*. Not the sixties, the nineties, affirmative action, Bill Clinton. Not cilantro, Salman Rushdie, rational suicide, Lily Tomlin, or Great Danes. While Philip parried, pouted, and pontificated, and my husband and sons stayed maddeningly silent, I rushed in with constructive interventions.

"Rosalie," I told Philip, "has a wonderfully wry sense of humor, was a junior-year Phi Beta Kappa, and contributes both time and money to many good causes."

"How truly fascinating," Philip said coldly.

"Philip," I told Rosalie, "plays the piano, has nine honorary degrees, and was once named Washingtonian of the Year."

"Thank you so much for sharing," Rose said coldly.

It seemed a good time to serve the dessert and coffee.

The moment we finished our coffee, Wally excused himself to go upstairs and study, and Jake excused himself to go phone Marvin, and Rose excused herself to go to sleep, and Jeff excused himself to go—he mumbled something vague about needing to check out some documents down at his office.

Philip insisted on helping me clear the table.

"Alone at last," he actually said, and he backed me

against my six-burner restaurant stove. "I thought they'd never leave."

"Okay, enough," I said to him, pushing him away. "I'm not available. My sister is. And despite—I'll have to admit—a not-too-terrific first impression, you're going to find that to know her is to love her."

Philip closed in on me again. "Don't talk foolishness. We love each other."

"Wrong," I told him, slipping out of his fevered embrace and starting to put the perishables into the fridge. "This isn't an earthquake. It's simply a shock. It isn't the real turtle soup. It's merely the mock."

Philip, his self-esteem awesomely unassailable, smiled tolerantly at me and shook his head. "Brenda, Brenda, Brenda," he said. "Stop fighting it."

With a real edge in my voice I told him, "There is no *it* to fight. I don't—" I started again. "Look, I really liked going to bed with you. I liked it a lot. It was fun. It was great fun, but it was just one of those things."

"A thrillingly total soul/body experience," Philip stiffly replied, "is considerably more than just one of those things."

I took a deep breath and decided to go for the truth—well, for part of the truth. "Why don't we just forget about that thrillingly total stuff," I said to him firmly. "I have something to confess: I used you, Philip."

As I scraped the plates and loaded them into the dishwasher, I described my forty-sixth-birthday sex-and-mortality crisis and my need, before I died, to explore my sexual nature in another man's arms. I decided to make it "another man" instead of "other men" because I was convinced that I'd look better and he'd feel better if I omitted Louis and Mr. Monti. I was correct.

"So out of all the men in the world, I was the one you chose to . . . as you say . . . use." Philip was looking extraordinarily pleased with himself. "You *are*"—he ruffled my hair—"a wicked creature."

"So you forgive me?" I asked, relieved that everything—more or less—was out in the open.

"I not only forgive you, *querida,* I understand you," Philip replied, "better, I think, than you understand yourself. Death becomes sex. Sex becomes love. Love becomes guilt and shame and renunciation."

"That isn't quite it—" I began, but Philip hushed me up and said, "I'm yours to use but I shan't press you now. Let's just say we have . . . unfinished business."

"Let's just say good night," I said. "I'm exhausted."

I walked him to the front door and gave him a chaste kiss on the cheek. "I'd like to leave you with one little word: Rosalie."

Philip wound his sporty red scarf twice around his neck and flipped it dashingly over his left shoulder. "I'd like to leave you with one little word: Never."

Early the next morning, while Jake met with Marvin and Wally met with his client, Dwayne, I ran Rosalie out to National Airport. When I stopped at the shuttle, she warned me, "You can forget about palming Philip Eastlake off on me. A jerk like that—I could never be interested. Never."

I thought about informing her that she and Philip had finally agreed about something. I smiled instead and said, "Never say never."

"Anyway"—she grabbed her suitcase and tote bag—"my current career plans leave little time for romance." She gave me a hug and a kiss and said, as she rushed to catch her plane, "Hubert and I will be seeing you next week."

A group-dynamics friend of mine had put me onto AFGO, the nickname of the Northern Virginia Displaced Homemakers Support Group to which, on Thursday evening, I escorted a docile but dubious Birdie Monti. The house in which we were meeting belonged to Frances, one of AFGO's seventeen members, all of them former (or soon to be former) wives in their upper forties or fifties and sixties, who had either been dumped by their husbands or (less commonly) had decided to do the dumping. Urged by counselors and comforters to regard their new unattached status not as a loss but as a chance to grow, one of the ex-wives had groaned, "Yeah, right. My husband walks out and gets a sexy young girlfriend. *I* get Another Fucking Growth Opportunity."

Which is how, group leader Ginger told Birdie and me as we helped ourselves to some wine and cheese, this local support group got to be known as AFGO.

"Okay, let's do Good News," Ginger said as we settled down to business in the family room. "Molly, did you pass your driver's test?"

"I've still got that problem with parallel parking," said Molly, a plump brunette with a lot of blue eye shadow. "But I keep getting closer. And next time I know I'll make it."

Everyone clapped for Molly, who, according to Ginger, had never attempted to drive until her divorce had left her beached in the boondocks. "You're dynamite," Ginger told Molly, her expressive freckled face alight

with approval. "Now who"—she addressed the group—
"has more Good News?"

Two women, Paula and Betty, stood up and announced they were going to London together next
spring. "We just signed up for a cheapie tour," said
Paula. "This is a really big first for us," Betty said.
"We've never traveled before without—" her lower lip
quivered; her pale eyes filled with tears "—without
Sam and Oscar."

"But now you *can*. And now you *will*," said Ginger.
All of the women clapped for Paula and Betty.

Another two women reported Good News: Helen had
found a job with a small foundation. Gail had invited a
widower to brunch. Applause rang out again and I started
mentally writing a column called THE WOMEN OF AFGO
PROVE THAT DIVORCE REALLY *Is* ANOTHER FUC ... How
would I phrase this for a family newspaper?

Again the clapping faded. In the silence Ginger
waited, her frizzy head cocked, her bright eyes scanning
the room. "Okay then," she said. "If there's no more
Good News, let's move on to Venting. Who wants to go
first?"

Everybody wanted to go first.

"He looked me straight in the eye and he swore that
he wasn't involved, that there wasn't another woman.
Then I find out that eleven months before he even *mentioned* a divorce, he already was sleeping with ..."

"Sometimes the only time the telephone rings the entire weekend is if I call myself up on the other line."

"They say they're my friends, but he's the one they
always ask to dinner when they're having some famous
columnist or some senator. *I* get asked to dinner when

they're having the aunt with the lisp from Bayonne, New . . ."

"It's scary to be in that great big house alone."

"The son of a bitch looks better than he ever looked in his life, while I've gained twenty-five pounds from the aggrava . . ."

"I can't believe how much I miss making love."

"So how come, if they *all* agree that it was all *his* fault, the kids are going to *him*—not to *me*—for Thanksgiving?"

Betty was sobbing loudly now. Frances was shrieking, "All I want is my life back." Helen was pounding a pillow and chanting, "Die. Die." Gradually the pain in the room, which was lacerating my heart, gave way to unreserved expressions of anger, as several of the women—nice-looking women with freshly done hair and well-tailored pants suits—started shouting the F-word, and the P-word, and the (pardon me) C-S-word like gospel singers in some devil's chorus.

Birdie Monti sent me an appalled get-me-out-of-here look. I smiled and pretended I hadn't received her message.

When the sobbing and shouting and moaning and chanting and cursing had reached a crescendo, Ginger—raising her voice to be heard above the din in the den—declared, "All *right*! You did good. You did great. Venting over."

In just a few seconds the women, their clothes smoothed down and their tears mopped up, had settled back into a state of pre-Venting decorum. After which they turned, under Ginger's firm guidance, to Resolutions—the next item on the busy AFGO agenda. More clapping was heard as Linda resolved to throw her "first time ever without him" cocktail party and Sally resolved to take a real estate course and Ruth, on a roll, resolved to give up gray and color her hair, plus ask for a raise, plus answer some ads in the Personals column.

"You're brave and beautiful women," said Ginger, after the last of the resolutions was made. "And now it's time for New Business. Let's listen to Birdie."

Seventeen pairs of eyes beamed in on an instantly blushing Birdie, who protectively held up her hand in front of her face. "I don't think—" Birdie's voice faded. She cleared her throat and started again. "I really don't think I have that much to say."

Ginger walked over and gently tugged her up to the front of the room. "Just say what's in your heart. Whatever feels comfortable."

Birdie looked at me pleadingly. "Talk to them," I mouthed. Her sumptuous body sagged in her gold-and-gray silk. Then, seeing that there was no way out, she straightened her back and lifted her stately head. Her voice now steady and clear, she started to speak.

"I put up with plenty, until I couldn't put up with any more. So I left. I moved in with my daughter. I cried and I cried. But after two days I stopped crying and two days later I was thinking that maybe I should have left him a whole lot sooner."

"We hear what you're saying," Ginger said, when Birdie, still wrapped in her dignity, finished speaking. "Would anybody like to make a comment?"

"Temporary euphoria," said Paula, sighing heavily. "You're feeling good. You're feeling good. You're feeling good. You're feeling good. Then one day you wake up—you're feeling rotten."

"The walls start closing in on you," said Linda. "Time starts hanging heavy on your hands."

"I don't know about that," Birdie said. "I'm with my grandchildren two whole days a week. I volunteer at a nursing home. I volunteer at a library. I'm taking Spanish. And I'm talking to some florists about letting me be in charge of their flower arrangements."

"You better get paid for your work," Frances warned. "You're going to need the money. You may be in for quite a shock financially."

"I don't know about that," Birdie said. "The house, the cars, the stocks, the bonds, the savings accounts? They're all—for business reasons, he said—in my name."

"Must be some tax dodge," said Frances. "But just wait, he's going to try to get them back from you."

"Trying," said Birdie mildly, "is different from getting."

Molly, looking pained, spoke next. "I just want to say—and I'm speaking from experience—that this living with your daughter is guaranteed to lead to friction and to heartbreak."

"I don't know about that," Birdie said. "We don't seem to bother each other. Besides, I'm moving back home again as soon as my lawyer gets Joseph out of my house."

Betty, eyes brimming over, said, "And once you're home you'll see—they hate me to say this—you'll see you're half a person without your husband."

"I don't know about that," Birdie said. "I think I was half a person *with* my husband."

Birdie Monti was given a standing ovation.

When Birdie returned to her seat, Ginger announced,

"There's another New Business." Everyone looked around expectantly. "We know she's a public figure, but she's got her private pain," Ginger continued. "So come on up here, Brenda, and tell us about it."

Before I could stop her, Ginger had me up and facing the group. "No!" I protested. "I'm only here to help Birdie."

"Birdie," Ginger said sweetly, "doesn't seem to need anyone's help."

"And I have this funny feeling"—this was Birdie, an inscrutable smile on her face—"that Brenda is needing more help than she is admitting."

I folded my arms across my chest and made myself perfectly clear. "My husband and I are together, we're staying together, we're happy together," I intoned, each of my "togethers" more emphatic (or was it defensive?) than the last.

"Whatever you say," said Ginger.

"Whatever you say," said Paula and Linda and Frances and Helen and Gail.

"Whatever you say," said all the other women.

"Well, that's what I say," I said. At which point the floor and the ceiling tilted, the walls lurched sidewards, the room started whirling around.

"Excuse me," I said, as my knees gave way and I slowly sank to the ground. "I seem to be having one of my dizzy spells."

After convincing the AFGO group that yes, I was able to drive—this was after a cup of tea and a lot of advice about vitamin C, acupuncture, and imaging—I chauffeured a cheerful Birdie to Gloria's house.

"Ginger says I should lead a group. She says I've got

the right stuff," Birdie informed me. "I doubt if I have the time, but I'll give it some thought." She paused and looked into my eyes. "But in the meantime, if there's some way I can help . . ."

I hastily changed the subject. "You know, we never even talked about Wally and Josephine."

"You're right," she said. "And I think that's how they want it."

"Wally and I have a very close relationship," I somewhat testily told her.

"That's what I hear from Josephine," she replied.

"And Jake and I," I felt compelled to add as I pulled the car into Gloria's driveway, "also have a very close relationship."

Birdie smiled and squeezed my shoulder gently. "Whatever you say."

Heading back home to Cleveland Park, I was feeling a little—how was I feeling?—unsettled. Visions of venting AFGO women—angry, frightened, sad—danced in my head. I admired their brave commitment to making a life, a new life, a husbandless life for themselves. I admired them, but I didn't want to be them.

I didn't want to be them because I wanted to be, forever, with my husband, who, thanks to selective amnesia, was looking better to me with every passing mile. Indeed, by 11:30, when I walked through our bedroom door, I couldn't think of anything but the good . . . great . . . perfect times we'd had together.

Like the winter Jake so patiently taught me to iceskate on the C & O canal, shouting sweet encouragements—"One small step for a man, one great leap for mankind"—whenever I stayed on my feet for more than two seconds.

Like the last months of my pregnancies, when he'd join me in the shower and wash my hair.

Like the day he said we had to see our tax accountant in Maryland, and instead he drove us to Wilmington, Delaware, where (surprise! surprise!) he'd booked us into a deluxe room at the deluxe Dupont Hotel to celebrate our twenty-first anniversary.

Like the time I announced my decision to be cremated when I died, and he said, "Sorry, Bren, I can't let you do that," and I said, "That's for me to decide. It isn't your decision," and he said, "I've been sleeping beside you almost all of my life, and I want to sleep beside you all of my death," and I burst out crying and told him, "That's the most beautiful thing that anyone ever said to me."

I mean, when I said I wanted to be forever with my husband, we're talking *forever*.

Jake was asleep—or so I thought—when I climbed into bed. I kissed his long-lashed lids, but got no reaction. I pressed my breasts against his back, draped my legs over his thigh, and gently plucked at his richly hairy chest. "I'm lonely. I miss you. I love you," I whispered softly, but not that softly, in his ear. "Please be my friend again. Please don't be mad at me."

Jake shook me off and sat up on his elbows in what was clearly not a welcome-home mode. "I heard at the deposition today that you paid a little visit to the Tesslers. How—dare—you?"

"This is your response," I asked, "to a gesture of warmth and love?"

As huffy as one can get lying down, I huffily scooted

to my side of the bed, turning my back away from him but prepared to forgive and forget at the touch of a hand. Instead, Dr. Iceman said, as if I were someone he barely knew and did not like one bit, "This is my response to an offensive and unacceptable intrusion."

My response to his response was not, I will admit, the most mature. I rolled around and kicked him in the ankle, adding, as he roared with pain and grabbed his wounded part, "And furthermore, you can just go to hell, Jacob Kovner."

"So can you," said Jake, moving into full-fledged counterattack. "Maybe that would keep you from butting in where you don't belong and—as usual—totally fucking up."

The "as usual" stung. "And suppose I hadn't butted in about buying those stupid stocks? And suppose I had just stood by and let the contractor put our new tub the wrong way in our bathroom? And suppose, as you had suggested, I had minded my own business and then that widow had ruined your father's life? You have a short, and very ungrateful, memory."

"And you, my dear, have a very self-serving one. You want to talk about Cookie Beckerman growing a mustache because you knew more about hormones than her doctor? You want to talk about our water heater almost exploding because you knew more—"

"No, I want to talk about the Tesslers. I thought that I could reach them on a human heart-to-heart level and make them see that they should drop the suit."

"In other words, you thought you knew more than the lawyers."

"No. In other words, I was trying to help you."

"Some help," said Jake. "The Tesslers think I sent

you to see them. They think I'm running scared. We were hoping to shake them loose. But now—and for this I give you full credit—they're really dug in."

Jake's voice was arctic. I gave him arctic right back.

"They're dug in," I said, "because Joseph Monti is helping them with their legal bills."

I suddenly had his attention. "They told you that?"

"No," I said smugly. "Joseph Monti told me."

Instead of asking what else Mr. Monti had said and why he was financing these lawsuits, all Jake wanted to do—the rat!—was reproach me. "Didn't it ever occur to you"—his words were curt and clipped—"that Marvin Kipper might want to know about this?"

"I figured it wouldn't matter once I'd had my talks with the Tesslers and the Ma—"

"Don't tell me"—Jake glared down at me—"Don't tell me you've also been talking to the Malones."

I pulled the blanket up to my shoulders and answered, "Just Mrs. Malone. But if I want to talk to Mister, I will. This lawsuit affects me too, you know. It isn't just your lawsuit. I'm your wife."

Jake brought his Jewish Sean Connery face very close to mine. My heart leaped. He was going to kiss and make up. Wrong again. "Your hubris," he said to me softly, "is apparently unalterable. But just remember, your marital status is not."

At Jake's unpleasant insistence, I telephoned Marvin the next morning and told him about Mr. Monti and the malpractice suits. Marvin, who's one of those lawyers to whom everything alien is human, was not impressed. "The man's a nut case," he said. "But there are lots of

folks out there using the courts as an instrument of destruction. It's dirty stuff, for sure, but not illegal."

"Just as I thought," I snapped. "The law lets everybody get away with everything unless you're two
seconds over on your parking meter."

"Now Brenda—" Marvin protested.

"No," I argued with him, "it's true. I'll bet if a person threatened to harm some perfectly innocent person,
you'd say that there was nothing the law could do."

"People make threats all the time," Marvin said. "We
have to wait until a crime is committed. And then . . ."

"And then," I said grimly, "it's too late."

When Marvin and I hung up, I tried to write a column about the women of AFGO. Instead I found myself
writing a column entitled UNLESS YOU MEAN IT, DON'T
THREATEN DIVORCE. I didn't finish writing it because I
had to get dressed and meet Vivian Feuerbach. I also
didn't finish it because I kept thinking of what Jake had
said last night and wondering, Did he mean it? Did he
mean it?

I was almost out the door when the telephone rang and
a gravelly voice asked for Wally Kovner. I explained
that he was at school and said I'd be happy to take a
message. "Then listen carefully," the voice replied. I
started to shiver even before I heard the jeering words,
which made me completely forget my marital woes.
"Tell Wally Kovner," the messenger said, sounding sincerely sinister, "that Sunday was fun day but pretty
soon it gets serious."

The caller slammed down the phone before I could
ask him who was speaking and how "it" and "serious"
were being defined. But why did I have to ask? I al-

ready knew. I knew that a sentence of death had been pronounced upon my son. And I knew that the pronouncer was Joseph Monti.

I never cancel appointments, but without a moment's thought I canceled my dates with Vivian and Louis. I told them I felt really sick and was going to bed for the rest of the day, but only the first half of the tale was true. For though I was feeling as if I'd been injected with stomach flu, I dashed out to People's Drugstore to purchase assorted body lotions, two bottles of hair oil, some medicated eye pads, and foaming bubble bath, stowing them in the trunk of my car along with the wig and the uniform and the other essentials that I had purchased on Monday. Buying these items seemed, at the moment, more urgent than persuading Vivian Feuerbach to buy Jeff's properties over in Anacostia. And now that I was equipped I intended to spend the rest of the day reviewing my plans for murdering Mr. Monti.

Which, prompted by the "Sunday was fun day but pretty soon it gets serious" telephone call, I decided I'd do on Saturday. September 26. Tomorrow.

From what I knew of his habits, Mr. Monti was likely to be at home on a Saturday. I furthermore felt quite confident that he was going to be at home alone. His wife and kids wouldn't be there because no one in his family was currently talking to him. His housekeeper wouldn't be there because, as I'd learned from Birdie Monti, Carmen only worked from Monday to Friday. And even if, since Birdie's desertion, he'd already taken up with another woman, I knew for a virtual certainty that he would not dare to bring her to his house. He had once brought a woman home, he'd confided to me in an intimate moment, while his wife and daughters were off on a winter vacation, and that very same night he had had this hideous dream where his long-dead mother arose from her grave, cursed him for defiling the marriage bed, and recommended his office or even an automobile for all future assignations.

Yes, Saturday was the day to kill Mr. Monti. I was going for it.

On Saturday morning, I left my house at twenty minutes to ten, explaining to Jake and Wally that I was planning to shop for clothes the entire day. I drove my Ford to the underground parking lot of the Georgetown Park mall, took a taxicab to Sixteenth and L, rented a car, and drove back to the mall. There, unobserved, I removed the various items stowed in my Ford and placed them with shaking hands—they were shaking so hard I dropped the clothes, wig, and folding table—in the spacious trunk of my rented Buick. After which, in the Buick, I left Georgetown Park, drove up M Street, turned onto Key Bridge, and headed for Mr. Monti's house in McLean.

How does a nice Jewish woman feel on her way to committing murder? I can tell you just exactly how. I felt as if I was breathing that nitrous oxide I get when my dentist fills my cavities—there but not there, aware but not aware, knowing that something truly unpleasant is going on somewhere but not especially fearful or concerned about it. I floated above my life with an almost Zenlike philosophical detachment, though every once in a while (as I do when the gas starts wearing off) I'd come into painful contact with reality. My God, I'm going to kill a man! I'd think, breaking into a sweat and barely able to hang on to the steering wheel. But then I'd take another whiff of that soul-soothing nitrous oxide, and float off again.

On the way to McLean I found a deserted stretch where I could pull off the road and change into the white uniform, the sensible shoes and stockings, the pageboy wig, and the very large dark glasses. Pitching my voice an octave lower than my usual tones, and laying on a deeply Swedish accent, I practiced—as I'd been practicing all yesterday afternoon—"I am Ingrid Svedenborg, certified masseuse. Our Institute is offering, this day only, a free home massage to a few selected residents in this area. Ve offer it free because ve believe that, vonce you have experienced it, you are going to vant to sign up for the entire *otrolig*—that's Svedish for fabulous—series."

(Now that you get the idea, I'm going to stop with the ve's and the vonce's and the vant's. But think of me as sounding like Ingrid Bergman and Liv Ullmann with just a little Greta Garbo thrown in.)

I'd sketched out some fairly plausible story to lay on Mr. Monti if, God forbid, my cover failed to work. I figured I'd know immediately, one way or another. I did.

When Mr. Monti answered the doorbell, he showed not the slightest hint of recognition. Nor did he grow suspicious when I launched into my "I am Ingrid . . ." spiel and handed him one of my quite sincere-looking flyers.

THE INSTITUTE OF BODY CARE
SWEDEN-GENEVA-WASHINGTON-NEW YORK
INTRODUCES

THE TERRA-AQUA MASSAGE
DEEP THERAPEUTIC BODY MASSAGE ON TABLE AND IN TUB
INGRID SWEDENBORG, CERTIFIED MASSEUSE

"Sounds good," said Mr. Monti. "But I'm kind of tied up right now."

"Oh, you have company maybe?" I raised my eyebrows and widened my eyes in benevolent concern, although nothing, I knew, could be seen behind my huge glasses.

"Nobody here but me, but I'm doing some work I've got to get finished over the weekend."

"You are working so much you cannot spare just one hour and thirty minutes to recharge your body and clear the *spindelnät*—that's Swedish for cobwebs—from your brain?"

(In case you've been wondering whether these are really the Swedish words for cobwebs and fabulous, the answer is certainly.)

"How about next weekend?" he suggested. "Could you come back then?"

"Then is a hundred dollars." I smiled winningly. "Now is free."

"A hundred next week, but free today," Mr. Monti said musingly. "Okay. Come in. You've got yourself a deal."

I excused myself to go back to the car and remove what I called "my equipment" from the trunk. Then we went upstairs, where I unfolded my folding table in his bedroom, assembled my lotions and oils on a nearby shelf, and started the hot water running—with a double dose of bubble bath—in his tub.

"So you want me to take off my clothes?" Mr. Monti suggestively inquired, eager to plumb the full meaning of "massage."

Mobilizing my thickest accent and sternest, most no-nonsense voice, I let Mr. Joseph Monti know what was what. "Before I leave the bedroom," I said, "you will give to me your glasses"—I put out my hand to receive them, feeling much safer as soon as his eyesight was impaired. "Then, when I go, you will take off your clothes and place yourself on this table"—I patted the table—"and cover yourself with this"—I gave him a fresh unopened sheet—"up to the armpits. We have here very strict rules: No eye contact, ever, with private parts. No touching between the top of the thighs and the belly button. And, to guarantee the very highest, most strict standards of physical health"—as well as no fingerprints—"the masseuse is at all times required to wear latex gloves."

Without quite clicking my heels, I turned and left.

When I reentered the bedroom, Mr. Monti lay on his back upon my table, his body dutifully covered up to the armpits. I switched on the radio, drew the drapes, gently placed the eye pads on his lids, and, after pouring apricot body lotion into my hands, I went to work on Mr. Monti's body.

His body was almost rigid. "Please to try to relax," I said. "Banish all unhappy thoughts from your mind."

Mr. Monti groaned. "You want me to banish unhappy thoughts? When my life has been destroyed, when those people—I'll crush them! I'll smash them! I'll pulverize them! I'll chew them in little pieces and spit them up!—have stripped me of my children and my wife?"

"Later you'll crush, smash, and pulverize. Now

you'll relax," I said, my voice (despite the terror I felt) authoritative, my fingers (despite the terror I felt) adroit. Joseph Monti delivered himself of a few more alarming pronouncements and then he yielded to my ministrations.

You may be surprised to learn that if I weren't an extremely successful columnist, I could probably make good money as a masseuse. After years of massaging Jake (which I do because it blisses him out, which makes him tell and promise me things that he'd otherwise never tell or ever promise) I had learned to relax the facial muscles, release all those knots in the neck, banish stress from the shoulders, eliminate islands of tension from the arms and legs, and introduce the palms of the hand and the bottoms of the feet to sensations that might well be called ecstatic.

The object of this exercise was to make Mr. Monti putty in my hands. From the long, soft sigh that issued from his lips, I knew he was exactly where I wanted him.

As I was gazing triumphantly at this sighing, supine blob, my hands freeze-framed—I all of a sudden was paralyzed. All of a sudden I could barely breathe. All of a sudden I found myself distressingly aware that this creature beneath my fingers was a naked, vulnerable, flesh-and-blood human being. Are you really, I asked myself, really going to kill him? And then I saw the van crashing through the hedge and the pachysandra, heading for Wally. And then I heard that sinister voice on the phone. And then I heard the words "I'll chew them into little pieces and spit them up." And then I said, You bet!—and resumed the massage.

A few minutes later I checked the tub, now filled to

the proper depth with steaming hot water. I adjusted the water to cool it off enough for Mr. Monti to endure it, then asked him to climb into the tub (his naked body discreetly concealed by the bubbles) for the aqua part of the terra-aqua massage. After he'd settled into his bath, I draped a steamy washcloth over his face and then I began massaging his scalp with the oil, rubbing and kneading and rubbing and kneading until—soothed, smoothed, and stewed—he sank into a semicomatose state.

After which I set the radio on the edge of the tub and plugged it in.

"Let the music fill your soul," I whispered in his ear, and then I quietly slipped into the bedroom, where I folded my table and stowed my gear, preparing to make a clean and rapid getaway. Then I returned to the bathroom and gave his head one final soporific rub before—averting my gaze to spare myself the sight of his death throes—I decisively shoved the radio into the bathtub.

And, still averting my gaze, rushed from the room.

Death by electrocution. A household accident. The most serious accidents happen at home, in our bathtubs. A man drifts off to sleep in the hot steamy water and moves his elbow just the wrong way and the next thing you know he is . . .

Well, I didn't feel it was necessary to visualize the hideous details. Nor, though I knew I would have my moral torments and my dark nights of the soul, was now the time to work myself up some heavy-duty Raskolnikov-type guilt. I had murdered Mr. Monti but I would think about it tomorrow. At the moment I needed to leave the scene of the crime.

Which I was about to do when I heard my name.

"Ingrid," said this drowsy voice.

I dropped my gear and screamed, but the only sound that emerged from my throat was a harsh hiss of air.

"Ingrid." That drowsy voice again! From the bathroom!

I crossed my arms against my chest and huddled into myself, groaning oh-God-oh-God-oh-God-oh-God-oh-God-oh-God in a state of near-panic. On the one hand I knew Mr. Monti was dead. On the other hand I knew that he couldn't be calling across the Great Divide. One of these statements was wrong, but I would have to return to the bathroom to find out which.

In fear and trembling I edged my way back to the bathroom.

Mr. Monti, the steamy washcloth still draped over his face, lay in the tub in the same semistupefied state. Joining him in his bath, though he appeared to be unaware of it, was the instrument of his destruction—the fatal radio I had knocked into the water. Except that it wasn't fatal, because in the process of briskly knocking it into the water I seemed to have jerked the plug right out of the socket.

Unmechanical I may be, but even I understood that electrocution won't work without electricity.

As I stood there aghast and appalled, Mr. Monti spoke my name again. "Ingrid, please," he murmured, barely audible, "please just do me once more with the hair." He was sinking back into his trance but roused himself long enough to add, "And turn the radio up. I can't hear the music."

What could I do? I did him once more with the hair.

Kneading his head with my oiled left hand, I fished the radio out of the tub with my right, humming a little melody that I hoped he would in his stupor mistake for the radio. I continued with both my hands, working his head and then his neck and then his shoulders, by which time Mr. Monti was babbling with pleasure.

I considered trying to kill him again but the radio was so wet that I feared that I'd kill *myself* if I plugged it back in. Instead I said, preparing to scram, "I have to leave you now. But you will stay in the tub and relax ten more minutes."

Mr. Monti jolted awake, sat up, and pulled the washcloth from his face. "No, wait," he said. "This was wonderful. I want to sign up for the whole *otrolig* series. You certainly cleared the *spindelnät* from my brain."

He started to stand up but I placed my hand on his shoulder and pressed him back into the tub. "You forget—no eye contact, ever, with private parts."

"No, of course not, excuse me," said Mr. Monti, looking abashed at my reproof. "Hand me a contract. I'm ready to sign right now."

I assured him that the contract would be in the mail on Monday morning. A hundred dollars a session, not counting tip. Worth every penny, he told me. Never felt so relaxed in his life. Couldn't wait to have me back again. He closed his eyes and sighed, and I sidled softly out of the bathroom, then made my way downstairs and out the front door.

No nitrous oxide floated me off as I headed back to the District. Reality pressed upon me sharp and clear. I had attempted murder. I had tried to kill a fellow human being. Reality was more than I could bear. The contents of my stomach, defying gravity, rose up swiftly into my throat. I swerved to the side of the road and was very sick in somebody's very expensive bushes.

But then—and this is a testament not merely to the value of throwing up but also to the resilience of the human spirit—I started feeling better, and better, and better.

Granted, I had tried to kill a fellow human being. Granted, I was capable of murder. Granted, I had—once again—stared into my private heart of darkness and found bad news. But was it really bad news to learn that a loving, protective mother was ready to kill in order to save her young? Or was it something that, if it weren't so terribly illegal, one could unabashedly be proud of?

I chose option two.

I also chose, while fully admitting that my mission had failed, not to be too hard on myself for my failure. I certainly wasn't denying that my reach had exceeded my grasp—but what a reach! I'd devised the perfect crime, and though the execution left something to be desired, I had to give myself credit for possessing a quite remarkable talent for murder.

Or as Geena Davis, having embarked on a life of crime, so gleefully put it in *Thelma and Louise*, "I just feel like I got a knack for this shit."

8

•

THIS IS A HOSTAGE SITUATION

*A*fter returning the Buick and grabbing a cab back to Georgetown Park to retrieve my car, I made a quick stop at the market to pick up some swordfish, which—topped with fresh salsa and teamed with pasta dressed with garlic and olive oil—would serve to show my husband that no matter how insensitively he behaved, I'd always meet my culinary commitments.

When I got home, however, two brief notes were waiting on the kitchen table—a "Mom, I'm with Jo. I'll see you Sunday" from Wally, and a "Brenda, I need a time-out. I won't be back until tomorrow night" from Jake. Wally's note had a "love" in front of the signature. Jake's did not.

In all of our married life, Jake had never before gone off for the night without advance warning. He had never gone off for a night without providing a telephone number where he could be reached. Nor had he ever gone off because he needed—what was that nasty phrase?—"a time out."

My *Thelma and Louise* euphoria vanished.

Big bad bleak black thoughts clouded my mind.

I shoved the food into the fridge and removed a chilled, unopened bottle of Chardonnay, deftly yanked out the cork, and filled up a glass. No, in case you are wondering, I am not a secret drinker, but sometimes a woman has to have a drink. A Saturday that includes attempting murder and being abandoned by your husband is—in my view—certainly one of those times.

My big bad bleak black thoughts grew bleaker and blacker.

Had I, in trying to kill Mr. Monti, lost my moral moorings? Had I maybe lost my husband too? Had I, in addition, lost my looks? A glimpse of my haggard self, as I carried my drink past the front-hall mirror into the living room, suggested that this might indeed be the case. I seemed to be a dead ringer for that woman in *Lost Horizon* who aged a hundred years when she left Shangri-La. No one would mistake me for Goldie Hawn's first cousin.

For a few shaken moments I almost—along with my moorings and husband and looks—lost my self-confidence. I felt myself surrendering to despair. But then my can-do attitude—enhanced with several swigs of the Chardonnay—came, as it so often has done, to my rescue, allowing me to review and reconceptualize the current situation.

So I said to myself, If Anne Archer, in defense of herself and her family, is entitled to kill Glenn Close in *Fatal Attraction*, surely you are entitled to kill Mr. Monti.

Ergo I have *not* lost my moral moorings.

And I said to myself, If Angelica Huston, in spite of many obstacles, can get Jack Nicholson back in *Prizzi's Honor*, surely you will be able to get back Jake.

Ergo I have *not* lost the man I love.

And I said to myself, Tomorrow morning, after a good night's sleep, your skin will be brighter, your eyes will be wider, those brackets between your nostrils and mouth will vanish, and you'll stop resembling that lady in *Lost Horizon* and start resembling Goldie Hawn's first cousin. Furthermore, I reminded myself (although I still didn't want him) that, just a few days earlier, in my kitchen, Philip Eastlake had found me wildly attractive.

Ergo I have also *not*—not in such a short time!—lost my looks.

By the time I had finished ergo-ing, I had finished my third glass of wine, which—since I'd skipped eating lunch—winged straight to my head, from which all thoughts had fled except for the oddly comforting thought that Philip Eastlake found me wildly attractive. A naked woman quoting James Joyce while on her elbows and knees in the moistly receptive Jumping White Tiger position is Philip Eastlake's notion of wildly attractive. My mind traveled back to March 18, half a year ago, when I'd been that woman.

Arriving at noon that March day at the John Hay suite of the irreproachable Hay-Adams, I had found Philip eagerly poised at the open door, elegantly but improbably clad in a flowing silken black-and-gold kimono. He helped me off with my coat, continentally kissed me on each cheek, and told me he was delighted that I had come. Then he gestured grandly to a table set for two, next to a window that offered one of the most theatrical views to be found in the city: the White House, with its amicable majesty. And behind it, solemn and pure, the Washington Monument. (And in front of it, in Lafayette

Square, a homeless fellow napping on a park bench, though Philip, when I pointed this out, insisted that some of the homeless in Lafayette Square are really the Secret Service working incognito.)

I was on an adrenaline high, having spent from 6:48 until 11:10 in Joseph Monti's vigorous embrace, after which I had scooted home to shower and dress and perfume myself for my second bout of adulterous activity. Which, in sharp contrast to my morning encounter, Philip eased us into with great tact.

Indeed, as we chatted over a meal of lobster bisque, grilled lamb chops, and champagne, you never would have believed we had sex on our minds, for we seemed to be getting together for the sole and exclusive purpose of discussing Yeltsin, the Middle East, the greenhouse effect, education, and the fluctuating state of the economy. I can't quite remember how we got from the deficit to Oriental erotica, but that's where we'd got to shortly before 1 P.M., when Philip opened his robe to display what he called—as he gently urged my hand upon it—his Weapon of Love, his Precious Scepter, his Jade Stalk, his Crimson Bird, the Lingam with which he yearned to fill my Yoni.

"Excuse me," I told him, "I grasp the idea, but I don't grasp the context."

Philip was happy to help me with the context.

It seems that while he was doing research for his TV program on Oriental art, he learned that this art included the art of erotica—exquisitely painted and highly graphic and (to him) profoundly arousing portrayals of often esoteric acts of love. By the time he had finished pursuing his intriguing line of research, he had had— well, let him tell it—"an epiphany. I understood that the interpenetration of the esthetic and the erotic was my path to a thrillingly total soul/body experience." (Which, of course, is how I picked up that damn phrase.) Philip had also acquired, in the course of his thorough review of the material, a vivid and varied vocabulary of arcane sexual postures and bodily parts, legitimized by references to the Taoist and Tantric teachings of Eastern philosophy.

He spoke knowingly of these matters in his aristocratic voice. He spoke with his hands.

"The union of woman and man," he explained, unbuttoning my blouse, "precisely mirrors the mating of Earth and Heaven. In making love"—he adroitly unhooked my new red peekaboo bra—"we recapitulate, microcosmically speaking, the macrocosmic harmonies of the spheres." He paused to taste what he characterized as the Immortality Peach Juice of my breasts, causing my breathing to quicken and his Crimson Bird to flutter under my fingers. And then he went on to say—as he unzipped my skirt and dropped it to the floor, along with my stockings, lace garter belt, and panties—that what we were embarking upon wasn't mere carnal contact but the merging of Positive Peak and Pleasure Grotto, of Yang Pagoda and Purple Peony.

"This just isn't me," I started to say as Philip removed his robe and stretched me out on the rug with my legs in the air. But then I reminded myself that I was here precisely *because* I didn't want to be the old sexual me.

As Philip straddled my hips and draped my ankles around his neck, preparing my Honey Pot to receive his Ambassador, I huskily whispered, "Philip, wait. The Trojans."

"We'll try that one later," he promised, resuming his efforts with an ardor that almost made me forget about safe sex. Fortunately, my purse was on the floor, within reach of my hand, and despite great distractions I finally extracted a condom. Which, after a few more moves that took me up to, but not over, the brink of bliss, he paused to put on. But instead of returning to what he proudly informed me was an inspired variation of the ever-popular Pawing Horse position, he sat me upon his lap, easing my Precious Conch Shell onto his Jade Flute, and swayed us backward and forward, not to mention from side to side and round and round, in the even more inspired Shouting Monkey Embracing a Mountain Goat variation.

Once again Philip brought me to the very portal of paradise and stopped an instant before the bell was rung, a tantalizing tactic that he repeated again and again with impeccable timing. My nerve ends revved and ready, I eventually attempted to accelerate, but Philip—twisting our bodies into increasingly improbable positions—said we must move to the music of the spheres. And so he bent and folded me into the Mysteries of the Clouds and Rain position. And then he stood me on my head in the Donkeys in the Third Moon of the Spring position. And then he arched me over into the—

"You're asking a lot of my lower back," I was about to complain, when the music of the spheres picked up its beat, and Philip's Faithful Servant addressed itself without restraint to the final requirements of my Valley of Joy.

And yes I said yes I will yes (I am, of course, quoting Molly Bloom in Joyce's dense but deeply rewarding

Ulysses) as inner and outer . . . and heaven and earth . . . and micro- and macrocosm interpenetrated.

While the floor, two pink chairs, a floral print couch, and a Chippendale conference table had served as the sites of our acrobatic amours, we never got anywhere near the bed until after. But after our passions were spent, we summoned the strength to crawl between the pristine sheets, where Philip napped and I evaluated.

Had I liked it? Hey, I'd *loved* it. All my molecules were humming. The sheets could ignite from the heat coming off of my skin. Every inch of my body— including my earlobes, my eyebrows, my belly button, my toenails—quivered with voluptuous satisfaction. My big Oriental O had been, without any question, a once-in-a-lifetime experience.

But once was enough.

Yes, even if I had been into long-term adultery, once with the Pair of Tongs position and the Bee Buzzing Over Man position, not to mention the Fixing a Nail and Soaring Seagulls and Spinning Top positions, was quite enough.

Why? Because it's a miracle that I didn't wind up in traction after all of those tricky gymnastic gyrations.

But also, and mainly, because Philip never smiled.

What I mean is, he brought to his efforts to wed the esthetic to the erotic a dedicated, unrelenting solemnity. What I mean is, the man was remorselessly sincere. There were times when I wanted to laugh—when I thought I'd explode if I didn't laugh—when the only response was to laugh—but I didn't dare. Now believe me, I am willing—just as willing as anyone else—to be reverent about acts of sexual love, but how can a person feel reverent when doing a back bend? And while I was truly grateful for the attention that Philip's Warrior had lavished so warmly on my Pleasure House, how could he speak those names with such a straight face?

Lying beside him in bed, I began to giggle—softly at first, and then dementedly. Yes, I thought, clamping both hands on my mouth so I wouldn't disturb his rest, once was enough.

I drifted off to sleep, and when I awoke I found Philip gazing upon me adoringly. Adoringly, but as I was later to learn when we met at the zoo, with full awareness of each and every physical imperfection from laugh lines to . . .

Anyway, there was Philip, gazing and quoting—I guess—from some Eastern book of love: "How delicious an instrument is woman. How capable is she of producing the most exquisite harmonies, of executing the most complicated variations, and of giving the most divine of erotic pleasures." His Precious Scepter was showing some definite signs of perking up as he continued. "With minds freed from doubt and shame, we have not cooled the natural urges of our passionate—"

"Philip," I interrupted, not wanting to deal with any uncooled natural urges. "It's getting late. I've really got to go." Which is when he insistently asked how soon we two could meet again. After which, complications set in.

My Philip Eastlake reveries and my end-of-the-bottle-of-Chardonnay golden glow were banished in a flash by the sound of his-and-her voices quarreling on my front porch. The voices belonged to Wally and Jo, who weren't supposed to be at the house this evening. Their words, despite the closed windows, came through sharp and clear. I don't think you call it eavesdropping when people are speaking so loudly that you'd actually have to leave the room not to hear. I did not leave the room.

"I said I'd drive you home, but I didn't say I was coming in with you," said Josephine.

"You're not staying here. I can't stay with you at your sister's house. What," Wally angrily asked, "is going on?"

"Separation-individuation," Josephine said, "is what's going on."

"That's fine. You go and separate-individuate from your father. That's probably an excellent thing to do. But, damn it, Jo, we love each other. I'm the guy you're marrying. Don't separate-individuate from *me*."

Wally's voice broke as his hurt and bewilderment overrode his anger. He (and his loving mother) were close to tears.

"I won't feel guilty," Josephine snapped. "I won't let you make me feel guilty because I want some psychological space." She let out a heavy sigh. "Oh, Wally, don't you understand that I can't just go from my dad's domination to yours?"

Wally shouted "Christ!" and pounded his fist against the front door. "That's nuts!" he said, and pounded the door again. "I am *not* your father. I do not *want* to dominate you. And if that's what your shrink is telling you, then tell her for me that she's totally full of—"

Josephine, sounding more like her father than I could have ever imagined, snapped, "Don't tell me what to tell her. Don't you dare! And don't you start putting her down just because she's got me—" she paused, cleared her throat, and continued unsteadily, "to ask myself some questions about our relationship."

A long silence followed her outburst, and then Wally grimly said, "So what are you asking?"

Josephine's voice dropped so low that I had to—I still don't think you could technically call this eavesdropping—move from the couch to a nearer-the-window chair. "I'm asking," she told him nervously, "if our feelings for each other are based on—uh, you know—love or just on need."

"I need you," Wally exploded, "like I need a hump on my back. You and that family of yours—that's what I need? There are plenty of nice Jewish girls around who don't have crazy fathers and fear of botulism. God knows I don't need you, Jo, but"—Wally's voice turned sweet as syrup—"honey, I *love* you."

A rustling on the porch suggested that Wally was conveying his love nonverbally. "Don't kiss me. It mixes me up," I heard Josephine groan. "Okay, so you say you don't need me but maybe you need me to need *you*. And maybe that's what I'm doing instead of *loving* you."

Now Jo was crying, and Wally was crying, and I started crying too, for Jake and me as well as for Wally and Jo. I cried for young lovers everywhere and for middle-aged lovers too, for the way we were—and the way we screw it up, for that please-believe-me-I'll-die-if-you-leave-me, that are-you-pretending-it-can't-be-the-ending, that high-as-the-mountain-and-deep-as-the-ocean devotion which ends with our lonely heart calling, in the chill still of the night, lover come back to me.

"Oh God, oh God, it's so sad," I wailed. My body shook with sobs—two-thirds sorrow, one-third Chardonnay. As tears streamed down my cheeks and my sobbing reached a loud crescendo, all of a sudden I heard somebody say, "Mom? Is that you?"

I had, in my grieving for love's labours lost, forgotten that Wally and Josephine were right there. Now they knew that I was right there too. "It's me," I said, thinking fast. "I was taking a nap, and I just woke up from a terrible nightmare. Come on inside and I'll make us all some coffee."

I opened the door to let them both in, but Josephine told me No, thanks, explaining that she had studying to do.

Wally grabbed her hand and said, "It's really important to me for you to come in."

Josephine slipped her hand away. "It's really really important," she said, "for me not to."

"It actually isn't that cold tonight," I said to Wally and Jo, trying for a constructive intervention. "Compromise! Have coffee out here on the porch."

"Forget it," said Wally, and stormed into the house.

"Good night, Mrs. Kovner," said Jo, and walked to her car.

Saturday night, I said to myself, is the loneliest night of the week.

I made myself a lonely cup of coffee.

And since Wally said no—a rather sharp no—when I asked if he wanted to talk, and since Jake was God-knows-where with God-knows-whom, I decided the best thing to do was to go to sleep. Tomorrow—when I was thinking more clearly and looking a whole lot better—I'd figure out how to make up with Jake and how (once again!) to murder Mr. Monti.

* * *

Sunday started out badly and got worse.

The phone rang at 7 A.M. with my sister Rosalie saying, "I didn't wake you, did I?"

There are three answers to this question. The direct approach: "Damn right you did. Who calls at seven A.M.?" The smart-ass reproach: "Certainly not. I had to get up to answer the telephone anyway." The comforting lie: "Oh, no, I've been up for hours."

In the interests of sisterhood, I chose option three.

"So why," Rose persisted, "are you sounding so groggy?"

"Maybe I'm getting a cold," I said. "Rose, I'm up."

"Because if I *did* wake you up, you could tell me. I can deal with that. I'd rather have you say it right out than secretly thinking I'm selfish and irresponsible."

"That's not what I'm thinking," I fibbed. "I'm thinking that if my sister is calling at seven A.M., it must be important."

"In other words," Rose said triumphantly, "I did. I did wake you up. And you hate me for it."

As I think I've already mentioned, ours has never been an easy relationship.

It took about ten minutes to get beyond this opening gambit to the purpose of Rosalie's early-morning call, which was to let me know that she and Hubert would be coming down on Wednesday. They would need to stay, she reminded me, two or maybe three weeks, till the work on Carolyn's yard was well under way. "Unless—and you can be honest with me, Brenda—" she tensely said, "you'd rather that Hubert and I went somewhere else."

"You're more than welcome," I assured her.

"Is that 'you' as in me or 'you' as in Hubert and me?"

"You're both welcome here," I said. This was not the truth.

"I know you don't really like dogs, Bren, but I couldn't come without Hubert."

"I wouldn't want you to."

"I mean, a Great Dane is a sensitive breed, and Hubert happens to be especially sensitive. And intelligent. And intuitive. And dignified and proud. And deeply devoted."

"I don't know Hubert that well," I said, trying to stanch the flow, "but I'm looking forward to getting to know him better. And now, if you'll excuse me"—I employed my old trick for getting off the phone—"my doorbell is ringing."

"Who would be ringing your bell," asked Rose, "so early in the morning? Don't they care about waking people up?"

"Wednesday, Rose," I said, and hung up the phone.

When I went outside to bring in the Sunday papers, I saw something on the windshield of Wally's car. Stuck under the wipers, a raggedy note announced in big block letters, ON HALLOWEEN THE CLOWN TURNS INTO A GHOST.

I had no problem deconstructing this terrifying message. It obviously was naming the date on which Mr. Joseph Monti intended to do in my baby boy.

The sidewalk lurched under my feet. The sky started falling. A full-scale dizzy spell was about to begin. No, I said to myself, I won't let this happen. I won't let them hurt him. I won't be helpless. I won't, I won't, I won't let that bastard win.

The dizziness passed.

I reminded myself, as I tore up the note and tossed it into the trash can, that Halloween was more than a month from today. Which meant that Wally was safe for a while, that I didn't need to feel pressed to swing into action and rescue him right away. There was time, and I had to have time, to prepare another foolproof plan to kill Mr. Monti.

How much time did I have to win back Jake?

I was brooding over this question during a meager breakfast of coffee and dry toast when I got a telephone call from Vivian Feuerbach.

"I wanted to check on your health, my dear," she said to me in her Katharine Hepburn voice. "You sounded so dreadful on Friday when you canceled."

What in God's name was she talking about? For a moment my mind was blank. And then I remembered. "Oh, right. But I'm fine today."

"And I also wanted to tell you that I'm going out to the shack for a couple of weeks"—this shack was her two-hundred-acre estate in Middleburg—"so whatever you wished to see me about will have to wait until I have returned."

My mind, no longer a blank, flashed, *That's too late*.

I guess I must have moaned, because imperious Vivian quickly, graciously added, "Unless—well, if it's important, I could make the time to see you this afternoon."

I told her it was important. I told her I'd get back to her immediately. I called up Louis and asked could he meet us today. "We'll take her to Anacostia, and then we'll take her to Harmony House, and then you'll make your pitch about converting Jeff's properties into group

homes for the homeless, and then she'll agree it's a
great idea, and then she'll agree to buy them, and then
Jeff will be all right, and then maybe Jake ... maybe
Jake ... maybe Jake ..."

"Brenda! Brenda! Slow down! You need me to meet
you and Ms. Feuerbach, I'll do it." Louis's voice was
soothing and concerned. "But—no offense intended—
you are *strange*, I mean sincerely strange, today."

I took a deep breath and told Louis that I was suffering from a case of sensory overload—"I need to unjam
a few circuits and I'll be okay." I decided I wouldn't
say that I needed this real estate coup not merely to bail
out Jeff but to score some urgently needed points with
my husband, whom—I also didn't say—I seemed to
have significantly alienated.

"I don't want your praise or apologies," I imagined
cooing to Jake, when—having been told (dramatically)
about Jeff's ruinous real estate deal and (modestly)
about my brilliant solution—he looked at me with new
respect in his eyes. "I don't want your praise or
apologies—just your love."

In the early afternoon Vivian Feuerbach and I—and
Jeff, who of course we needed to come with us—were
crammed into Louis's Honda on our not-so-merry way
to Anacostia. To one of the meaner sections of
Anacostia. To, in fact, one of the meaner streets of one
of the meaner sections of Anacostia.

The day was gray but mild, and a silent cluster of
teenage boys, in the hanging-out mode, looked us over
when we stopped at a light. As I, in turn, looked them
over—looked at their unsmiling faces and what-you-
doing-here eyes—my hand, without my permission,

reached out to push down the locks and roll up all the windows. Red light, red light, turn green, I nervously said to myself, this chant of impatience dredged from the mists of my childhood. But when the light turned green, our way was blocked by a wiry lad in high hair and a headband, who darted into the street and, rhythmically pecking his head and jabbing out his elbows, started dancing to an improvised rap song.

> So they come across the river
> From the other side.
> Now they got no place to run—uh uh!—
> And no place to hide.
> Gonna make tomorrow's headlines—
> This is where they died.
> Get 'em. Go get 'em. Go get 'em. Go get . . .

When some of High Hair's pals danced into the street and joined him in the "get 'em, go get 'ems," Louis backed up, swung around them, and pulled away. None of us expressed any wish to stay for the rest of the boyz-n-the-hood performance. Especially me.

I mean, I was scared. I also was ashamed of being scared. I also was much more scared than I was ashamed. I was scared to be in this blighted place with its overflowing trash cans and dismembered cars, not to mention its alienated inhabitants. Would I be feeling more welcome if I were wearing my sixties WE SHALL OVERCOME T-shirt? I doubted it.

I was looking across a gulf that was missing a bridge, that I wished could be bridged, that required a lot of encouragement to be bridged. Which is why, when we parked in front of a battered brick building—one of

Jeff's sorry set of eight—with its door swinging off its hinges and its first-floor windows methodically smashed in, the sign saying KOVNER PROPERTIES— EFFICIENCIES FOR RENT displayed a desperate addendum: FIRST MONTH FREE.

In spite of which, as Jeff had already informed me, the occupancy rate was no more than 30 percent.

I had warned Vivian in advance that I was taking her on "a magical mystery tour" of a part of the city that she had never seen. I also had warned her in advance that I might, for the very first time in our relationship, be asking her to make what I termed "a substantial contribution to a good cause." (I chose to avoid specifics until later.) I also had warned her in advance to wear her casual clothes, which for Vivian meant low heels with her Chanel. Leaning on Louis's arm, with Jeff leading the way and me warily covering the rear, Vivian made a regal entrance into the front hall—and bumped into Jeff, who was frozen in his tracks. He was staring—we all were staring—at a man in a Rolex watch and designer running suit, who seemed to be holding a gun to another man's head.

Forget about "seemed." This man was positively holding a gun to another man's head.

"We're doing some business. Please move on," said the man who was holding the gun, though he phrased his request in far more colorful terms.

Jeff began backing out. "Yeah, right. We don't want to interrupt." Vivian, however, stood her ground. "Are you going to whack him?" she asked. "Is this a drug deal that's gone sour? Or one of your pushers skimming off the top? It's important to show some muscle, but everyone knows you can't collect money from a dead man."

Billy (the name was embroidered on the pocket of his running suit) tilted his head and squinted his eyes at Vivian. "You been seeing too many TV shows, Mama."

"I happen to be of the *reading* generation," said Vivian proudly, "and quite a connoisseur of detective fiction."

"Mama, get your ass out of here or you gonna be quite a *corpse* of detective fiction." Billy was clearly not charmed by Vivian's style. He was even more annoyed when, moving up close and shaking a finger in his face, she told him, "No one, not even my son, calls me 'Mama.' And furthermore I consider threats a repugnant and unacceptable form of discourse."

While Billy, cursing vividly, was pushing Vivian's chastising finger away, his erstwhile victim chose to exploit the distraction. Moving with serpentine grace, Elton Jr. (his name was embroidered on his running suit too) swiveled around and wrestled the gun from Billy. After which he grabbed Vivian, held her up in front of him like a shield, and announced, "This is a hostage situation."

Somebody down the hall, his interest aroused by the commotion, poked out his head, said, "Oh, shit!" and quickly withdrew.

Somebody from the second floor, a baby on her hip, looked down from the top of the stairs, said, "Oh, shit!" and withdrew.

While Jeff (aloud) and I (silently) concurred in this estimate of the situation, Louis asked Elton Jr., "What are your terms?" But Vivian—eyes ablaze and all of her ninety-six pounds aquiver with indignation—said, "No terms, Louis. Never. I am, have been, and will continue to be, opposed to any negotiations with hostage-takers."

"You with the big fat purse," said Elton Jr., looking at me and ignoring all talk of terms and negotiations. "Open it up and put it here by my foot."

I did what he said.

"Your jewelry. All of it. Off and into the purse."

I did what he said.

"Now you two dudes. I want wallets and watches and, hey, that's a fine-looking belt you wearing there, white boy. Lizard?"

"Lizard," said Jeff.

"In the purse."

Jeff and Louis did what he said. Vivian, after protesting, did so too. "And now it's your turn," Elton Jr. told Billy.

"Hell, kill the hostage," Billy replied. "Ain't gonna bother me."

"Ain't gonna be the hostage who gets it," Elton Jr. told Billy.

Billy, like the rest of us, anted up.

Pointing his gun at the four of us now, Elton Jr. released his grip on Vivian and used his free hand to scoop up the loot at his feet. "Catch you all later," he said as he backed down the hall and out the front door. "Catch you all later," said Billy, who followed soon after. Before disappearing, however, he turned to Vivian and said, "Hey, Mama, he was skimming off the top."

We tried to phone the police from one of the first-floor Kovner apartments, but there were no apartments, exactly, on the first floor. There were two what once were called crash pads but what I guess you'd now have to call crack pads, and they lacked not only telephones but furniture, intact windows, and other niceties. What they didn't lack was people, a Dante's Inferno collection of people, semireclining on the filthy floors—so drugged, so wrecked, so out of it that they barely could lift up their heads when we four E.T.'s pushed open their unlocked doors. As for the other units, four were vacant and triple-bolted, and two belonged to tenants who demanded a warrant before they would let us in, and one appeared to belong to a foreign student who informed us—through the keyhole—that he was too busy studying for an engineering exam to be disturbed.

"We'll go to *my* house," Vivian said, showing her leadership qualities. "We'll call the police from there and then we'll have tea. Unless"—she turned to Jeff—"your other buildings are more . . . ah . . . together than this one is."

· We went to Vivian's house.

It was clear that the trip to Harmony House, though on *our* side of the Anacostia River, had been scrubbed for the day, and—in Vivian's case—forever. Pouring tea in her paneled and chintzed and English-antiqued library, she characterized our adventure in Anacostia as "an enlightening experience which shall, I believe, suffice me for a lifetime." (Kind of the way I felt about sex with Philip.) When we pointed out that Jeff's buildings could be turned into eight more Harmony Houses if someone like her would make—I repeated the phrase I had used with her earlier—a "substantial contribution to a good cause," Vivian briskly noted that in surrendering her jewelry to Elton Jr. she already had made a substantial contribution.

"We all feel real bad about that," Louis said.

"It's my fault," moaned a deeply demoralized Jeff.

"Vivian," I began, winding up for one of my no-holds-barred abject apologies, "I can't begin to tell you how unspeakably, inconsolably sorry I am, how anguished, appalled, incredibly sick at heart. Anguished that you were robbed. Appalled that you were put in physical danger. Incredibly sick at heart that you were exposed to—"

Vivian stopped my words with an impatient wave of her hand. "You don't have to apologize, my dear. And I"—she cocked her head to one side and gave me a shrewd smile—"don't have to buy any buildings in Anacostia. Yes?"

I swallowed a miniature blueberry tart and wiped the crumbs from my lips. "Of course yes," I said with false heartiness. "Of course yes."

Vivian turned to Louis and Jeff. "My passion, you know, is music. It has always been one of my chief philanthropies. If you get your new homeless houses set up, I'd be happy to give each one a nice CD player."

Driving away from Vivian's house, Louis tried to cheer up the kvetching Kovners, who had banked a whole hell of a lot on a positive outcome. When he failed to dispel our gloom he began to beat out a rhythm on the steering wheel, pecking his head and chanting, "Get 'em. Go get 'em. Go get 'em. Go get 'em," and then swinging into a vigorous "So we come across the river from the other side . . ." He gave Jeff a nudge.

"Now we got no place to run," said Jeff, "and no place to hide. Mom?"

"Gonna make tomorrow's paper. This is where—uh-huh!—we died."

And all of us, laughing hysterically, screamed out, "Get 'em, go get 'em," all the way home.

The swordfish was marinating and the salsa was freshly made when Jake returned around eight on Sunday night. I had set the dining-room table with candles and flowers. I had also—in the interest of privacy—managed to ease glum Wally into going out for a meal and a movie with Jeff. Dressed in a dark-green hostess gown with a gilt-edged plunging neckline, I looked like what I was: a woman whose game plan for the evening was seduction.

My mood was positive.

Jake strode into the house as if he'd only been gone for ten minutes. "I assume you got my note," he said, dropping his overnight bag onto a chair. Then Mr. Never Explain-Never Apologize-Never Justify took off his jacket and grabbed himself a beer, waiting for me to do what he was confident I would do—zap him with bitter where-were-you's and how-could-you's. I had a surprise for him.

"Go sit down with your beer," I said. "I just need a moment to toss the angel-hair pasta. Oh, and sweetie"—I knew for sure he wasn't expecting any "sweetie" from me—"would you please take these matches and light the candles."

Before I tossed the pasta, I put on the music of Nat "King" Cole, whose songs could soften the heart of a Saddam Hussein. "Oh, how the ghost of you clings," I sang along as I popped the cheese bread into the oven. "These foolish things"—I took off my apron, smoothed my hair, and got ready for action—"remind me of you."

Having a cozy and vivacious conversation that omitted, among many other burning subjects, all of what Jake had been doing since Saturday morning, much of what I had been doing since Saturday morning, and can this marriage be saved?, was something of a challenge. I rose to it. I told Jake, in a moving but not-at-all-maudlin manner, that Wally and Josephine seemed to be going through a difficult time, obliquely making it clear that I in no way was advising—or interfering with—them. (The reason for this, of course, was that they wouldn't let me advise—or interfere with—them, but why trouble Jake with all the boring details?) Next I told Jake, in a really quite charming and entertaining manner, about my sister's early-morning phone call, making many wry observations on sister-sister and sister-dog relationships. Halfway into the swordfish, I actually got him to laugh. And then I moved on to how wonderful he was.

"You're being so nice about Rose coming down to stay with us," I said warmly. "A lot of brothers-in-law would not be that tolerant." In the background, Nat "King" Cole complemented my words with, "Unforgettable, that's what you are. Unforgettable, though near or far . . ." Jake kicked off his shoes. The man was relaxing.

"Rose isn't all that bad," he said. "It's actually kind of exciting to see who she is going to be this week."

"You mean like her Melanie Giffith wild-thing phase?"

"I was thinking more of her Mother Teresa phase."

This led to some funny recollections of Rose in her assorted incarnations, which led—by associative leaps—to Great Danes, to great Danish, to a new production of *Hamlet*, to "O death, where is thy sting?" (which I insisted, incorrectly, came from *Hamlet*), to a recent D.C. police department sting operation, to the hernia operation Jake had performed on two-month-old Claire on Friday morning.

"Tell me all about it," I urged, as I served the apple crisp with the frozen yogurt. "The shore was kissed, by sea and mist, tenderly," crooned the legendary Nat "King" Cole. Jake, while I listened closely, told all about it.

"I like how you look in that thing you've got on," Jake interrupted his story to observe. "Especially the part that isn't on." He traced a path from the base of my throat to halfway down to my wrist, which was where the plunging neckline finally stopped plunging.

". . . lipstick's traces . . . romantic places." The tapes were on their second time around. Leading Jake to an open space in our long front hall, I put my arms around him and said, "Shall we dance?"

I once wrote a newspaper column which, opposing conventional wisdom, was called It's Sometimes Better to Shut Up. It starts by noting that though married couples are deluged with advice to say what's in their hearts and on their minds—to ventilate, to communicate, to share—this may not always be a great idea. It goes on to observe:

> A full and frank disclosure of every stupid (or worse) thing we've done could lead to alienation instead of to intimacy. An utterly truthful description of exactly how we feel about each other's mother could leave us feeling bruised instead of informed. And must we really tell our mate that last night's performance in bed

was down three points from Friday's 8.9? And couldn't we—instead of rehashing every painful detail of our last argument—sometimes use our mouths just to kiss and make up?

Though I don't necessarily follow my own advice, I was, in this instance, enthusiastically doing so. And though Jake hadn't read my column, he was enthusiastically doing so too. At least that's what I thought as, without any full and frank disclosures, we danced our way upstairs and into bed. It wasn't until ... after ... that Jake was moved to move into the confessional mode.

"Nothing major happened," he said, "but I have to be honest with you." (Who told him he had to?) "I spent ... I spent last night with Sunny Voight."

"Ain't misbehavin', I'm savin' my love for you," sang Nat "King" Cole, the words floating into our bedroom as honest Jake delivered himself of that wonderful news.

I didn't—not for a moment—believe either of them.

9

•

THE MYTH OF THE G-SPOT

*A*lthough, as I've already mentioned, I do not believe in God, I nonetheless believed that God was punishing me. I believed that God was punishing me for sleeping with another woman's husband by letting another woman sleep with mine. Jake had denied this, of course, but I knew he was lying—just as I, in his place, would have lied. I furthermore knew that Sunny and Jake had gone to bed together for just one reason: Because, on Wednesday morning, March 18, I had gone to bed with Joseph Monti.

Actually the bed we shared on the morning of March 18 was the unfolded seat of his chauffeured stretch limousine, the very limousine in which he and I, just eight days before, had already dallied. I had not been aware at the time that with a simple flick of a switch the back of the limo converted into a bed, although I had observed that—thanks to the smoked-glass windows and the stereo system—we could do and say whatever we wished, while driving all over town, in perfect privacy.

That morning, a busy surgery day, Jake had left for

Children's at 6 A.M. At 6:45 I was down on Connecticut Avenue. At 6:48 the limo glided slowly to a stop and picked me up in front of the Cleveland Park Library. I had dressed for my first adultery in leather cowboy boots, a long brown woolen skirt, and hacking jacket, a Waspy Western Ralph Lauren look that contrasted, I felt, quite charmingly with my down-and-dirty peach bustier and peach panties.

Which, as soon as I closed the car door, Joseph Monti reached under my skirt and removed.

After which his head vanished under my skirt.

Shortly after which I found myself trilling *eee-eee eee-eee-eee eee-eeeeeeeee,* and revising a view I had once espoused in a column I had entitled SEX WITHOUT LOVE—NOT REALLY ALL THAT TERRIFIC.

"You thought we didn't do that," Mr. Monti said accusingly, after I had finally quieted down.

"Do what? You mean, engage in or—"

"I know what I mean. You know what I mean. You don't have to say the words. You thought we didn't do that fancy stuff, right?"

"Who's we?" I asked, as I tried to return to reality, where, I now noticed, the two of us lay naked (except for my leather cowboy boots) on the car-seat bed.

"Italians. Blue-collar backgrounds. Lowbrow types. You figure that we're all a bunch of animals."

"Certainly not," I said, the word "animals" getting me excited all over again.

"Yeah, you do," Joseph Monti persisted. "You think we only care for our own satisfaction."

"How could I think that, Joseph?" I said, "when you just finished giving me the most glorious org—"

"I would like you, Brenda, please, to watch your language."

"I was only trying to say," I started to say and then forgot what I was saying. Joseph Monti was stroking me, he was melting or was it igniting me, he was even—though with a disapproving frown at such female forwardness—wearing the Ramses condom he had received from me. And then, having made some exquisite incursions into (could this be?) hitherto unexplored territory, he once more had me crescendoing *eee-eee eee-eee-eee eee-eeeeeeee,* and once more retracting a view that I had expressed in an earlier column, this one with the title THE MYTH OF THE G-SPOT.

"You think that because we didn't go to some classy Ivy League college, we don't know about those parts of a woman's body." Joseph Monti, his weight on his elbows, his eyes boring into mine, waited for me to catch my breath and reply.

"Joseph," I told him, "believe me when I say even *I* didn't know. I mean, what you just did, it was a new and whole different kind of orgas—"

"Silence!" Joseph Monti roared. "I don't want to hear any words that begin with 'Or.' I don't want to hear them—even from women like you."

I gasped. The muscles in my throat contracted. My stomach muscles, such as they were, contracted. I pushed Joseph Monti off me and sat up. We were driving, I noticed, along Rockville Pike in Maryland, heading toward Toys R Us and Bloomingdale's. I was almost angry enough to leap out of the limo, minus my clothes, and hitch a ride.

"Women like me?" I screamed. "Women like me? What's this—the old Madonna-whore routine?"

"You probably think," Joseph Monti was back to being defensive again, "I'm not educated enough to get
the reference." He pressed me back down and rolled
over on me, turning my face to face his with one of his
powerful hands held under my chin. As my anger
turned to hurt and the tears started welling up in my
eyes, I could feel him—well, not all of him—suddenly
softening. "That's not what I meant," he said gruffly.
"I'm not calling you a whore. That's not what I meant."

He then, for the first time since I'd entered the limo,
embarked on a normal human conversation. We discussed the kids, including Josephine's problems. He described his dream with the message from his dead
mother. And he swore that he'd never reveal—"or may
my daughters only give birth to female children"—what
we had just done, and still appeared to be doing.

For as we continued speaking he rolled around so
that I was on top—"I bet you thought," he said, "that
we were too macho for this position." "Oh, why don't
you just shut up," I sweetly replied—and slowly, very
slowly he started us rocking.

"You still haven't had an—ooops!" I censored the
word that began with "Or."

Joseph Monti chose to ignore my remark. Still gently
rocking he said, "What I told you before? You misun-
derstood. You shouldn't think I think that you're a
whore."

"Yeah, well," I said, "but when we talk about our
families and all, I start to feel cheap."

"I can respect that."

"And when I think about your wife—"

"She's a wonderful woman."

"—a wonderful, wonderful woman—I feel guilty."

"I can respect that."

"And then when I think that someday you and I could be sharing a grandchild . . ."

Joseph Monti quit rocking. He was silent for quite a long while. And then he said, "That's revolting. Wait, I mean—"

"You mean," I said, "that you wouldn't want your grandchild's grandma and grandpa commiting adultery."

"With each other," Joseph Monti corrected me. "With each other's the part that wouldn't be right."

His line of thinking fit perfectly into my one-time adultery plan. Great as this was, I didn't want to repeat it. Joseph Monti's aptitude was way ahead of his attitude, sexually speaking. I mean, sometimes a woman simply has to say "Or—."

"Then this morning," I whispered huskily, glad that the matter was being resolved so easily, "is going to have to be our final encounter."

"Yeah, but not yet," he whispered back. "I'm going to make you—you know what—with me. Together. Both together this last time."

"I can't. I couldn't possibly. Not again," I protested. "Go ahead, Joseph. It's your turn to . . . enjoy."

As Joseph resumed his rocking, our driver slammed on his horn and his brakes. The limo jerked to a sudden screeching stop. With a sickening thud that had us clutching each other tighter than ever, another car plowed into us from behind. Metal groaned and glass shattered as the laws of thermodynamics (or whatever) rolled us forward—then back to our prior position.

Our driver shut off the engine and leaped from the limo.

Astonishingly, Joseph Monti kept on rocking.

I peeked out the one-way smoked-glass window and saw that we were on upper Wisconsin Avenue, just at the Maryland-Washington district line. Out on the street our driver and the driver of a vintage Fleetwood Cadillac were hurling recriminations at each other as they inspected the limo's smashed taillights, the Caddy's fractured headlights, and the rest of the not-as-bad-as-it-sounded damage. Our cars, which were messing up traffic, were unable to pull over because, improbably, their bumpers had locked, the Cadillac's front bumper entangled with the back bumper of our limousine. Beneath me, Joseph Monti continued rocking. I swear he was humming "Volare" in my ear.

After a while, the recriminations ceased. Insurance information was exchanged. And a small crowd had assembled, eager to offer helpful advice on how to disentangle the locked bumpers.

Joseph Monti kept on gently rocking. For sure he was humming "Volare" in my ear.

A few of the helpful citizens tried to unlock the bumpers by leaning on them and rocking them up and down. Both bumpers were tightly engaged, as were Joseph and I. And despite my firm "I can't. I couldn't possibly. Not again," I was beginning to feel that maybe I could.

Outside and inside, up and down, the rocking continued in perfect synchronicity. Joseph kept humming "Volare" in my ear. Bumpers and bodies rocked up and down, and up and down, and up, until, with some mighty manly roars and one last *eee-eee eee-eee-eee-eee-eeeeeeeee*, both outside and inside achieved release and I was persuaded to reconsider a view expressed in a column that I had called SIMULTANEOUS—IT'S NOT THAT BIG A DEAL.

When, a bit later, the limo stopped a couple of blocks from my house, I bade Joseph Monti a truly grateful goodbye. "I never had a lover before," I told him, in all honesty. "And I'll never have one again." (Okay, so I lied.) "I want to thank you for a . . . quite special morning."

"I'm glad you found it fulfilling," Joseph Monti, with deep solemnity, replied. "You shouldn't go around thinking of us as animals."

"And you, sir," I told him, half-jokingly, as I covered my sex-drenched body with my clothes, "shouldn't go around thinking of us as whores. Even"—and now *I* was speaking with deep solemnity—"even though I feel guilty about your wife."

"I can respect that," Mr. Monti replied. "My wife is a wonderful—"

"Woman. Yes, I know. And I guess I really deserve some kind of punishment for doing this to her."

"Don't worry," Joseph Augustus Monti reassuringly said to me, as he handed me my crumpled underpants. "You don't have to worry about it—you'll be punished."

And now, at the end of this very demanding weekend in late September, Joseph Monti's prediction had come true. My husband had returned to the woman for whom he had once almost left me. I had been punished.

"So do you swear on your children's heads that you didn't make love with Sunny?" I inquired. It was, I'm the first to admit, a desperate question.

"I never swear on my children's heads. Never have. And never will," was my husband's maddening reply.

"Look, Jake, I didn't ask you—just remember I didn't ask—where you were last night. You volunteered the goddam information. But now that you have started it, I want to know the truth. Did you go to bed with her?"

Jake shook his head, though I wasn't prepared to take that as a denial. "That's not what I went for."

"Which was what?"

"Comfort. Sunny's a very comforting person."

"And what does she wear when she's comforting you? Where does she conduct her comforting sessions? And how come she's so available—didn't she get married a couple of years ago?"

"They just broke up."

"Nice. So she's back in the business of looking for a husband. Anyone's husband."

I got out of bed and covered myself with one of my vast collection of T-shirt nightshirts, this one emblazoned with a SO MUCH TO READ, SO LITTLE TIME across the chest.

"That remark," Jake said to me as he pulled on his pajamas, "is unworthy of you. Sunny didn't go looking for me. I went looking for *her*. And she tried to help me put this whole thing in perspective."

"What whole thing would that be?" I asked, as we stood on opposite sides of the bed and glared at each other. "You and me? You and Sunny? Or is it the three of us—together again?" A sudden wave of dizziness made my words come out shakier than I'd intended. I steadied myself by grabbing hold of the bedpost. "What whole thing?" I stubbornly persisted.

"You wear me out, Brenda. You wear me out." Jake sounded truly sad, which scared me more than anything else he had said. "Tonight, with the dinner, the love-making, you were a genuine pleasure. But I've got to tell you, most of the time you are work."

I gripped the bedpost tighter. "What exactly," I asked, "is that supposed to mean?"

"That this need of yours to be in control of everybody's life is driving me nuts. That you're out of control with trying to be in control."

"A nice turn of phrase," I murmured, as the room spun around and around and I started to sink. "Though it sounds a lot more like Sunny's than like yours."

"Brenda! What's wrong?" Jake shouted, as I crumpled to the floor. "Are you having those dizzy spells again?"

"You see, I can't control everything—yet," I said to him, smiling weakly. Then, for all kinds of reasons, I started to cry.

Jake joined me on the floor and tenderly leaned my reeling head upon his shoulder. After a while the room settled back into place. "Okay," Jake said in a gentle voice, "I'm willing to grant that you're only trying to help."

"Is that what Sunny told you?"

"Shhh," Jake said. "You're only trying to help, but a lot of the stuff that you're doing is—iatrogenic."

"What?"

"Iatrogenic. That's when the treatment causes—instead of cures—the disease. And that, let's face it, Bren, is what's happening here. You've screwed up the Monti marriage and you've screwed up my malpractice suits, and I shudder to think what else you've been screwing with."

Oh, baby, I thought, if you knew—would you ever shudder!

Jake went on. "It's like, these past few years, you almost can't stop yourself. There's nothing that you don't think you can fix. At least"—he sighed—"I've learned when I shouldn't operate, when to call in another surgeon, say no to a case." He kissed the top of my head and stood up. "Brenda," he said, "say no. Quit being a fixer."

"Or else you'll divorce me and marry Sunny Voight?"

Jake walked across the room and dug a rolled-up parcel out of his overnight bag. Then he came back and pulled me up on my feet. "I went to one of those T-shirt stores"—he handed me the parcel—"and had this made especially for you." He watched me closely as I unfolded the shirt and read its message: FOR PEACE OF MIND, it said, I HEREBY RESIGN AS GENERAL MANAGER OF THE UNIVERSE.

"You've got to do it, Brenda," he said. I clearly heard the unspoken "or else" in his voice.

"Maybe you're right," I insincerely replied.

Maybe he's right, I even thought, a fleeting thought that I rejected immediately. For what, I would like to know, would become of the universe if I decided to hand in my resignation?

Even without the assistance of my managerial skills, something remarkable happened the very next day.

I was on a plane to Miami to give a lecture at a women's mental-health seminar. Sitting directly behind me two men—on their way, I learned, to a coroners' convention—were discussing interesting autopsies they had performed. I was not especially interested in even the most interesting of autopsies, but something one of them said to the other suddenly had me sitting straight up in my seat.

"And we'd never of known what killed him. We didn't have a clue. Ain't nothin' showed up on any of the tests."

"So if that empty container hadn't been found—"

"That's right. And even so, the prescription was just for this innocent-seeming drug—these pills he took once a day to prevent the gout."

"Then what made you think he used them to commit suicide?"

"The label was dated three days before his death. The quantity of pills dispensed was sixty. And like I said before, the container was empty."

"So you figure he took all sixty of them at once."

"You got it. He probably mashed those mothers up—they're teeny, smaller than peppercorns—mashed them up and took them all at once. And he wouldn't even of tasted them if he drank them in something sweet, like a strawberry Daiquiri."

Keep talking, I telepathed to the men behind me. Give more details. And please, please name your poison.

"He almost got away with it," my coroner continued. "This stuff gets absorbed in the system very fast. All we knew was, two days before, he caught what everyone thought was the stomach flu. And then he wakes up dead, and no one—until we found that container—could figure out why."

"And the name of the medication?" his companion asked him aloud and I asked him silently.

"It's called" (he not only said it; he spelled it!) "_____."

And so I learned the name of a painless, easy-to-obtain, undetectable poison. You'll forgive me if—out of prudence—I don't pass it on. You'll also forgive me if—though I do not believe in God or in signs from God—I nonetheless believed that this was a sign directly from God to go ahead and murder Mr. Monti.

My Tuesday-morning lecture, on Emotional Support Systems, focused on the importance of finding time in our busy lives to take care of each other. In a rousing conclusion I told the attentive women in my audience, "Make friends of your sisters and sisters of your friends." I then flew home to Washington, where I worked on feeling friendlier about the impending arrival of Rose and her dog.

Rose showed up on Wednesday in a rented minivan, in which she'd installed—in case Hubert wanted to nap—a full-size mattress covered in pink crushed velvet. Driving, she explained, was less of a strain on Hubert's nerves than going by plane. Pink, she explained, was Hubert's favorite color. And the box she was dragging into my house was filled, she explained, with Hubert's special supplies, including—and I'm going to quote her directly—his "yummy yum-yums" and his "favorite blankie."

It remains for me one of life's mysteries that a number of folks who are more or less basically sane can speak to and of their dogs in unabashed baby talk,

oohing and cooing and lisping and using words like
"yum-yums" and "blankies" without the slightest suggestion of self-consciousness. I also find it mysterious
that some of these folks—my sister, for example—
would never in a million years do for their children
what they do for their dogs. Believe me, my sister
would not be renting minivans with velvet-covered mat-
tresses to ease the strain on the nerves of her only child.
But the sky was the limit for Hubert, a.k.a. "snookums,"
a.k.a. "my lovey pie."

Anyway, there was Rosalie—who had never called
her daughter snookums or lovey pie, who indeed had
never gone in for what she once termed "that mommy
shit" of snuggles and hugs—crawling around on my
living-room rug and drowning Hubert in praise for being the "bestest doggie traveler ever." Several minutes
passed before she stopped with the kisses and coos and
managed to address a "Hi, Brenda," to me.

Hubert, thrilled to be free of the car, exuberantly ex-
plored his Washington lodgings, loping from room to
room and then up the stairs, returning—as I boiled Rose
some tea—with my Donna Karan panty hose in his
teeth. The panty hose for which I'd paid eighteen dollars. The panty hose I had worn only once—last night.
The panty hose which, when I lunged for them, were
shredded into bits in a game of tug-of-war with the
bestest doggie traveler, and panty-hose wrecker, ever.

Afterward, to show me that he was not a gloating
victor, Hubert nosed me up against the wall, rearing up
on his back legs and putting his front legs on my shoulders and moistly licking my face from forehead to chin.
"He seemed a whole lot calmer at your apartment," I

grumped to Rosalie as I tried to escape this damply dogged embrace.

"He's telling you that he likes it here, that he's feeling right at home," said my sister serenely. "You should be flattered."

Flattered was not exactly what I was.

But, as I tell my readers, once you've agreed to do whatever it is you're doing, get credit for it by (as I called my column on the subject) DOING IT GRACIOUSLY.

My point is that once you've agreed to dine with your husband's boring former college roommate, be perky and charming—give it your absolute all. And once you've agreed to go shop for a dress with your cheap and hard-to-please cousin, be patient and sweet-natured—give it your absolute all. And once you've agreed to allow your sister's panty-hose-chomping Great Dane to move his two-hundred-plus pounds into your house, be . . .

I tried. I did. I gave it my absolute all. Which, I'm sorry to say, was nowhere near good enough for Rosalie, who kept telling me, as she bustled about her business, "If you'd spend more time with Hubert, Bren, he'd be a happier dog, and you, I can promise, would be a better person."

Rosalie was a dynamo: Preparing her yard plans for Carolyn. Taking bids from carpenters. Comparing the relative merits of flagstone and slate. Discussing the outdoor lighting and the underground watering system. Checking out shrubs and plants at various nurseries. "How did you learn to do all this stuff?" I once inquired uneasily. "You don't think I know what I'm doing?" she replied. "You figure out how we all should live, but I can't figure out a lousy backyard?" I dropped the subject.

Most of the time Hubert accompanied Rosalie on her rounds, but on a few occasions she left him behind, assuring me that I would find him "an angel—no bother at all" and adding, "It wouldn't kill you if you got down on the floor and played with him."

I had no wish to get down on the floor and play with him.

Besides, I had serious business to attend to.

During the first week of Rosalie's stay, I kept three different appointments with three different doctors, acquiring three prescriptions—each for twenty of the painless poison pills. All the prescriptions were written for a Mrs. Yvonne Kaiser, of Stamford, Connecticut, a dear but forgetful woman who was visiting her son and had left her gout-prevention pills at home. A friend of her son's, whose name she couldn't remember, had recommended this doctor, she told each one. That modest fib, and payment in cash (instead of by a revealing personal check), evoked not the slightest tremor of suspicion.

Now all I had to do was go to three different pharmacies and fill my prescriptions, and my foolproof murder weapon would be in my hands. How it would get from my hands into Mr. Joseph Monti's belly was my next challenge.

Though Jake and I had declared a tacit truce for the duration of Rosalie's visit, my mood (though I concealed it well) was not merry. Jeff was calling me every day with the latest in his impending financial disaster, explaining that by October 19, if he didn't come up with three hundred thou or a miracle, he would be handing over his Jaguar, his Rockville houses, and his Watergate condo to Monti Enterprises. After which he might find himself in need of temporarily moving back home.

"You still don't want me to mention this business to Dad?" Jeff, not—I confess—for the first time, asked me.

"Not with those lawsuits on his mind," I replied. "Obviously, if you move back home, we'll have to tell him why. But maybe that won't be necessary. Maybe"—I had one more avenue to explore—"there'll be a miracle."

I didn't have any miracles to offer my suffering Wally, who refused to turn to me in his hour of need, although he indeed was in need, as the slump of his shoulders, the pain in his Mel Gibson eyes, attested. As that recently overheard quarrel on the porch and subsequent snippets of phone conversation informed me, Wally and Jo were in a relationship crisis. And while I yearned to tell Wally that this speedy emergence of Josephine's fierce sense of self might eventually augur well for their relationship, he wasn't sitting still for any augurs. He ached, so I ached; he was cut, so I bled, as a good Jewish mother should. But my once-so-accessible son would not let me help him.

With his love life, that is. He did, however, allow me to give him a hand when he paid a home visit to one of his more intransigent socialwork cases. It seemed he'd been trying for quite a while to persuade his client Dwayne to move out of his mother's apartment and to sign himself into a psychiatric hospital. Dwayne, who was manic-depressive, not to mention somewhat paranoid, urgently belonged—Wally said—in a hospital. But so far he had refused, and his mother, no mental-health triumph herself, was going to pieces watching him going to pieces.

"She can't stop blaming herself—for his manic-depression, his paranoia, even his athlete's foot. And she can't," Wally said, "stop interrupting my sessions with Dwayne to explain to me yet again why it's all her fault."

I had a terrific idea: I'd go with Wally and kind of sit there with Dwayne's mother while he did some undisturbed one-on-one with Dwayne.

"No, thanks, Mom," my son replied.

"Just this once," I pressed. "Maybe you and Dwayne will have a breakthrough."

Wally reconsidered. "Well, it might be worth a try. But please," he added, "don't give her advice. I've got my own way of working with her, and I think it's the right way to go. So make sympathetic noises, but no advice."

We drove over to Eleventh Street, to a not-quite-middle-class block of peeling three-story houses and brick apartment buildings. The building we entered stood tall between a pungent carry-out and a laundromat.

A skinny mid-twenties man with thinning dark hair and dark darting eyes opened the door a crack, then tried to shut it, vanishing into his bedroom when his mother, in too-tight pants and a fuzzy pink sweater, invited us into her overly knickknacked apartment. Five seconds later, the introductions made, Dwayne's mother was into nonstop mea-culpa-ing.

"So you're Wally's mother. So pretty. So calm. So relaxed. Yeah, relaxed—not like me. From the moment they handed me Dwayne I was tense as a tick, and they pick up your tensions, you know, even babies do. And when he was three and he ran in the street, I lost my temper—I'm so ashamed!—and I smacked him, and I promised to come to his second-grade play, but I couldn't because of this crisis at my office, and I'll never forget what he said when I bought him a blue ten-speed bike for Christmas. 'If you would have listened better,' he said, 'you would have remembered the color I wanted was black.' " She wiped away a tear from her careworn Shirley MacLaine-ish face. "You do wrong by your kids," she said, "and they never recover."

Wally joined Dwayne in the bedroom, while his mother, perched anxiously on the living-room couch, continued her psychological self-flagellation. "I should have read to him more and not let him watch all those violent programs on the TV, and when he was twelve I divorced his dad, which I wouldn't have done if I'd known it would drive him crazy, and—"

"I won't. I won't. I won't. I won't." The reedy refusal drifted through Dwayne's bedroom door. "I won't let my enemies lock me up in some mental hospital."

"And who," my shrewd Wally asked him, "are your enemies?"

"I don't have to tell you," Dwayne whined. "You know who you are."

"I know I care about you. I know I'd like to help," Wally said gently. "Can't we—?"

His soothing words were interrupted by a high-pitched yowl. Dwayne was terminating his therapy session. "Out out out out out," he yowled. "Out out out out out." "Can't we—?" Wally tried again. Apparently they couldn't. "Out out out," yowled Dwayne. "Out out out out."

"See you in a couple of days then." Wally, who knew it was time to withdraw, withdrew, pausing to tell Dwayne's mother, "Try to be patient. I think we're making a little progress."

"I hope and I pray that the hospital can undo the damage I've done," she mournfully told him. "But how can they ever make up for that time I went to New York for the weekend, and he wanted to come but I forced him to stay with the sitter? Or that time—"

I couldn't keep quiet another minute. "Don't dwell in the past," I said. "Get out more, take an art class, train for a marathon, study French cooking, read to the blind, go join a—"

Wally pulled me away and, as we drove home, he observed, with a tad of irritation, "You can't quit doing it, can you, Mom? You can't lay off. You've always got to fix it."

I gave him some irritation right back. "That's your father's complaint. But it didn't, I'd like to remind you, used to be yours. In fact"—I warmed to my subject—"I have a few things to say about Josephine that might help you reconceptualize your relationship, plus make you feel much better."

Wally reached for the radio and turned up the music, loud, a trick—I regret to say—he learned from Jake. "Thanks for coming this morning," he said, "but I don't want to talk about reconceptualizing. Jo and I have to figure that out for ourselves."

Jo, who had not been around for a while, dropped by our house after lunch and instantly fell in love with Rosalie's Hubert. Instead of cuddling with Wally, she was down on all fours carousing with the dog. "I'd forgotten what a delightful girl this Josephine is," said Rose, beaming with approval at the sight of the two of them rolling around on the floor. To Josephine she presented what I'm certain she believed was the ultimate compliment: "You're got a magnificent way with dogs. I can tell that you're a lifelong animal person."

"Not really," said Jo. "I never had pets because I had so many allergies. But now I don't have allergies anymore."

"But I thought you were scared of big dogs," said Wally, who clearly wished he, not Hubert, were getting Jo's hugs.

"I used to be scared of all kinds of things," said Jo, "that I'm not so scared of anymore."

She continued cavorting with Hubert. Wally looked hurt.

"Stay for the rest of the afternoon, and I'll make us an early supper," I urged Josephine, hustling on behalf of my forlorn son.

"Thanks, but I can't," Jo replied. "I'm meeting my mom to go to the top of the Washington Monument."

"The top of the Washington Monument?" Wally was amazed. "But how can you do that, Jo? Heights give you nosebleeds."

Josephine glanced at her watch. "Oh, hey," she said, "I've got to leave." She leaped to her feet and then addressed Wally's question. "Before my therapy, heights gave me nosebleeds," she rather coolly informed him. "But heights don't give me nosebleeds anymore."

Going to this therapist, I thought, as Jo made her farewells, was surely the next best thing to going to Lourdes. Even though, at the moment, her impressive improvement was breaking my baby boy's heart.

Philip's heart, on the other hand, appeared to be mending nicely, or so his most recent phone call seemed to indicate. "Just checking to see if you're feeling the need to use me again as a sex object," he had said, chuckling. This time he took my refusal with cheerful aplomb.

On Friday, October 9, I lunched with Edmund Standish Voight, Sunny's zillionaire uncle, who, with his pointy chin, pointy nose, and neatly trimmed mustache, could have been a suaver David Niven. We met at the Jockey Club, where the tables that day were mostly occupied by exes—retired ambassadors, defeated senators, once-numero unos of the CIA, and other former Washington stars, all of whom had now become consultants. A consultant, as I understand it, uses the contacts and knowledge obtained before he was exed to offer his clients access and information, much of which these clients—with a couple of telephone calls—could obtain for themselves. These clients, however, can bill *their* clients for the consulting fees, and these clients' clients can probably bill someone else. Besides which, people seem willing to pay for consulting and consorting with a former ambassador (from a well-known country), a former senator (from a well-known state), and (any) former head of the CIA.

"Awfully nice to see you." Edmund pumped the pudgy hand of a former (and never should have been) cabinet officer. He also greeted three ladies who lunch—in the latest Ferre, Ungaro, and Saint Laurent—each of whom (I had learned on the highest authority) had once been his mistress. After dispensing a few more hellos and ordering our meals, and after some flattering words and some casual chat, Edmund leaned back and said, "And now I'm eager to hear why you called and suggested this meeting."

He listened most attentively as I spoke of the noble purpose of Harmony House. He continued to listen attentively as I urged him, over our creamy seafood pastas, to purchase Jeff's eight buildings in Anacostia and donate them to CBBF to turn into the Voight Homes for the Homeless. The amount of the check I hoped he would write was precisely the same amount that Jeff had to pay Mr. Monti a week from next Monday. That $300,000, I noted to Edmund, was a mere three-fourths of the original down payment.

For those of you who are interested in the exciting world of high finance, let me explain the arithmetic of this enterprise: The down payments had totaled $400,000. Jeff had come up with $65,000. Joseph Augustus Monti had lent him the rest. To stall off Mr. Monti when he started demanding immediate payment in full, I'd given Jeff my personal check for $35,000—$25,000 of which was a loan to be repaid when he reached age thirty, and $10,000 of which was all of his birthday and Chanukah presents until he reached fifty.

I had nothing more to offer, financially speaking. But I hoped that my last-ditch pitch to super-rich Edmund Standish Voight could—while helping the homeless—solve my son's problems.

It didn't.

"The only thing that sounds better than the Voight Homes for the Homeless is the Voight Neonatal Center of Children's Hospital." Edmund gave me a warm and rueful smile. "I do so hate saying no to my favorite columnist, but that's where our family foundation money is going."

"And it couldn't spare just three hundred thousand dollars to contribute to another worthy cause?"

Edmund looked startled. "But surely you know that if we bought and donated those buildings, their mortgages would be part of the purchase price. And once you include the mortgages"—he spoke in the patient tones of a preschool teacher—"you're asking us for a total contribution of maybe a million, a million two."

In other words, in my eagerness to cut a deal with Edmund, I seemed to have made a few miscalculations.

In other words, if you're interested in the exciting world of high finance, don't depend on me to do the arithmetic.

I could feel from the heat that my face had turned red with embarrassment. I could tell from his face that Edmund felt sorry for me. "Not that we're unwilling," he was quick to reassure me, "to give consideration to other good causes. Your request was quite legitimate, and I thank you for thinking of me and the foundation. Perhaps some time in the future—"

"Yes, of course, some time in the future," I interrupted, still aflame with terminal embarrassment. "But right now could we please just change the subject?"

Boyohboyohboy, did we change the subject.

For without a moment's pause, Edmund said, "I've got a little surprise. I've invited my niece to join us for dessert. Won't she be astonished when she sees who I am dining with today."

It was clear from his guileless expression that Edmund knew nothing about the Sunny-Jake affair—neither about the original show nor about its very recent revival. For a fellow who had spent his life in the diplomatic corps, he had really screwed up.

"You girls—I mean, you young women—used to be such constant companions," Edmund continued. "So I thought, well, why don't I do this, for old times' sake."

Right, I wanted to say, and while you were getting folks together, you should have invited Ivana Trump and Marla. I buttered a second roll instead, while chipper Edmund chatted. Except that, all of a sudden, I couldn't hear him.

In fact, the entire horsy room, with its crowded red banquettes and too-small tables, was wrapped in silence. I looked around and all I could see were mouths. Thin-lipped, fat-lipped, chapped-lipped, lip-sticked, all of these mouths were in motion—talking and laughing and yet not making a sound. Oh my God, I thought, as my pulse accelerated, my heart began to pound. Oh my God, I've been struck with hysterical deafness.

A moment later my deafness was cured when a Leslie-Audrey voice greeted me with a melodious "Hello, Brenda." An exquisite blast-from-the-past kiss-kissed my cheeks, then kiss-kissed Edmund's, then sat down. Now who, I would just like to know, can go for eight years without aging a day? The answer, annoying to say, is Sunny Voight, who also displayed remarkable poise as she murmured, "What an unexpected pleasure," and ordered a double decaffeinated espresso.

Wearing a chocolate-brown body suit and a chocolate-brown wrap-around skirt, she looked like a gorgeous elf with a high I.Q. Her intelligent oversized eyes displayed the only discernible makeup on a face that otherwise seemed to be dipped in dew. I have to confess that I, if I weren't basically fond of fellows, could have fallen in love with Sunny, who was effortlessly laying on the charm.

"I've been following your career. You must be so proud of what you've accomplished," was Sunny's opener. She ran her fingers through her gamine hair. "And the boys—I still remember how adorable they were. Those gorgeous smiles—exactly like their mother's."

The trouble with Sunny Voight was she probably meant it.

"You're too, too kind," I said, though I'd never spoken like that in my life. I was struggling to regain my self-command. It certainly was my plan to behave with dignity and maturity and grace, which is why I will swear on my children's heads that I didn't do it on purpose when I knocked the espresso into Sunny's lap.

You want to know how much liquid there is in a double decaf espresso? Plenty.

A waiter arrived with fresh napkins. A waiter arrived with club soda. Another waiter brought Sunny a dry chair. Everyone blotted and patted and mopped while I, in addition, apologized, with Sunny who's not into Freud or his slips—exclaiming, "Of course it was," every time I wailed, "It was an accident."

As I believe I've already mentioned, apologizing is something I do really well.

"This is terrible, just terrible!" I told Sunny.

"Please don't feel upset," Sunny replied.

"What a nasty mess I've made," I told Sunny.

"Don't worry. I'll be all right," Sunny replied.

"Can you possibly forgive me?" I asked Sunny.

"I doubt it." Sunny—ha-ha-ha—was making a little joke. "But let me think about it."

As we were speaking it dawned on me that, considering which of us had really hurt whom, Sunny (husband snatcher) and I (betrayed wife) should have been delivering each other's lines.

"This is terrible, just terrible!" Sunny should have said to me.

"Please don't feel upset," I would have replied.

"What a nasty mess I've made," Sunny might have conceded.

"Don't worry. I'll be all right," I would have lied.

Sunny: "Can you possibly forgive me?"

Me: "I doubt it—ha-ha-ha ha-ha ha-ha ha-ha—but let me think about it."

Sunny went off to the ladies' room to do a few more repairs on her sopping self. I bounded from my banquette and went right along with her. As we stood in the white, mirrored room, I stared searchingly into her Leslie-Audrey eyes and, using a tactic I'd once proposed in a column called PRETEND YOU ALREADY KNOW, I said, "You slept with my husband this weekend. Why are you starting in with him again?"

And then—and I'll be the first to grant this was not mature behavior—I made a fist and punched her in the shoulder.

"I can't say I blame you for doing that," Sunny said to me, slowly rubbing the place where I'd landed my punch. "Not only don't I blame you, but I love and admire you, Brenda. I always have."

"Then why are you fucking my husband again," I shrieked, as one of Edmund's former mistresses half-entered the rest room and instantly backed out.

"It was"—Sunny rewrapped her wraparound skirt so the coffee stains wouldn't show—"a regrettable lapse. It happened, yes"—she emptied espresso out of her brown suede shoes—"but that's not what he came for. It happened and it was—" She silenced herself; a sensual shiver shook her fragile frame. "But truly, Brenda, that's not what he came for."

Sunny's admission, however, was what I had come for.

"I hope you gain forty pounds," I said to Sunny. "I hope you start sprouting unsightly facial hair. I hope the Smithsonian fires you for conduct unbecoming a paleontologist. I hope every night you go home and nobody's there. I hope your tax returns are audited annually. I hope—" I took a deep breath "—that all four quadrants of your mouth require gum surgery."

In the horrified silence that followed, I noticed that all of Edmund's exes had entered the ladies' room. Sunny and I departed, our heads held high.

"Don't tell Jake I had lunch with Edmund," I said to Sunny as we approached our table. "And I won't tell him I tricked you into telling me that you two went to bed."

"Tell him whatever you wish," Sunny said, her legendary poise still fully intact. "I don't plan to see him again—as either a lover or a friend—unless he leaves you."

I hated "regrettable lapse" and "unless he leaves you." But it was something else Sunny said that seared my soul, something that she whispered to me while Edmund was saying goodbye to his former mistresses. "I know you'd never do to me—or to any woman, Brenda—what I've done to you. I acknowledge how cruel and destructive this can be. And I just want to say"—she swallowed hard—"that in a better world, all of us would have your kind of purity, integrity, and decency."

I went right home and called up Birdie Monti. Toward whom, on March 18, I'd been cruel and destructive. Toward whom I'd failed to display any kind of purity, integrity, or decency. Toward whom—although I'd been trying to forgive myself—I continued to feel astonishingly guilty.

I reminded myself that she didn't (and never would) know I had slept with her husband and that I wasn't the one who had broken up her marriage and that, aside from adultery and (okay) attempted murder, I was basically, a decent human being. I still, however, felt guilty toward Birdie Monti. I needed to hear that she was doing okay.

"Definitely okay" was Birdie's cheerful response to my query. "My grandbabies are a blessing—the lights of my life. I'm sure going to miss my little Brittany when I move out of Gloria's."

"You're moving?" I asked. "Where are you moving to?"

"Why, back to my house, of course. I think I mentioned it's in my name." Birdie sounded magnificently serene. "My lawyer told Joseph yesterday that he had to be out of my house by October eighteenth."

"But where will he live?" I asked.

Birdie, busy burbling words of endearment to baby Brittany, somewhat sharply replied, "That isn't my problem." A few burbles later she added, "He told my lawyer that he'd probably move to the city. Let him call real estate agents. They'll find him a place."

This conversation returned to me as I drove, the next

morning, from pharmacy to pharmacy, filling my three innocuous prescriptions for what added up to deadly poison pills. To murder Mr. Monti I needed the will (which I had) and the way (which I'd just acquired). But how, I needed to figure out, would I find the opportunity to get close enough to slip him the fatal dose?

I'd been brooding about this question since Miami.

It came to me in a flash as I was paying (in cash, of course) at the third pharmacy, that Birdie Monti had given me my answer.

10

●

BANANA, BANANA, BANANA

*A*ttempted murder was getting awfully expensive.

What with the long blond wig, the rental car, the uniform, the table, and so forth, my Swedish masseuse disguise had cost three hundred dollars: By the end of Monday afternoon I had spent almost four hundred more (including the past week's doctors' appointments and poison pills) to prepare to present myself to Mr. Joseph Augustus Monti as Elizabeth Fisher-Todd, ace real estate agent.

"Hah there," I said in a husky honeyed *Cat on a Hot Tin Roof* drawl when I reached Joseph Monti by phone on Tuesday morning. "Ah unnerstan' y'all's lookin' to fond a place to live in the District. Ahm your puhson."

(I'll return to Standard English, but keep in mind that I'm sounding a lot like Blanche DuBois, with just a little Scarlett O'Hara thrown in.)

"I only now decided to move," Joseph Monti growled. "How did you already get that information?"

"We got it because it's our business to get it, and we're the best in the business," I silkily soothed him. "Fisher-Todd is a low-profile outfit with very high quality clients. We only work with"—stroke! stroke!—"the cream of the crop."

"Well then—" he softened; I knew that he'd be a sucker for "cream of the crop"—"what do you have to show me in, say, a luxury two-bedroom condo in northwest Washington?"

"Oh, no no *no!*" I replied. "That isn't at all how we do business at Fisher-Todd. Our slogan has always been More Than Realtors—Matchmakers. And to make the perfect match between you and the place that you next will call home, I'll need to meet you and buy you a drink and chat a bit so I can grasp your essence."

"Grasp my what?"

"Your essence. I can promise it won't take long. This evening? Caucus, on Capitol Hill? Six o'clock?"

Mr. Monti resisted. "No, I don't think so. I don't think I want—"

"I'll be the kind of . . . bosomy one . . . with the violet eyes and black hair and a little mole—like Liz Taylor's—on my cheek."

My fish was back on the line. "It sounds as if maybe more than your mole is like Liz Taylor."

I sighed with becoming modesty. "Well, actually, people say like a *younger* Liz Taylor."

With my black bouffant wig and my penciled-on mole and my violet-tinted contacts, I did—in the dimly lit Caucus—look somewhat Lizish. And I figured I'd look a lot more so when Mr. Monti, as I was counting on him to do, took off his glasses in order to impress me with his big blind bedroom eyes. But I knew I must have a backup plan in case my disguise didn't wash, and, while praying I wouldn't need it, I had prepared one, intending to tell Mr. Monti—if caught—that I'd tricked him into this meeting to beg for mercy. And then I'd say, "So I'm asking you, I'm pleading with you, I'm urging you, to please please please please let my family be." And if he agreed (unlikely), I would happily flush the poison pills down the toilet. And if he refused (highly likely), I'd suggest that we have one last drink, for old times' sake. And then he'd either sneer and leave or sneer and have that drink—in which case I'd kill him.

"Easy to find you among these yuppies," Joseph Monti greeted me, sliding smoothly into a chair and immediately (whew!) removing his glasses.

"Charmed to meet you." I reached out my hand in a crisp but certainly not unfeminine handshake. "My clients call me Elizabeth. I hope that you will too. And I do hope you will forgive my unbusinesslike garb."

"Yeah." Mr. Monti nodded his sleek head. "I see what you mean."

I should note that the way I was dressed was meant to serve as a crucial part of my disguise. For what I was also banking on was that Mr. Monti's eyes would be studying not my features but my breasts, whose bared rosy mounds had been pressed (by a shrewdly engineered bra called Lover Cups) above and beyond the neckline of my dress, and whose truly spectacular cleavage (also courtesy of Lover Cups) housed, in its perfumed depths, a simple gold cross.

My alibi for the dress, a slinky, satiny, silvery number, was that I was going from there to another engagement—"a dinner being given by Secretary and Mrs.—whoops!" I interrupted myself. "Sorry, we never mention the names of our clients. Suffice it to say he's a man upon whose shoulders might rest the survival of the world."

Mr. Monti, pleased to be numbered among my exalted clients, and even more pleased with my unbusinesslike garb, fixed his liquid gaze on my cleavage and huskily observed, "That's a beautiful cross."

I thanked him and said, "I've already ordered us something special to drink. It's an old and famous Fisher-Todd tradition. And while it's being prepared, perhaps you could say some more about what you have in mind."

Joseph Monti's eyes swept the room, where the Young and Ambitious were gathered, speaking—as they sipped Chardonnay—with the borrowed importance of their congressional bosses. "We've got the votes." "We told HHS." "We met with the Speaker this morning." Clearly these kids believed they were running the world. It struck me, as I watched them playing mine-is-bigger-than-yours, that this was a perfect place to poison a person.

"What I have in mind—" Joseph Monti swallowed hard as I leaned forward, the better to hear him, breasts rising to the occasion magnificently, "what I have in mind is that you skip that dinner party and let me take you to eat at the Lion d'Or."

"Would that I could," I sighed. "Would that I could. These Washington do's, with the great and near-great, are really such a bore. I mean, yet another evening with Bobby Dole and Nino—pardon me, Justice—Scalia is not at all my idea of a high old time."

"Then why not—" Mr. Monti persisted.

"One night soon," I promised. "But business first, Mr. Monti, and pleasure later. So would you please an-

swer me this: If you were a tree—think carefully now—
which tree would you be?"

Mr. Monti's eyes drifted up from my cleavage to my
face. Uh-oh, he was studying me. His forehead was fur-
rowed. He cocked his head and knitted his brows and
examined me some more. My bared rosy chest grew
damp with perspiration.

Mr. Monti kept staring at me. And then—at last—he
spoke. "They're wrong," he said. "You're really not a
Liz Taylor."

"I'm not?" I asked him, anxiety slipping some northern sharpness into my southern-fried drawl.

"It's somebody else you remind me of," Mr. Monti
replied. He continued to study my face. "Someone I
know."

I sat there reviewing my backup plan, which on second thought seemed unbelievably lame. I mean, what
if—after I tell him my story—he gets really mad and
telephones the police and has me arrested for imperson-
ating a real estate agent, and then the police take me
down to the station and then they frisk me and find the
poison pills, and then—I flashed on Susan Hayward,
locked behind prison bars in *I Want to Live!,* and per-
ishing, though innocent, in the gas chamber. Large
drops of sweat were dripping down my cleavage.

"I've got it!" Mr. Monti snapped his fingers—one,
two, three. "You know who you are? You're a brunette
Goldie Hawn." He paused. "Well, maybe Goldie Hawn's
first cousin."

I almost choked with relief but I somehow managed
to get a grip on myself and my drawl. "Actually," I replied, "I've heard that before. Now tell me—this may
sound silly to you, but it helps us compose a psycho-

real estate profile—tell me what kind of tree you think you'd be?"

Mr. Monti leaned back in his chair and sighed impatiently. "I don't do trees."

Across the lively room I could see our waiter slowly making his way to our table, two foamy pink drinks aglow upon his tray. "Then let's look over my listings," I said, adding hastily, "and would you be a lamb and kindly go and fetch my briefcase from the checkroom?"

Mr. Monti left. The drinks—two oversized strawberry Daiquiris—arrived. The waiter left. I whipped out the poison pills. Which, of course, I had already mashed and which, when stirred, dissolved most gratifyingly into the contents of Mr. Monti's glass.

Did my fingers tremble as I poisoned my former lover's drink? I'll try to answer the question honestly. I'd already resolved my ambivalence and made peace with homicide. I was now, as Nietzsche once put it, "beyond good and evil." I was also, as Yeats had wisely advised, looking "on the motive, not the deed," while keeping in mind noble Seneca's instructive observation that a "successful and fortunate crime is called virtue." Furthermore, I was guided by— But enough with the citations. You ask, did my fingers tremble? The answer is no.

Mr. Monti gave me my briefcase and settled back into his seat. I removed the listings I'd typed up for the occasion. Pushing his drink a bit closer to him, I adjusted my cleavage and asked, "How central is a fireplace to your happiness?"

"My happiness?" Mr. Monti laughed softly, bitterly. "I have no happiness."

"Oh," I said in a most tactful tone, "is that perhaps why you're moving? Domestic problems?"

"Not domestic. Foreign." Mr. Monti's eyes were burning. "An outsider attacking the sanctity of my home." His eyes were searing mine. "Destroying my family. Turning my wife and children against me. But he is going to pay. They all will pay."

I knew who "they" were but I had to ask, "Pay what?"

"Their blood, their sweat, their tears, their grief." Mr. Monti's voice ran up the scale. "Their misery, torment, agony, and anguish. That's what they owe me. And that's what they will pay."

When he finished his loathsome litany, he clenched one fist and bit into his knuckles, which definitely underscored his point. And though I had felt no further need to justify this . . . this assassination, his words and gesture hardened my heart even harder.

"I do," I said, dredging up a smile, "I do admire a man of strong opinions."

"And I," said Mr. Monti, his rage retreating, his eyes returning to my cleavage, "do admire your cross."

I'll nail you to it, I said to myself. Aloud, I kept smiling and said, "If I might change the subject, it's time for a toast."

I raised my glass and gestured to Joseph Monti to do the same. He picked up his drink, examined it, put it back down. "What"—his caressing voice had acquired an unexpected edge—"is this you're giving me?"

For one wild moment I thought about leaping out of my chair and trying to make a getaway. Surely the jig was up. Surely he knew. I fought back my panic and told myself that he couldn't possibly know, that I had to stay cool, that I had to see this through. Clearing my throat, I replied to his what-is-this question with a reassuring chirp. "Why, it's the Fisher-Todd drink, the traditional drink we always offer our new clients. A strawberry Daiquiri."

"Sorry. No. I can't drink this." Mr. Monti shoved it away as if it were . . . poison.

"Of course you can," I insisted, anxiety once again playing havoc with my drawl. "All of our clients drink it. Even Justice Souter drank it. You've got to! You must!"

"I'll have something else." Mr. Monti summoned our waiter back to the table. "I'd like a—"

"No!" I interrupted. "Listen, okay, I'll grant that it's sweet and I know that a lot of men aren't crazy for sweet. But please, just this once, drink it down. It's really important to drink it down. It's . . . a tradition."

I knew I was pushing too hard. I knew I risked rousing his suspicions. But I couldn't—so very close to my goal—bear to fail. I took his drink in my hand, reached out, and pressed it to his lips. "You can't"—I batted my lashes—"you can't refuse me."

"I'd like a scotch and soda," Mr. Monti told the waiter, moving my hand away and ignoring my lashes. Then, with a sort of sheepish smile, he explained, "I have the greatest respect for tradition. But the reason I can't drink your drink"—he did a sue-me-sue-me-shoot-bullets-through-me shrug—"is because I've got this bad allergy to strawberries."

During the forty minutes required to extricate myself from this fiasco, one cruel word kept tormenting my brain: Banana! Banana, banana, banana! Banana, banana, banana! If only, I thought, as I fought back tears of regret, if only I had ordered *banana* Daiquiris.

It took me eleven days to regain my shattered equilibrium after my failure to poison Mr. Monti. It took me until Saturday, October 24, to once again be able to say "Can do." Where were my organizational skills, where was my resilience, I had to wonder. For it took me until Halloween was one short week away to turn my thoughts to another murder plan.

It had been, to be fair, a stressful eleven days. While struggling to regain my equilibrium (and while, of course, writing my column three times a week), I had, in addition, been fighting with Jake, desperately seeking Hubert, enduring attacks with sharp instruments, lecturing in Berkeley and Indianapolis, trying my damnedest not to throttle Rosalie, and assisting shell-shocked Jeff to move back home.

I'll address these matters in chronological order.

On Wednesday, despite daily flossing and my submission, four times a year, to the preventive periodontia of Sherman Schwartz, I nonetheless had surgery—part one of a two-part series—on my gums. (Why me? Why me? I wanted to know, but according to Dr. Schwartz, in matters of the mouth there is no justice.) I spent the rest of the day adrift on a sea of self-pity and painkilling medication, in no condition to concentrate on murder.

On Thursday night and on Friday night I lectured. I flew to San Francisco Thursday morning and talked about growth to Berkeley students that night, urging them to set aside some time in their lives to do community service. (This could, I said, be simple volunteer work. It's fine, I said, to be Indians, not chiefs. "Native Americans, please," one of the students, another Adrienne, had corrected me. Where will this end?)

On Friday I spent all day attempting to get to my next lecture, in Indianapolis. (Or should I be saying Native Americanapolis?) The trip to and from Indiana was not a good time. Engine trouble, fog, high winds, and many screaming babies diverted me, during my travels, from plotting a murder.

Late on Saturday afternoon Jeff, having no place to live, returned to the room in which he had spent his childhood. It seems that Mr. Monti, in lieu of buying himself a condo in the District, had decided to take over Jeff's plush Watergate pad (which, as you recall, Jeff had to forfeit). The only good news was that Jeff, by vacating Watergate immediately, had received an extension on the rest of his loan, with munificent Mr. Monti postponing the due date—what a prince!—till December 1.

Preoccupied with assuaging Jeff's depression, I didn't have a moment to think about murder.

On Sunday, Monday, and Tuesday Jake and I had nonstop fights, both in person and by telephone. For Jeff's glum move back home had forced me to notify my husband not only about Jeff's real estate problems but also about my efforts to resolve them. I had hoped to tell Jake the minimum, but under his stringent questioning (which came close to violating my human rights), I confessed about Vivian Feuerbach ("Billy? Elton Jr? You've got to be kidding!") and Edmund Standish Voight ("And Sunny joined you for dessert? Uh, what did she say?"). I didn't say what Sunny had said until the third day of our fighting, until Jake's righteous scoldings had gone too far, until he had moved from "Incorrigible!" "Reprehensible!" and (he learned this from me) "Narcissistic!" to "Liar" and "Sneak." After which I coldly observed, "Speaking of liar and sneak . . ." (significant pause), and then proceeded to tell him every word that Sunny had said to me at the Jockey Club.

My ensuing recriminations, extensive and colorful, left me no energy for murder plots.

On Wednesday I returned for part two of my gum surgery.

On Thursday, while I was occupied with signing a FedEx receipt, Hubert streaked out the front door and disappeared. I called his name, searched the neighborhood—both on foot and by car, rang doorbells, searched some more, shrieked, whistled, implored, impelled by the vision of Rosalie's face if I had (God forbid!) to inform her that Hubert was lost. Two hours after my search began, I dragged myself over to Carolyn's, hoping for some tea and sympathy. And there in the back was Rosalie, with Hubert at her side, supervising the digging of Carolyn's lily pond.

"You let my dog run away," said Rose accusingly, her muddy hands planted on her blue-jeaned hips. "He could have been hit by a car. He could have been taken to the pound and put to sleep. He could even—a gorgeous creature like this—have been kidnapped."

Hubert woofed a reproach and went bounding blissfully through the crunchy autumn leaves, returning to Rosalie's side and woofing once more. "I just want to ask you this," I said to my sister, blowing my bangs out of my eyes. "Did you hear me before—like an hour ago, and also an hour and a half ago—did you hear me out there screaming my heart out for Hubert?" Oblivious to the red-and-gold glories of Keats's "season of mists and mellow fruitfulness" (the poem is "To Autumn"), I awaited my sister Rosalie's reply.

"If you'd found Hubert right away," Rose actually had the chutzpah to say, "you wouldn't have appreciated how terrible it was to have let him escape. So you'd let it happen again, and then the next time he'd be hit by a car or kidnapped."

"You're telling me you heard me calling earlier," I said, my voice robotic. "You heard me calling but you didn't answer."

Rosalie, shameless, admitted that this was true. "It's one of the things people do—I read this in some book translated from the German—to get kids to be responsible for their animals."

She paused to give the lily-pond diggers instructions and Hubert a scratch behind his ear. "And Brenda, you'll have to agree," she said, "that spending all morning looking for a dog will make a person think twice before that person lets that dog run away again."

Just as I was about to say something stupendously unsisterly, Rosalie made an announcement that saved the day. "I'm almost finished with Carolyn's yard. The rest of the planting can't be done until spring. I'm planning on leaving early on Saturday. So tell me"—she paused, smiling slyly, looking for trouble, looking for love—"are you going to miss me?"

I didn't skip a beat. "My house will not be the same"—I spoke from the heart—"without you."

Friday the twenty-third was Wally's birthday. My baby boy was twenty-four years old. The Kovner Four, plus impossible Rose and elusive Josephine, had tickets to the Washington Ballet, after which we were coming home to my Death by Chocolate birthday cake and champagne.

It's difficult enough to bake a tricky cake like that without at the same time figuring out a murder.

Josephine met us at 7:15 on the top floor of the Kennedy Center. "Wow! Wow! Wow! Wow! Wow!" all of us said. Indeed, we hardly knew her, with her radiant hair piled artfully on her head and her tall, slim body's perfection displayed in a well-cut black crepe suit instead of hiding out in one of her many where-have-all-the-flowers-gone numbers. Her fingernails were not only not chewed; they were polished. Her shoes were not only not scuffed; they were high-heeled. And color, deftly applied to the angles and planes of her heart-shaped face, revealed the full dimensions of her beauty.

In response to our chorus of wows, Josephine giggled and explained her transformation. "I was starting to feel like my outer me wasn't matching my inner me anymore. And so—and so—I decided to get a makeover."

"Your outer you was fine with me," Wally said to Jo, adding with some bemusement, "Besides, I didn't even know you knew about makeovers."

Josephine blushed prettily. "I didn't," she told him. "It was my doctor's idea."

We walked through the Terrace Theater's tasteful but totally purpled lobby and filed into our center orchestra seats—first Jeff, then Rose, then Jake, then me, then Wally, and then Jo, an arrangement which allowed me, though the lovebirds were speaking softly, to hear their conversation without really eavesdropping.

"So tell me," Wally asked Jo, "does your shrink do the makeover all by herself or does she subcontract?"

"If I'm not mistaken, that is a hostile remark."

"I'm not being hostile. I'm being concerned that—"

"Shush!" warned a voice behind us, as the curtain went up on four ladies in classic tulle, who broke from their prettily posed tableau to embark upon a charming pas de quatre. During the applause and the little pause—not a full intermission—that followed this piece, Wally resumed his defense with "I'm only concerned that your shrink is too involved in your life, like she's Pygmalion and you're—you're what's-her-name."

"Galatea," I said, but not out loud.

"That just isn't so!" Jo said hotly. "She's isn't *creating* me. She's only helping *me* create *myself*."

"Nicely put," I said, but not out loud.

Dvořák's stormy music squelched this dialogue and swept us into *Nocturno*, where we watched a muscular bare-chested dancer engage in—and I'll defer to the program notes here—"a seduction promising the splendor of eternity." The object of his affection, who was not exactly playing hard to get, molded, melded, melted into his body as he executed a series of moves so gymnastically erotic that Philip would have gnashed his teeth with envy.

"That's how you used to be with me," my wistful Wally whispered to his Jo.

"Submissive," said Jo.

"Receptive," Wally countered.

"Engulfed!"

"United!"

"Consumed!"

"Content! Complete!"

"Wally," Jo said, "It's awful to have to tell you this on your birthday, but—"

Thunderous clapping obliterated the rest of Josephine's sentence, though I almost fell out of my seat trying to hear. But as we rose for the first intermission, Wally's anguished response floated back loud and clear. "I can't believe you mean that. I can't believe it."

Wrapping our coats around us, we stepped outside to the rooftop terrace to admire the city lights, the river, the sky. Wally, who had started to cry, grabbed Jo by the arm and left our happy group, which wasn't all that happy what with Jeff morosely contemplating the Watergate (which, alas, was not only right next door, but you actually could see his former condo), and with Jake and me in what I would have to call an exceedingly tenuous rapprochement, and with Rose (still in her man-bashing mode) declaiming, "So after the splendor of eternity, you know what he's going to do? He's going to dump her."

"That wasn't a sexist tract. That was a goddam ballet," I said, but not out loud.

Wally and Jo were not in their seats when the curtain went up on *Lucy and the Count*, the Count turning out to be the blood-sucking Count Dracula. Who, to Rose's delight ("Once a victim, not necessarily *always* a victim," she crowed), is offed by ex-victim Lucy in the end.

Back out on the terrace during the second intermission, I saw Jo and Wally wrapped in each other's arms, an embrace that to my practiced eye looked far far more like "parting is such sweet sorrow" than it did like "and they lived happily ever after." My suspicions were intensified when, just as the last ballet started, the star-crossed lovers announced that they were leaving.

Jo (with quivering lips): "Thank you so much for a lovely evening. I have to go now."

Wally (with deadened voice): "I'm driving Jo home to McLean. I'll meet you back at the house as soon as I can."

They left. I gave my divided attention to *Colorful Fantasies*, which was very ... colorful, and then we headed homeward to what threatened to be a real downer of a birthday party.

Wally surprised us by getting back from McLean by 11:30. He had obviously composed himself on the way. "I only have this to say," he said, as he joined us in the dining room, "and I won't be taking questions after my statement: Jo and I, though still engaged, have agreed to date other people for six months. After that, the plan is that we'll either split up or set a wedding date." His voice cracked a bit at the "split up" part but he valiantly pressed on. "So is this my birthday or what? Where's my cake?"

I don't want you thinking I'm vain, but I need to explain that my Death by Chocolate chocolate cake has been known to bring tears of joy to an eater's eye. I'm only mentioning this in order to help you understand why, despite assorted tension and dissension, we were starting to relax, mellow out, have something resembling having a good time when—it was almost midnight—the doorbell rang.

The first response was from Rosalie: "Where's Hubert? Did he get out? No, he's here. He's safe."

The rest of us just kind of froze, hands poised in midair with flutes of champagne and forkfuls of cake.

The doorbell—shrill and spiteful—rang again and

again and again. "I guess I'd better go answer it," said Jake.

Looking rather stern, he pushed back his chair.

All of us followed behind him as he walked down the hall to the door where, visible through the glass pane, stood a Harpo-haired clown in a striped and polka-dotted clown suit. With a garish red smile gashed across his dead-white face and a bunch of black—black!—balloons clutched in one hand, this clown made me think of *A Clockwork Orange* (one of the scariest movies I've ever seen) rather than your basic benevolent Bozo.

"Go away and leave us alone," I shrieked at the top of my lungs. But not out loud.

"I was here earlier. You were out. I'm from The Clown Connection," the clown, balloons waving, told us through the glass. "Birthday greetings for Mr. Wally Kovner."

Just as I started to say to Jake that he shouldn't let him in, Jake opened the door and let the clown inside. "So which one is the birthday boy?" he inquired, looking around. Don't answer, I wanted to say, but Jake replied. Shuffling over to Wally on pink-and-orange oversized shoes, the clown bowed ceremoniously and handed him the creepy black balloons. "Courtesy of an anonymous admirer," he said. "And so is this song."

Hubert, who had been sniffing the clown, wagged his tail approvingly and started chewing the pompom on one of his shoes. "He doesn't do that with everyone," Rosalie told the clown. "That certainly is a compliment to you." The clown looked unconvinced, his eyes, beneath mobile Groucho brows, casting uneasy glances at his foot. Then, with a hitch of his droopy pants (and with Hubert still chomping away), he started to sing.

> Walked the walk.
> Talked the talk.
> Never questioned why.
> Had some fun.
> Now it's done.
> Time to doo da die.
> Rode the bumps.
> Took the lumps.
> Learned to laugh and cry.
> Ran the race.
> Ran out of space.
> Time to doo da die.
> Time to doo
> Time to da
> Time to doo da die.
> It won't be long now.
> Time to doo-oo da die.
> Yeah!

In a combination final bow and fruitless attempt to pry Hubert off his pompom, the clown, his song completed, bent low to the ground. I leaned against the wall and managed—barely—to prop myself up as the room began to spin around and around. Knowing what I knew, I understood the brutal meaning of Mr. Monti's mocking messenger. But while his cavortings choked me with nightmarish horror, the rest of my family seemed merely bemused by the spectacle.

Then Wally burst out laughing. "Too much! Everyone's sent me these birthday cards about aches and

pains and gray and needing a cane and wearing a truss
and getting old. But one foot in the grave? Give me a
break!"

"You'd be surprised," said Rosalie, ever Miss Merry
Sunshine, "how fast it all goes."

The clown, after one last struggle, finally ceded
Hubert his shoe and, holding his stockinged foot high,
hopped out the door. While my sons, Rose, and Jake returned to the cake, I—fighting off my dizzy spell—
excused myself and hurried after the clown.

"Just a minute," I yelled. I was going to say, "I know
who sent you," or maybe, "This is a citizen's arrest."
But the clown, pausing only to reach in his pocket, said,
"Here. I almost forgot. The birthday boy's card," put on
a sudden burst of speed, and vanished into the dark October night.

I opened the card before I went in and scanned its
black-bordered message, although I already knew what
it would say. I had not shared the previous warnings
with Wally, nor would I show him this, for I planned on
making the danger go away. But the witching hour was
near. Halloween was next Saturday, just a week from
today. And as this message, like the last message,
threatened: ON HALLOWEEN THE CLOWN TURNS INTO A
GHOST.

11

•

MY MOM IS A SLUT

/n the very few hours I slept, I dreamed I was watching a pas de trois at the Kennedy Center. Mr. Monti, the clown, and Count Dracula, all wearing oversized shoes, were doing a stylized dance-of-death ballet. I screamed, "You can't get away with this," and the terrible trio vanished from the stage. And now I was watching *Nocturno,* whose unabashedly erotic pas de deux was being performed by . . . a naked Louis and me.

The shame woke me up—the shame, that is, of dreaming of sexual pleasure when I should have been figuring out how to save my son. On the other hand, since Jake and I were currently making war instead of love, this was the only kind of sex I was getting. So enjoy it a little longer, I indulgently told myself. You'll decide how to kill Mr. Monti later today. I snuggled under the blankets and—half-sleeping and half-awake—entirely gave myself over to sexual reverie.

Having banished shame, I let my mind drift drowsily, dreamily back to Louis. To satin-skinned, loose-limbed Louis, with his long narrow face and tell-me-about-it eyes. To Louis, whose close-cropped head seemed always cocked in the yes-I'm-listening-to-you position. To Louis, with the shade and sweetness of a Milky Way, and the strength of ten because his heart is pure. To Louis and March 18, when I'd removed my no-nonsense Jockey For Her pants and undershirt (yes, okay, I was making a statement), lain down beside him on his sofa bed, and in less than thirty seconds fallen . . . sound asleep.

It had been a hard day.

As you recall, I'd been up at six, dressed in my long-skirted Waspy Western ensemble, rushed to the corner and into the limousine, where from 6:48 A.M. till roughly 11;10 A.M. I'd—under the tutelage of Joseph Monti—revised a number of my newspaper columns. After which I'd rushed home, leaped into the shower, dressed in red undies and a suit très Julia Roberts in *Pretty Woman* (post-, of course, not pre-Richard Gere), and cabbed to the Hay-Adams John Hay suite where, from noon till roughly 4:20 P.M., under the tutelage of Philip Eastlake, I'd deepened my knowledge of Oriental philosophy. After which I'd rushed home, leaped into the shower, put on my authentic equal-rights Jockeys (plus something authentically working class from the Gap), and promptly at 6 P.M. joined the board of Harmony House (and Chloe the social worker) for a very authentic brown-bag dinner meeting.

During the next three hours we heard reports on the various residents from Chloe—Ilona, for example, had just been hired by a bakery and would soon be ready to move to her own apartment; Alfred was back to beating up on Laverne. We heard from the head of our ever-harried maintenance committee that the furnace had been deemed beyond repair. We heard from our desperate treasurer: Would we give some serious thought to doubling our annual contribution? And we heard, at the end, from Louis, who—having written four grant proposals and lined up several more business groups to find jobs for the grownups and mentors for the kids and talked an orthodontist friend into doing Ilona's daughter's braces free and spent last Sunday helping repair the Harmony House front stairs and attending Sam's sobriety celebration—wanted us all to know how terrific we were and what a wonderful job we were doing.

At nine, when the meeting broke up—it had been held at our treasurer's house in Bethesda—Louis and I, in separate cars, drove down to his apartment in Adams-Morgan.

I mean, please, where else would you expect Louis to live?

It's true that Adams-Morgan is just a five- or six-minute ride from Cleveland Park. And it's true that some of the houses on some of the side streets harbor, behind their modest facades, dazzling no-expense-spared renovations. Nevertheless, Adams-Morgan—with its colorful ethnic and economic mix, its store-front *abogados,* its Ethiopian and other exotic cuisines, its dance clubs and bars, its antique shops and frame shops and wig shops—is a far, far funkier neighborhood than mine. (That is, if they're still using words like "funky.") There was plenty of action on Eighteenth Street as I cruised behind Louis that night—action and an edge, just an edge, of risk. Finally—it took quite a while—we managed to find two places to park and walked the three long blocks and the four long long long *long* flights of stairs to his top-floor apartment.

Where things did not, initially, go too well.

I suppose in a way I started it when, having huffed and puffed up those endless stairs, I plopped down into the nearest chair and proceeded to use my pocketbook to fan myself, complaining as I fanned, "My God, I'm positively dripping with perspiration."

"Yes, and your face is really red," Louis said sympathetically. "How long do these episodes usually last?"

"Excuse me?" I answered, mopping my brow with a Kleenex.

"It's a normal, natural process, and I'm glad it's come out of the closet," Louis said. "I'm glad that people like you and me can discuss it without embarrassment—frankly and openly."

"Discuss what, Louis?" I didn't quite catch his drift.

Louis sat down in the chair next to mine, took out a hankie, and finished mopping my brow. "The night sweats. The irritability. The mood swings, insomnia, migraines. The—"

"You've lost me," I said to Louis, but he marched on.

"—urinary incontinence. The short-term memory loss. The vaginal dryness. And, of course, the hot flashes, which I can see that you are experiencing right now."

"Did you say hot flashes?" I asked, my face burning up all over again—with indignation. "What are you talking about?"

"The Change. The Big M. The Silent Passage," Louis answered cheerfully. "Menopause."

I was, as rarely happens to me, rendered speechless. Louis, now tenderly holding my hand, pressed on. "I've been reading up on the subject lately—it's something we men need to know about—and I think I'm getting a sense of what it's like."

I still found myself with nothing to say, but Louis, it seemed, had plenty more to tell me. About hormone-replacement therapy. Osteoporosis. Menopause support groups. Vaginal lubricants. "And I just want to add, and then I'll shut up—I get that you're feeling uncomfortable with this, Brenda—that to me a woman in menopause is as vital and as sexy as one who is . . ."

While he cast about for a tasteful phrase ("ovulating"? "menstruating"?), I finally regained the capacity to speak.

"You promised to shut up," I told him, "so shut up and listen to me. These aren't hot flashes. I'll say that again. These aren't hot flashes, Louis. I'm not menopausal."

"They aren't—? You're not—?" Louis fell silent, hanging his head and staring down at the rug, and then he started to laugh—a low rich sound—a low rich sound that grew louder and richer and wilder and so contagious that I quit being miffed and started laughing too.

"I was trying to be—" he began, but a new wave of laughter intervened.

"You were trying to be," I helped out, "a sensitive male. I appreciate that, Louis, and I promise you that the minute the Big M strikes, I'm racing to the phone and letting you know."

Louis tossed me a rueful glance and eased out of his chair. "What I'd really like to know," he said, heading into the kitchen, "is whether you like your omelet well done or runny."

He moved around the small kitchen with efficiency and grace while I watched from his book-lined, minimally furnished living room, trying to act like I wasn't pretending I wasn't menopausal, which I wasn't. I didn't fully recover until Louis served up gorgeous platters of herb-flecked eggs, put something with mandolins on the CD, and began to probe my life as a girl, daughter, wife, mother, writer, and woman with such gently insightful questions and such rapt attention to my every reply that I practically forgot that I had come for sex, not eggs and understanding.

I didn't doubt for a minute, as I talked nonstop about me me me me me, that Louis would totally understand what I'd done that day with Philip and Mr. Monti.

I didn't doubt it. But I didn't tell him.

"I really respect and admire you as a person," said Louis, finally making his move—a slow, sweet kiss on each of my eyes, followed by a soft kiss at the edge of my mouth, followed shortly thereafter by a kiss upon my lips of such scorching intensity that I urgently needed to fan myself again. My whimpers of pleasure encouraged Louis to open the sofa bed, divest himself of his clothes, and climb under the sheets, from whence he warmly invited me—"though please don't feel that there's any pressure whatever"—to join him. Passion warred with exhaustion as I swiftly stripped and threw myself into his arms. Exhaustion won.

I woke to the ring ring ring of the phone. Louis reached out, picked it up, listened long, and frowned. "Okay, yes. I'll hold. It's Darryl" (the resident manager of Harmony House), he whispered. "There's sort of an emergency. He first tried calling Chloe. She's not around. So . . ."

I looked at my watch. It was almost one. "My God,

it's late," I said. "Jake is out of town tonight, but still . . ."

"You don't want to go before we—" Louis caught himself and shuddered with embarrassment. "Whoa, sorry. Don't mean to lay expectations on you. Hey, just because you took off your clothes and got naked with me in bed doesn't mean I'm entitled"—he tactfully covered himself with the sheet—"to make any kind of sexual assumptions."

"Feel perfectly free," I said to Louis, reaching under the sheet, "to make assumptions."

Which, for the next several moments, he deftly did.

He kissed the hollow of my throat while one gentle hand took a leisurely trip down my body, stroking my breasts, my belly, my inner thighs. He had just established beyond any doubt that I wasn't yet in need of commercial lubricants when Darryl was urgently back on the telephone.

Louis listened intently while caressing me firmly but gently. I returned the favor fervently. We were heading with all deliberate speed from separate but equal to total integration when Louis was called upon to respond to Darryl.

"Okay, let her stay in the bathroom," he said, "while you try to get Paulie down to your apartment. Tell him I'm waiting to talk to him on the phone. Then while I'm talking to Paulie, go on back up"—he slipped on the royal-blue condom I handed him—"and say to Joan that she's got to come out of the bathroom."

Although I am ordinarily a woman of more than average curiosity—some have even called it nosiness—I was remarkably unconcerned about the current domestic problems of Paulie and Joan. I had other matters to contemplate when Darryl put down the phone and went to get Paulie, leaving Louis free to inquire—as I lay panting beside him—whether penetration was permissible.

"You still could get up and walk away and there wouldn't be any hard feelings," he quickly added.

"Thank you," I told him, "for reassuring me."

"No matter how far things have gone, a woman always retains the right to change her mind."

"Or not to change her mind, as the case may be."

"Nor do I agree," Louis said, "with those who hold that silence means assent."

With every cell in my body warbling "I'm in the mood for love," this dialogue was becoming just a tad tedious. Not to mention the fact that at my back time's winged chariot was hurrying near.

For I could visualize Darryl running up the stairs at Harmony House and quickly getting Paulie away from Joan. And now he and Paulie were coming down the stairs to Darryl's apartment, where Paulie—any minute, any second, any instant now—would be talking to Louis at length on the telephone. "Listen to me, Louis. You've got my assent. Believe me, you've got my assent," I moaned. "I'll put it in writing, Louis. I'll get it notarized."

Too late. Alas, too late. For, just as I feared, there was Louis on the phone with Paulie. "You're right. Yeah, that's a bummer, man," he said. So was this a bummer, I thought, and—seizing time by the forelock—I pushed Louis down on his back on the sofa bed. And I . . . impaled myself.

"Paulie, excuse me," I heard Louis say as I began to undulate enticingly. "I'll have to put you on hold for a little while." Then, laying down the phone, he com-

menced to attend to the subject now under consideration
with zest, imagination, and great style. He was on his
way to the moon—I had already been there—when I
stopped the proceedings and said with a sweet little
smile, "You still could get up and walk away and there
wouldn't be any hard feelings. A man retains the right
to change his mind. Hey, just because you took off your
clothes and got naked with me in bed . . ."

Here's what's so great about Louis. A little bit later—
not right at the moment, but later—he laughed.

On Saturday morning, before Rose left, we took a walk
to Carolyn's house so Rose could show me the finished
work on the yard. "Can't stay. I'm late for my facial,"
said Carolyn, large and lush in her blue-and-white cash-
mere warm-up suit, blowing kisses as she rushed to her
car. "But go see how divine."

On Thursday I'd been too angry at Rose to notice
what she had done. It indeed was divine.

"You never believed—now admit it, Bren," Rosalie
challenged me, as I lavishly admired the latticed tree
house, the three-tiered lily pond, the delicate Japanese
garden, the pebbled walkways, "that I was capable of
doing this job. You thought I'd screw up."

"If that's what I thought," I said, amazed and impressed by the beauty before me, "I take it all back." I
knelt to examine a bronze baby walrus that Rose had
artfully set on a rock by the pond. "You're a born landscape architect."

Rosalie's usually tense, alert face surrendered to a
six-year-old's blissful grin, a testament to the trans-
forming power of praise. "You really think so?" she

asked, reluctant to let the moment go. "You really think so?"

I unstintingly assured her that I did.

Rosalie twinkled with pleasure. "Thank you," she said. "And thank you for letting me stay at your house. I know I'm not the easiest to live with."

I was on a magnanimity roll. I shrugged my shoulders and quietly said, "So who is?"

Sisterhood sang in the treetops as we walked home.

Later, when Rose had packed the car and settled Hubert onto his velvety mattress, she buckled her seat belt and looked me straight in the eye. "I have to count on you, Brenda, being all alone in the world, and I want you to promise me that if I die—"

"You do," I reminded her, "have a daughter."

She waved a dismissive hand. "I want you to solemnly promise me, Bren, that if I die, I'll be able to count on you to take care of Hubert."

When Rose had roared happily off (I am now the designated guardian of a Great Dane), I sat on the porch in my wicker rocking chair. Rocking back and forth in the bracing late October air, I turned my thoughts to murdering Mr. Monti. I rocked and racked my brain. I rocked and I racked. I racked and I rocked. I came up with zilch.

Jake strolled out to the porch and sat across from me on the hammock. "You're thinking," he said. "I get nervous when you think." Wearing a tight black turtleneck, a pair of soft khaki pants, and an amiable expression on his face, he crisply reviewed the sexual and the real estate revelations we'd been fighting and brooding about for almost a week. When he finished his review, he made a proposal.

"Suppose I forget what you did," he said, "and you forget what I did, and both of us swear we'll never do it again."

"Not good enough."

"Suppose I concede, in addition, that what I did was a lot worse than what you did."

"Not good enough."

"Suppose I add to the previous package a statement of deep remorse, accompanied by a genuine plea for forgiveness."

"Not good enough."

"Suppose I fall on my knees to the ground and kiss your fucking feet."

"Now you're talking."

Jake had to leave for the hospital. He didn't kiss my feet. But he did take my hand and plant a long kiss on the palm. "I'm sorry I slept with Sunny," he said. "But now you know all my secrets." He gazed deep into my eyes. "I hope I know yours."

In the months that have passed since March 18 it has never once entered my mind to confess to Jake about my three adulteries. And whenever my readers ask, "If he tells about his, should I tell about mine?" I always say no. Presumably, what's sauce for the gander ought to be sauce for the goose, but in sexual matters this simply isn't so. "So of course," I said to Carolyn on Saturday afternoon when she stopped off at my house to borrow a book, "when Jake made that crack about did he know all my secrets, I didn't say a word."

"Damn right you didn't," said Carolyn. "He'd never

have forgiven you. There's no such thing as equal-opportunity adultery."

"I guess. But, God, that seems so unfair," I complained. "It's so unfair that Jake could feel entitled to not forgive *me,* and yet he's just assuming that I'll forgive *him.*"

Carolyn shook out her shining blond hair and said sure it was unfair but that's how it was. "Because, when our husbands cheat on us, they only break our hearts," was her explanation. "When we cheat on our husbands, we break their balls."

Hearts, we both agreed, were far more resilient.

Carolyn left with her borrowed book, a novel by Rosellen Brown called *Before and After*, a novel that spoke to concerns that consumed my soul. How far—to what lengths—should a parent go on behalf of his or her child? the book inquired. I'd already answered that question for myself.

And so I sat down again and gave my full attention to implementing that answer. I needed to figure this out for once and for all. I needed to find a way, a safe and simple and foolproof way—a *final* way to murder Mr. Monti.

On Sunday I thought about gas—perhaps I could turn on the jets in Mr. Monti's kitchen and somehow persuade him to stick his head in the oven. Or perhaps I could get him to park in a shut-tight garage with the motor running in his car. On Monday I thought about plastic bags—I might, as he lay sleeping, ever so gently slip one over his face. On Monday I also recognized that—tidy and simple though they well might be—these were not the murder plans of a rational person.

You will note that in the head-in-the-oven plan as well as the plastic-bag-over-the-face plan, I presupposed access to Mr. Monti's condo. I presupposed access because, when Jeff had handed over the keys, he forgot about mine. And of course I had a key—what Jewish mother would not have a key to her child's condominium? In case of emergency. In case he's too sick with the flu to open the door. In case she wants to murder the next tenant.

With no murder plan in sight by the end of a sleepless Monday night, and with time running out, I made the desperate decision to let myself into the Watergate condo and look around. Somewhere on the premises there must be, had to be, would surely be found, some obvious opportunity for homicide. I was going to find it.

I needed to go unrecognized to the Watergate condominium. Once again I needed a disguise. Who should I be? I asked myself (I must admit I was getting into disguises). And after I had rejected dressing up as a policewoman or a nun (though I loved both outfits), I had my answer. Three stops—at a hardware store, a uniform store, a costume shop near Dupont Circle—and I was (not too expensively) equipped. I had just tried everything on in a gas station ladies' room to check out the effect when a woman walked in, gave a shriek, and fled out the door. My disguise was a triumph!

On Wednesday morning I put in a call to Mr. Monti's office and established that he was already there and that he was expected to be there all day. I then called the Watergate desk—this time I spoke as Mr. Monti's private secretary—and explained that Mr. Monti would be sending someone to work in his apartment. I then drove my car past the Watergate and parked it right next door, in the underground parking of the Kennedy Center. Finally I dialed Mr. Monti's Watergate telephone number to make absolutely certain that no one was home.

No one was home.

Just a bit before noon a man with a small black Chaplinesque mustache walked over to the Watergate desk. Dressed in heavy work boots, a white peaked cap, and blue-and-white-striped industrial coveralls, he explained in broken English that he was Mr. Garcia Fuentes, here to do a job in apartment 10 C. He carried a bucket of paint, a paintbrush, a ladder. He said Mr. Monti had given him the key.

"We're expecting you," said the man at the desk, pointing him—I mean me—to the service elevator.

And here I was, in Mr. Monti's—previously my poor son Jeff's—condominium.

And a very nice place it was—two bedrooms, two baths, eat-in kitchen, huge living room, handy dining area, and a wraparound terrace reached through sliding glass doors. Though Mr. Monti's furniture (which, I presume, he had rented) lacked the high-tech flash of Jeff's former decor, I observed, as I put down my ladder and other equipment and wandered slowly through the rooms, that he had already settled himself in. Indeed there were paintings hung on his walls and photographs set on his tables, photographs of him and his family. A studio portrait of Birdie. Snapshots of his daughters and his grandchildren. A photo with his parents and his twin brother. A photo of—

O, my God! I gasped, as I suddenly saw, on a shelf

in his bedroom, a picture that made the blood freeze in my veins. Smiling and festively dressed, there we were—Jeff and Wally, Jake and I—in a silver-plate frame, a brutal black X slashed across each of our faces. The photo had been taken on the night of April 4. The night of my birthday party. The night that was the beginning of the end.

Some people like to throw a big blast for the birthdays that mark their decades, but I never wanted a thirtieth or a fortieth. Yet, as you will recall, the year of my forty-sixth was deeply symbolic to me. Without telling Jake exactly why I wished to celebrate this particular birthday, I made it clear that was what I wished to do. Which was how come there were sixty-two guests at our house on Saturday evening, April 4, swearing that I was looking real good for my age.

In my tush-hugging midnight-blue crepe, in honor of which I had lost five pounds, I had to agree with my guests: I was looking real good.

I also was feeling good, though a little peculiar because beneath my roof that night were all the men with whom I had slept in my lifetime. Jake was there, of course, and so were Wally's future in-laws, Mr. and Mrs. Joseph Augustus Monti. Louis had been invited as my colleague at Harmony House and as my pal. And then, at the very last minute, I got a telephone call from Nora telling me that her husband had fallen ill and could she please bring Philip Eastlake.

At one point I watched as all four of my lovers converged upon the Design Cuisine buffet and attacked the sirloin filet and grilled baby vegetables. A question came to mind: Was I a star on a Donahue show called

"My Mom Is a Slut"? or was I Lady Brett in *The Sun Also Rises*? But then I told myself that I was allowed not to answer that question on my birthday.

Our guests took their plates to the tables for eight set up all over the house, filling the rooms with laughter and conversation. I heard Hillary . . . lowered the interest rates . . . CDF . . . CEO . . . NBC . . . great pedicure . . . they still don't get it . . . the Vineyard. I heard carjacking . . . cut the defense budget . . . Jack Nicholson always plays Jack Nicholson . . . EEOC. Philip, having lobbed a couple of soulful glances at me, was pontificating on the Middle East peace talks, while Marvin was demanding proof from the woman on his right that a sixty-five-dollar silk tie was really superior to the beauty he was wearing—"nine-fifty, two for eighteen bucks."

Josephine, with the camera that Wally had bought her and taught her to use, was shyly photographing the happy event, posing us four cute Kovners for a couple of family shots before we drifted off to our separate tables. When she held up the camera to shoot, however, her hands were shaking so hard that she couldn't, at first, even manage to push down the button. No matter what she does, that girl turns into a nervous wreck, I said to myself impatiently—and unfairly. For later that evening I learned that it wasn't photography that was making Josephine tremble.

Later, after our guests had finished their meal and crowded together in the dining room to watch me blow out the candles on my cake. Later, after Philip had bent to deposit a birthday kiss upon my cheek, murmuring a throaty "I want you. I need you." Later, after Louis had whispered, "Best-looking premenopausal woman I know," as he wrapped me in a warm but platonic embrace. Later, when people had started to leave, though several still remained, one of whom was Gilda, who happened to be not only our neighbor but our rabbi Emmanuel Silverman's assistant rabbi.

Wally, Jo, her parents, and I were standing off to one side, sipping coffee and chatting, when Gilda—bright-eyed and bouncy, broad in the beam and beaming broadly—presented herself to Joseph and Birdie Monti.

"I didn't want to go without meeting Josephine's mom and dad," she said, a warm rabbinical hand on Birdie's arm. "This is not the time and place for a whole big discussion—"

"That's right. It's not," my son interrupted.

"—but I'd just like to reassure you that conversion doesn't mean you lose your daughter."

All of us stared at Gilda. "What?" asked Mr. Monti. "What was that you said?"

"That just because your daughter's converting to Judaism," said Gilda, "doesn't mean she's any less your daughter."

Our stunned little group collectively gasped. Jo's cup and saucer dropped from her trembling fingers. Birdie Monti, bending to pick up the pieces, looked up to scan the clouded face of her mate.

"We were going to t-t-tell you all t-t-tonight," Jo stuttered, utterly undone. "It was Wally's b-b-b-birthday surprise for his mother."

"And mighty surprised I am," I said, with a desperate please-don't-blame-this-on-me heartfeltedness. "When"—I turned to Jo—"did you decide?"

"Decide? What did she decide?" Mr. Monti demanded in a voice that silenced all conversation at the party.

"I think the rabbi just told you, sir," said Wally.

"Let Josephine tell me," Mr. Monti replied.

Gilda, red in the face and gasping apologies for breaking the news too soon, began to back away from our shell-shocked group. "I guess I first ought to let you all discuss this among yourselves," she whispered nervously. "But please feel free to call if you have any questions. You know, like about the conversion classes"—Gilda kept backing away—"the Hebrew lessons, Leon Uris, the *mikva* . . ."

Gilda was out of there.

"Talk!" Mr. Monti bellowed to Jo. He cast a glowering glance around the room, where the guests who remained were maintaining a gape-mouthed silence. "Please," he said oleaginously, smiling his sharky smile; "don't let us interrupt your conversations."

When the room started buzzing again, Joseph Monti turned to Josephine. "Okay," he said to her, "you decided *what*?"

"To convert"—her voice could barely be heard—"to Judaism."

"And why? Why are you doing this to me?"

"She isn't doing it *to* you, sir," Wally interceded.

Mr. Monti ignored him and imperiously repeated his question to Jo.

Jo, who had just finished chewing off all her fingernails one by one, now directed her small, perfect teeth to her cuticles. "It's because of what you said about conversion," she replied in a hoarse whisper.

Her father threw up his hands. "What did I say?"

Josephine opened her mouth to explain. Not a word

emerged. She tried again. No words. Wally came to her rescue.

"You told us," he said, "that conversion was the kind of accommodation, perhaps even sacrifice, that people in love should be more than willing to make." He swept his expressive Mel Gibson eyes from Jo to Birdie to me. "That's what he said."

"And so beautifully put," I added in an effort at a constructive intervention.

Mr. Monti ignored me.

"You knew what I meant," he told Wally and Jo. "You both knew who was supposed to convert to what. I made"—his voice grew louder—"my wishes clear."

Wally and Jo said nothing. Mr. Monti, his voice still louder, pressed his point. "Did I or didn't I make my wishes clear?"

"Yes, Daddy," Jo whispered. "You did. But then we decided—"

Wally and Jo explained that they had decided that if Jo converted to Judaism, and if Wally joined her in her Jewish studies, it would be a truly meaningful experience. Plus good for the marriage, not to mention the soul. Even if it involved, on Josephine's part, some accommodation, even sacrifice.

Unfortunately, I was forced, though I could hardly bear to do it, to excuse myself and tear myself away. The rest of the guests were leaving and I was obliged to say some very long goodbyes. What was I missing? I wondered. What were they telling one another? Was Mr. Monti adjusting to the news? The occasional phrases that I could hear—like "mocking and disdaining me"—suggested that Mr. Monti wasn't adjusting.

Indeed, by the time I rejoined the group, the man was

taking exception most unattractively. Throughout the whole diatribe, Birdie Monti stood mute. "I'm sure it'll all work out," I warbled, hoping to soothe an acutely strained situation. But everyone's eyes were on Wally, who (in a sensitive, sweet, not one bit defiant way—that boy was *born* to be a social worker) had embarked upon a response to Mr. Monti.

"You know," he said, "Rabbi Gilda was wrong. You're going to lose your daughter."

"Losing isn't my thing," Joseph Monti replied.

"But you aren't going to lose her because she's converting," Wally persisted.

"I'm not losing—period," he replied.

"You're going to lose your daughter because she'll be leaving you," said Wally. "She'll be leaving you to cleave to another man."

"That's not," Mr. Monti said, "how it's done in our family."

For a couple of endless moments no one spoke.

"Daddy, please," Jo whispered, breaking the silence.

"Not now, Josephine," her father replied. "It's getting late. It's time for us to go home."

He turned to Wally and me and, once more mobilizing that sinister sharky smile, placed one arm on my shoulder, the other on Wally's. "A decision gets made," he said. "It can get unmade, especially when that decision is making certain people real unhappy."

"I'm sorry you're unhappy," Wally replied.

Mr. Monti sighed. "When I'm unhappy," he said, "everyone's unhappy."

He pressed on our shoulders, forcing the three of us into a tight, tense embrace.

"Talk to your son, Mrs. Kovner," he said to me softly.

"Listen to your mother," he said to my son.

"And in case you forgot what I mentioned before, I'll mention it again. Losing"—his dark eyes glistened—"isn't my thing."

Still Doing It

● *The Rest of October 28
and On into the Last Day of November*

12

•

A LEAN MEAN KILLING MACHINE

"*L*osing isn't my thing." The warning words rang in my ears as I stood in the condo this late October morning. "Losing isn't my thing." The brutally X-ed out photograph of us four Kovners wobbled back and forth in my trembling hand. I set it down and continued methodically casing the condominium, desperate to find a way to murder the man who intended to X out my whole family. The photo, to which I kept coming back for another horrified look, fortified my homicidal resolve.

I was staring at it, transfixed, determined to do this man in—but how? but how? but how?—when I noticed another photo on that same shelf. This one showed a tuxedoed Joseph and a white-gowned Birdie Monti coming out of church on their wedding day. It also—albeit circuitously—showed me the way to murder Mr. Monti.

For twenty-four years ago I had seen that same scene, that very same scene, of a bride and a groom coming out of the door of a church. *What* was it telling me? *Where* had I seen it? The answers danced into my head.

It was telling me about killing people dead, and I'd seen it in a French film—a sinister François Truffaut film—called *The Bride Wore Black*! *The Bride Wore Black*, starring Jeanne Moreau, whose husband was shot at the church on their wedding day. *The Bride Wore Black*, with Jeanne Moreau avenging herself on the men who had done the deed. *The Bride Wore Black*, where Jeanne Moreau, using five clever techniques, methodically murders the men who had murdered her husband.

I remembered every detail of every murder.

The second man was killed with a poisoned drink, a method which—remember?—I'd tried already.

The fifth was stabbed to death—too sordid for me.

And number four, a bit esoterically, was executed with a bow and arrow.

The first of Jeanne Moreau's victims, however, had perished when she pushed him off a terrace. This Watergate condo had a terrace too, a terrace with a crenellated concrete waist-high barrier on which a man could quite easily climb and from which he could quite easily jump—or be pushed.

Now it's true that I had initially abjured anything so directly hands-on violent. But with time running out and my dear Wally's life in danger, I was starting to think a bit less fastidiously. Like Jeanne Moreau, I would have to consider a fatal shove from the terrace a definite option. A definite option. But not, let's face it, my favorite.

My favorite option and clearly—as I checked out the condo, found what I wanted, and ran through my plan a few times—the best way to go was the way Jeanne Moreau had murdered her third victim.

Yes, that was the way to go. It was simple and certain, involved no blood, and was considerably less violent than shoves off terraces.

Now that I knew what to do, it was time to get the hell out of Mr. Monti's apartment. But Mr. Garcia Fuentes would be back.

Before I left, I paused to review my Garcia Fuentes disguise in the living-room mirror, smoothing my mustache and tucking my hair into my cap. I slightly loosened my coverall straps so no hint of a bosom marred my manly form. It struck me, as I studied myself, that I looked like Charlie Chaplin when he played a factory worker in *Modern Times*. I looked like Charlie Chaplin, but when I practiced speaking aloud, I was Charlie being dubbed with a—well, it's difficult to characterize this accent.

"I'm a come-a feex-a you kitchen, mon," I said to the reflection in the mirror. "The management send me up here. I'm a-gonna to paint you cabinets a leetle beet."

"In that case I'm glad I caught you," said a darkly familiar voice from the front hall. "There's a couple of other places that need some patching."

A year ago, in the midst of my my-life-is-about-to-be-two-thirds-over pre-birthday crisis, I was in New York having lunch with my sister Rose. "Don't you ever worry," I asked when we got to the key lime pie (one slice; two forks), "about dying?"

Rosalie put down her fork. "If that's what we're talking about at lunch, then you are the one who is picking up this check."

"Fair enough," I said. "So tell me—do you?"

"No," answered Rose. "And now can we change the subject?"

"But, Rose," I persisted, "all of the women on Mom's side of the family died at the fairly young age of sixty-nine. Which means—and honey, I don't intend in any way to upset you—that you might have only ten and a half years left."

Rosalie laughed a mirthless laugh. "I canceled an appointment with my chiropodist. I was going to have an ingrown toenail removed. I canceled the appointment because I—hah!—thought that lunch with you would be more fun."

"Rose," I beseeched my sister, "answer the question."

Rose leaned back in her chair and said, "Honey, I don't intend in any way to upset you. But you look exactly like Mom, so I guess you take after her side of the family, genetically speaking. And I look like all of Dad's sisters, especially Pearl." She sipped her Earl Grey tea. "And since Aunt Pearl is almost ready to get birthday greetings from Willard Scott on the *Today* show, I'll start worrying about death when I'm around ninety."

I nodded in silence at her flawless logic. Then I picked up my fork and attacked the key lime pie. "Oh, well," I said when I'd finished every morsel. "I still have twenty-three years and four months left."

"No," Rose said. "You'll live longer than that. You'll figure something out. Here"—she called to our waitress—"I'll take that check." She cast me a comforting smile. "I'm sure you'll figure something out. You may have bad genes but, Bren, you're so resourceful."

You're so resourceful, I told myself, when I heard Mr. Monti's voice in the front hall.

Pressing my mustache firmly in place and pulling my cap down low, I resourcefully rushed to the kitchen and started painting.

"I no expecta you home, mon," I said, when Mr. Monti joined me in the kitchen and poured himself an eight-ounce glass of milk.

"Yeah, well, my gut started acting up. The docs think I'm getting an ulcer. I had to cancel the rest of my day and come home." He took off his glasses, rubbed his eyes, and stared broodingly into his milk. "Did I say home? Hey, that's a laugh. *This* place isn't home. My wife took my home and left me with this ulcer."

I put down my brush, raised my eyes toward the heavens, and waggled my mustache up and down sympathetically. "Ai, women," I said. "They treat us vary bahd."

(I won't do the accent anymore, but imagine, please, an Italian Desi Arnaz, with just a smidge of West Indian thrown in.)

Joseph Monti waved his hand. "Keep painting," he said. "Keep painting. For eighteen bucks an hour or whatever you guys are raking in these days, you can paint and have a discussion at the same time."

I dipped my brush in the paint and resumed the painting.

Mr. Monti, sipping his milk with obvious distaste, announced, "Here's my philosophy of life. You work to get what you want. And when you get what you want, you keep it. Whatever you have to do"—he slapped his hand down hard on the table—"you do to keep it."

"*Absolutamente,*" I said, and kept painting.

"And if your enemy takes it from you," Mr. Monti

continued, "you squash him like a bug and then you tear out his liver and feed it to the gizzards."

I decided I wouldn't point out that the word he wanted was *buzzards*, not *gizzards*. Nor did I plan to ask him if bugs had livers. *"Positivamente,"* I replied to his remarks, and kept painting.

Mr. Monti stared at some vision beyond the kitchen walls, some vision of vengeance too monstrous for me to imagine. "Soon," he rasped. "Without any mercy. I will be striking soon."

I shuddered silently. And I kept painting.

Two hours later Joseph Monti was still at the kitchen table, complaining about his life and cursing his enemies. I had finished painting two kitchen walls. I'd also tried to leave several times—"You're sick. I come back later. I come back tomorrow"—but Mr. Monti insisted that I remain. He insisted that I remain and keep on painting while he kept muttering things like "She threw me out of the house." And "How could this happen to me?" And, most unnervingly, "I'll tear out his liver."

Not if I can stop you, I thought. But first I needed a hammer and nails and some masking tape. Without them, I couldn't do him in that day. Besides, with my muscles aching—throbbing and burning and twitching and aching—from my unexpected workout with the walls, I didn't have the strength to commit a murder.

"No more paint!" I finally—thank God!—had an exit line that Mr. Monti would buy. "I go get more and come back early tomorrow."

"Be here before I leave for work," Mr. Monti told me. "I'll show you these other places I want you to patch."

"Absolutamente," I said. "I be here before you leave. *Absoluta-* and *positivamente."*

During the afternoon I went to the store and purchased another can of white semigloss, though I had no intention of doing any more painting. I did, however, expect to make full fatal use of my other purchases: the roll of tape, the hammer, and the nails. But my plan to return in the early A.M. and do to Mr. Monti what Jeanne Moreau had done to victim three was thwarted— temporarily—by circumstances beyond even my control.

Groans awoke me at five that morning, terrible kicked-in-the-stomach gasping groans, oh-god-oh-help-me groans that came from the room above my head—from Wally's room. (Needless to say, Jake snored at my side, undisturbed.) I flew up the stairs, convinced that Joseph Monti had somehow gotten to my boy, though the green letters on the panel of our security system still read "all secure." When I reached the third floor I found no suggestion that anyone had breached our electronic fortress. (I didn't even find Jeff, who was out for the night with, I figured, another unsuitable babe.) Wally was up there alone. He was writhing and thrashing on his bed. His face was soaked with sweat and contorted with pain.

"Mom," he moaned, "I'm hurting so bad. You've got to do something, Mom. You've got to do something."

I put my hand on his forehead. It was on fire.

"Jake," I roared in a voice that I had cultivated for major domestic emergencies, a voice that could waken the dead—and sleeping mates. Faster than the speed of light, my husband the doctor arrived at Wally's bedside.

One phone call and two minutes later, the three of

us—Jake and Wally and I—were on our way in Jake's Volvo to Sibley Hospital. And at 9 A.M., after whispering, "I guess maybe Jo should know about this," Wally had an emergency appendectomy.

While Wally was having surgery and Jake rushed off to Children's to perform some urgent surgery of his own, I went to a phone booth and made a number of calls. To Josephine, as Wally had requested. To Jeff, except he had not, as yet, returned home. To Dwayne's mother, who, upon hearing that Wally wouldn't be seeing his clients for a while, took full responsibility for his appendix. And to Mr. Monti's office, where I explained to his secretary that though Mr. Fuentes had not showed up today, he would be at the condo early on Friday morning. Indeed, though I was aware that it might be hard to get away, I *had* to be at the condo on Friday morning. Halloween, after all, was Saturday.

Jo arrived at Sibley while Wally was still in the O.R. Birdie, looking ten years younger, was with her. "Family should stick together," she said, explaining her presence in the visitors' lounge. "Your boy is a lovely boy, and I'll count him as family until Jo returns his ring."

Josephine bit her lip and wandered off to stare out a window. Birdie joined me on the tan vinyl bench. "I guess with how mean my husband's been about the kids' engagement, you wouldn't mind so much if she broke it off."

Mean? I said to myself. She's calling him "mean"? How about "vicious," "evil," "homicidal"? Aloud I murmured mildly, "We all love Josephine. But I guess right now she's deep into self-discovery."

Birdie Monti laughed. "Self-discovery, yes! I left Joseph over Josephine's self-discovery."

Even though Birdie Monti was about to become a widow, I felt strangely compelled to set the record straight. "I honestly think," I said, "that your husband never did anything sexually inappropriate. I mean"—I hastened to add—"as far as Jo or your other daughters are concerned."

Birdie nodded. "We know that now. At first we were kind of confused. Until the doctor explained to Jo, and Jo explained to me, that the problem"—Birdie paused, then dived in—"was not her father's unconscious incestuous yearnings, which, Dr. X says, even nice people have. She said that the problem was his larger pathology."

My jaw dropped as Birdie swam briskly through these dark psychological waters. I cleared my throat and inquired, "Larger pathology?"

"That's right," said Birdie calmly. "His narcissistic need for control and domination."

I couldn't, I thought, have put it better myself.

Wally's green-suited surgeon came out to the lounge to tell us that everything had gone well and that Wally was now being monitored in the recovery room. "Strong lad. No complications. He can go home on Saturday morning. And with this laser surgery, he'll be back in business within a week to ten days."

Birdie hugged me hard. "Oh, Brenda," she said, "I'm so happy that Wally's okay. Thank God."

Hugging her in return, I prayed to To Whom It May Concern that this lovely lady would also be okay.

For despite (or because of) the fact that I was her husband's former lover and future murderess, I was feeling responsible for Birdie. And despite her stellar performance that September night at AFGO, I still worried about how well she would do on her own. But as we continued talking together that morning at Sibley Hospital, I realized that my concerns were quite misplaced. Her contentment, her composure, and her quiet self-possession made Gloria Steinem look like a co-dependent.

"So," I said to her, deeply relieved that I wouldn't have her unhappiness on my conscience, "I guess you're not planning to get back together again."

"Planning to get back together again? Oh, I can live without him. I can live without him very well." She smiled somewhat abashedly. "Except—and you know, they never talked about this at AFGO—I sometimes worry that Joseph can't live without *me*."

Birdie stood up to leave, patting her thick dark hair into place with one well-jeweled hand. She walked to the window and said goodbye to Jo. Then, bending to peck my cheek, she whispered, "I want to tell you something before I go. I don't think it's right that Joseph took Jeff's condominium."

"It may not be right, but it's legal," I said. "A contract is a contract. And Jeff signed over his life to Monti Enterprises."

Birdie tucked her cream silk blouse into her slim boot-length skirt. When had she attained that firm, flat stomach? "Yes," she said, "a contract is a contract. But what is Monti Enterprises? That's what the lawyers are trying to figure out."

Soon after Birdie left, Jo and I were told that Wally was out of the recovery room. We fluttered around his bed solicitously. I did not in the slightest resent it that when Wally fully focused on our presence he was far more thrilled to see Josephine than to see me.

While Wally and Jo held hands, I tactfully gazed out the wall-wide window at the autumn-burnished trees in their final glory. While tactfully gazing, I tactfully eavesdropped, too, but—mindful of my presence—the troubled lovers exchanged the most irritating inanities.

"I know that it means a lot to him that you're here," I said to Jo, when weary Wally wafted off to sleep.

"I'm glad to be here," she said, "but I wouldn't want him to misunderstand. I think we really need this trial separation."

I assured Jo that my son wouldn't use his operation to make undue demands upon her. I, however, wished to make one small request. Could she please come to the hospital and keep him company tomorrow morning? I had some pressing business—some extremely pressing business—to attend to.

What kind of person asks the daughter of someone she plans to murder to give her a hand so she will be free to murder him? I answer, without apology, "A mother person." Indeed, I'd like to quote a letter I got a few years ago, signed, "Memphis Mom":

DEAR BRENDA:
    Some four-year-old creep has been mocking my little William, who is a stutterer. I told this creep he better cut it out. When he wouldn't cut it out, I twisted his arm behind his back and told him next time he mocked William, I'd break the arm. I also tracked down the car that had deliberately cut me off though the driver could plainly see that William was

with me. I tracked down that car and threw a rock at the windshield and what I've been wondering is, if a mother doesn't protect her child, who will?

"Memphis Mom" had inspired me to write a whole column on mother love, which I called (all exceptions granted) the most primitive, unconditional love in the world. Forget about Heathcliff and Cathy. Forget about Romeo and Juliet, I wrote. If you're looking for love that a person will sacrifice everything for, lie for, steal for, cheat for, die for, kill for, look no further than your average mother.

I noted in my column—and decided that it would be best to end it right there—that, fortunately for all of us, most mothers aren't called on to kill for their children.

I didn't say what we ought to do if we are.

But as "Memphis Mom" so eloquently put it, if a mother doesn't protect her child, who will?

On Friday morning, I drove through drizzle and fog to Rock Creek Park and, in a deserted picnic area, again turned into Mr. Garcia Fuentes. I looked like Charlie Chaplin and spoke like an Italo-West Indian Desi Arnaz, but as I entered the Watergate condominium, I was strictly Arnold Schwarzenegger in *The Terminator*.

Mr. Monti stood at the door. I looked at his shabby shoes instead of his face. I didn't want to see a human being. I only wanted to do what I'd come to do without further ado. I wanted to be a lean mean killing machine.

Okay, I commanded myself. Okay, let's do it.

"Excuse me," I interrupted when Mr. Monti began to talk. "There's something I got to show you in the kitchen." I gestured for him to follow me into the room.

"The other day, before I leave, I was looking inside"—I pointed to it—"that broom closet. I find something strange in the back, behind the broom. Something vary strange, and maybe important."

I opened the door of the closet, crouched down, and peered into the back. I shook my head with convincing perplexity. "Please," I told Mr. Monti when I was standing up again. "I don't think I should touch it. You go see." And when he knelt down in the back of the closet to see what I'd said I'd seen, I slammed the closet door and quickly wedged a kitchen chair under the door handle.

(If you remember *The Bride Wore Black*, you'll know that I added my own special variations to the suffocate-him-in-the-closet plan. Nevertheless, Jeanne Moreau deserves full credit for the fundamental concept.)

"What the hell's going on!" Mr. Monti shouted.

I decided not to answer. I turned on the faucets and dishwasher instead, hoping the running water would mute the loud and extremely reproachful things he said as—just in case the chair didn't hold—I methodically nailed the door shut with my hammer.

Mr. Monti banged on the door and screamed more unpleasant things. I didn't wish to hear what he had to say. I turned on the exhaust fan. I turned on—top volume—the little TV on the counter. I turned on the water faucets the rest of the way. I hardened my heart against him, and kept hammering.

Mr. Monti was pleading now. "You've got to let me out. There's hardly any air. It's hard to breathe."

And it will be getting harder, I thought, as I reached in my pocket and whipped out my roll of masking tape.

Mr. Monti was bargaining now. "You want money?

I'll give you money. Tell me how much you want and I'll get it for you."

I re-hardened my heart against him, as I was fiercely determined to do, and started to tape up the cracks where the air came through, between the closet door and the door frame.

Mr. Monti was weeping now. "This just doesn't make any sense. This just doesn't make any sense at all," he said. "I fly down here to visit my little brother. And bing, bang, boom, the next thing I know, I'm dead."

Visit his little brother? I put down the masking tape.

After which I turned off the faucets, the dishwasher, and the exhaust fan. After which I turned off the little TV. "Who," I asked, remembering that I should speak not like me but like Mr. Garcia Fuentes. "Who, *por favor,* is your little brother?"

"Joseph," whispered the voice inside the closet. "We're twins but he was born eight minutes later."

"So you are—?" I asked, but of course I knew the answer.

"Vincent Theodore Monti," he said, "but please call me Teddy."

Do I need to tell you that this was very very—I mean, extremely—upsetting news?

Do I need to tell you how badly this sort of thing can shake one's confidence in oneself?

Do I need to tell you again that, as Rosalie mentioned last year at lunch, I happen to be a really resourceful person?

Before I got resourceful, however, I first got one of my dizzy spells. The kitchen twirled like a merry-go-round run amok. I slid down onto the floor, bent my head, and listened to Teddy Monti as I waited for the return of my equilibrium.

Teddy explained, through the door, that he had flown down the previous evening to visit "Joey," who was having "some family problems" and feeling "depressed." Joey had left for a business meeting in the early A.M. and had asked him to show me where to patch up the paint. "He mentioned that you were an excellent painter. However," Teddy said gloomily, "he forgot to mention that you were also a killer."

"A killer?" I laughed most merrily, my dizzy spell done, my resources fully mobilized. "A killer? What kind of gringo talk is that? You got some kind of problem here?" I sounded slightly hurt. "You can't take a joke?"

I then told Teddy that where I came from—I didn't mention where—it was considered hysterically funny to shove a person into a closet and nail it shut. If you wanted to go for the big guffaws, I said, you added the masking tape, but that was optional.

"This is a really sick—" Teddy started expressing his heartfelt feelings, but apparently realized that wasn't the shrewdest move.

"Yeah, yeah, it's a famous custom," I told him, adding, with a menacing hint of annoyance, "You never heard of it?"

Picking up on my cue, Teddy murmured that now that I'd jogged his memory, he was starting to recall that he had indeed heard of it. He furthermore agreed that it was—ha, ha, hee, hee, hee—hysterically funny. "So when," he casually asked me, in between chuckles, "do you jokers let your victims out of the closet?"

I explained that I was about to remove the masking

tape from the cracks and pull out all the nails with the claw of my hammer. "But when I remove the chair," I said, "you must stay in the closet until you count up to three thousand, or else I have to shove you back in again."

Teddy swore on all he held dear that he'd stay in the closet until he reached three thousand.

I was out the condo door by the count of three.

The near-murder of the wrong Monti gave me much food for thought, but not immediately. Immediately, I had to go relieve Jo at Wally's bedside and also come up with another murder plan fast. I felt frenzied. I felt frantic. Halloween was on its way. I now had less than a day to save my son. And having seen *Godfather* one, I knew that killers could get to their victims even in hospitals. I also knew that when Teddy told his brother about what Garcia Fuentes had done, it wouldn't be easy to, say, return to the condo and push Joseph Monti off his terrace. (Which was, at the moment, my only backup plan.)

Before I went to the hospital, I stopped off at the house. I wanted to bring some soup to Wally for lunch. I also wanted to check the mail, our answering machine, and our new fax.

There was nothing of interest in the mail. Nothing on our answering machine. Our fax had nothing whatsoever, too. But just as I started to leave, I heard that special little ring that announces that a fax is coming through.

I walked back to the machine. I waited, filled with a feeling of dread. But when the message arrived, there was good news and bad news:

FORGET HALLOWEEN. NO TRICK AND NO TREAT.
THANKSGIVING THE TURKEY TURNS INTO DEAD MEAT.

The way I figured, this message contained not only a threat but a stay of execution.

Early on Halloween morning, thrilled that I didn't have to kill anybody that day, I quietly removed my A WOMAN'S PLACE IS IN THE HOUSE T-shirt/nightshirt and put on a long string of pearls and one blue lace garter. I then awakened Jake to introduce him to my G-spot and other adulterously acquired lore.

"This doesn't mean," I said later, as we lay in a sweatily satisfied embrace, "that I forgive you."

"Nor does it mean," Jake replied, as he gently stroked the side of my face, "that I can be happy living with a control freak."

"A charming phrase!"

"An even more charming character trait!"

"Not nearly as charming as screwing Sunny Voight!"

"So what are we doing?" Jake sighed. "Are we going to go a few more rounds on this? Let me know so I can put on my gloves."

I started to lob one back. (Yes, I am aware that I'm mixing metaphors.) I shut my mouth and searched my heart instead, where feelings of the fiercest love, and also the fiercest hate, mingled ambivalently.

I searched my heart. And then I made my move.

I sat myself on Jake's belly, facing away from him. I slipped my hands under his legs, and raised his knees. Once they were fully bent, I, holding on to his knee-caps, slid just slightly southward.

"Forget about the gloves," I said as I settled my Yoni

upon his Precious Scepter. "Have you ever heard of the Turtle Dove Embracing Two Eucalyptus Trees position?"

I could thus, with some sincerity, tell Philip—when he phoned me later that day—that I had been thinking of him. He said I'd been very much on his mind as well, that indeed he'd been going through hell as he searched for some graceful way to tell me that he was seeing someone.

"I feared that the news would upset you," he said.

"No, not the tiniest bit. Not the teeniest, tiniest little bit. Not even," I continued, "for a minute, a second, a micro-mini-second."

Okay, I was wrong.

Look, I didn't feel upset when he said she was beautiful, brilliant, fiery, plus principled and dedicated, plus very young—but "wise beyond her years."

Nor did I feel upset when he said that this paragon had "turned his life around."

I didn't feel upset until he told me he had found her while doing a TV program in Northern Ireland. And that, though she lived in Belfast, she was American. And that—this shouldn't surprise you—her name was Adrienne.

13
•

AND THEN
THERE WERE NONE

*P*hilip had wished to notify me about the new love of
his life because we would all be seeing each other on
Sunday, when the Cranes—she a lifelong Republican
and he a ditto Democrat—were throwing one of their
big bipartisan bashes. Nobody understands how Drew
and Blake Crane have stayed married for almost thirty
years when on every political candidate and every political issue they publicly and passionately disagree. Nevertheless they have been together since 1964, when her
Goldwater Buick sideswiped his Johnson VW. And
once a year they pay back a great many social obligations by filling up their house with wall-to-wall (and
sometimes truly off-the-wall) people.

The food is always terrible, but that's okay with me.
I think of the Cranes as a diet opportunity.

That night I not only watched my weight, I also
watched Philip and back-from-Belfast Adrienne. He
was fawning and drooling all over her. She was treating
his adoration with cool disdain. My (admittedly child-
ish) annoyance about their relationship began to fade,
however, when I heard Philip say, "May I bring you a

fruit tart, *querida*?" and she said, "Philip, can it with the *queridas*," and he, having brought her the fruit tart, said, "It is always a pleasure to serve you," and she, having taken the fruit tart, said, "But it doesn't make up for centuries of oppression." I figured that if Philip had chosen to move from seasoned me to PC Adrienne, the man was going to get what he deserved.

I also decided that I deserved to be spared any further discussions with right-wing Republicans, one of whom seemed to be advocating death by lethal injection for welfare cheats.

It was time to go home.

The next morning, as I considered—and rejected— lethally injecting Mr. Monti, another fax message warned that the end was near:

NO MORE DELAY

DEATH'S ON ITS WAY

THANKSGIVING IS EXECUTION DAY

THANKSGIVING DAY THE TURKEY TURNS INTO DEAD MEAT

I realized that I was reading an ultimatum.

I needed a murder plan, and I needed it soon.

I went to Potomac Video and rented *And Then There Were None*, where many people are killed—one by one—on an island. No useful ideas.

During the second week of November, Wally returned to school, having made a fast and full recovery. He also seemed to be making his peace with Josephine's "trial separation," especially since—to his thrilled surprise— she actually was attending conversion classes.

As Jo explained it to Wally in one of their occasional phone conversations, all she was really doing was keeping her options open. "I could convert and marry you," Wally told me she told him. "I also could *not* convert, and still marry you. I also," she continued, "could neither marry you nor convert. And I also could even convert and still *not* marry you."

She did, however, warn Wally that if she both converted and married him, he'd damn well better know about Tu B'Shevat and Tisha B'Av, not to mention Brith Milah and Pidyon Haben.

"I think it's looking good," said Wally who—with no Jo to turn to—found himself turning back to his faithful ma. "And I think I'm going to look up Tisha B'Av."

I went to Potomac Video and rented *Monsieur Verdoux*, where many wives are killed by Charlie Chaplin. No useful ideas.

On Wednesday, a gray and drizzly day, I walked over to Carolyn's house for some biking and bitching, beginning with my complaints about Jeff as we pedaled side by side in her sumptuous bedroom.

"Everyone else in our family," I said, "feels some duty to mankind. But Jeff's always been this wheeling-dealing hedonist." I wiped my brow with the back of my hand. "I was hoping these real estate problems of his would have prompted some agonizing reappraisal. But he's still dating women with hair twice as long as their skirts. And he changes the subject whenever I bring up the Peace Corps."

Carolyn laughed indulgently. "I've always loved your

Jeff. But he always gets into trouble. And he never agonizingly reappraises."

"Then it's time for him to start," I said. "I wish he were more like—"

"Wally. And that," said Carolyn, puffing hard, "is the problem. Wally's already the designated saint in the Kovner family. Why would Jeff even try to compete with that?"

The timers dinged, releasing the two of us, sweating and wheezing, from our metal steeds. "Anyway," I said, "he's not sitting still for advice from me. And Jake, well, you know Jake. He says our kids aren't kids anymore and we have to let them make their own mistakes."

Having mentioned Jake, I moved on to assorted complaints about him, while Carolyn showered and I emeryboarded my nails. "He's expecting me to forgive and forget and to keep on working on being less controlling. I'm the one who's supposed to do all the changing. But what exactly do I get in return?"

"Love and sex and companionship," said Carolyn, shouting through the stall-shower door. "And he's basically one of the good guys. And, you'll never meet anyone else who owns a gorilla suit." She laughed. "So he's still having trouble finding your G-spot. Hey, nobody's perfect."

Carolyn and I have always been staggeringly frank about our sex lives, frank in a way that men—I'm convinced—can't even begin to imagine that women can be. But then Carolyn and I have always been staggeringly frank about virtually everything. Everything, that is, with one recent exception.

For although I had told her plenty about the Kovner

difficulties with Mr. Monti, I had never let her know that I believed he was homicidal or that I intended to be homicidal first. Supportive though she could be, I knew she'd undoubtedly try to stop me, as she always tried to stop me whenever I planned to do something that she deemed deeply dumb.

"We're trying to make up," I said, "but every time things improve, I get to brooding about that night with Sunny." I closed my eyes and sighed. "I mean, I honestly don't know if I'll ever get over it."

Pearly Carolyn stepped from the shower, wrapped herself in a towel, and cleared her throat to prepare for a pronouncement.

"And here's what I think, Brenda," she said, her blue eyes opened wide. "Get over it."

"Get over it?"

"Yes, like right away." Carolyn shook out her glorious hair. "Look, you're the one who kept telling me that you only had twenty-three—now it's fewer—years left. You don't have any time to waste. So, get over it."

I went to Potomac Video and rented *Kind Hearts and Coronets*, where Alec Guinness dies many unnatural deaths. No useful ideas.

On Thursday, November 12, I got a call from Birdie Monti.

"I met with Joseph last night," she said. "We had an interesting talk."

"Anything you'd like to share with me?"

"Not at the moment," she said. "Except I heard about all those real estate tricks and also about Jake's two malpractice suits. And I'm calling to apologize for the not-nice things that Joseph has done to your family."

Not-nice things, I said to myself. What about vicious? What about reprehensible? Aloud I merely inquired, "Is your husband joining you in this apology?"

"Not at the moment," she said. "but we'll be having another interesting talk real soon."

I went to Potomac Video and, just to relax, I rented *Mary Poppins*.

That weekend Jo told Wally that among the options she was keeping open were becoming a rabbi, becoming a psychotherapist, becoming a lesbian, and/or applying to medical school. She said she was calling to tell him all this so he wouldn't be taken aback if he heard that she was dating Vanessa Pincus.

Wally, quite agitated, brought me this news on Sunday morning, while I was setting the table for a dinner party we were throwing next Friday. (As I often tell my readers, one certain way of making a dinner party go smoothly is to do as much as you can well in advance.) "I'm worried about that shrink," Wally said, as he helpfully placed two forks on each cream-colored napkin. "I think she needs to set some limits with Josephine."

"Maybe," I said carefully, laying a cream-and-green plate beside each napkin, "Josephine needs to learn to set her own limits."

Wally, stormy-eyed, threw down the rest of the forks. "You don't think she's overdoing it with these options of hers?"

"She probably is," I told him. "But she'll calm down. And when she decides who she wants to be and what she wants to do, she's going to feel that they're *her* decisions—not yours and not her father's and not her psychiatrist's."

"And I'm just supposed to wait around and hope she decides on me, not Vanessa Pincus?"

"Don't think of yourself as waiting around," I told him. "Try to think of yourself as poised for action. I mean, things happen. Jo could hit a rough patch, a disappointment, a loss—even a serious loss. And then you'll be there, coming through for her, providing support and comfort in her grief."

Wally gave me a baffled glance. "Her grief? What kind of grief?"

"I haven't any idea," I replied, stepping back to admire my gorgeous table. "But it wouldn't hurt a bit to be poised for action."

I wasn't telling the truth when I told Wally I had no idea. I had two ideas. My first idea was that Jo would turn to Wally in her grief when she lost her father. My second idea—which had come to me as the result of a major new insight into myself—was how to arrange for Jo to lose her father.

The next day, in addition to making my soup for Friday night and writing a column entitled POISED FOR ACTION, I swung into action on my murder plan. I rented a P.O. box. I purchased a dowdy tweed suit and a dowdy brown hat and a dowdy brown wig that curled just below my ears in one of the less felicitous styles of the 1940s. Dressed in my matronly duds, I hailed a cab, went off to Jeff's block of buildings in Anacostia, and stopped at the one I had visited back in September. There I reached into my purse, where I had placed a note and two thumbtacks, and tacked up my note on the badly splintered front door.

"Dear Billy or Elton Jr.," the note said. "Your talents are sought for a short-term, high-paying job. A.S.A.P. Time is of the essence. If you are interested, write immediately to"—here I provided my P.O. box information—"with the day and the hour you can meet me at"—here I named the location—"to work out our business arrangements." I read my note over and added a P.S. "You won't know who I am, but fear not, I will know you." Then I added a P.P.S.: "Dress discreetly."

That evening I borrowed ten thousand dollars from Carolyn (for such a small sum she does not have to ask her trustees), making up a fib about how I needed it to pay off one of Jeff's debts. I certainly couldn't tell her that I needed it in order to hire a hit man.

I know what you're saying. You're saying, "This woman has lost it." I recognize how you could see it that way. For, tossing caution to the winds, I was planning to violate my cardinal rule: Never use an accomplice in a murder.

Billy and Elton Jr.? What was I, crazy?

No, not exactly.

I wasn't crazy because I'd decided I couldn't do this alone—that I'd never kill Joseph Monti without assistance. This astonishing conclusion flowed from the aforementioned major new insight into myself. I had been watching *Mary Poppins* when I suddenly understood that my failure—three times!—to murder Mr. Monti was due not to ineptitude but to some kind of stubborn psychological block. Hadn't I pulled that radio plug from the socket—a Freudian slip—when I'd tried to electrocute him in the tub? Hadn't I failed to poison him by means of a *strawberry* Daiquiri because I unconsciously knew (he had pushed them aside when he ate my lemon sorbet back in August) that he didn't eat strawberries? And hadn't I *deliberately*—though unaware I was doing so—wound up stuffing the wrong Monti twin in the closet? I mean surely, when I had looked at my victim's feet instead of his face, I had seen that he was wearing something that Joseph Monti would never wear—shoddy shoes!

In other words, while my mind was screaming, "Kill the s.o.b.," my superego was whispering, "Murder is wrong." In other words, I unconsciously was sabotaging my efforts to kill Mr. Monti.

And so I wasn't crazy to seek an accomplice to help me outwit my superego. Nor was I crazy to seek Elton Jr. and Billy. Look, I desperately needed a hit man, and how many people with hit man potential does a woman like me get to meet in the course of her life? It struck me that my September hallway encounter with these two bad dudes was, if not preordained, a stroke of good fortune.

Nor—final point—was I taking the major risks that most people take when they use an accomplice. I wasn't risking blackmail or betrayal. Why? Because my accomplices were never going to know that I was me.

On Wednesday I went to my P.O. box and found a letter from Elton Jr. *and* Billy. Having forgiven each other for past transgressions, they were happily working together once again. They wanted to hear my proposal and would meet me where I requested—on Thursday, November 19, at 10 A.M.

On Thursday, at 10 A.M., Prudence Gump was waiting for them.

Our meeting place was Union Station, surely one of
the world's great railroad stations, a grand historic pile
that had gone from beauty to schlump to ravishingly
renovated, a building I always do the honor of pausing
to admire—even on my way to confer with hit men. I
love its combination of columned majesty and mall, its
stately halls and bustling buy-me shops, its arching ceilings and movie theaters and sleepers to Chicago, its
statues and fountains and restaurants galore. I've had
dinner there. I've bought blouses there. I've seen a couple of movies there. I've taken Metroliners from there
to New York. I once met Rosalie there—she was coming to visit for the weekend—and we got into such a
fight before we even left the station that she turned right
around and took the next train home. A few times a
year I lunch there with Nan, who works for a senator
known as The Fool on the Hill, and decide what she can
do to help him along. The fact that Union Station is so
versatile, vast, and anonymous, plus so easy to get to by
Metro from Cleveland Park, made it, in my opinion, the
ideal meeting place at which to plan a murder.

And there, as instructed, were Billy and Elton Jr.—in
pinstriped suits! with attaché cases!—browsing among
the hats at The Proper Topper, and quick to follow me,
when I had identified myself, to one of the station's less
populated locations.

With my dowdy duds, droopy hair, and splendid
upper-class British accent, I made a truly persuasive
Prudence Gump, briskly describing to an attentive Billy
and Elton Jr. the kind of high-paying job I had in mind
for them.

"So how come," Elton Jr. inquired when I had finished my spiel, "you know about us?"

"Yeah, right," said Billy. "Like, who told you our names?"

"I say, that's a jolly good question," I said. "You chaps are veddy clevah. It's immeedjitly cleah that you chaps are too clevah by hahff. I'm teddibly pleased to be working with a criminal element of such high caliber."

(I won't belabor the point, but I hope you're hearing Queen Elizabeth and Julie Andrews, with just a little Winston Churchill thrown in.)

"However," I continued, "the rule of Her Majesty's Secret Service is to never identify another agent."

"You're doing a job for Her Majesty's Secret Service?" Billy inquired.

"Not this time," I answered. "This is personal. It's a seamy private matter involving financial as well as sexual indignities."

Billy nodded knowingly. "He dissed you."

"Dissed you is American," Elton Jr. translated, "for showing you some real bad disrespect."

"Perhaps," I stiffly replied, "you could put it like that."

"He dissed you," Billy said, "so you want us to kill him?"

"Five thousand dollars for each of you. Half in advance. Half upon completion."

"I like it," said Elton Jr.

"Hold it," said Billy.

He drew Elton Jr. aside for a *sotto voce* conversation which, because of my finely honed eavesdropping skills, I could hear while appearing tweedily unconcerned.

"Something funny here," Billy told Elton Jr.

"What's so funny?" Elton Jr. inquired.

"Me or you I can understand—we get dissed, we smoke the mother. But a la-di-da English broad like that, she gets dissed, she cries in her crumpets. Am I right?"

"Used to be right," Elton Jr. replied. "But you're not reading the papers. All the morals in England, they have *de*clined. The Queen's son Charles—the heir—he's fooled around. Her horsy daughter Anne—she's fooled around. And both her daughters-in-law—that Princess Di and that Fergie of York—they've fooled around."

"Fooled around?"

"Yeah, fooled around. You're not supposed to say fuck when it's the royal family. Anyway," Elton Jr. continued, "if that could happen right up there in the palace, this English broad and the common people gonna be doing all kinds of crazy shit."

It was clear from Billy's "uh-huh, uh-huh" that this lecture on the demise of British morality had been persuasive. When they rejoined me, both were prepared to go over the details of my murder plan. Everything could be settled, I said, except for deciding the night of the murder itself. This item of information would depend, I explained to Billy and Elton Jr., on the victim-to-be's response to a decoy dinner invitation from my associate.

"Who is this here associate?" asked Billy.

"A woman who has already made herself known to the v-t-b," I replied. "Her code name is Elizabeth Fisher-Todd."

We went over the plan.

1. Elizabeth Fisher-Todd makes a dinner date with the v-t-b and arranges for him to pick her up downtown.

2. She pretends she forgot something urgent at her (fake) apartment building, to which they drive so she can pick it up.

3. She tells him to wait in the parking lot of her (fake) apartment building, and saying, "I'll just be a minute," she disappears.

4. Billy and Elton Jr. join the v-t-b in his car and drive him to a location of their choice. There, in a manner they solemnly swear will be both swift and painless, they murder him.

"As soon as Elizabeth Fisher-Todd makes the dinner date," I said to my accomplices, "I'll ring you chaps with all the final details. You'll find the second half of your payment beneath the passenger seat of the v-t-b's car. The first half"—I opened my purse—"will be paid right now."

High fives were exchanged, by which I mean I gave each gentleman twenty-five hundred dollars. After which I took the Metro back to Cleveland Park, climbed up the hill, and telephoned Joseph Monti.

In the honey-toned drawl of Elizabeth Fisher-Todd, I invited Mr. Monti to join me for dinner. Since Jake would be off at a conference from Saturday until late Sunday and tied up with meetings on Monday and Tuesday nights, I could offer my prey a choice of four different evenings. To guarantee his acceptance I made it lubriciously clear that the dinner I was proposing would be but the appetizer of long and very satisfying feast. I knew that I was making him an offer he couldn't refuse.

He refused.

"You're a beautiful woman," he told me, "and I

won't deny that I'm tempted. But I have to say no. I am a married man."

Since when did that ever stop you? I wanted to ask, but instead I drawled mildly, "Why, honey, I'm quite perplexed. I thought you told me you were a *separated* man."

Mr. Monti astonished me by conceding that although this was the case, he was hoping it wouldn't be the case too long. He said he missed his family, most particularly his wife, to whom, he further conceded, he had done wrong. He said he was mending his ways and that forsaking women like me was number one on the list of the ways he was mending. And when, in desperation, I urged, "How about one final fling before you tread in the paths of righteousness?" I was—I could hardly believe this!—given a lecture on the sanctity of marriage. A sanctimonious lecture from the very same brutal beast who had violated my body and who intended to kill my boy in exactly one week!

"So tell me," I quickly regrouped, "will you and your family be getting together for Thanksgiving?"

"No," Mr. Monti replied. "My wife isn't ready for family occasions yet, she says." He sighed. "They'll all be eating turkey together. And I'll be eating turkey all alone."

Without really thinking it through, I jumped in with, "Why eat turkey alone? I'm invited to the home of"—I named a major figure in government—"and you're more than welcome to come with me, I'm sure. Strictly," I hastily added, "as a friend."

Mr. Monti pondered my new and safely nonsexual offer. "It depends on what time," he finally replied.

"There's something important I have to do—something I have to do personally—in the evening."

And I know what it is, you murdering monster, I said to myself. Aloud I said, improvising frantically, "Well, they"—the So-and-So's—"will be serving their meal mid-afternoon. It should work out jes fahn."

But how could it work out jes fahn when fifteen people were dining at *my* house on Thanksgiving? How could I be with them if I had to be in a car with Mr. Monti too? Well, I couldn't be in that car, so there was only one thing to do and—resourceful type that I am—I promptly did it. I changed the plan.

"Our hosts," I told Mr. Monti, "will send a limo to pick us up. And I guess"—I pretended to calculate—"they should probably stop to fetch you before they fetch me. So let's see." I pretended once again to calculate. "You should look for their limo and drivers around one o'clock."

"Their limo and drive*rs*?" asked shrewd Mr. Monti.

"That is right," I drawled. "Their regular driver and their driver-in-training. All of the better people"—I spoke in my surely-you-know-this voice—"have a spare."

Billy and Elton Jr., when I chatted with them on the phone, did not love Plan B.

"We'll have to steal a limo," said Elton Jr.

"How will we get our final five grand?" asked Billy.

"I've got my own Thanksgiving dinner to go to," said Elton Jr.

I promised them that it all would work out—except I was speaking British, not Southern—jes fahn.

* * *

On Friday morning I unexpectedly ran into Josephine at Elizabeth Arden's, where my very own Lawrence had slicked back her rich red Botticelli curls into a sleek, straight, somewhat . . . masculine hairstyle. Her clothes— she dressed as I disrobed—worked well with her new do: a gray pinstriped pants suit, a buttoned-down shirt, a pale silk paisley tie, and a soft slouchy hat. "You're looking very . . ." I paused for a moment and then came up with the obvious word—"very handsome."

"Thank you," Jo said solemnly. "I appreciate the adjective. I've been getting in touch with the masculine part of my psyche."

"How interesting," I murmured, as I hung up my blouse and wrapped a green robe around me. "And how does it compare"—I slipped my feet into paper slippers for my pedicure—"with your feminine part?"

Whoosh—it was as if I had pulled out the cork in a bottle of champagne. Jo was burbling, bubbling, effervescing. "Stronger. Braver. More independent. Less eager to please, to compromise, to sell out, to—" She stopped, ducked her head in embarrassment, and then continued at a calmer pace. "We need to become aware of the full spectrum of our sexual identity before we can make an informed sexual choice."

Elisa, ready to wash my hair, peeked into the dressing room. "One sec," I told her, hating to break away. Surely, I thought, before we part I could come up with something to say that would help Wally's cause.

I could. And indeed I did. I sometimes astonish myself.

"I think it's great you feel stronger, braver, more independent, and all that good stuff," I told Jo. "But why do you call these *masculine* characteristics? Isn't that sexual stereotyping?" Josephine looked abashed. "I mean, why can't we call these *feminine* characteristics. *Feminine* characteristics that any good, decent man would embrace in the woman he loved."

Jo was chewing her lower lip, chewing on what I said. She straightened her shoulders and tightened the knot on her tie. "I see what you're saying," she told me as she buttoned up her coat. "I'll discuss it next week with my friend Vanessa Pincus."

Who has a dinner for twelve six days before she's serving turkey to fifteen? What can I tell you? I am an overachiever. My Friday night fete was a smash and the very next day I was setting the table for next Thursday, this time with place cards to artfully mesh my more-disparate-than-usual Thanksgiving guests, which included Rose and her daughter Miranda, who planned to fly in from L.A. and who'd already let me know that she wished to be seated as far away from her mother as possible.

It was going to be a very intense Thanksgiving. Nevertheless, I was feeling completely relaxed.

My mellowness could be attributed to two different but deeply mellow-inducing conditions: The fact that I was saving the life of my son. And the remarkable improvement in my marriage.

For on Carolyn's recommendation I had tried to be more forgiving toward my husband, whose response was to be more appreciative of me, which made me even more forgiving and him even more appreciative, and so forth. You could call it, as I did in one of my wittier newspaper columns, AN UNVICIOUS CYCLE. I found my unvicious cycle powerfully soothing to the soul.

But nothing could be more soothing than the certainty that Wally was safe from harm, that—having enlisted the aid of two professionals—I had ensured Mr. Monti's death. This time there'd be no slip-ups. This time his fate was sealed. I had beaten the beast at his homicidal game. There's nothing in the world, I thought, reveling in my monumental triumph, that can stop a can-do woman who is propelled by the primitive passions of mother love.

I had won. Yes, won! I had rescued my son. Joseph Augustus Monti was a dead man. My victory had swept away my tensions and anxieties. My victory had left me sweetly serene.

On Sunday the telephone rang and someone said, "Gobble, gobble, gobble," and hung up. Unpleasant though this was, I remained serene.

On Monday Jo told Wally that she was going to have a drink with Vanessa Pincus. Unhappy though he was, I remained serene.

On Tuesday Jeff, who'd been trying to sell his Anacostia buildings at what was a truly desperate cut-rate price, dropped the price of his buildings even further. Insolvent though he was, I remained serene.

On Wednesday, at lunchtime, Rose arrived. With Hubert.

Hubert announced his doggy delight at being back in D.C. by bounding into the dining room and seizing one end of my tablecloth in his teeth, the tablecloth on which the silver and dishes and glasses and napkins were already placed, along with the candlesticks and the three sets of salt and pepper shakers, plus the centerpiece of Indian corn and gourds.

"Don't yank!" I pleaded with Hubert as I rushed into the room to avert disaster.

Hubert yanked. I remained serene.

On Thursday, Thanksgiving Day, sweet Wally was planning to rise before dawn to drive to Dulles, where Miranda, who had taken the 10 P.M. plane, also known as the Red Eye, from Los Angeles, was due to arrive at 5:42 A.M. Well before dawn, however, Wally already was quite otherwise engaged, having received a phone call from Dwayne's mother.

"You've got to come over here right away. He's acting awfully crazy. He's acting awfully crazy, and it's my fault. If only I'd let him keep that snake when he was eight years old, and I took his pacifier away way too early, and I should have—"

Wally interrupted. "Look, I need to hang up and get going. Meanwhile you should try to make him talk. Talk with him about anything—positive stuff if you can—but just try to keep him talking. I'll be there soon."

I'd picked up the extension on the first ring—Jake never stirred—and listened, along with Wally, to the news. Now I went up to his room and said, "I think I ought to come with you. I'll keep her calm while you are dealing with Dwayne."

Wally said, "No, I don't think so," thought again, and changed his mind. "Yes, okay. She knows you. She trusts you. Come. But, Mom—"

"I know, I know," I said. "This time, no advice."

Five minutes later—Wally preoccupied, I planning to give Dwayne's mom just a *little* advice—we were on our way.

Dwayne's mother, her eyes red and swollen, greeted us

in one of Victoria's Secrets. She pointed to Dwayne's bedroom where, she explained, her son had triple-bolted the door. While Wally tried to gain entry, I gently led her to the couch and whispered comforting words into her ear, to which she replied with a torrent of lacerating self-reproach that never stopped until Dwayne finally said to Wally, through the door, "Yeah, what do you want?"

Wally said, "Let me in. Whatever it is, we'll talk about it. We'll work it out."

"It can't work out," Dwayne said. "It's useless. Hopeless."

"I know it *feels* hopeless," said Wally, "but I promise we'll find a way."

"No way. No way out," said Dwayne. "I'm doing it."

"What are you going to do?" Wally asked.

"Kill myself," said Dwayne. "I'm going to jump out the window. I'm jumping right now."

And though we heard the window thrown open, and Dwayne climbing up on the sill, and the thud of his body as it hit the ground, none of us—as we raced outside to despairing Dwayne's prostrate form—felt terribly panicked.

The apartment, you see, was located in the basement.

It was only after I looked at Dwayne, who'd suffered nothing more than a chipped front tooth, that terror started surging through my veins.

Not because poor Dwayne had jumped out the window.

But because he'd jumped out the window wearing a turkey costume.

14

•

I-THINK-I-CAN-I-THINK-I-CAN

*A*s you know, I'm deeply proud of my (truly mature) capacity to apologize, to unflinchingly admit it when I've been wrong. And since, as Pope has observed, to err is human, I have—a goodly number of times—been wrong. Never, however, let me concede, have I been as massively wrong as I'd turned out to be in the case of Mr. Monti. I mean, if errors were earthquakes, this would be a 9.9 on the Richter scale.

Dwayne, not Mr. Monti, had been sending those murderous messages to Wally. Furthermore, Dwayne saw *himself* as the turkey and clown. Furthermore, those messages had been warnings not of *homicide* but of *suicide*.

I'd made a big mistake. A big mistake.

Now it's true I'd been right in believing that somebody out there was threatening death. THE CLOWN TURNS INTO A GHOST, as well as THE TURKEY TURNS INTO DEAD MEAT, have, you'll agree, a decidedly fatal sound. All that I'd actually erred about was who, exactly, intended to do in whom. But this was the kind of error which, if I didn't stop Elton Jr. and Billy immediately, would end

315

up with Joseph Monti's being in no condition to accept my apology.

I had to stop Elton Jr. and Billy immediately.

For ratty though Mr. Monti had been—and continued to be—I no longer could claim that he deserved to die.

Since Wally was going to need to be spending some time with Dwayne and Dwayne's mother, I offered to drive to Dulles to pick up Miranda. But first there was one imperative piece of business I had to attend to: I had to find a telephone so I could tell my hit men to cancel the hit. I cruised the darkened streets till I found a pay phone which not only worked but which I'd be able to use without being mugged, and hastily deposited twenty-five cents.

"Yo, this is Billy and Elton Jr. Limited Partnership, Inc.," said Billy on the answering machine. "We're out on a job right now but if you'll please leave your name and number we'll get back to you."

I hung up the phone and had a 9.9 on the Richter scale dizzy spell. I also gave serious thought to throwing up. Never in my entire life had I yearned to converse with a person the way I yearned to converse with the absent partners of Billy and Elton Jr. Inc. With trembling hands I picked up the phone and dialed their number again—and again a machine, instead of my cohorts, answered.

"I say," I said at the sound of the beep, doing my British accent, "it's Prudence Gump here. I'm calling to inform you that the business meeting planned for today has been canceled. Definitively, permanently, nonnegotiably, now-and-forever canceled. I'll be phoning again to make sure you received this message."

I jumped in the car and drove, far faster than my usual cautious pace, to Dulles. As soon as I got there I hurried to the phone. Please let a human being answer, I prayed to To Whom It May Concern. "Yo, this is Billy . . ." et cetera, said the recording.

This time I left them a message to leave me a message that they had indeed received my message. "If you put it on your machine, I'll be able to get it," I said, "the next time I ring you up." I told them that though I much preferred to speak with an actual person, "I would find such a message"—this was the understatement of the ages—"quite *quite* reassuring."

It was time to greet my niece at the mid-field terminal.

Miranda, brown bangs and dark glasses obliterating half her face, arrived in skinny jeans and a well-cut sports jacket, striding along on funky shoes with the odd giraffelike grace of Diane Keaton. "Hi, hi," she said, enveloping me in a warm but speedy hug. "So how's The Rose—impossible as ever?" After which, from baggage-claim area right up to my front door, she obsessed about her mother, my sister, "a woman who," she rat-a-tat-tat complained, "can't even remember—my friends don't believe this—which programs her daughter produces, and has yet to take the trouble to sit down and watch one, though you know—admit it, Aunt Brenda—that if Hubert was doing some dog-food commercial on television, The Rose would not only be watching, she'd be sending engraved announcements to the whole world."

I murmured something intended to be nondenigrating to Rosalie while deeply sympathetic to Miranda, a tightrope walk I have mastered over the years and can do with minimum attention. Which was all I had available since most of my attention was consumed with concerns about stopping Billy and Elton Jr. from murdering Mr. Monti.

They were picking him up at 1 P.M. It was now almost 7 A.M. I desperately needed to know that the mission was scrubbed. But restraining myself from rushing once again to the telephone, I decided I'd wait for an hour and use the time to do some work on my Thanksgiving dinner. By eight, Jake, Jeff, and Rose—Miranda was trying to take a nap—were drowsily making their way to the kitchen table. I gave them a brief report on Wally's predawn melodrama and left the room. "The coffee's done, there's muffins and juice, I've already eaten," I told them over my shoulder, as I hustled right upstairs to the telephone. And when yet again I heard the same thwarting "Yo, this is Billy . . ." message on the machine, it struck me for the first time that I might be unable to head off Billy and Elton Jr.

And it struck me for the first time that I had better try to head off Mr. Monti.

Hubert, my new best friend, was whining outside my closed bedroom door. "Beat it! I'm busy," I grrred. Hubert grrred back, grrrs becoming barks becoming howls as I sat on my bed, taking deep breaths and telling myself, You can handle this.

Actually, I found myself thinking, *How* am I going to handle this? Like, what was I going to say to Joseph Monti?

Hubert was trying to break down my door when Rosalie clattered upstairs, hollering, "Brenda, why are you torturing Hubert?"

Losing my composure, I answered, biting out each

word, "I. Want. You. To. Take. Your. Fucking. Dog. Downstairs."

"If that's how you feel," said Rosalie, escalating instantly, "I also can take him straight back to New York."

Outside my still-closed bedroom door Rose and Hubert had just been joined by Miranda. "Can't a person," she groused, "get some sleep around here? I'll tell you one thing, Mother, if Hubert was sleeping and I was the one who was making this noise, you'd—admit it, Mother—have strangled me by now."

"Blame your aunt for the noise. She's the one who wouldn't let Hubert—"

"Stop it!" I shrieked, then seized hold of myself. "I mean, please," I said calmly and sweetly, "go eat breakfast. I've got a call I need to make—some corrections on one of my columns—but I'll be back downstairs just as soon as I'm done."

"Maybe Hubert and I will be there, and maybe we won't," said Rose, huffily departing from my doorway. "You took a nap with your makeup on?" Rose had turned her attention to Miranda. "You want to have pores the size of dinner plates? Youth doesn't last for . . ."

I dialed Joseph Monti's number, having decided to say—in my Elizabeth Fisher-Todd drawl—that our hostess had fallen ill and had, to her everlasting sorrow, been forced to cancel. I also intended to say that she'd been unable to contact her drivers, who thus might appear at his condo door (I'd had to reveal his name when I switched to Plan B) to pick him up. "Being devoted employees, they might be real insistent," I also intended to tell him, "on taking you where their employers said they should. So you need to make it clear to them that the dinner has been canceled and that they can call their message machine to confirm."

Although this ploy was, I'll grant you, rather klutzy, it was also the best I could think of at the moment and it would, God willing, save Joseph Monti's life. Having figured it out, I could feel my panic begin to subside, a state of relief that lasted until Mr. Monti's voice on the telephone said, "Hello, I'm not home right now, but . . ." Where *was* everybody?

I left the message on his machine, said I'd be checking in again, and, pulling myself together, went downstairs.

Down in the kitchen Rose and Miranda already were barely speaking, in addition to which Rose was furious with me. Nor was she quick to accept my earnest apologies for, as I oh-so-grovelingly put it, using "insensitive language" about her dog.

"One of these days," she warned me, when she finally received me back into her good graces, "you won't get away with this 'I'm so sorry' routine. I'm a very forgiving person"—not true!—"but one of these days, Brenda, you're going to do something unforgivable."

But don't let it be today, I silently prayed, as a shudder of apprehension swept through me. "Excuse me," I said, and rushed upstairs to the phone.

Where, hyperventilating, I put in a call to Joseph Monti and then a call to Billy and Elton Jr. And got their machines.

Where *was* everybody? Where the hell *were* they?

I took a deep breath and told myself, You can handle this.

* * *

Wally, looking drained but relieved, came home a little past ten. "It's all turned out for the best, I think," he said, explaining that Dwayne, having scared himself with his suicide attempt, had agreed to sign into a psychiatric hospital.

"Incidentally, Mom," he said, "remember that van that was chasing me back in September? Dwayne told me *he* was driving it. He says it was a message—a cry for help."

"Mmmm," I muttered noncommittally.

"And it also turns out that Dwayne was the person disguised as that clown on my birthday. He says it was another cry for help."

"Mmmm," I muttered noncommittally.

"In fact, he says he sent a lot of messages to me, but I don't know where he sent them—I never got them." A sudden thought seemed to strike him. "Mom, did you ever happen to see any messages?"

I stopped being noncommittal. "Of course not," I lied.

Wally went up to rest and I stuffed the turkey and started it roasting in the oven, after which I yet again attempted—and yet again failed—to contact either my hit men or Mr. Monti. By now there was only one reason why I wasn't having my own psychotic break: I fully intended, if worse really came to worst, to drive down to the Watergate and stop Elton Jr. and Billy when they showed up.

This meant I would need, to be safe, to be down there no later than 12:45. It was now already 11:28. Fortunately, however—from a scheduling point of view—my guests would not be arriving till half past three. I think-

I-can-I-think-I-can-I-think-I-can, I chanted, as I showered and put on my holiday attire. Except—uh oh!—if I was meeting Billy and Elton Jr., I'd need to be wearing my Prudence Gump disguise.

I called again, got machines, and decided that Billy and Elton Jr. were out on the streets attempting to steal a limo. I couldn't imagine where Mr. Monti might be. A flash: Could Billy and Elton Jr. have somehow revised my plan, picked him up early, and already done him in? This was indeed a plausible thought, but such a hideous one that I immediately banished it from my brain.

Jake came into the bedroom. "Your sister and niece," he said, "are going at it again. It's the first time I've actually seen someone engage in sibling rivalry with a Great Dane." He tilted his head and smiled at me. "So how come you're not interceding with one of your . . . constructive interventions?"

"Qui, moi?" I answered innocently. "Why would I want to do that? I'm trying to work on being less what certain people insist on calling controlling."

I needed to try those calls again, but my portable phone was busted, and every room with a phone was occupied: Jake getting dressed in our bedroom. Wally attempting to nap on the third floor. Rose and Miranda sniping at each other while doing the dishes in the kitchen. And Jeff in my office staring glumly into the middle distance and reminding me (as if I needed reminding) when I asked what was on his mind, "December first is my deadline, when Monti Enterprises gets everything else I own."

I wished I had time to give him my whole maternal/supportive number, but unfortunately I had to cut to the chase. "Just remember, whatever material goods they

take away from you, they can't"—my eyes moistened—
"take *you* away from you."

"Yeah, right. I've already heard that song, Mom. But
thanks anyway," Jeff said, resuming his brooding. He
needed more work, but I couldn't do it right now.

I hurried down to the living room, occupied only by
Hubert, who was stretched out on my entire four-
cushion couch. There, having finally found some relative privacy, and some privacy from the relatives, I
dialed my two numbers for the final time.

Nobody home. I would have to go to the Watergate.

"Got to pick up a few things at the store," I called to
Rose and Miranda, firmly fending them off as each of
them offered, insistently, to come along. "I need some
private time and space," I said to Miranda, who understood such needs. "I need you to baste the turkey," I
said to Rose. Then, stealthily shoving certain items into
my canvas tote bag, I left the house solo.

First stop was a trip to the ladies' room of the National Cathedral, where I put on my Prudence Gump
hair and hat and suit, after which I drove to the Watergate, parked next door at the Kennedy Center garage,
and nervously paced the front entrance, awaiting the
longed-for appearance of Billy and Elton Jr.

One o'clock came and went. One-oh-five came and
went. So did one-oh-six, seven, eight, and nine. At ten
minutes after one I was forced to revive my banished
question: Had I seen the light too late to prevent the
execution of an innocent man? This was the kind of
miscarriage of justice that has made folks ferocious
opponents of the death penalty. Twelve minutes after
one, and after years and years of favoring capital pun-

ishment, I'd become a ferocious opponent of the death penalty.

At quarter after one a car—but not the car I'd expected—slowed to a stop in front of the Watergate.

And there was Joseph Monti—alive and well and exceedingly perky—climbing out of the passenger's seat, then coming around to the driver's seat, then bending down into the car to engage in a long, deep goodbye kiss with . . . Birdie, his wife. I guess it was quite a kiss because instead of saying goodbye, he tenderly loosened her seat belt, slid in beside her, and started in with the kissing all over again.

I looked up and down the street. If Joseph Monti was here and intact, could Billy and Elton Jr. be far behind? And if they weren't around, which they clearly weren't, then I needed to move almost instantly into my fallback position.

I ducked behind a parked truck and reached into my tote bag (equipped, of course, for this contingency), withdrawing my violet contacts and my Elizabeth Fisher-Todd wig and installing them on the appropriate parts of my body. I just had time to scrawl on a beauty mark, unbutton four buttons on my Prudence Gump blouse, and emphatically shove my breasts upward in search of cleavage, when Joseph Monti offered his beaming Birdie a final embrace and entered the lobby. I was right behind him.

"Hah there," I hummed ecstatically. "Lordy, lordy, I am so pleased to see you."

Joseph Monti was flustered. "Why are you here?" he wanted to know. "Wasn't the limo supposed to get me and *then* you?" He scowled and fingered the sleeve of my suit. "And, excuse me for mentioning this, but how come you're not more dolled up for this big-shot fancy-pants Thanksgiving dinner that you're taking me to?"

He was, of course, referring to my Prudence Gump ensemble, which even four unbuttoned buttons couldn't de-frump.

I explained that I wasn't dolled up because our dinner had unexpectedly been canceled. "I've been trying to call and tell you since eight A.M."

Joseph Monti actually blushed. "Well, you see," he said, "I didn't sleep here last night. My wife and I got together for dinner, and one thing led to another, and we . . ."

"That is so wonderful. That is so fabulous. I am so happy for you." My relief was turning me into a babbling idiot. "So it's all working out jes fahn, and you'll be having Thanksgiving dinner with your family?"

Mr. Monti shook his head. Why was he telling me no? "Why are you telling me no?" I impatiently asked.

"She doesn't want to spring it on the children all at once. She thinks they have to get used to the idea. So"—Mr. Monti clasped my hand—"since neither of us has a place to eat turkey today, you and I are going out to a restaurant."

My mind went into overdrive. "No, wait, I can't," I replied. "I mean, like you said, I'm not dressed for the occasion." But when Mr. Monti pressed ("What's your problem? A nice respectable meal. No monkey business") and refused to return my hand till I acquiesced, I made my escape by telling him that I'd go home and change my clothes ("I'll get all dolled up") while he called around and made us a reservation.

"Give me an hour," I told him, as I pushed/escorted

him to his elevator. "I'll phone you when I'm ready to be picked up."

Euphorically—I had saved the day!—I wafted through the front door of the Watergate building, and there at the curb, in the longest stretch limo I'd ever gazed upon, were a neatly liveried Billy and Elton Jr.

Luckily, I saw them before they saw me.

Darting behind the same truck behind which I had made the quick switch from Prudence to Elizabeth, I took out my contacts, rubbed off my beauty mark, buttoned my buttons, put on my limp brown wig, and re-emerged as Prudence once again. Leaping into the limo, I emitted a terse "Let's roll," and two seconds later Billy and Elton Jr. and I—Elizabeth, Prudence, Brenda—were cruising toward Virginia on Rock Creek Parkway.

I and the victim-to-be had worked out our differences, I notified my cohorts. Their services wouldn't be needed after all. I suggested that in the future, if they were hired for a hit, they should show up on time, not half an hour late. I told them that they could keep the five thousand dollars I had paid them in advance, and asked them to please turn around now and drop me off.

"Not till you give us the other five grand," said Billy.

"For what?" I protested. "You don't have to kill the man."

"And we won't," said Elton Jr. "We won't kill him— but only if you pay us the other five grand."

Having been made an offer I couldn't refuse, I reached in my tote bag and paid them the rest of the money.

"Pleasure doing business with you," said Elton Jr. when they stopped the car.

"Any time," said Billy, coming around and gallantly opening the door.

I was starting to walk away when Billy said, "Hold up there a minute," and scrutinized me meditatively. "I'm gonna give you a tip. You go out and get a hot red dress, you get some red shoes, you color up that hair, and you're gonna look like—what's that blondie's name?" He pointed his finger at me and said, "Yeah, right. You gonna look like Goldie Hawn's first cousin."

I was back at the house by two, prepared to lie about a flat tire, but no one seemed to notice how long I'd been gone. Everyone noticed, however, that I was totally manic with joy as I bopped around the kitchen stirring, sautéing, and singing, at the top of my lungs, a pull-out-all-stops "I'm Sitting on Top of the World."

The Thanksgiving dinner was beautiful.

Our dinner guests were beautiful.

The report on Dwayne—the hospital called to say he was doing very well—was beautiful.

I was sit-sit-sitting on top-top-top of the world.

On Friday Jo phoned Wally to say that her father had come to the house Thanksgiving evening and taken her mother off to a motel.

On Saturday Jo phoned Wally to say that she fully, without reservation, accepted the validity and the legitimacy of the lesbian lifestyle.

On Sunday Jo blazed up to our house on the back of a highly aggressive-looking motorcycle. Dressed in studded black leather, with an earring in her nostril, Jo wasn't looking any too gentle herself. I hovered out of sight but not out of earshot, and heard Jo tell Wally,

"You said you wanted to talk to me, so I'm here, but I don't have much time. Benito is waiting."

"Well, maybe that answers my question," said Wally, his voice on the borderline between anguish and anger. "I'm trying not to crowd you, but I need to know about you and Vanessa Pincus."

Josephine replied that although she fully, without reservation, accepted the validity and legitimacy of the lesbian lifestyle, she'd nonetheless concluded that she herself seemed to be of an alternative inclination.

"That's real good news," said Wally. "I'm glad—"

"And besides"—Jo hadn't stopped talking yet—"a woman can be a fully feminine woman, and still be strong and brave and independent."

"You're right," Wally said. "You're right and—"

Jo still wasn't finished. "But you will meet people who want to call these *masculine* characteristics. Which, as I certainly hope you agree, is sexual stereotyping of the worst kind."

"I agree," Wally said. "You're completely correct, and I—"

Jo kept going. "And also," she said, "a woman—it's not just guys who feel this way—can crave excitement, can want to—uh—walk on the wild side."

"Or"—Wally's patience was fraying—"ride on the wild side. So maybe you'd like to explain about that hulk hunched over the Harley. And why you're all done up like a Hell's Angels groupie."

"I'm not explaining anything," Jo replied with withering dignity. I heard her heavy boots clonk down the hall. "But I think you ought to know that Benito says the Hell's Angels have gotten a really bum rap."

* * *

Later on Sunday Birdie phoned. She wanted us to come to her house that evening. "I'm sorry it's such short notice," she said, "but Tuesday's December first, and I think we need to have a big discussion."

"You mean, about Jeff and his contract with Monti Enterprises?"

"I mean," said Birdie mysteriously, "about everything. So maybe after dinner—let's say eight-thirty—you and Jeff and Wally and Jake could join us."

"Us?" I inquired.

"Us. Joseph and me."

We joined them in the den because the Monti living room had been demolished. The furniture was gone. The drapes were gone. The beige-on-beige wool carpeting was gone. "I've sent out the couches and chairs to be recovered in golds and maroons," Birdie softly explained to me while her husband and my three men exchanged tense pleasantries. "And I'm thinking of doing the drapes"—she pressed some boisterous swatches upon me—"in one of these prints."

I nodded enthusiastically. "Very unstagnant," I told her. Then giving Mr. Monti my hand and one of my lesser smiles, I dissemblingly said to him, "Long time no see."

Joseph Monti didn't reply. He stared at me, a quizzical look on his face. He glanced away. He removed and cleaned his glasses. He put them back on and stared at me again. His silence was verging on rude when, picking up on my phrase, he echoed, "Long time no see. Except—it's funny—it just doesn't seem that long."

Birdie Monti—when had she started to look so much like Gina Lollobrigida?—got down to business as soon as we six were seated in the large and leathery den. "Just so you are aware," she said, "when the lawyers checked over the documents, it turned out to be that *I* am Monti Enterprises." Four Kovners snapped to attention as she softly repeated the phrase, "Just so you're aware."

Then Birdie turned to her husband. "Joseph," she said, "would like to apologize for all the troubles he's brought upon your family. He knows that this is very important to me."

Joseph Monti shrugged. "So I'm apologizing."

"He also"—she turned to Wally—"wants to apologize for picking on you. He knows that this is very important to me."

Joseph Monti shrugged. "So again I'm apologizing."

"He also"—she turned to Jake—"wants to say that he's getting those people who're suing you to stop suing you. It's going to cost some money but he knows that this is very important to me."

Joseph Monti sighed. "It's costing a fortune."

Birdie turned to Jeff. "So Joseph shouldn't be too upset, we'll be taking your Rockville properties, and we'll keep the money you've already paid on your debt. However," and she smiled at him reassuringly, "on your car and your condominium, which Joseph won't be needing anymore, we plan to make an equitable arrangement."

Joseph Monti groaned. "Equitable? A giveaway!"

Birdie frowned at her husband. "Just remember that this is very important to me."

Birdie turned in my direction and said, "There's been some feeling—and I agree—that my husband didn't do right by your son on those properties he's stuck with in Anacostia." She folded her arms across her ample bosom and declared, "We're going to make this right. I don't know how, but I promise we will. This is also"—she smiled at her husband—"very important to me."

I almost squealed with excitement. "You're saying you want to make it right with Jeff and those properties? You're saying that this is very important to you?"

"It is," Birdie Monti replied, raising an eyebrow. "Tell me, Brenda, do you have some ideas?"

Boyohboyohboy, did I have some ideas!

The subsequent discussion, which came to a satisfying conclusion some hours later, began with my suggesting mellifluously, "I'd like you to close your eyes and picture something: I'd like you to close your eyes and picture the Monti Homes for the Homeless, in Anacostia."

Before we left the Montis, Birdie Monti took Wally aside for a brief heart-to-heart. With a minor shift of position—so minor I honestly do not feel you could call it eavesdropping—I found myself able to hear every word they said.

"Jo isn't here tonight because she's out with—"

"I know," Wally said. "A biker. Benito."

"At least that girl she was dating—what was her name? Vanessa Pincus—was nice and clean-cut. But I'm asking you not to give up on Jo. She's trying things out. She needs to. And when she's through she's going to see that you're the one for her. Even my husband is finally beginning to see this."

"And why is that?" Wally asked.

"It's because"—Birdie ruffled his hair—"compared

with Benito and Vanessa, you're starting to look like John F. Kennedy, Jr." She paused. "And also because it's very important to me."

Although it was pouring rain when we four Kovners drove home from McLean, I didn't give Jake any navigational tips. Instead, I snuggled up close and said, as diffidently as I could, "I hope you didn't mind my coming up with that Monti Homes for the Homeless plan."

"Not at all," Jake answered. "You did great."

The opinion was not unanimous. "*I* minded," Jeff protested from the back seat. "I think you could have cut a better deal. I know you saved my ass, but I can't believe you're making me be the resident manager."

"Think of it," I said, "as a kind of Clintonian national service."

"Think of it," my adorable husband added, "as learning how to be in control of your life."

Later, as we stood side by side in the bathroom brushing our teeth, Jake—to my astonishment—whispered, "I love you." Caught with a mouthful of water, I gargled and rinsed and then replied, "I love you back." After which, I was moved to say—okay, I was being greedy—"So embroider a little. What do you love about me?"

"Jesus, Brenda," said Jake, but not unkindly, "you know that's not my kind of conversation."

"Okay," I said. "Then I'll give you a couple of hints. 'Yours is the breath that sets every new leaf aquiver. Yours is the grace that guides the rush of the river. Yours is the flush and the flame in the heart of the flower: Life's meaning, its music, its pride, and its power.' Doesn't that kind of sum up your feelings for me?"

Jake gave me a sideways glance. "Well, no, it doesn't. No, not exactly. I was thinking more along the lines of 'You may have been a headache but you never were a bore.' "

"That's what you call embroidering?" I gave him a jab with my elbow. "That is *it*?"

"That's it," said Jake. "That's a lot. We've got a lot." He sighed, sighed deeply, and shook his head. "And Brenda, I'm so glad we didn't blow it."

"Me too," I told him softly, so flooded with feeling I could barely speak the words. We smiled—almost bashful smiles—and hugged each other. And though I know very well that such things don't happen, can't possibly happen, except in the movies, our bathroom was filled with the sound of violins.

This morning Birdie Monti called to say that all bets might be off, that her husband had awakened in the middle of the night awash in anxiety. Yes, he'd replied to her questions, he most desperately wanted her back and would do whatever she said was very important to her. Which meant that he'd never ever be unfaithful again. Which meant that it was okay by him if she kept all the money and property in her name. And which also meant he was willing to make his peace—at the cost of a million plus—with the Kovners.

Except, Birdie Monti groaned, there was this obstacle.

"My husband says that he placed a curse upon the Kovner family, a serious curse, an irreversible curse.

And he says that unless he fulfills it, terrible things he can't even tell me about will happen to him." She tsk-tsk-tsked. "I know there's got to be a way around this, but, honestly, I can't think what it is. And meanwhile, whenever I say to him, 'Joseph, forget this curse,' the color goes out of his face and he grabs his—um—privates."

Oh, God, I thought. Joseph and his stupid superstitions. I sat there holding the telephone and mentally replayed his August curse:

"May I never see my wife or my children or grandchildren again, may I end my days in poverty, may my . . . thing . . . fall off, if I fail to exact full vengeance on your husband and your sons for what you have done to me."

No wonder the poor fellow was so panicked.

"Brenda," said Birdie Monti, who hadn't heard my voice in a while, "are you still there?"

"I'm here," I reassured her, "and I'm thinking. Believe me, I am thinking very hard."

I thought for a few more minutes and then—I tell you, sometimes I astonish myself—I had it. I'd figured out how to stop this crazy curse from messing up a happy ending.

"Birdie," I said, "tell your husband that I know a professional witch who's able to reverse irreversible curses."

Birdie laughed. "You're joking with me, right?"

"Do you want to solve this problem," I asked, "or do you really want me to answer that question?"

Birdie didn't hesitate. "Have your witch get in touch with Joseph today."

* * *

This afternoon I succeeded in removing the Monti curse. I did it on the phone. It was a triumph. For even though Joseph Monti had initially responded with great skepticism, he soon surrendered to my mystic charms.

"I hear your spirit's turmoil," I said, my tone kind of thin and quavery—think of the high lama in *Lost Horizon*. "I hear it, but I do not understand."

"What don't you understand?" grumped Mr. Monti.

"These words your spirit is whispering. Alien words like *otrolig*. And . . . *spindelnät*?"

"This is amazing!" Joseph Monti said.

"And now—ah, yes—it's starting to change into something I comprehend. Fish. I hear fish . . . fishing . . . fisherman . . . Fisher-Todd."

"This is amazing!" Joseph Monti said.

"And, hark"—do witches say "hark"? oh, well—"I hear yet another whisper from your spirit. Org . . . orgast . . . some words that begin with 'Or.' "

"Okay. All right. That's enough," Joseph Monti said. "Let's just work on getting this curse reversed."

Getting rid of the curse was a cinch once I'd established my supernatural bona fides. The nice thing about a curse is that it is gone as soon as the curser believes it to be. And indeed Joseph Monti believed it gone when I mumbled some arcane phrases which I characterized as a curse-reversing spell. (You'll find the full text of the spell in *Brenda's Best*.) But though he seemed convinced of my witchy powers, he expressed a few residual anxieties.

"You're sure it's all okay now?" he asked.

"I'm sure," I replied. "The curse is reversed and you have made peace with your enemy."

"And nothing bad will happen to me?"

. "Nothing bad," I replied. "Indeed, your spirit will soon be free of turmoil."

"That's nice about my spirit. Very nice," Mr. Monti persisted. "But what about the rest of me? Like . . . my body?"

"The curse is reversed," I witchily assured him once again. "And your body, I can promise, is safe—unless . . ."

"Unless?"

"Unless you should harm the Kovners or"—I figured I owed one to Birdie—"cheat on your wife. In which case, I can promise, your thing will fall off."

After talking with Joseph Monti, I found myself having further thoughts on the subject of cheating. Indeed, I found myself faced once again with the question I'd raised at my birthday party last April, the troublesome question that came to mind as I contemplated my husband and my three lovers. Was I, I had asked that night, a star on a Donahue show called "My Mom Is a Slut"? Or was I Lady Brett in *The Sun Also Rises*?

Here, after all these months, is my final answer:

First of all, I've decided that this is not the right question to ask, that the only right question is, "Are you sorry you did it?"

To which I've decided, second of all, that the only right answer for me is "no" and "yes."

No, because I have learned what *it* is like with other men. I have learned what *I* am like with other men. I have learned about the G-spot and the Jumping White Tiger position—though I never did learn what happened to Paulie and Joan. I've acquired carnal knowledge of a younger man, a married man, a genius. Of a man who belongs to a different religious persuasion. Of a black man, a celebrity, a committed political activist—and a twin. No longer can I complain, as I look back on my forty-six years, that I've been deprived of sexual variety. In one fell adulterous swoop, I have acquired enough variety to last for the final twenty-three years of my life.

So no, I can't say that I'm sorry, because I wanted to possess this carnal knowledge.

Except yes, I am sorry. Deeply deeply sorry.

I'm sorry because I hate the fact that I've slept with another wife's husband. I'm sorry because I still hold fidelity high. I'm sorry because I long to be—in addition to carnally knowledgeable—guiltless, blameless, virtuous . . . unadulterated.

Fortunately I am able to live with ambivalence.

It's 7 P.M. and I've lighted a fire in our living-room fireplace and the Chardonnay is chilling and I'm heating up a curried-crab hors d'oeuvre. Both Jeff and Wally are out and I await the arrival of Jake, with whom I am planning to spend a cozy evening.

Sinatra is bittersweetly singing "It Was a Very Good Year." I am feeling grateful.

I'm grateful there's no more curse on the Kovner family.

I'm grateful that Jake is back in love with me.

I'm grateful that I am still (despite many setbacks) a can-do woman (though far, far humbler than I used to be).

I'm grateful for my children, my friends (among whom I count Birdie Monti), and even for my sister Rosalie.

And I'm grateful—profoundly grateful—to my unconscious, dumb luck, and To Whom It May Concern that I didn't manage to murder Mr. Monti.

DONE

● *The Following June*

EPILOGUE

These last several months have been painful for Wally, but, as I've already mentioned, he happens to be a remarkable young man. Indeed, despite an aching heart, he showed (with just a few lapses) surpassing patience as Josephine moved from Vanessa to Benito to Zbigniew, then on to a saxophone player and a Tae Kwon Do instructor. His steadfastness has paid off: This Sunday Wally and Jo will be married, assisted—since Jo doesn't know yet if she wishes to convert—by a rabbi and a priest. And I'll tell you, what with her great mental health and Wally's enormous joy, I'll take my future daughter-in-law any which way whatsoever that I can get her.

We've seen a lot of the Montis since the wedding date was set—he subdued and uxorious, she vibrant and very much in control of her life. From time to time Birdie goes to an AFGO meeting and speaks to the women about the importance of knowing what's very important to you. She is also quite hands-on involved with the newly renovated Monti Homes for the Homeless, where Jeff, she has assured me, is doing well and "getting his shit together."

"Birdie," I gasped when she used that phrase, "where, for heaven's sake, did you pick up such language?"

Birdie, looking pleased with herself, replied, "From these men who sometimes help when we have problems at the homes. Two nice men named Billy and Elton Jr."

Billy and Elton Jr., in fact, are making themselves indispensable by keeping the Monti Homes free of guns and drugs. In gratitude, Jeff has sold his flashy Jaguar to Elton Jr., replacing it with a car more modestly suited to his role as resident manager. Jeff is also subletting his Watergate condo and currently living in Anacostia, since resident managers—Birdie Monti insisted and I concurred—ought to be residing among their residents. And though he's still dating women I cannot imagine becoming the mother of my grandchildren, he may be developing character at last.

He may even, my sister says enviously, have found himself a meaningful career, something Rose continues not to do. Which is why she is now taking a course to prepare for the LSATs and plans to apply to law schools this coming fall.

Speaking of Rose, I've been thinking she might be right about my resourcefulness, that I might find a way to outwit my short-lived genes. Indeed, with my dizzy spells gone and my body and soul in mint condition, I'm feeling convinced that I'll make it past age sixty-nine.

Which I certainly hope to do because I wish to walk into the sunset with the man who's lying next to me in bed, a man covered head to toe in a full gorilla suit (mask included)—except for a slit in a highly strategic location. I, in turn, am wearing Jake's most favorite

T-shirt-nightshirt, the one he had made for me, the one that says: FOR PEACE OF MIND, I HEREBY RESIGN AS GENERAL MANAGER OF THE UNIVERSE.

Jake finds it deeply comforting, he tells me, to see those words emblazoned across my chest.

But, as I'm not reminding Jake, but often tell my readers, people shouldn't believe everything they read.